Nothing much happened in this small, sleepy town, now everything was happening at once...

She must have sensed his shyness. Reaching up, she put a soft palm on his scratchy jaw. "Dear Jordan, you look just like I remember you—tall, dark, and rugged as a fence post."

"I promise I do look better when I haven't been routed out of bed before I could shave. Can I buy you a soda at Sara's Place?"

She frowned slightly. "Do you really think that place is fit to go in? I mean, it used to be the old jail and all. And I hear her customers are mostly...you know..."

"Black? Well, I'm a regular there now. Even got my own table unless someone gets there first. They do make room for pretty ladies, though. We can even have our own table outdoors if you want."

"Are you asking me on a date, Jordan Tanner? I thought you never would! Sure, I love to walk on the wild side, as long as you're with me." She looped her thin tanned arm in his. He was acutely aware he hadn't bothered to wear deodorant in a year. *Not since...when the hell am I going to stop tagging everything BCD and ACD—before and after Carolyn died?*

Melissa didn't seem to mind him smelling like a rank mixture of dog and sweat, however. She kept glancing up at him with those sparkling eyes like a girl on her first date. In spite of a mouth like the bottom of a chicken coop and a growling stomach, he felt as though the weary years had just been ripped away and he was immersed in the blossoming summer for the first time.

They hadn't strolled far before she had him laughing, rattling off incidents involving mutual friends, when his cellphone rang. It was Quade Walker. "I think you better come right on over to the police department, Mr. Tanner. Something else's just happened."

It is said that in the deep woods right outside of Julia Springs, Georgia, lives a creature of myth and legend, the Chinaberry Man, so named due to the sweet, pungent scent remembered by those who have remotely come across him. Remotely because very few have lived to tell of a close encounter, except one. Gina McFarland has always been special: predicting plane crashes, having visions and dreams that come true—mostly the kind that don't have happy endings. Now she sees the dead. And, of all people, the creature has chosen to save her. In a matter of days, several strange events threaten the peace of this quiet hamlet, all of which culminate in hatred and revenge, Mother Nature's wrath, pure serendipity—and the love song of the Chinaberry Man.

KUDOS for *Love Song of the Chinaberry Man*

In *Love Song of the Chinaberry Man* by Trisha O'Keefe, Kenya is a young teenager being abused by her stepfather. When she tries to tell her mother, the woman beats her and throws hot coals at her. Just another day in swaps of Georgia. Throw in another pregnant teenager, the murder of an old woman and a teenage boy, and you have a complicated stew of a mystery/thriller. But when you add in mythical creatures of legend, the story gets really complicated. The plot is strong, the characters well developed and intriguing, and the action fast-paced. Once you pick it up, you won't be able to put it down. ~ *Taylor Jones, Reviewer*

Love Song of the Chinaberry Man by Trisha O'Keefe is an fascinating and complicated paranormal thriller. Set in the bayous of Georgia, the plot revolves around several families in a small town called Julia Springs and the creature they call the Chinaberry Man, a Southern version of Big Foot. As the lives of the residents of the town and the deep woods/swampland, the locals call the Thicket, play out on a background of intrigue and murder, the Chinaberry Man exacts revenge for disrespect shown to a voodoo priestess, the rape of a young girl, the imprisonment of others, and generally helps the good people in the area. But is his help intentional or inadvertent? And who killed the wealthy dowager? And what about the "deacon" living in the swamp with all his wives and children? Oh, wait, they all moved out and started their own compound. Needless to say, it's a complex story. I love all the little subplots and the innocence skimming on the surface of evil. O'Keefe has crafted an intriguing tale of paranormal creatures, murder, greed, lust, superstition, and everyday life in rural Georgia. This one's a page turner you'll want to read more than once. ~ *Regan Murphy, Reviewer*

Love Song of the Chinaberry Man

By

Trisha O'Keefe

A Black Opal Books Publication

Black Opal Books

BECAUSE SOME STORIES JUST HAVE TO BE TOLD

GENRE: PARANORMAL THRILLER/WOMEN'S FICTION/SUSPENSE

LOVE SONG OF THE CHINABERRY MAN
Copyright © 2015 by Trisha O'Keefe
Cover Design by Jackson Cover Designs
All cover art copyright © 2015
All Rights Reserved
Print ISBN: 978-1-626943-54-4

First Publication: NOVEMBER 2015

Published by Black Opal Books **http://www.blackopalbooks.com**

DEDICATION

To my mother, Kathleen, who dutifully cleaned everything my father brought back from his hunting trips until I cracked a tooth on a piece of buckshot. After that, she drew the line at anything with feathers or scales.

To Bill, whose adventures inspired this story.

And to Faith, my long-suffering editor, who cleaned up my work.

Chapter 1

They heard her singing long before they came upon the
tall brown woman in the deep woods. The two hunters
had been following their dogs through the primeval
tangle of water oaks, sweet gum, sticky vine, and spiky marsh
grass since before dawn. The sun had climbed to its seventh
hour, searching for the forest floor with fingers of insect-filled
light. At the very moment when a shaft of light lit the huge
water oak ahead of them, an eerie sound seemed to come bubbling up through the green ooze beneath their boots.

The taller of the two, a skinny kid named Cole Prescott,
froze and raised his hand the way he'd seen infantry patrol
leaders do in war movies. "What the hell is that noise? Who's
she talking to?"

At his signal, they crouched down, watching the woman
standing beneath the mammoth tree, waving her arms as if
welcoming an invisible deity. Her mouth opened wide in song,
she swayed back and forth as if moved by the morning breeze
gently stirring the smaller trees around her.

"Sounds like some kind of hoodoo thing," his companion
whispered. He was seventeen with a fiery line of acne still
tracing his narrow jaw beneath the patchy start of a beard. "It's
not English, I know that. And it ain't Christian, neither."

Their raspy voices in the underbrush sent nesting birds
flying, but she didn't stop, so deep in prayer was Root Woman.
She raised her arms to the whispering canopy of trees far
above her head and chanted in Geechee, "Oh, come, Old One,

come and feast. Here are offerings of your children, come partake of food and drink. Oh, come, Guardian of the Deep Woods, you First One of the trees and streams, come guardian of those who hide behind your strength—the poor, the runaways, the outlaws, the outcasts. Come, drink and eat! Come."

Her deep voice wove through the green maze with a resonance only belonging to forest creatures. As if summoned, a chilly breeze lifted the gray Spanish moss like a child playing with an old man's beard. Then it grew into a stiff wind, bending the branches that held the moss until they looked like gray banners waving above a battlefield.

"Who the hell is she talking to, Cole?" The younger one glanced up as the breeze spiraled into a strong wind that moved the branches over the heads of the hunters. "What's that? Did you feel that?"

It seemed to him the very ground shook, sending vibrations through their bones. In the jungle behind them, the sky darkened and appeared to boil. The dogs crouched and whined, looking back at their masters for the call to retreat.

All except the Catahoula curs who sat down, fixing their glassy yellow eyes on the woman in the clearing as if they were waiting for a signal. They stretched their long dark bodies across the marshy ground, quivering like runners on the mark.

"Aw, just the military training ground across the river setting off bombs is all that is." Cole spat in scorn as if bombs were nothing to fear. Then he got to his feet, his body stiff with resolve. "I've had enough of this crap," he said, spitting at one of the dogs who had the sense to get out of the way. "What in hell you doing, old woman? Knock off your magic tricks and get the hell out of here! You're scaring off the deer." The taller of the boys, he advanced into the clearing pointing his rifle at the woman's turbaned head. "I said get the hell out, woman!"

His friend stayed back in the tall weeds, looking behind him into the thick underbrush where he heard branches knocking together like jungle drums.

"Go easy, Cole. She ain't' doing nothing, except the hoo-doo magic. They talk to trees and rocks and shit. It's just how they do."

But his companion ignored the warning, stopping just short of the woman, rifle pointing at her chest. "Snap out of it and scram, old woman! You're trespassing!"

The look she turned on him made him retreat a step. "No, son of Prescott, it is you who trespasses against me. Now, go on with your hunting or you will be the hunted."

"My dad bought this property for hunting and I said you're trespassing! Now, get going."

But with just a look, Root Woman had melted the resolve on the face behind the rifle. Prescott took another step backward in spite of having a length of shotgun between them. "You have no right to interrupt prayers, Cole Prescott. Go away, before—"

"Prayers! You call that caterwauling praying? Hey, Trey, she says she was saying her prayers. It sound like any kind of praying you ever heard?" Without waiting for a reply, Cole flared up. "I've heard about you, old woman. You do jou-jou magic, calling up spirits and crap like that. Now, quit doing your magic spells and clear off. You're trespassing and, what's worse, you're scaring off the game with all that howling you call singing."

Root Woman sighed and shook her head. "You don't respect nothing, son. That's a sad way to live." Leaning over painfully, she picked up her shawl which lay next to a turtle shell piled up with roots. Beside it were two more gourd bowls, one with berries and strawberry box wine, the other with dried persimmons and figs. "But listen to what I say, Cole Prescott. If I were you, I'd keep going along home or you'll soon be the game."

"I take that as a threat!! I said scram, you old bitch!" He was aiming a kick at her ample rear when a sudden burst of cold wind bowed down the towering trees. A whirlwind of leaves and dust clouded his vision and his kick missed its mark. Prescott lost his balance, falling backward, cursing, to the ground.

Root Woman straightened, her eyes fixed on the dense

forest surrounding the clearing. The younger sapling bent down as if bowing to a superior force and, here and there, branches crashed to the ground.

"Run," she said to the other hunter. "Don't look back!"

Woods and grasses began to shake and writhe convulsively in a mad dance and Root Woman fell to the ground, arms out flung, her forehead pressing to the earth in abject supplication. The last thing Cole Prescott remembered was a pair of saplings being uprooted and flying skyward as if they had wings. Then, like a supplicant pleading for his life, he followed them into the sky.

Trey Blake shrieked and turned tail, running like the deer he had come to hunt. Unfamiliar with the Swamp, he plunged into water up to his waist, clawed his way out again, and got upright. Stumbling and sprawling, gasping like an asthmatic, he put distance between himself and the sound of Cole's hideous screams. Then a gnarled tree root tripped him again and he sprawled out like a starfish. He lay there listening for death that would surely come, but the screaming had stopped and the ground was no longer alive with waving trees.

Chapter 2

She had grown up to the sound of singing in the morning. Even in winter, the whole earth seemed to burst into song. The winter wind whistling through the shutters, bright cardinals quarreling over the suet in the birdfeeders, people going to work in the fields, noisy chickens, hungry dogs, cows waiting to be milked, and the mules honking in the pasture—all had a morning song. Her aunt's voice, rich as cream pie, and Cousin Joy's lilting soprano tangled in harmony, seeped through the old walls from the kitchen like moisture from the shower in the hall bathroom.

To Gina Kelly, morning music was there, but no one else in the house seemed to hear it, except maybe Uncle Lane. In the kitchen from behind his newspaper, his deep voice rumbled, "It's like living with a damned church choir."

Across their room under the eaves, her sister Megan only jerked the bedcovers over her head. "Shut the window, damn it. Do I have to tell you every morning? I can't wait to get my own room! Shut the window, you moron!"

"Listen to them, Megan. There's a lead singer—a brown thrasher, I think—who starts out and then they all answer back. And they keep the same downbeat—birds, people, chickens, truck engines."

"I don't care if it's the Metropolitan Opera, shut the damn window, Ginny!" A shoe landed squarely between Gina's shoulders.

"I'm going to get breakfast," Gina told the mound on the

bed. "When you get yourself out of bed, you can shut the window."

This morning in early June, she was washing her face at the single washstand, trying not to see the new pimple arising—where else but on her chin—taking its place among the freckles the sun had glued there. It was real hell to be sixteen with corkscrew hair, freckles, *and* pimples. She was turning around to grab her robe when she looked out the dressing room window to find Cole Prescott standing in the side yard staring at the house.

"Geeez Loueeez! What's he doing out there?" She snatched up the robe to cover her full breasts—full because she'd just started her period. "Oh, gawd, he must be stoned again."

"Will you shut up and get out of here so I can get up in peace?" Her sister's whine, muffled by pillows, drifted past her, unheard.

He was standing there in Aunt Mildred's azalea garden—not looking at her or anything else—just staring at the house as if he could see through it.

"Oh, lord, Cole's stoned again," Gina said, loud enough for him to hear her through the half-open window, "and this early in the morning. I'd just be ashamed." The moment the words were out of her mouth, he was gone. "Huh, that's funny."

"Are you talking to yourself? What's funny?"

Gina looked back into the bedroom, still clutching her robe to her chest, half expecting to see Cole standing in the deep shadows by the curtains. He and Megan had a big thing going until she began going out with Arthur Gatewood, then Arthur had told him to get lost and he did, kind of. He came to school stoned more than once and got suspended. Megan's cell phone would ring at all hours and Megan would answer it with a snarl. "I know it's you, Cole. Quit bothering me or I'll tell Art and he'll put you away, understand?"

Gina walked slowly back into the bedroom, looking around as if Cole had somehow managed to sneak in and was hiding behind the flowered drapes. "I just saw Cole Prescott standing in the side yard, staring at the house, like he was stoned or something."

Under the mounded pillows, she heard her sister groan. "Why does that strike you as strange? Probably was. And you woke me up for that?"

Chapter 3

Down in the workers' row houses, Kenya was sick. She couldn't pick up her head without throwing up. She crawled like a dog over to the chamber pot and puked again. Her mama would be getting mad and would be there in a minute. Not even that long, if her retching woke up the little ones. "Keeeeeenya! Get in this kitchen, girl. I need more wood for the fire. Now!"

She walked herself up the wall to a standing position, weaving around like a drunk. Pulling on her shift, she made it through the door into the next room where her mother stood cooking at the fireplace. "Sorry, Mama. Had to get Pansy back to sleep."

"Go get me more firewood, girl. Go on. Your daddy will have a fit if the cornbread's not done. Go on, now. "

"He ain't my daddy, Mama. You know he ain't."

Pearlene wasn't listening and it was good thing she wasn't. "Quit talking to yourself and get on out there, now go on."

Revived by the fresh morning air, Kenya took a few deep breaths before negotiating the cabin steps, which were really just logs and could sometimes turn if you stepped wrong. She headed on out to the woodpile where the chickens picked at grubs and wood worms. Shooing them away, she nearly stepped on an egg and stooped quickly to put it in her pocket. Her heart began to race as she loaded up the firewood into the wood bucket, bending her knees to avoid bending all the way over to reach the pile. Her head reeled as she lost her balance and staggered back under the weight of the bucket.

"Let me help, girl." Like a great dark shadow, he came up behind her, quietly for a big person. His hands went around her breasts and then down to pull up her shift to her waist. Then they slipped between her legs.

"Don't," she said in a whimper. "Leave me alone."

"I got to. Bend over, girl. You know what I got to do. I fight it, but it comes over me like a spell." He pushed her against the wood pile and lifted her up enough to spread her legs. "Quit fighting me, now. Be good and I'll bring you something nice from town. A pair of cute undies like they got now."

She grabbed a piece of wood but he knocked it out of her hands. His organ went into her like a rod and she cried out. She flailed at him with her fists but in vain. "Mama! Help!"

When he was finished, he let her drop, sliding to the ground. "Don't you go telling your mama, girl, or I'll kill you. You know I will."

But she did. She tried, anyway. There was no opportunity after they came back from the field at noon because after dinner they slept in the next room, while she watched the four little ones play in the yard. Nor at night, when they all slept together, the adults in the one bed and the children in cradles or on the straw mattresses.

Only in the morning when he'd gone out with the early wagons to the fields until breakfast. "Mama, I've been sick in the mornings lately."

"Something going around. Don't spread it to your sisters and the baby, hear me? Wash your hands after you get sick, and then go get us some wood. Your daddy'll be home before noon-time bell." Pearlene was occupied with doing her hair up. In the dresser mirror, she saw Kenya still standing there with her stubborn look on. "What's you waiting for? Doomsday? I swear I never saw anything so lazy as you, Kenya!"

Kenya trembled but stood her ground. "He ain't my daddy. He your husband, not my own daddy. You know that's the truth. My daddy's Willy Jones and Lewis killed him in a bar fight and got off saying was self-defense when he started it."

For once, her mother met her eyes. Large, brown ones in a heart-shaped face. Kenya was beautiful and growing up tall. Pearlene had begun to hate the sight of her. She wished to God that someone would ask to marry her—some big farmhand—to get her out of the house.

"Why you saying that? You under his roof, ain't you? Eating what he provides, ain't you? He your daddy now since your own was killed over shooting craps and left me with two babies to feed."

"He ain't, Mama. No daddy does his own up that way, does he? He done got me with child. No real daddy would do that!" It was out and she burst like a dam, drowning them both in tears of self-pity.

She knew the wild-eyed look that took over her mother's face too well. She should have run, but she waited, begging for some morsel of pity, some relief from the humiliation and guilt. Instead, her mother launched into volcanic rage.

"No! You're lying, girl! Lying to my face! You been playing the whore all along!" Grabbing the butcher knife she'd been slicing fatback with, her mother raised it high and came at her like a crazy woman, jabbing the air as Kenya dodged around the table and chairs.

"Don't, Mama. I didn't do nothing, honest. Mama, don't kill me! Oh, help me, Jesus!" She dashed by the door to the sleeping room and saw three pairs of eyes wide with horror. "I didn't do nothing, Mama. Please!!" She cowered behind the three screaming children, certain her mother wouldn't harm them to get to her.

Seeing the children, her mother threw away the knife and grabbed a smoldering piece of firewood from the hearth, hurling it at her daughter with perfect accuracy. It struck Kenya in the left eye, sizzling as it came in contact with her tears. The children joined her screams, fleeing in all directions, two slipping out the door into the yard and two more huddling in the corners of the small sleeping room. Kenya had nowhere to run and more burning wood rained down on her bare back and shoulders. As she made her way toward the door, a mule whip caught her across the back and legs. Her mother pursued her like a demon, laying the whip across her body as if she were a draft animal down in its traces. Kenya knew if she wanted to live, she had to flee.

She left her mother screaming, "Whore!" in the front yard with neighbors running to her aid. Kenya sought refuge in what locals called the "Thicket" another hundred yards away. There, hiding in trees, mosquitoes feasting on her open wounds, Kenya said goodbye to her home. When it came to Lewis Spencer's support, her mother would never believe or forgive her. She knew her mother needed a man much more than she needed a daughter. Kenya traveled deeper into the Thicket, thinking about how to kill herself, because no one wanted a pregnant fourteen-year-old—not to work for them, for sure—because she would have to take off time to care for a child. No one wanted to feed an extra mouth, so she would die anyway.

A kind of delirium took over after a while. Her entire body seemed an open wound and her left eye had closed from the burn.

She hadn't eaten since the previous evening and had retched that up this morning. When she tried to put water from the brackish creek on her burned eye, she fainted from the pain, falling across the mossy bank. When she revived, to even take a sip of it, she vomited again.

Finally, she came to her senses in a place near the creek where it deepened and widened enough that she could throw herself in. But as she stood teetering on the bank, a gator dropped into the water with a splash, anticipating a meal.

Her idea of death was not to be eaten by a gator, so she crouched on the shore, watching another and then another drop in the water, smelling the blood oozing from her cuts, gathering for the feast.

Getting to her feet, Kenya wandered on and on through the woods, getting more and more disoriented until finally the sky held up by the trees began to spin and she fell to the ground.

cɔeɔ

Later that morning, a couple of fishermen found Cole Prescott's pickup parked at the edge of the sprawling Thicket. The gunlocks were empty in back of the truck, and bees and flies clustered on the bait bucket. Fishing rods were locked in place and a six-pack in the cooler was untouched. Something was clearly wrong.

They were making their way down to the creek that wound through the thick vegetation when they noticed freshly uprooted trees and turkey buzzards in a slow orbit around a small clearing. Climbing over the tree trunks and through blackberry brambles, they looked around at what appeared to be the path of a tornado funnel.

"Hell, I didn't even know there was a storm in the area," one of them said, picking his way around the debris.

"Weatherman said sky was clear and eighty-nine degrees today. No rain in the forecast."

"You know how much they know," the other commented sourly. "Half the time they're wrong and the other half they're just guessing. Besides, the Thicket's got a weather system all its own. Like some alien planet."

"Wonder what them buzzards are after?" Following the spiraling path of the turkey buzzards to where they perched, flapping their wings as they sparred over their carrion prize dangling from a broken limb. "Holy shit! Poor bastard got caught in a twister, looks like."

His companion joined him. Together they stared upward at what remained of Cole Prescott, hanging upside-down from the loblolly pine some twenty feet above them. "Geeezuz, would you look at that? I ain't going up there to get him down. Let's call that dumbass sheriff and tell him they need to get an extension ladder out here. And a body bag."

✌︎つ℮つ

Tinker Pierce was there within the hour with a lineman from the power company, the fire truck, and as many volunteer fireman as he could round up. The firemen carried an enormous ladder across the Thicket into the clearing and propped it against the towering pine. The lineman climbed the ladder and up the tree, retrieving the body from its tortuous perch on the limb where it hung like a child's rag doll. The firemen handed the bloody body of Cole Prescott carefully down the line until it reached the last of them.

Only then did the paramedics waiting on the ground realize the truth. Cole's right arm was missing entirely and the jagged shoulder bones protruded from what remained of his checkered shirt. Tinker Pierce was immediately sick, rushing down to the creek to vomit in the dark water.

Chapter 4

When Gina came down the hall stairs, her uncle and cousin Chris were already in the big yellow kitchen, where sunlight and Joy's humming had turned it into a beehive.

"Morning, Miss Poptop," said her Uncle Lane, leaning down for a whiskery kiss without putting down his morning paper. "Pork futures are up. That's a plus."

"Great," she said as if she could care less. She tried to get Cole Prescott out of her mind. "Could I just have fruit, please? I'm on a serious diet—seriously, just fruit."

Joy had already fixed her grits and eggs which she plunked down on the grotesque placemat Gina had made in kindergarten. She was in high school now, but still had to face her name spelled out in finger paint with imprints of her hands or someone's hand surrounding it.

It was like a daily testimonial to how awkward she was, even at that age. "Eat up, buttercup. If you're going to be helping Dad out around here this summer, you need fattening-up some."

"Wrong," Gina replied. "You know Megan calls me lard-ass because my butt shakes when I walk."

Her uncle rattled the paper for silence. "Watch your mouth, Ginny. Ladies don't use that kind of language."

"Sorry. My behind. You know I hate buttermilk, Joy. Can't I just have juice for once?"

"It'll take those freckles off your face, so drink it up." Either her cousin believed the old Southern myth or she was afraid of what Mildred would say.

"Nothing but a blowtorch is going to get my freckles off, but I'll take the freckles any day before I drink that stuff. Tastes nasty, like that stuff you drink for constipation."

Joy went back to the sink, giggling. "Don't you want to go to prom with somebody handsome and rich like Clay Winfield? He's got a cool car. Sports convertible, right?"

Gina stirred the melted butter into her grits, creating a whirlpool. "Clay Winfield is dumb as dirt and he also brags on his family too much. How they built this and donated money for that. Besides, I heard he told a bunch of kids at lunch the other day that I was so ugly, my daddy took off and left my mama when I was born."

"I'll get on him for talking that kind of trash." His concentration now thoroughly shattered, Lane McFarland crushed the morning paper to his lap. "He doesn't have any room to talk, that kid doesn't. His family might have money, but his great grandfather Clay was the biggest hoodlum around here and his daddy is another story entirely. Clay wouldn't even be a Winfield if his great-grandpa hadn't got some girl pregnant, before he got killed in the Pacific, and her family laid claim to his money. If the Winfield Foundation hadn't agreed to cut a deal with the girl's family to make his granddaddy a Winfield, he'd be driving around in some rattletrap pickup instead of the slick job his grandma bought him."

"I don't think you ought to go into all that, Daddy," Joy said from the sink where she was washing up. Something in his daughter's voice always brought McFarland's anger under control. "That's all in the past, anyway."

"That's right, Pop. The Winfield kid's okay—just kind of wild, is all." Chris winked at Joy and made the time-out sign with his fingers. "Wants to be a racecar driver I heard."

"Wouldn't last but one round at Indianapolis. Nearly ran me over in town yesterday, his car full of kids. Speaking of that, Dr. McFarland, hadn't you better be going along up to

Macon for your exams, instead of sitting around listening to gossip?"

Her cousin Chris rose to his feet, tall and so good-looking. Gina wondered how she could be even distantly related to him. Where his hair was dark reddish-brown and his features classically handsome, her eyes were a murky hazel and her nose tilted slightly upward. Her curly red hair, a garish copper color, sprang from her head in all directions as if she were permanently flying through the air.

"A doctor has to know his patients, right?" Chris picked up his backpack and car keys. He slapped his free arm across his chest. "We who are about to die salute you," he said. "Have a good day, Poptop." He threw a kiss to Gina. "And tell Winfield to shut his mouth or I'll make him eat dirt."

After the front door had slammed, and they heard Chris's car start up, Lane picked up the paper again, giving the limp pages a firm shake. "Can't wait until he starts cutting on people so he can pay me back for medical school."

The two families had merged when Gina's father, Mark Kelly, left his wife and two children to work for a technology firm in New York. The McFarlands had volunteered to take the girls while Maureen "got on her feet" again. Gina always interpreted that phrase. Recalling her father knock her mother to the ground, she visualized Maureen struggling to stand upright, something she was certain she had witnessed as a younger child. As much as she loved the McFarlands and the farm, she ached all over to be with her mother in Atlanta. However, Maureen had rarely extended that invitation, "seeing as the girls are so happy where they are."

Lane was still waiting for peace to settle so he could put in a word before returning to his paper. "All I'm saying is, Ginny, your daddy loved your mama. May still, for all we know. Now, c'mon eat your breakfast. I'm leaving in about ten minutes." The newspaper came back up to form a print wall between them. "And comb your hair. You look like you slept with your head in a mixing bowl."

Joy came over to sit down across from Gina at the table. "Your daddy works real hard up there in New York City. And it's a long way between there and down here in Georgia."

One of those eternally sweet and softhearted women, Joy had a crush on her boss at the mill, Holland Baker, grandson of one of the Winfield brothers, and, therefore, a lynchpin in the local oligarchy. He'd been married and divorced twice, and her girlfriends told her she was wasting her time and her life, waiting for him to even look at a farm girl, even one who looked like Joy. Because that's what the McFarlands were, an old family in the region, not landed gentry but good yeoman stock nonetheless. Fighters in the Revolutionary War, they had settled here after being given land in Creek Country as a mustering-out allotment by General Washington. They had produced producers and good citizens, veterans in all the subsequent wars, large broods of children who all left the farm for industry, only to return home at the end of their lives.

Lane himself had fought briefly in the Middle East, received shrapnel wounds over the lower half of his body, and returned to McFarland Land, as the family called it. His oldest son, Doyle, graduated high school and returned after two years at Auburn to help run the place. The real mastic in the construct of their lives was Mildred McFarland, wife of Lane, mother of Joy, Chris, and Doyle and the girls' aunt by marriage. Stout, energetic, and practical, Mildred was the power behind her laid-back husband's success, goading him into new ventures like aqua-farming. She managed the finances and gathered the Kelly girls under her wings like a broody mother hen.

"I appreciate you making excuses," Gina said. "We don't need it sugar-coated, though. Life is what it is."

"My, aren't we the hoary, old philosopher, though?" Her uncle's attempt at humor did little to gloss over the seriousness of the subject of divorce.

Spoon halfway to the grits, she stared at Lane, appalled. "A what kind of philosopher?"

Joy broke down in fits of laughter, nearly spilling her coffee on the sports section.

"Hoary," he repeated, getting choked as he tried to swallow his coffee.

At the sink, Mildred was soaking the morning eggs in disinfectant. "It means like ancient, honey. Your uncle shakes everybody up with that one. You know, old guys with white hair and long white beards. Confucius, you get it now?"

"I get it." Studying her grits bowl, Gina saw the world as it really was, a microcosm of obscure motives and devious explanations. "Maybe what Clay said is true. I was so scary-looking, he didn't want to stick around. And anyway, Joy already told me it was because I wasn't a boy. You don't have to sugar-coat everything. I'm sixteen going on seventeen now. You can tell me the truth."

Her cousin had the grace to look embarrassed when her father put down the paper to stare at Gina. "My lord, girl, now what in the world put that idea into your head? We'll talk about this later on, but right now, you, Miss Ginny, are going to be late for your very last day of school. So if you don't want to end up in detention, missy, get a move on."

"But it's only a half day," she whined. "Everybody skips. Please? With sugar on it?"

Joy swatted at her with the dishtowel. "Skip is a big no-no to McFarlands. Get dressed, girl."

"Right," Lane said. He was neatly folding the paper with a defeated sigh. "We don't skip school. We flat out run."

The kitchen door creaked and Megan stuck her dark, curly head into the large, airy room. There were dark circles under her eyes which, combined with her smeared eye makeup, created a zombielike effect. "Morning, everybody. Don't want breakfast, not hungry. Just some coffee with milk. Arthur's on his way to pick me up, so toodles for now, kiddies." Blowing a kiss off her hand as if it were a bubble, she let the door swing behind her.

"And was that this year's Julia Springs Prom Queen?" Joy looked around for someone to appreciate the joke. No one did, so she mumbled, "Must have been the Zombie Prom."

Normally, Gina would have laughed at any joke about her sister, but today had been anything but normal—and it was only eight-thirty.

"Megan, wait for me! I'll ride with you." Throwing down

her napkin, she bolted out of the kitchen, breakfast untouched.

Before the kitchen door swung closed, she heard her uncle's voice raised in annoyance. "Now, what'd you have to go and tell her that for, Joy? You know that wasn't it at all."

And her cousin's whiny reply. "She asked me and I didn't know what to tell her, Papa. You ought to tell her the truth, then. She's right."

Before she was halfway up the stairs, Gina heard the front doorbell jangle and went down to answer it. When she opened the door, Brice Johnson came through it so fast, she barely had time to tell him, "Morning, Mr. Johnson."

"Is your uncle here? I've got to talk to him."

"That you, Brice? Come on in and have a cup of coffee," Lane shouted from the kitchen. "Slow start this morning."

The foreman wiped his muddy work boots on Mildred's new doormat and without waiting for Gina to accompany him, strode to the kitchen door. He hit it so hard with his muscular shoulder, it flew back, striking the cooler behind it.

"Sorry," he said to no one in particular, even though Mildred was about to remind him the kitchen had just been repainted and charging in like a mad bull out of the chute wasn't too helpful.

Considering the state of her hair, Megan would take forever to get ready, keeping Artie Gatewood simmering behind the wheel over his overheated pickup. Curious to see what was so urgent that Johnson didn't even have time for the usual pleasantries like "Today the last day of school, ain't it?" or "What you going to do with yourself all summer, Miss Ginny?" she hung around on the hall stairs.

Johnson was always worried about something, this lanky, saddle-tan farmer who managed 520 acres of McFarland land in return for a percentage of the produce and a minimum wage salary. Usually, it was the price of feed, or soybeans, or some commodity, that people of the land depended on.

When she heard the name Root Woman, Gina moved closer to the kitchen door and with her bare toes, pushed it open a crack.

"What I mean is she was doing jou-jou medicine, like that

old Evil Eye kind of stuff. It's about time she was arrested, practicing Satanism in broad daylight. My nephew said when he and Cole approached her, she was there doing some kind of talking to spirits like they do."

At the table, Joy covered her mouth with a napkin in an effort to hide a smirk. Instead, it came out in her tone. "She's a healer, Mr. Johnson. You all know that. Why, even white people go to her. Even old Mrs. Winfield had her come to the Glory Hall when she had the tumor in her belly and Root Woman took that tumor away. At least that's what Mrs. Winfield said."

"I'm sorry, but that ain't the point, Miss Joy. I mean, everybody knows only ignorant people believe that kind of thing. Taking tumors out of people and the like."

Joy got up to take her plate to the sink. "Well, you were the one asking if she was doing some kind of voo-doo stuff. Just telling you she's a healer, is all. Nothing wrong with that. Asian people believe in that way of thinking. We don't know everything about curing people here in the United States."

"Where's all this leading to, Brice?" Lane was a patient man but there were times when Brice got on his nerves. This was one of them. "You look to me like a man who could use a good cup of coffee. Pull up a chair and join us."

But the foreman remained on his feet, alternating between grasping his John Deere cap and slapping his dusty jeans with it. "Yeah, okay, well, Trey's hard to make sense of sometimes, but he was going on and on about some kind of eyes coming at him. And Root Woman telling him to run and hearing Cole screaming like some kind of wild animal had ahold of him."

Lane put his paper down and stared at the farmer. "Well, did he go back and see what was happening or did he just take off?"

"He didn't go back, so he don't seem to know what happened." Johnson's voice spiraled upward. "But I'm telling you she was a-practicing some kind of witch craft, Lane. She's about scared that boy about of his mind!"

"I'm just asking, how come he didn't go back and help him. He had a gun, didn't he?" Lane squinted distrustfully at his foreman. "Now, sit down, Brice. You look right spooked.

Joy, bring him some coffee." His voice dropped to a level he used with nervous animals. "What time did all this happen?"

"I don't know. Real early, the boy said. And they took Prescott's pickup to go hunting and fishing all night, my sister said."

"And Trey came back on foot, you say? That's a helluva long way. About six or seven miles, I'd say. Go on. Maybe their truck broke down."

In the hall, Gina pushed the heavy door open a crack so she could hear. *Six or seven miles? But how could he have been standing in the side yard just half hour ago, just staring at nothing?* She listened, unaware she was pressing her body to the swinging door.

Johnson crumpled up into a chair, his bony frame collapsing beneath his denim overalls as if it had been constructed of paper. "I'm damned if I know what's going on. When they didn't show up for breakfast, my sister asked me to go flush 'em out of the Thicket. So I drove down there and found Trey flapping around in the road like a chicken, in such a state I thought he'd gone stark staring crazy. Took drugs or drank and took drugs. Talking all about eyes and eyes coming down out of the trees. And kept saying, 'Run, he's right behind us! Run, or he'll catch you!'"

When he was thinking deeply about something, Lane lit a pipe and sent an aromatic cloud through the sunlight slanting down through the tall windows.

"Prescott. Scottie Prescott's kid?"

"Yeah. I can't get nothing else out of Trey but this run, run, run stuff. Says last thing he remembered was hearing Cole screaming. What in hell could have happened to him, Lane?"

Suddenly, the door gave way and Gina was thrown into the kitchen.

Trying to regain her composure, she said, "I just came to tell you Cole's okay, Mr. Johnson. I just saw him about fifteen minutes ago." The adults around the table simply stared at her so she took advantage of the pause. "I saw him when I got up and went into the bathroom. I just looked out the window and there he was standing in Aunt Mildred's azaleas. He was fine,

except a little dopey looking. He is a druggie, you know. Probably still stoned. Sorry, Mr. Johnson. I mean, everybody
knows he uses…stuff."

Joy was trying not to spit her coffee all over the paper.
However, Aunt Mildred, who had come in from the backyard
with the morning's eggs, gave her a horrified stare. "Gina
Kelly! Why, I never! Excuse her, please, Mr. Brice. You know
how these teenagers talk! It's all drug talk these days."

Johnson kept twisting his big hands together and nodding
absently. "It's okay. I know how kids are. Anyway, thanks for
telling me, Miss Gina, honey. I'm so relieved to know he's
safe and I'll let his mama know. I wonder what in the world is
Trey so scared about then?"

Suddenly, she was the bearer of good news instead of a
complete dork, falling into the kitchen like a plaid meteorite.

Trying to strike a nonchalant pose, she affected a shrug,
one hand on hip. "Probably just had a bad trip. Drugs can do
that to you, they say. Makes you see things that aren't really
there."

Her laconic uncle merely glanced in her direction. "We'll
talk about it later, okay? And where did you get that T-shirt?"

She looked down at her flat chest, realizing her robe had
fallen open. Her T-shirt read, *ADAM AND EVE HAD PRE-
MARITAL SEX. WHY CAN'T WE?* "I—I—It's Megan's. I
couldn't find a clean one so I borrowed it from her." She
jerked the robe closed. "I'll be ready in five, Uncle Lane. Just
wanted to tell you—" She left the kitchen so fast, the door
swung back, hitting her on the heel.

The relieved laughter in the kitchen was cut short by the
phone ringing.

Upstairs in the rambling farmhouse was an attic that Mildred and Joy had turned into a quasi-office, game room, and
storage facility. She found Megan sprawled on her stomach
with a text book in front of her, talking on the phone to Arthur.
She knew it was Arthur before even hearing his name, the way
Megan had that whiney tone in her voice she got when she
wanted her way.

"Hold on, I can't get a bit of privacy around here. The

wobbly just came in," she said as Gina opened the door. "I'll call. See you in a few, okay? Love you, baby. Kisses."

Gina made a gagging sound. "You don't have to hang up because of me. I don't want to listen to your drivel anyway. Kisses. Baby. How disgusting is that? I just wanted a ride to school."

"We're not going to school, dummy. It's senior skip day. We're going to a skip party. But if you tell, I swear I'll kill you." Megan sighed and lay back on her cushion, gazing at the painted heavens on the ceiling. "God, I loathe Arthur. Utterly hate his guts."

Trying to straighten her hair with a round brush, Gina stared at her sister lying on her flowered cushions like the doomed Maid of Shallot, dark hair spread all around her. "I don't know how to answer that except, 'Huh?'"

Megan kept staring straight up like she did when she said her prayers at night. "I know what you think. I crawl all over him, but I can't quit now. I'm in such trouble, Ginny. And I'm so scared. I don't know what to do. Sometimes I think I'll just die."

It was so unlike her older sister to confide in her, much less ask advice, she simply couldn't think of a reply. "It can't be all that bad," sounded really lame.

"Three months pregnant is bad when you aren't married. That's why I'm trying to get that dirt bag Arthur to marry me secretly, like down in Florida or something before—before everybody finds out." Megan rolled over to face Gina, perched on the edge of the old day bed the dogs slept on in winter. "Don't you dare tell anybody, even Joy, or I'll kill you, I swear. God forbid, if Maureen finds out. She'll have a cow and make me wear a scarlet letter 'A,' like on Arthur's football sweater—and it won't stand for Arthur, either."

The announcement was still filtering through the cement wall enclosing Gina's mind. Always practical, she started with the cause rather than the result. "Pregnant? Didn't you use—I mean, isn't there stuff you can use not to get that way? Like pills or…whatever?"

The horny Lady of Shallot sighed, her chest heaving. Gina sneaked a look at her belly. Flat as ever. Megan was so slim, a full-blown pregnancy would make her resemble an olive stuck on a toothpick.

"He was using a condom and it broke one night. Just my luck. I don't want to have a kid right now. If it makes you feel this bad, maybe never. I've got that scholarship and I'm going to music school in Boston." Suddenly, almost violently, Megan sat up. Fixing her younger sister with a wild stare in her green eyes, she said in a tight voice, "I've got to get rid of it, Ginny, and you've got to help me."

A hundred questions flooded into Gina's mind in a heartbeat. *What does it feel like? Did it hurt? Is it as good as they say in songs? What does he do? What do you do?* "Then why did you keep doing it with him?" It sounded like a normal thing to say, but Megan threw her a scathing look.

"Because I want him to marry me, stupid. Just marry and get it over with and then we can divorce and go on to college. I'm not forfeiting that scholarship. Hell, no!"

Megan was a talented pianist—so talented, she had outgrown several music teachers in the community, or exhausted them with her tantrums. The McFarlands decided she'd take lessons at the Mercer School of Music where they didn't have to put up with histrionics. That meant someone had to drive her some seventy miles up to Macon three times a week.

For her senior year, that someone was usually Arthur Gatewood and it was on one of those trips, they had skipped the lesson and gone to a motel for another set of lessons, Megan confided. That lesson had created the maxim "never buy cheap condoms."

Mildred had never checked in with the teacher so the missed lesson went unnoticed.

Momentarily stymied by the moral and physical implications of having a child, Gina left her sister lying on the bed and pulled on a short blue cotton dress she had thought would look sexy. Instead, it hung on her like the strange events of the morning—heavy with portent, but empty of meaning. When she checked the rear view in the full-length mirror on the door, her rear end seemed to stick out like a set of stairs.

When she came out again, the room was empty.

"Megan?

There was no answer. Megan and her awful secret were gone.

Chapter 5

Her uncle was usually a taciturn man, but as they drove down the road leading to town, he cut loose with such a diatribe Gina was a little afraid of him. When McFarlands were angry, their blue eyes caught fire and their faces flushed dark under the habitual tan.

"Would you like to tell me why you lied to Mr. Johnson this morning? I want to know why you can never tell the truth, Gina. You're always making up some kind of exaggerated story. That was an awful thing to say to Mr. Johnson, to tell him you saw Cole Prescott and he was fine!"

She had rarely seen her uncle angry, and never at her. Now he was furious with her, with a scathing stare that caused her to choke back tears. All the more hurtful because she didn't understand why he was accusing her of lying.

"But I did see him, Uncle Lane. In fact, Megan heard me ask out loud what was he doing out there. Just ask her. She'll tell you I wasn't lying. I saw him plain as you see me."

"You can be very certain I'll do just that." Her uncle gave a deep sigh, the sudden rage depleting with each mile. After a long silence he said, "Okay, so maybe you just thought you did. Maybe it was somebody else and you just thought it was Cole. But it couldn't have been him, Gina, honey. He's dead. Torn apart and thrown up in a big old pine tree. They found him up there this morning. The sheriff called me, asking me to tell Brice Johnson."

She was so relieved to be off the hook, she hardly processed the news. "Maybe that happened to him later on after I saw him. I know I saw him. He was wearing a checkered shirt and jeans and—and he had a red bandana in his..." Here she closed her eyes, seeing him again, staring at the house. "Right hand. I just thought he was there to see Megan. You know they were going out before she went steady with Art Gatewood." She stopped, checking her uncle's face again. "But how did he get up in a pine tree? Maybe something was chasing him and he climbed a tree. You know, panthers do come up from Florida sometimes when they get brushfires down in the Okefenokee."

McFarland knit his brows and played with his cell phone as if he were deciding whether to make a call. "What time was he—I mean, what time was it you said you saw him in the yard again?"

"Seven-fifty exactly. I know because my alarm goes off at seven forty-five exactly and I hung around in bed for a few minutes just listening to the singing."

"Singing?"

"Yeah, outside in the road where the workers line up to fill their water coolers. I even heard the old pump squeaking." She suddenly had a funny feeling something wasn't right. She sneaked a peek at her uncle again out of the corner of her eye. He looked the way he did when he couldn't guess the word that fit in Sunday's crossword puzzle.

"Honey," Lane began and then stopped, even more doubtful than ever about the right word, "we got running water now. The hands fill their water containers at home. And nobody went out this morning—yet." His brows knit over his nose. "Maybe you were dreaming about the whole thing."

"No, I wasn't asleep. I was talking to Megan." Overwhelmed with confusion, she wanted to spill the news about Megan's pregnancy before he heard it from anyone else. He'd been the father she never knew and never would have. His was the strong arm to lean on, the guiding hand, her teacher and protector.

"So you think it was about seven-fifty when you saw him, do you?"

She nodded emphatically. "Yes, sir, I do."

"Okay, we'll just leave it alone for now, honey." Uncle Lane still wore his worried expression as he gripped the 150's wheel. "It's all right."

"I guess it wasn't him I saw, then." She looked at her uncle's grim face, putting all her displaced love on the man she regarded as her father. "Uncle Lane?"

Her voice seemed to shake Lane out of deep thought. "That's right. Couldn't have been. Probably just some bum looking for a day job. Been a lot coming around lately."

Neither of them believed him. They rode in silence the rest of the way to the high school where half the usual number of students were gathered, mostly the geeks who didn't want to skip and underclassmen who wouldn't dare skip.

With relief, she spotted Holly, holding forth with her famous monologues to a racially mixed group. Light-skinned and green-eyed herself, Holly fit in with both black and white cliques, with no fear of scorn from either group. She and Gina were buddies, BFF's on the social media and in real life. They had each other's backs, literally and figuratively, from grade school cat fights to big girl gossip.

Others called Gina a geek and ragged Holly not to be associated with such a dorky kid. The pure white crowd called Gina a "crossover" and "wobbly-butt" to find favor with Megan, her older sister, homecoming queen, *and* prom queen in two successive years.

Holly, however, had nothing but praise for her friend. "Look, Gina doesn't have a mean bone in her body, unlike Megan who's a real snake. Gina stood up for me in first grade and beat up a bully who called me the 'N' word. She's going to be beautiful, wait and see. And if she doesn't turn out good, I love her anyway. And no, she's not gay. She just doesn't sleep around unlike someone we know."

That put a stop to all the catty gossip and Gina was on good terms with both sides but never one of the cool kids.

Getting out of Lane's truck, she hurried to Holly's group, hanging on the edges of it as if it were a raft in a choppy sea. She was greeted by halfhearted compliments.

"Hey, Gin, cute dress."

Holly waved her audience away. "Your bra shows," she whispered, taking Gina's arm and steering her to one side. "There I've fixed it."

"At least, I'm wearing one. Does my butt stick out too bad?"

Holly laughed in her usual carefree way that was as contagious as the newest germ. "Honey, don't you know that's sexy to the max? Megan just calls you that 'cause she looks like a broom with legs, is all. Get it? She's jealous, honey, because you've got curves. So use 'em! We call it a back porch worth sitting on."

"Holly, I've got to tell you something weird that happened this morning."

"Let's cut before the first bell." Holly led her away from the school steps. "Hustle that booty, girl."

"Where're we going?"

"Over to Saranji's or Sara's Place, as you white folks call it. I'm starving. My mom's got nothing in the kitchen to eat. Played the Lotto with the food money. Sara always gives me something. You look cute in that dress. I remember you wore it to Megan's party, right?"

"Have you ever seen something that wasn't there?"

Holly stopped and turned to look in her eyes. "Yeah, lots of times when I was tripped out. Why?"

"Because I saw Cole Prescott this morning. After he was dead."

Chapter 6

Jordan Tanner felt old. He felt it more every time the seasons changed and the temperature switched from cold to hot, and back again, as if some central thermostat had gone haywire. He felt it in his old war wounds and particularly in his foot and ankle—which had nearly been torn off by an animal trap. He still wrote the occasional article for sports and outdoor magazines, bringing in some extra money he didn't know what to do with, but Carolyn did. Correction, Carolyn had. She would use it to spend a lot of time away from the farm, traveling up to Atlanta to see the grandkids and lavishing presents on them, all the while talking about putting money away for their college. That it was a contradiction in terms never seemed to occur to her.

But the house behind him was quiet since she'd been gone, as if it, too, had died. The female life had gone out of it and the place was barren as an old woman now, never to reproduce chattering, squalling, and racing offspring again. Tanner found the purpose of money had died along with it. It just sat in the bank, neglected, unless he sent a birthday check or paid a bill with it. The funeral bills were all paid, a stone erected, death cards sent. Only the memories refused to quit the earth.

Carolyn's stark blue eyes, full of pain for the life and love she had lost, had followed him around the polished halls of the hospital. "I hate leaving you like this, Jordan. You need someone to look after you."

Slightly annoyed by being talked to like a child, he had nevertheless squeezed and patted her pale hand. "I'm not a dog. I can opened cans and go outside to pee."

"That's exactly what I mean. Marry somebody, but don't love her like you did me. And certainly not like you loved Francesca. Show some good sense in your old age."

"I'll have you know my grandfather the judge—"

The pale hand slid from his like a silk handkerchief and waved the air. "I know, married a sixteen-year-old girl when he was eighty. Talk about one foot on a banana peel."

"He had five kids before he got both feet in the grave."

"Who aren't right in the head, I heard."

He smiled, reliving the conversation and what he should have said. He'd been doing that a lot lately—reliving old conversations, old fights, and recreating a new self who was faster with a comeback and stronger with an uppercut. Lord God, had he ever been able to fight the way he remembered fighting?

At six-thirty in the morning, Maybelle was doing his washing and singing gospel music, in hopes it would persuade him to go to church again. He was like an old barnacle clinging to the bottom of a sunken boat. No purpose except to breathe and take in nourishment, that is, whenever Maybelle decided to quit singing and start breakfast.

Maybelle interrupted his revel in self-pity. "Miss Melissa Bulloch whatever-her-last-name-is is back in town. Looking real good for her age an' all."

His reply was typically cynical when it came to women who were rich and of a certain age. "Probably. She ought to be the poster child for the Plastic Surgeons of America by now."

"Maybe so." Maybelle wiped her hands on her apron and studied the mirror beside the door where Carolyn used to primp at the last minute before going out. "But she sure is rich. Driving a brand new Mercedes. Bronze, it is, with wire wheels. Eeewee, that's some smart-looking automobile. So what if she's had plastic surgery to look better. Wish I could. I'd jump at the chance."

"Okay, Maybelle, what's your point?" He was on the front porch, cleaning a shotgun which he rarely used anymore.

He was afraid he would mistake some misguided hunter for a deer.

"Nothing," she said in a way that always meant something. "Just you ought to get out more instead of sitting around like an old sourpuss." She went back in the kitchen, humming next Sunday's hymn. "You know, Miss Carolyn wouldn't like the way you been acting. Drinking and smoking."

The morning sun put him back to sleep in the middle of Maybelle's lecture. Somewhere he was awakened by a distant sound which translated into his dreams as an alarm. He rose and fell back like an old war horse to the bugle call. *Damn, where was the coffee?*

"I'll get it," Maybelle said. "Since you ain't getting out of your rocking chair yet." She reached the receiver around the screen door. "Don't disturb yourself now, hear?"

"Who's calling at this ungodly hour? If it's not the president, hang up."

Maybelle handed him the phone, "It ain't him on the Hotline, but you'd better answer it just the same."

"What?" he snarled into the phone, silently cursing Edison.

"Jordan, come over here quick."

He recognized the squeaky voice as belonging to Desmond Clark retired minister of the Julia Springs Church of the Miraculous Waters.

"What in hell? Des, do you realize it's only...damn," he cursed the clock for being in unreadable numerals from this distance. "The sun's barely up."

"Jordan, get over here now." Clark's voice mounted the scale like a mountain goat in full flight. "You don't know what's happened?"

"How can I know? I just got up, dammit! What's the matter, Des?"

"She's here—dead! Mother's dead! Foully murdered, poor dear."

"Now, Des, calm down. She's ninety-five years old going on a hundred. By all rights and purposes, she should be dead. I mean, we've all got to go—"

"No, you don't understand. She's been killed. Murdered! Her head's...oh, my dear God, Jordan. You've got to come right now. Please, Jordan. I'm at her house. Please."

He started to ask what in hell Des was doing at his mother's house at seven o'clock in the morning, but thought he wouldn't get a straight answer anyway—not the shape Desmond was in. "Did you call Pierce yet?"

"God, that bumbling idiot! I don't want him here. She wouldn't want him here. She even thought his father was an idiot! No, please come now, Jordan. Now!" The minister burst into tears and hung up, sobbing.

Jordan called Chief Tinker Pierce, pulling on his trousers at the same time. Finding his fishing shirt hanging on a chair outside, he slipped that and his moccasins on, found an earwig crawling in one and shook it out, hopping on one foot out into the warm, damp morning.

Tinker Pierce answered in a mumble, "Julia Springs Police, Chief Pierce speaking." It was clear he was still at home from the background noise—still in bed, most likely.

Chapter 7

"Maybe she fell down the stairs. Old people do fall down a lot, Des."

Pierce's SUV was there at Farebourne in the Clark mansion's circular drive when he got there. Pulling up behind it, he vaguely wondered how a town like Julia Springs could even afford a police chief, much less afford to supply him with such a lavish vehicle, being only 21,000 in population, counting the livestock and recently deceased.

On the other hand, Tinker was the one senior of two fulltime member of the police force, the other three being parttime deputies. Also, it was rumored the Clarks and Winfields supplemented his salary.

The other fulltime policeman on the Julia Springs force was Detective Sergeant Quade Walker, a strapping ex-US Marine veteran and son of a dirt poor farmer from somewhere down around Albany. After two tours in the Middle East, doing some kind of mission he didn't like to talk about, Walker had returned to Julia Springs, of all places, to start a farm of his own. Organic stuff, the locals would say with a twisted smile that really meant "moronic," except nobody dared to use the word in reference to Quade Walker, in case it got back to him. A taciturn, grim Walker returned from Iraq and Afghanistan even more grim and silent than death itself. For whatever reason, people whispered about him, no doubt having something to do with the deep scars on one side of his face. He had then been excluded from combat and served two more years with the military police at Camp Lejeune where he got his detective stripes.

Needless to say, his very appearance on Sunday morning was enough to sober the Saturday night drunks who ended up in jail to sleep it off.

Along with a whimpering Desmond Clark, Pierce was conducting an investigation which consisted of stepping over pools of blood while one of his officers threaded around upstairs in search of clues. He peered down at the crumpled, broken form of his late benefactress with obvious distaste at the sight of her crushed skull, split to the cranium.

"Poor thing," he added, shaking his head. "She was such a nice lady."

Desmond became unglued, straightening his skinny body to his full height like a fishing bird defending his nest. "Oh, just shut up! Shut up, you fool!" His vehemence shocked the entire room full of people, all except Tanner. He knew Clark did not suffer fools lightly and it was no secret what he thought of Pierce, whose expression had become an adolescent pout. "No, she wasn't nice at all. She was an old demon in disguise, full of guile and inconsistencies and weak, weak as sin, that's what she was."

"Take it easy, Des." They hadn't seen Tanner standing in the marble foyer. He realized too late that he still had his bedroom slippers on. "I brought the flask, Des. Come on over to the library and tell us how you found her."

Tanner led him shuffling across the entrance hall in blood covered slippers to the enormous library built by his great-grandfather. In fact, he noticed Desmond's jacquard silk bathrobe was almost covered with blood, as was the hand he placed on Jordan's arm to steady himself.

"I don't know what happened, J.T.—I just found her like that. Honestly I did." He looked at Tanner, urging him to believe in his innocence.

"Of course, you did, Des. It was an accident, that's all." As soon as the words were out of his mouth, Jordan Tanner was struck by another thought. *But what if it wasn't an accident?*

When they were seated on the leather couch, Tanner pulled out the flask of brandy and offered it to Desmond but the minister waved it away. "I don't drink. It's bad for my heart."

Knowing how finicky Clark was about germs, Tanner filled up a shot glass from the bar and handed it to him. "'Drink it and think of me,' isn't that what the good Lord said? Go on, down the hatch."

Clark made a face but gulped it down, making Jordan smile when his eyes nearly popped from his head. Then he handed Des a glass of water, and the minister nearly strangled getting it down. "Oh! Oh!" he warbled. "Oh, that burns going down!"

After that he settled down and began to make some sense. Detective Walker had joined them, as quietly as his feet would allow him to move across the hundred-year-old pine floors. "Mind if I listen, too? Strictly off the record."

He took a seat where he could watch Desmond's hands and face in the light while sheltering his own, Tanner noticed.

"I was spending the night here because Marilyn was having her ladies' club over to play bridge. It's just like trying to sleep over a henhouse when she does. They just squawk and giggle and eat until all hours, and she insists on doing the dishes afterward, even though I'd help her in the morning. But no, she's just got to get her kitchen cleaned up, which takes her until three in the morning. I'm exhausted the whole next day."

Tanner interrupted to attach a memory to Desmond's train of thought. "I remember when Carolyn used to do that stuff, but she always left the dishes for Maybelle to do in the morning. Go on."

"So I was sound asleep when I heard Mother calling my name. I jumped out of bed and put on my robe and then called out, 'Holly? What's going on?'"

Walker looked up from his notebook. "Who's Holly?"

"She's a local girl from the Springs Mother hired to sit with her at night. Oh, don't worry, she's just a teenager and I know her grandmother. Used to iron for us. This is her wayward daughter's child. Daughter's in prison for drugs and I don't know what all. Father ran out years ago. We checked her out and she sits with old people and new mothers and that sort of thing."

The detective made a brief scribble. Though he said nothing, Tanner suspected the bulge in the officers left pocket was a cell phone with the microphone open. Sort of an unofficial statement, which wouldn't stand up in court, but could be solid gold when mined for clues or discrepancies.

"Where is she right now? This Holly?" Walker's voice barely raised an octave. He might have been asking about the weather.

"That's just it. She wasn't there. I haven't seen her. She must not have come in."

The detective's expression didn't change, but something about him did. It was as if an internal switch had been activated, subtly releasing a burst of energy. "You mean she hasn't been here at all?"

The liquor had left spots of red on his otherwise pale face and before Des covered his eyes with his hands, Tanner thought he saw a look of terror in his eyes. "I don't remember. I'm so confused! The sight of her when I came downstairs...so horrible, you can't even imagine."

Tanner pressed on, knowing his friend had always had a flair for drama. "Des, you've got to pull yourself together, man. Did you see Holly? Anywhere, any time?"

The door opened slowly and Tinker Pierce stuck his head in. Motioning to Walker, he whispered, "Coroner's here. You can come, too, Tanner, but Desmond better not."

Slipping off the arm of the couch, Tanner left Desmond in a shivering heap dwarfed by the huge leather chair that was his grandfather's and stepped outside into the hall. "This is one helluva mess," he said to Pierce as they walked across the harlequin tiles that formed the foyer. "He's hysterical."

"Hell, I would be too if that happened to somebody in my family." One thing about Tinker, he was a softy, Tanner thought. He commiserated with everybody—down and out farmers, wealthy landlords, edgy shopkeepers and swampers— alike. "So damn much going on around here, I feel like a one-armed paperhanger on steroids." Then, his face reddening at his own blunder, he said, "With what happened to Cole Prescott earlier, I mean."

They all looked at him, a question in their eyes except, Quade Walker who said, "Let's just take one case at a time. Okay, Chief?"

Chapter 8

Quade Walker had played football in high school and still looked like he was wearing shoulder pads. Everybody thought of Walker as the real police chief and that Tinker Pierce just had the job because his dad was a sheriff before him. Still, it was who you were in Julia Springs—not who you wanted to be.

Tanner liked the young man because he was obviously a survivor of any number of harrowing ordeals and had remained reasonably sane. Moreover, he got straight to the chase without the usual polite talk around the subject. Within the hour Walker had made a thorough check of the old mansion and was returning to the library when Tanner came in, followed by Pierce and Newton Tapley, the local undertaker who doubled as the county coroner.

"What's going on, Q? Good to see you, except bad right now," Tanner said.

Walker stuck out an enormous hand with a grip like a bear trap. "Mr. Tanner."

After that brief greeting, he got on with an explanation of what he had found. "Looks like somebody got in through the carport door, which for some reason was unlocked. I didn't see any sign of forced entry anywhere. Dusted the area for prints and took infra-red pictures. Have to talk to Mr. Clark to see if anything's missing or not."

"Maybe somebody left it open on purpose." Pierce stood with his hands on his love handles, draping over the sides of his cowboy belt. He always wore cowboy boots, custom made in Texas, and sported a cowboy hat in summer. Since he had never been on a horse and was afraid of large animals in general, it was hard to imagine Tinker Pierce riding to someone's aid in anything other than an SUV. Still it boasted of Julia Spring's western frontier heritage as the edge of Indian country in the early 1800s.

"I imagine it gets pretty warm in here during the day," Walker said, dismissing any allusion to conspiracy before his boss got carried away with theory. "Maybe someone just forgot to lock it. There's very little crime in Julia Springs— stealing livestock is more common than stealing expensive things that have to be fenced."

Pierce nodded as if he, too, had thought that was the case, and turned back to Newton Tapley. "So what do you think, Newt?"

"Think we ought to take her over to the morgue at County General and do an autopsy just to make sure it wasn't a blow that cracked her skull. Appears to me, on the face of it, that she fell all the way down those stairs," Tapley said, waving at the enormous spiral staircase in the hall. "Elderly folks wake up in the middle of the night thinking they're young again and just go walking downstairs like they used to. Had one old gentleman with Alzheimer's go sliding down the banister, just like he did when he was a kid, except he shot right off the end of the thing and broke a whole lot of bones. Went into a coma next day and died."

"Hell, at least he died happy," Tinker chortled. "That's how I want to go. 'Cept sliding down a balustrade ain't my idea of a good time, if you know what I mean?"

Everybody did but nobody laughed as the joke died in midair. The police chief had the grace to look embarrassed and even relieved when the overweight coroner got up with a groan. "I called Doctor Morrison to meet me over here. Since I'm not a licensed physician anymore, I need one present to certify death."

A car door slammed and the doctor hurried in, a good-looking young man fresh out of medical school and trying to establish a patient base in the area. When he entered the foyer, his bright blue eyes widened as he glanced at the towering staircase and frescoed ceiling of the front hall. "Hard to imagine this place existing in the middle of nowhere," he said with a grin.

"We're just full of surprises around here," Pierce said, coming forward as if he owned the place.

Shaking hands, he introduced the young physician as Chad Morrison. Morrison was all business after that, checking the body briefly for a pulse, examining the head with gloved fingers, gently probing the body and then indicating it should be covered. The ambulance pulled up outside, strobing the immediate neighborhood with its red Cyclops eye.

The whole thing took less than fifteen minutes, then the frail body of the last daughter of Cecil Clark, railroad pioneer, banker, and white-collar crook, left the great house on Church Street. The great double doors of Farebourne were opened briefly as the gurney was lifted over the door jam, allowing the assembling townspeople a glimpse into the house which had been a landmark for tourists and people who could afford the garden walk and Christmas fund raisers, but never them. They stared in awe to think that such a grand mansion was here right under their very noses, a dowager princess from yesterday. Before now, they had never once glimpsed its magnificent interior. They maintained a humble silence as the tiny bump on the stretcher was rolled past them and into the ambulance. The last of an era was passing by and they knew it, most without resentment. What had been, back in the day, remained back in the day.

As the ambulance attendants closed the doors, they did so without haste. They leaned against their vehicle, chatting and having coffee Ronda Wilkes had sent out to them. Their whole attitude was one of relaxation. Death was not a reason to hurry when it had already claimed their passenger.

Their attitude wasn't lost on the onlookers. One little child in footie pajamas said, "Mommy, did the mean old lady die and will she go to hell for making you cry?"

"Hush, you promised you wouldn't say nothing about

that," his embarrassed mother said in a low voice. "That's disrespecting the dead."

Someone standing nearby over heard the child. "He's right, though. Meanest old thing ever was, Miss Delia. I remember when she had her handyman out at Halloween, running those kids out of her yard. Like putting out some candy's going to hurt her old rich self. I know it's bad to speak ill of the departed, but wherever she's going, she's going to take her money with her, that's for sure—thinking she's going to buy her way into or out of wherever that is."

"Did she have her purse with her?" asked the little boy, looking up at his mother. "'Cause she better go in and get it if she don't."

Gradually, the crowd dispersed, but several small bouquets of flowers were put on the porch in the early morning. That morning was the first time the gates to Farebourne had ever been unlocked for even the postman.

Tanner was wandering around the kitchen, trying to make coffee, when the kitchen door opened and Deli's cook, Ronda Wilkes, came in. She stifled a small scream when she saw Tanner, unshaven and in his old fishing shirt and slippers, standing there with a coffee pot. Ronda was a plump farmer's wife, well past fifty, who had been presiding over the Clark kitchen and everything else for thirty-something years.

"Mr. Tanner, you gave me a start," she said, putting her hand over her shelf-like chest and giving it a couple of reassuring pats.

"I admit I'm no prize to look at this early in the morning, Ronda."

"What on earth has happened? I saw all the cars and people outside. Could hardly get the pickup through the crowd. My sister called me, saying her husband's saying Mrs. Clark's been hurt. Is she going to be all right?"

"'Fraid not, Rhonda. She's dead. Looks like she might have fallen down the stairs or something."

He glanced behind him where the two policemen were waiting for the county's crime scene people to call neighboring Bibb County's crime scene people for assistance. After all, they had better lab equipment and military expertise at their disposal.

"You don't want to go in there. Just make some coffee, will you, please, ma'am? "

As a newspaperman, I used to stay out until dawn and operate on four hours sleep. Not any more, he thought.

"Sure, I will, Mr. T. Never got to tell you how sorry I was about your wife. She was such a fine lady, Miss Carolyn was. So pretty and all. A darn shame." Ronda bustled around the kitchen, fixing not only a pot of coffee, but ham and eggs and biscuits to go with it.

"Say, Ronda, did you happen to go out the carport door sometime yesterday?"

"Why is everybody interested in that carport door? You're the second person to ask me that in an hour. No, I never use that door. I told Detective Walker I always use the front door and the kitchen door, never use that one. Now, call the others before these eggs get cold. Nothing in the world makes me madder 'n' cold eggs."

Chief Pierce took time out to eat heartily and Tapley had coffee, but Walker kept going from room to room, taking pictures and making notes.

"I'd hate to have that fellow on my tail," Newton Tapley commented as Walker passed by the kitchen door to the library. "He'd find me sure enough."

Tanner kept checking on Des who was laid out on the library sofa, snoring away. He smiled, thinking how his friend would wake up with the hangover of his life—no doubt his first and only. He took his coffee and went into the huge living room—the parlor, Delia used to call it. "Living rooms are for family living. A parlor is for receiving callers."

He could almost feel her disapproving eyes following him around as he looked for a place to put his coffee mug down. Paintings of ancestors top-lit with small brass lamps frowned down on him, echoing Delia's sentiments about him. "That Tanner fellow—uncouth and uncultured. Only got where he did because his grandfather was a judge. I must say, however, his great-grandfather served in the Civil War and was made a

captain. That's the only reason I allow him to associate with
my son. The DOC wouldn't appreciate my discriminating
against a descendant'"

Then there was the time he got drunk at Des's graduation
party and threw up on her oriental rug—*a gift to my great-
grandfather from the Sultan of Qatar who took a fancy to my
great-grandmother*. The more he thought about it, the more
Tanner felt uncomfortable. It was not a comfortable room, full
of prickly dried flower arrangements in oriental bowls and por-
traits of equally prickly generations of Clarks.

Returning to the kitchen, he passed through the library
where Des was stretched out and found Marilyn Clark standing
there, looking down at her sleeping husband. She saw him before he could decide what to say—her expression instantly
changed to one of relief.

"Hello, Jordan. Thanks so much for your help. Chief
Pierce told me what you did to comfort Desmond and I so appreciate it. Terrible thing, isn't it? Her passing like that."

If it hadn't been for the solemnity of the occasion when
one says the things they ought to say but don't really mean, he
would have laughed. It was no secret Delia despised her
daughter-in-law, calling her "that silly little fat cow" and
"humpty dumpy country bumpkin"

It was equally well known that, despite her quiet, ladylike
manner, Marilyn Clark smoldered with mutual loathing for her
autocratic and venomous mother-in-law. The old dowager had
forbidden Marilyn to come into the house unless invited to an
occasion where her absence would have been noticeable.

Marilyn, in return, refused to have her mother-in-law at
Christmas or any other family occasion, which had caused
poor Desmond, caught in the tug-of-war between spouse and
parent, to have to attend two of everything—two Thanksgiv-
ings, two Christmases, and even two Easter dinners. His skills
as a clergyman withered in the face of Delia's scorn and Marilyn's quiet resolve until, over the years, he had given up. Tanner had always liked Marilyn, having felt the bite of Delia's
withering scorn himself. "You doing okay? Kids all good?"

She looked at him with dancing brown eyes that said she

would join him in laughter in another time and place. "Never better. Oldest one just graduated from Georgia. You?"

"Ready to get up and boogie." They shared a quiet chuckle. He gave her a quick, earnest hug and nodded toward the kitchen. "Let's let him saw some more logs. He's quiet now. Must've been one helluva shock."

Tanner paused to glance toward the carport door where a small sliver of sunlight fell across the heart pine floor. Like all mansions of its Victorian era, it had a canopied driveway on the side leading to the street. This was originally to allow hearses to pick up coffins from the side door rather than the front entrance to shield the deceased from curious glances. Later, it was a place to park several family cars before the stables at the rear of the house were converted to garages.

"Hey, buddy," he said as Desmond rubbed his eyes and fumbled for his glasses. "You looking for these?" Tanner handed Des the glasses and he put them on, peering around like a surprised barn owl.

"Tanner? Have they…taken her out?" Satisfied after looking around that the body was gone, he adjusted his glasses and repeated. "Have they taken Mother away yet?"

"No, not yet. She's in the ambulance though. They're waiting for CSI to show up. You'll see her later at the funeral home." He didn't add the fact that Delia's body was to take a detour to the county coroner's office to be autopsied for evidence of foul play. "Sit tight, Des. I'll get Marilyn and some coffee."

"They're here," Walker said from the door. He had his gloves on, looking around like a coon hound smelling bait. The detective came over to the couch and sat down. "After you've had some coffee, I've got to get your statement, Mr. Clark."

On his way to collapse in the great leather chair Tanner had vacated, the minister stopped and stared at the detective. His eyes widened in sudden panic. "Statement? Why? I didn't do anything wrong, did I?"

"Just routine, that's all, Mr. Clark. It's okay now." The big police officer talked in a low voice guaranteed to calm soldiers with PTSD and drunks in fights. It had little effect on

Desmond Clark, however. He sat down and then leaped up to his feet.

"I can't just sit here gabbing. I've got things to do. A memorial to organize. Funeral arrangements. My wife! She must wonder what happened. I have to explain it to her. I can't just sit here gabbing—" He charged past Walker into the kitchen where Marilyn put down her coffee cup and hugged him to her ample bosom like a child.

"Oh, my dear," Des hiccupped into her flowered shirt, "I simply can't believe this is happening. It was so terrible. The worst thing I've ever seen, except in the war."

"I know, honey. I know. It's all over, now. All over." She rocked him, pressed against her flowered shoulder, her dark eyes empty and far away. "Did you check the wall safe, Mr. Walker? Just to make sure there's nothing missing? It's behind that picture of Man O' War on the wall."

"No, ma'am." The detective hovered in the kitchen doorway, which looked too narrow for his wide shoulders. "I was waiting to ask Mr. Clark if there was anything missing. I didn't know about the safe."

"Of course, there's something missing," Des screeched in a shrill voice. "My mother's missing!"

"Forgive my husband, Mr. Walker, he's just very upset. You understand, I'm sure."

Trust Marilyn Clark to have her head on straight, Tanner thought. *Just like Carolyn, at her best in a crisis.*

"I believe Miss Delia kept quite a bit of cash in there and some jewelry as well. When my husband is better, I'm sure he'll give you a list of the contents."

As soon as Desmond was coherent again, Tanner went into the library where the detective was peering around at the great room lined with bookshelves to the ceiling. Covers of embossed leather volumes shone in the lamplight, polished but rarely opened throughout the centuries.

Then Walker went to the engraving of the race horse on the wall and whistled. "I love these old places." Walker's hand brushed the mahogany bookshelf, his calloused palm caressing the smooth surface. "Lots of beautiful wood. Got more secrets than a fifty-dollar hooker. Yeah, man. The little safe is open and empty except for some papers and little velvet bags." Walker put on a clean pair of rubber gloves and reached in the wall safe. "Yep, everything of any value is gone, leaving Mr. Clark in the clear. The robbers broke in, got the old lady to unlock the safe, then hit her in the head. Probably got in through that side door."

While Tanner was still reflecting how much prices had risen since Vietnam, the detective said, "That's interesting. Mrs. Wilkes says she never uses that door. So who could have opened it for the thieves?"

Tanner thought of the possibilities. There was Holly of course. She worked at Saranji's after school and on weekends. Just a teenager. And there was Des himself and Marilyn, both of whom had keys. And Mrs. Wilkes who hadn't shown up last night. Or Holly either.

The detective must have taken his bemusement for a senior moment. "Why don't you go on in the kitchen with Mr. Clark," Walker said, "while I get the CSI folks in here. You look like you could use another cup of coffee."

The solicitous tone in the younger man's voice translated into: *You're a geezer, old man. Let us young bloods take over and go sit yourself down with the boomers in the kitchen. We got this under control. You're just in the way here.*

"I was just thinking. Desmond said there was supposed to be somebody staying with Mrs. Clark last night. I wonder if Holly could have gone out or something and left the door open."

That got Walker's attention. "Maybe. Or she let them in and then left. This place is so big, you could hide for days and no one would see you."

"Yeah, but I'll let Desmond tell you all about it, in case I don't get something right. Be bad to start rumors and then put suspicion in the wrong place."

But Desmond kept moaning and rubbing his receding hair saying, "I don't remember anything. I was so tired. Mother always wears me out, 'a pillow behind my back,' 'warm up my milk and put more cinnamon in it,' 'make sure the cat is inside,' 'come read to me a bit.'"

To which Rhonda Wilkes rejoined smartly, "Well, I know who was supposed to be at her beck and call, Holly Parsons. She always stayed with your mother on Tuesdays, Thursdays, Fridays, and Saturdays. She knows I can't stay because I've got Bible Study on Thursdays." The cook looked around for approbation.

"What time does she come in, Miss Rhonda?" Walker accepted a cup of coffee as though he was still on sentry duty in dangerous territory, holding it in both hands, as if anytime an IED would go off and he'd spill the precious liquid. It's the little things you treasured most on the frontlines. A hot cup of coffee. A cigarette. A candy bar.

Noticing the cup was shaking in Walker's large brown hand, Tanner wanted to apologize for feeling smug just because he had the advantage of friendship and this young ex-soldier didn't.

Rhonda Wilkes took her country time thinking about it. "Oh, around five, usually, around the time I leave. Miss Delia always eats around five-thirty and I leave her plate in the microwave in case it gets cold. Let's see, last night it was a slice of turkey with dressing, pickled peaches, and green beans. She loves my snap beans even though I got to mash them up." Suddenly overcome with tears, she dabbed her watering eyes with the tea towel. "Poor thing, to go like that and not peaceful in her sleep. Darn shame, I say."

Walker prodded gently. "So in that case, did you see her last night? This Holly person?"

"What? No, as a matter of fact. I just thought she was late, as usual. Now, Mrs. Pate's always on time, she cleans for Miss Delia, but not Holly. She works at Sara's Place and don't get finished up sometimes 'til six, but I think she's been taking time to see her boyfriend. That fellow from Warner Robins she's been seeing."

Walker had taken out a small notepad and was furiously making notes. "The air force base close to Macon? Go on. So you say she didn't show up on time?"

"That's right and my husband, Gary, was outside to pick me up at five sharp 'cause we have Bible Study on Thursday nights, you see?"

Desmond was quiet up until now, but he suddenly interjected. "That's why I didn't see her then. I got here around five-thirty, didn't I, dear? To eat with Mother or keep her company more like, and she was upstairs alone. So I just brought her dinner on a tray and then I heard Holly call out she was here, sorry to be late, all that. So I just went down in the library to read the papers and, later, I went to the church service around seven and came back around nine. The light was still on in the bedroom, but I knew Mama was asleep by then so I just went to bed."

"Didn't open the door to say "hey" or anything, then?" Walker seemed preoccupied with taking notes, but the question sounded anything but casual.

Desmond's rabbit-red eyes blinked, even fluttered at the suggestion. "Oh, no. I wouldn't dare do that! That might wake her. She sleeps like a…a guard dog or something. Always one ear always open for trouble. Thinks burglars are at the door. Tornadoes in the area. Shootings in Atlanta, she's sure they're on their way to shoot her. Anything, everything," which set everyone —Ronda, Marilyn, Desmond—nodding in agreement.

Ronda rejoined, "Then she'll be awake half the night and Holly or whoever has to read to her until dawn, poor things. Done it myself a few times."

Everyone agreed, except Tanner and the ever vigilant Walker.

"So this Holly who stays on Thursday nights eventually did show up." Walker tapped his pencil on his firm chin, thinking. His dark eyes darted around the kitchen like a night moth. "This house doesn't have an alarm system, I noticed."

"In Julia Springs?" Desmond chuckled as if the suggestion was absurd. "Hardly a high crime area, would you say?"

Marilyn smoothed his sparse hair. "The world is changing, my dear," she said softly. "Not for the better, I'd say."

"So when did you discover your mom—mother, Mr.

Clark?" Ever to the point, Walker allowed everyone to arrive there after he had planted the flag.

"Well, I was telling Jordan here, I heard a kind of bumping noise and I think I heard a shout or shouting, I can't really recall clearly."

"Take your time."

"And I thought she'd fallen out of bed or something so I got my robe on." At this point, he saw his robe was spotted with blood stains. "Oh, dear Lord! Look at me! I look like an assassin!"

He scrambled out of his wife's embrace and stood up on trembling legs. "It's her blood! I must have tried to pick her up! She was—was all crumpled like a little doll."

Walker frowned, pencil poised. "You didn't try to move her?"

"Of course, I did. It was my first instinct. To take her to the sofa, make her comfortable. Or to the hospital or somewhere besides the marble floor."

Meaningful glances flew around the group at the table. At that point, Pierce and the coroner stepped into the kitchen, caught the moment, and stood quietly in the hall doorway.

"But I put her down. I had to put her down." Desmond stood up, his jaw hanging as he stared around for approbation, realizing he had violated a basic tenet of first aid. "I just—just wanted to make her comfortable is all." His thin voice evaporated in silence, and only his jaw moved. "She was past help."

Chief Pierce was about to yell something about tampering with a crime scene but Walker intervened. "Naturally, that's your first instinct. You don't think about nothing else. She's not evidence. She's your mother, for Pete's sake." He nodded. "I know you've been in a war. That's how it is. You don't just leave people out there dying, do you?"

They all looked at the young policeman with renewed sympathy and gratefulness in their faces. All except Pierce who was fuming about being overruled by an underling. Then the county people took over, wanting to talk to Desmond and Ronda again, but Marilyn stepped in, saying her husband had to rest. She slipped her strong, plump arm through his and nearly dragged him up the steep stairs. "No more questions for now," she said, with her sweet smile that meant business.

Chapter 9

After a cup of coffee, Tanner's head cleared. He gave a brief statement to Walker about what he had found on arriving at the Clark mansion, evidently satisfying the detective's curiosity about something the way he kept grunting and nodding his head.

Looking in the kitchen where Des was being comforted by Marilyn, Mrs. Wilkes, and, to Walker's obvious discomfort, Chief Pierce, Tanner decided to pay a visit to Sara's Place.

For one thing, he had missed breakfast and couldn't eat in that scene of what could possibly be a murder. The second reason he hated to admit even to himself. He wanted to ask Saranji what she knew about Holly before Walker did. Holly worked for Saranji—Sara was a Christianized version of her African name. Holly who should have been sitting with Delia Clark all night, Holly who could have left the carport door open. Holly who was nowhere to be found, in the house, when Desmond discovered his mother's body lying on the harlequin tiles like a broken puppet.

Though Sara's Place was packed—all seats taken and a line trailing out into the mild summer morning—Saranji personally found him a place at the counter and poured his coffee.

"What's going on up there at Miss Delia's, J.T.? I heard the sheriff and the ambulance was up there a couple hours ago."

Tanner shook his head as the coffee scalded his lips. "Helluva mess, Saranji. Miss Delia's passed, that's about all I can tell you, but don't broadcast it right this minute. There's something I got to ask you."

"Ask away, honey. You know, I'd tell you anything and darn near have. You're the reason I got this place, big mess as it is. You and only you. If it wasn't for that woman, I would've had it long before that, but I ain't talking bad of the dead. Least not till the Good Lord's got hold of 'em and I bet He turns that one loose like a hot skillet. Come on out to the back porch, where we can get some quiet and I can have a smoke."

Grabbing a bacon biscuit from the plate of four that always came with coffee, he followed her as she threaded through the tiny kitchen, that would have been the old jail's bathroom, and out to the back porch that was no more than four foot square with an overhang.

With every bone in his lanky body yelling for help, Tanner folded himself up beside her on the top step while she lit up a cigarette. "No, I owe you, Mr. Jordan, more than I can ever pay you. Now, ask away."

"First thing, I want you to forget about that little loan to start your own place. That was business, Saranji. We were friends long before that. You helped me and Carolyn out when she was sick. When you should have been looking after your business, there you were. Now look, this isn't going anywhere, you dig? Strictly between us, okay?"

She looked at him with amusement. "I get it now. You playing detective. There you go again, like Mr. James Bond OO7 on afternoon reruns! I swear you're so cute, baby."

"Holly Gibbs works for you, right?"

Saranji exhaled with a hiss and choked back a laugh. "She do and she don't. About half the time, that girl don't show up for her shift from noon to five. Says she's got a sitting job with Miss Delia, but people've seen her with her boyfriend from Benning. Her man from Benning," she repeated in a prissy, singsong voice. "Says he just pops in anytime and sweeps her off to dinner in Macon at the best places and takes her dancing all hours 'til they've done all the clubs. Oh, Lord, I'll never hear the end of all the places they've been and things they've done. Why? She was supposed to be sitting with Miss Delia last night, right?"

"Yeah," he said, around the last bite of biscuit, and then wiped his buttery fingers on his pants.

"Oh, Lord, if she left that old lady alone and something bad happened, she's going to be in deep doodoo. That what they're thinking?" She looked at Tanner's face and then said again, "Oh, Lord."

When he had swallowed the biscuit and taken a sip of coffee to wash it down, Tanner said, "I take it she wasn't here, then," not able to decide if it was to be a statement or a question.

Saranji cut her eyes at him. "I'm not giving that girl no alibi, un-uh. Yeah, she done her shift from twelve to five and then left. Yeah, she was definitely here. I can show you where she signed in and out in the employee books like you all said I should keep. Got all them business tips from the foundation, I did, along with the loan. And guess what? I almost paid that sucker off. With interest. Got one or two more payments to go. Ain't that something, though?"

"Looks like you're doing a land-office business every time I'm here. Cars all over the place." He knew Saranji better than to press her for information, but Walker would eventually get to her and she'd get stubborn. "Did Holly say what she was doing after work?"

Saranji flashed a golden tooth in the morning sun. "You up to that old bird-dogging again, now, ain't you? Can't resist some super sleuthing, right? I know you, J.T. She said she going to Miss Delia's but I overheard her talking to somebody on the phone. I couldn't tell what she was saying, but it sounded like she was sweet-talking her boyfriend to me."

"Look, honey, Reverend Desmond was there when it happened, the police think. He says he didn't see Holly but was sure she was there in the house. So if Holly wasn't there, that's one thing. If she had something to do with it, that's something the cops are going to have to handle. I'm just worried about Desmond, you know? Miss Delia was worth whole lots of money and he stands to inherit everything—lock, stock, and barrel. He'll be rich as a king. That's motive enough to bring down suspicion on him like almighty thunder. Never mind he must have been in the house when it happened."

Saranji narrowed her eyes as the smoke drifted back on the morning breeze. "Oh, crap, I see what you mean. Holly's being there would be kind of an alibi for him, wouldn't it? I'll be honest with you, J.T., I just plain don't know what she did. But I know she was headed over there when she got off here."

One of the cooks stuck his head out the screen door. "We out of bacon, Saranji. Got to send somebody to the Piggly Wiggly to get some more."

"Already? We can't wait for somebody to go clear to Lumpkin to the Piggly Wiggly. Take some money from the kitty and go up to the highway convenience store."

"Don't do that. I got a freezer full of the best bacon you'll ever eat," Tanner said, happy to be useful to somebody. "Luther, go on over to my place and ask Maybelle to give you all the bacon you need. You know where it is. Tanner Farm Road. Got to stop at the Feed Store and Barber Shop while I'm in town. I'll call to let Maybelle know you're coming."

He was embarrassed about how long it took him to get back to his feet, even holding on to the stair rail. "Got to quit hunting at night," he said trying to be offhand about it. "Thanks, Saranji, honey. Remember, it's between us for now. And I'd appreciate it if you didn't tell Detective Walker I've been here."

Chapter 10

Before he left town, Tanner stopped to get chicken feed, kibble for Rollo, and a haircut since he had caught a glimpse of himself in one of Delia's accusing mirrors. The last person he expected to meet was Melissa Bulloch getting out of her car, wearing something short, revealing the legs that won her Miss Union County. Her auburn hair touched her shoulders and lifted in the morning breeze. She was seven years his junior but looked twenty years younger.

He was acutely aware of the rip in the pocket of his old fishing shirt, that the stubble of beard on his chin was gray and that he still had on the moccasins that doubled as bedroom slippers.

But Melissa was as gracious as if he were standing there in his tux. "Jordan Tanner, of all people, I was just about to call you up."

"To see if I was still around, you mean? Just barely. But you haven't changed a bit. Amazing what getting away from here does for you." If there was one thing he remembered about Melissa, it was her smile. Poster girl pretty, it set her green eyes laughing—in the old days, mocking the less fortunate or the socially awkward. Now it seemed full of benevolence, even fondness. *Amazing how time changes things,* he thought, *even social classes.*

She brushed off the compliment with a toss of her hair. "Oh, thanks. Heard about Carolyn. I'm so awfully sorry, Jordan. She was such a lovely girl."

They said the polite things and then she looked up at him. "I remember now. If I caught up with you, I was supposed to say Delia wants to see you. Got time to run by with me?"

For a moment, he got lost in those clear eyes, remembering the first time he ever saw her. She was wearing a green dress and wide-brimmed white hat, sitting in the back of her father's convertible. He thought then she was a flirt and she hadn't changed, still depending on money and looks for the world to do her bidding.

"You hadn't heard then?"

"Heard what?" She stared up at him, time, place, and memories tying them together. "I just got back from Atlanta."

"Delia passed away this morning. Or last night, I don't know for sure. Anyway, Desmond found her. Needless to say, he's a mess."

"I'll bet he is." Melissa shook her head slowly. "Well, she was awfully old. I guess you have to expect that." Then she wrinkled her nose in an impish imitation of embarrassment. "Isn't it nice to call somebody else old at our age? Anyway, I'll send some flowers and a note." There didn't seem to be any love lost there, simply polite sympathy like the rest of the little community. Miss Delia called Melissa "shallow as a creek in drought, a flirt, and a prom trotter" behind her back— while trying to throw her and Desmond together at every tea dance and Christmas supper she gave. Melissa, on the other hand, referred to her as "that old trout" and "walking death."

"How old was she, do you know?"

"In her nineties, I believe. She was pretty active up until a couple of years ago. Age finally got to her, I guess. Happens to all of us." He didn't know why but he always lapsed into platitudes around beautiful women. He'd always felt self-conscious around any of them, except Carolyn. "You write a whole lot better than you speak," she would say, laughing. "When you talk, you sound like a red neck."

And he sounded like one now, hooking his thumbs in his jeans and looking down at his big feet, aware of her pretty sandaled feet with pedicured toes.

She must have sensed his shyness. Reaching up, she put a

soft palm on his scratchy jaw. "Dear Jordan, you look just like I remember you—tall, dark, and rugged as a fence post."

"I promise I do look better when I haven't been routed out of bed before I could shave. Can I buy you a soda at Sara's Place?"

She frowned slightly. "Do you really think that place is fit to go in? I mean, it used to be the old jail and all. And I hear her customers are mostly…you know…"

"Black? Well, I'm a regular there now. Even got my own table unless someone gets there first. They do make room for pretty ladies, though. We can even have our own table outdoors if you want."

"Are you asking me on a date, Jordan Tanner? I thought you never would! Sure, I love to walk on the wild side, as long as you're with me." She looped her thin tanned arm in his. He was acutely aware he hadn't bothered to wear deodorant in a year. *Not since…when the hell am I going to stop tagging everything BCD and ACD—before and after Carolyn died?*

Melissa didn't seem to mind him smelling like a rank mixture of dog and sweat, however. She kept glancing up at him with those sparkling eyes like a girl on her first date. In spite of a mouth like the bottom of a chicken coop and a growling stomach, he felt as though the weary years had just been ripped away and he was immersed in the blossoming summer for the first time.

They hadn't strolled far before she had him laughing, rattling off incidents involving mutual friends, when his cellphone rang. It was Quade Walker. "I think you better come right on over to the police department, Mr. Tanner. Something else's just happened."

Chapter 11

Ernest Schultz was the grandson of German immigrants who had come to the United States after WWII. He had been grudgingly accepted by the little community only after the Catholic priest, on his rounds of churches in the parish, had spread the word that the Schultzes were anti-Nazis who lived in the Alsace Lorraine Valley. Father Carmichael said the family had hidden French Freedom Fighters at their own peril—so that one uncle had been tortured and shot for harboring enemies of the Reich.

The taciturn farmer had been out plowing a muddy field that ran along the creek when his shepherd dog came out of the Thicket dragging something behind him. Something dead. It was easy to see that from the dog's attitude. He stopped every few yards to sniff his trophy, to the point that Ernest got curious and went over to see what Teufel was bringing him so proudly. It was Cole Prescott's missing limb. At first, Schultz thought it was a calf's leg until he saw the hand attached to the ligature. Without bothering to change his dirty overalls, the bewildered Schultz wrapped the arm in some old newspaper he kept in the milking shed and carried it to the sheriff's office in town.

Walker and Tinker Pierce had just come back from dealing with an incoherent Desmond Clark and trying to take Trey Prescott's incoherent testimony about Cole Prescott's death. It had been a rough morning in a community usually as placid as a backwater pool. Quade was unshakeable, having seen enough blood and body parts in the Middle East, including those of his friends who were riding in the same Humvee, which blew up and sent him home from Iraq. Pierce, however, vomited for the second time that morning at the sight of a detached, putrefying arm lying on his desk.

"Holy Jesus! What in hell is that?"

His pale secretary hovered in the doorway, pinching her nose against the smell. "Mr. Schultz brought it in just now. Says he found it out in the creek on his property. He's waiting in the waiting room getting mud all over the floor. Can I go home now?"

Reaching into the bottom drawer of his paper-piled desk, Pierce got two paper cups. Poured two shots of Jim Beam in each and offered the other one to Walker who just shook his head.

Downing the whiskey, Pierce wiped his mouth, still not taking his eyes off the appendage in the newspaper. "No, you can't go home—send him on in. This has been one helluva start to a Tuesday, ain't it?" he said more to himself than to anyone else.

Walker just reached in his own desk and took out a box of disposable gloves, tossing a pair to Pierce. "I'll call Mr. Tapley to get over here as quick as possible."

An equally shaken Schultz shuffled in and recounted how his dog had been hiding the limb in a fallow field. The deputy quickly covered the limb with the stained pages of the *Macon Telegraph* and made two calls, one to the coroner and one to Jordan Tanner.

Tanner and Melissa lingered on the sidewalk outside the police station, making what both of them knew was small talk. Finally, Chief Pierce himself opened the door in desperation. "Are you coming, Tanner? It's a bad situation we've got here."

He slammed the door and Tanner started to chuckle. "With Tinker Pierce, it's always a bad situation," he said, wondering if he had bad breath the way Melissa drew back a few steps.

"I'll let you go now," she said, "but I'm not letting you off the hook that easy. I'll call you about that date tonight.

Don't go anywhere, hear?" And with a wave of her manicured hand, she strolled away down the Main Street the way only Southern girls walk, so their hips swayed easily from side to side.

Tanner walked into the Julia Springs Police Department to be greeted by a solemn group of men standing around the remains of Cole Prescott's severed arm and the distinct odor of rotting human flesh. "Hope they didn't send that thing through the mail," he said, nodding at the severed limb. "Old Postmaster Casper's so nosy he'd probably have heart failure if he saw what it was."

"No, I found it—or my dog did." In his dirty, faded overalls, Schultz stood like a gritty monument to farm life.

He doesn't understand that humor relieves the grimmest of occasions. It would take an act of God to make the big farmer laugh under normal circumstances, Tanner thought.

Faced with a detached human limb, Schultz held his battered straw hat in front of him as though he were at a funeral.

"All the way at your place, Ernst? Wow, that's a good distance from the Thicket. That's where Prescott, was hunting, right?" The chief was known for asking the obvious, but distance was something Schultz could relate to, a quantity to be measured.

"'Bout seven miles," he said, pride glowing in his plump face.

"Point is how did it get there?"

Leave it to Walker to focus on the facts, Tanner thought.

They refocused on the arm, bent at the elbow in the shape of a boomerang. "Hell, nothing can transport anything that heavy seven miles that fast," Tinker Piece said.

"Except wind and water," Walker said, looking closer at the limb. "Twisters have been known to deposit debris for two hundred miles or more."

"I know all that," Pierce replied petulantly, "but nobody's reported seeing a funnel, not even high winds. How in the hell would it have happened and no one saw it?" Tinker Pierce looked at the other men for agreement. "Naw, that's bogus, Q."

But Tanner, who had been quietly studying the grisly object, spoke up. "The Thicket's got a climate all its own. It's a marshland that turns into a swamp. I know, I live right across from it. All that moisture in the air turns to mist and the mist turns to rain. You mix that, and a windstorm with lightning, and you have the makings of a downspout, a funnel cloud that just zaps down out of nowhere. You can tell this arm has been banged around a lot before it landed in Schultz's field. Probably traveled some distance in the creek that's running high from spring rains, too."

"We got no idea who in the hell's arm this is 'til Newt Tapley gets here. Where is that guy anyway? Been fifteen minutes since I told him to get over here, and where is he? Probably still over to Farebourne gabbing away with Martha Wilkes like two old ladies." Pierce punched a speed dial on his cell phone and clapped it to his ear.

"You know anybody else who is missing an arm beside the Prescott kid?" Walker just threw the question out there, sending Tanner into a coughing fit to cover his laughter. It had been such a grim morning, even Walker's dark humor provided a little relief.

The chief was not amused, however. He fixed a holier-than-thou glance on the detective. "It's nothing to joke about, Q. How would you like it if a part of somebody you knew was found seven miles from where the rest of him was?"

Walker said nothing. He simply stared into the middle distance as if seeing something no one else could see.

⌘

After leaving the police station, Tanner drove to the rambling farmhouse that had been his childhood home. Although he and Carolyn had modernized it to the point his parents would have thought they had the wrong house, he felt both welcome and sorrowful each time he came up the winding approach. Those feelings were immediately replaced with uneasiness when he saw his son's huge truck in the driveway.

RSTBN. Reginald Sterling Tanner/Brandon Nesbitt. The

very sight gave him a sick feeling he could only identify as revulsion. He pulled up beside the enormous vehicle which dwarfed his dust-covered SUV by several inches. Luther had parked his humble pick-up behind the behemoth and left the engine chattering to itself as if debating whether to go or stay like old Luther did himself sometimes.

Reg was sitting on the porch, making an effort to look relaxed, but Tanner could tell something was wrong—mainly because something was usually wrong. *Thank God his playmate isn't with him for a change and we can have a discussion without his butting in with "Let me just reframe that." If he uses "reframe" one more time, I'm going to reframe him.* Tanner sometimes wondered if they didn't trust each other out of their vision range, so precariously did their relationship seem to pivot, like on a spider web in the wind, hanging from a single thread.

He brought the bacon slab out to Luther who reached in his pocket for a few dollars, but Tanner waved him away. "I expect I'll eat most of it up if you fry it anyway," he said to the waiting driver. "Tell Sara I'll be back for my supper. I think I'll get it to go so I can come back and hit the bottle. But don't you tell her I said that, hear?"

When Luther had rattled down the road, Tanner sat down beside Reg. "It's been a helluva a morning," he said, hoping Reg would take the hint and be brief about whatever he had come all the way over from Alabama about. Usually it was to complain about Brandon the Bimbo and how he couldn't trust him and how he thought he was having an affair with a soldier or some other damned thing and that he would never change. Tanner got ready to listen to his son who had everything a human being could wish for except good sense.

"No kidding," Reg agreed, rubbing his palms together and glancing up at the blue ceiling as if looking for some cue to blurt out what he really came over for, his aquamarine eyes so like his mother's, it hurt to see the uncertainty in them. It was the way she used to look around like a butterfly looking for someplace to land—uncertain, but passionate. "So, what's up in the Springs?"

"Nothing much. What's up in 'Bama?'"

"About the same. Just came to see how you were doing."

They both knew that was a lie. Knowing his son would eventually get around to revealing the real reason for the visit, Tanner told him about Delia's death.

As usual, Reg was unmoved by anything but his own troubles. Though he had his mother's looks and money, he lacked her innate curiosity about all things scandalous, a trait which had made Frenchy a top-notch society reporter.

"No kidding," he said again. "That must have given old Desmond the shock of his life. But she was really getting up there, wasn't she? I mean, like ninety something."

There followed a strained pause. Conversation usually lapsed when either Tanner's age or Brandon's name came up. "Yeah, old as God himself and twice as rich. How're the horses?"

"Great. Just great. Sold two mares the other day. Brought a nice chunk of change. The top blood line went for one twenty-five, the other just for fifty."

"Are you talking thousands? One hundred and twenty five thousand dollars? Fifty thousand? Geez, Reg!" Tanner was more than impressed. He was stunned but he tried not to let on. "Who's got that kind of money these days?"

"Oh, the guy's a trainer and he might even double that figure. I mean, in some circles that's a steal for a top bloodline and trained to the max. But that's not what I came over to talk to you about, Dad."

Here it comes, the real reason my oldest son is sitting forward in his chair, twisting his big palms together like interlocking wrenches.

"Geez, not Brandon again." Tanner didn't mean to say it out loud, but it came out in a groan. Too little sleep and he always said what he thought. "When are you going to get smart and throw him the hell out, Reg? I don't know why you want to waste your time on somebody like that." He didn't mean to come across as mean, but he could tell by the expression, the loss of hope which faded from his son's almost beautiful face that he had sounded harsher than ever before. No, take that back. He had tangled with Brandon the Bimbo once after too much to drink and threw him out of the house. He and Reg hadn't spoken for nearly six months afterward. "Sorry," he mumbled. "Too little sleep, too much coffee."

The surprise was that this time Reg didn't go sulking off like a girl not asked to the prom. He took a deep breath and began in a conciliatory tone. "Look, I know how you feel about my partner. Although it hurts me to—to know you despise him, and probably me as well, I wanted to let you know—you to be the first to know, that is—Dad, we're having a baby. Brandon and I."

"Jesus, you aren't pregnant?" The very thought made him burst out laughing.

Reg smiled, visibly relaxing. "No, surrogate mother. Very nice girl. Needs the money and has two kids of her own. Financially, that's all she can handle with her husband out of work."

"Is this one of those Rent-A-Womb deals? Where you donate the sperm and such?"

"Yeah. That's about it. It's—he's due in about four months."

He. A boy. So that'll be three guys together. Tanner savored the thought and couldn't help thinking how Carolyn would have reacted.

She would have nodded, given her stepson a hug, and said, "Congratulations, Reg, you're going to be such a good daddy. I thought it would never happen."

And they would have broken out the champagne. Reggie would have gone home feeling accepted once again into the fold instead of slinking off like a wounded animal. That is, if anyone six-foot-three could slink off in a one-ton dually.

Sounding as false as a counterfeit twenty, Tanner raised his beer. "Congratulations, buddy. That's great. How're the girls taking the news?"

Reggie had twin girls from his previous marriage to Stephany, a debutante he had met in college, but had left shortly after their honeymoon to Bermuda. Apparently, Reg had felt revulsion at having to fulfill his marital duties as well as a complete failure as a male. Post-divorce, he had spent three years in therapy only to be told he preferred sex with men. Tanner could have told him that and saved him a small fortune as well as years of self-loathing. His heart ached for his first-born, who with all his looks and money, couldn't have been more unhappy.

In the meantime, he hadn't failed as badly as he thought. Shortly after the divorce was final, the twins were born. Though delighted as a man delivered from a death sentence, he retreated to Spain to the Vargas finca, which was going broke by that time, and occupied himself with trading on the Net and ferrying the Vargas prize Andalusians back across the Atlantic to Alabama where he had inherited from his mother the Weatherall family lands, all eighteen thousand acres of it.

Now, he actually smiled, chasing the agony from his face. "They're actually excited about having a baby brother. Marisa's okay with it. She's always so nonjudgmental. Rosalee was iffy at first, but finally, last time I talked to her, she said, "Can I name him, Dad?"

Tanner grunted and nodded. That was his son, Reggie, a man blessed with more money and good looks than anyone needed. Yet, he had the heart of a woman. Maybe it was because his mother, Francesca "Frenchy" Weatherall, had been as peripatetic as a butterfly, not knowing which flower to pollinate because the love of her life turned out to be her own half-brother.

After taking their baby son and leaving Tanner for a series of husbands and lovers, Frenchy had finally married her adoptive uncle who was like a father to her. The old pain of rejection came back as Tanner now looked at his son with her aquamarine eyes framed in his heavy dark lashes.

Reg saw the look. "I only bring you pain, don't I, Dad? Every time you see me, you look so sad, I go away thinking I should have never come."

"It isn't you, Reg. You are more precious to me than you can ever guess. Just because you're one of a kind. You look so much like her, your mother. Yeah, it does bring up hurtful memories, but beautiful ones, too. I loved her so much and she—I guess it wasn't enough for Frenchy and she went away. I know what she'd say about all this. Frenchy would say, 'Hey, baby, why not be happy? I don't believe in being sad one more second than you have to, so live it up!'"

The strained look faded from Reggie's face. "You mean, you think she'd approve?"

"Of course, Frenchy—Francesca—would be wild with joy and go on a shopping binge to prove it. And Carolyn, too, although she'd be trying to work around all the legal hoops you'd have to jump through. It's just me, your old man, who's kind of uncomfortable with it. I believe in begetting the fun way, not with a test tube."

He tried to make light of it, but Reggie never could see the humor in things. He took life so seriously it was hard to believe sometimes that Reg was his and Frenchy's child. But then, that was when life was so simple, it just went sliding down like oysters on the half-shell with champagne.

Reg leaned forward, earnestly pouring out like sweat, except he didn't ever sweat. "But you're not happy and I so wanted you to be. I understand. I've violated a basic law of nature, having a relationship with another man. We're only people who love each other. We want to just be a family, is all." Reg stood up, towering over him, but slumping to average height. "Thought we'd name him Jordan after you. Sterling Jordan Tanner, II."

"Reg, sit back down and have a drink. I must be getting senile, but let's drink to the little fellow. A real man's drink, bourbon on the rocks."

Though it sounded condescending, Reg Tanner grinned broadly. It was a relief to see him smile.

"Okay. But don't get up, Dad. I know where you keep your secret stash. While I'm gone, you be thinking of a toast. Remember, his name's going to be Sterling Tanner."

Tanner's heart lurched in his chest. Did his son know the doubt that surrounded his birth? "Where'd you get the Sterling part?"

"Don't worry, Dad. Mom told me everything. About the romance with the prizefighter who she thought was my father.

Turns out it was you and I'm glad, even if she wasn't. I'll get us that drink now."

Tanner was still trying to wrap his mind around that when Lane Mcfarland and Johnson came up the road in his nephew's new Dodge truck. Immediately, he knew it involved some crisis because he didn't get that many visitors since Delia Clark and Clarissa Winfield had taken over the Winfield Foundation. The whole thing had turned into a nest of hornets anyway, as various Winfields jockeyed for control of Clay's legacy. Delia weighed in because she controlled most of the money in Julia Springs and was automatically on the board of directors of anything pertaining to the village. Defeated, the Winfield oligarchy had to part ranks and give her a seat on the Foundation's board, where she sat like one of gargoyles, on the bank her father the railroad magnate had founded. They would one-by-one grow old, waiting for her to die.

His nephew parked in a cloud of red dust which settled down on the shiny surface of Reg's truck. Tanner smiled. These days, one of his few pleasures was seeing nature get revenge on the civilization that blatantly ignored its gifts, as if they were some hideous Christmas present to be returned for money. Lane's foreman, Brice Johnson got out the passenger side, a rawboned country man with dirt farmer etched all over his lined face.

"Hey, how are you?" everyone said at once and they all shook hands as it were in the male DNA.

"Carolyn, we've got company," Tanner yelled toward the screen door and then said, "Oh, hell, I meant Maybelle. She's getting deaf anyway. Tell her to bring some iced tea or better yet, Reggie's bringing me something stronger. How 'bout it? A little bourbon and branch to take the dust out of your throat?"

Both men nodded and Lane said, "I'll go help Reggie, Uncle Jordan." Lane let the screen door bang behind him like he'd been told not to do since he was big enough to open it. All the hunting dogs started to bay, thinking it was a shotgun blast.

"Damn," Tanner said. "Now, even I can't hear. What

brings you this way, Mr. Johnson? You come to take one of these mutts off my hands? Lots of good hound puppies out there." He didn't mention Cole's death or that his arm was lying wrapped in the *Macon Telegraph* on Pierce's desk.

"Thanks, I just might do that." Johnson wasted no time dancing around the reason for the visit. "Tell you what, Mr. Jordan, there's been something weird going on around here lately."

"Weird is nothing new for Julia Springs. Care to elaborate on that?" Tanner got his pipe off the nearby table and lit what was left of a previous bowlful. "Go on." The reporter in him, long thought dead, rose Lazarus-like, beckoned by the word "weird." Somehow he had become known to specialize in weirdness since he had solved the Boyer murder case nearly forty years ago. Residents of the hamlet of Julia Springs had memories like elephants and pigeonholed individuals because of one event or another in their lives.

By the time Johnson had finished about Cole Prescott hanging up in the tree, one arm gone, Lane had returned with a tray of drinks. The porch table had to be swept clean of Tanner's ashtrays and pencils before he could set it down.

"Still about as tidy as a litter of pups, I see," Lane said. He looked from Johnson to Tanner. "I see he's told you. What do you make of it, J.T.?"

Tanner stuck his pipe in his teeth while the two other men shook their heads, waiting for him to say something. Finally, he said, "What exactly does Root Woman have to say about all this? You said Trey said she was there. Anybody talk to her yet? Pierce? Anybody?"

Both men looked at each other. Lane gave Johnson a slight nod, indicating he should start first.

"That's the problem. Not yet." Johnson studied his big, gnarled hands. Even though he washed up after work with lye soap, the dirt wouldn't come out of the grooves, a testimonial to his occupation as a hard-scrabble farmer.

"Why not?" Tanner knew all along what they were getting at, but he just wanted to hear them admit it.

He had felt neglected by the community he had served so

unselfishly. There was a generation growing up ignorant of
their roots, and the sacrifices their parents had made for them
by accepting the humility that came with doing without the
luxuries life in the city could offer. Things like central air conditioning, cable television, and computers—all deemed neces-
sities by their whining offspring.

Johnson burst out in frustration. "Because Pierce just says
he can't find her, that's why, Mr. Jordan. Shit, he couldn't find
his own shoe if was on his own danged foot. And Trey don't
remember anything about it, except he kept hearing Cole
scream and her singing and calling to something or somebody.
He's right tore up himself—mentally, I mean."

Aware his uncle was playing with them, Lane said,
"Pierce says he can't find her down in the Swamp. Nobody
knows where she lives, except Saranji and she don't want anything to do with it. And Lou Owl, of course, but good luck
finding him either. Hell, that place eats people alive. Quick
mud, snakes, gators, and meth dealers like Ham Phillips and
Goat Williams."

Tanner stuck a match to rekindle his pipe. "Dr. Phillips is
not a meth dealer, although he does grow some first class weed
for medicinal purposes—had a few samples in my day, I admit."

"I hear he's crazy as a bedbug," Johnson said, baring his
untended teeth in a grin, "all them machines running around
there, they say. Wish he'd fix me up one to cook better than
my wife. Don't tell her I said that, though." The bourbon had
put him at ease for the first time that morning. He sat back in
his chair and shook his head. "Damn, if this hasn't been a
morning. I heard about poor old Miss Delia Clark. She had
some years on her. My nephew Cole was just twenty last
week. It'll kill my wife. She practically raised that boy." Sudden tears formed in Johnson's eyes. He wiped them away
quickly and took a big gulp of bourbon.

Lane sipped his drink in thoughtful silence. Reggie came
out and pulled up a chair. He had a drink in hand but Tanner
knew he wouldn't touch it.

"Lane told me about your nephew, Mr. Johnson," Reggie said. "You have my sincerest sympathy."

He would, Tanner thought. His son was nothing but sincere and courteous. He tried desperately to fit in to this society where sarcastic wit was valued highest of any trait except skillful deceit.

Turning back to the conversation, Tanner wondered what Cole blundered into down in the Thicket. As Johnson said, the place was full of meth labs in fishing shacks by the creek, in old rusted trailers, even old abandoned trucks. Or maybe he had gone there with the intention of making a deal. Everybody knew Cole was a druggie, even his uncle.

Occasionally, the ATF or some task force of the feds made a raid down there, but as soon as the heat was off, the dealers flocked down there again. It was said locally that Chief Pierce was afraid to go down there.

"As long as they don't start selling in Julia Springs," he said. "Then you'd better believe I'll bust 'em."

They already had started selling in Julia Springs on the street corners by lamplight after the chief had gone home to Maria and church.

They drank in silence while Johnson regained his composure.

Finally, Lane spoke up. "A lot goes on down there in the Thicket. Sheriff Pierce told me one day some express mail guy went down there to his place trying to deliver a package or something. Old Mophead had one of his robot things scoop that poor guy up and carry him all the way back to his truck, just a-hollering like a baby. Came back into town white as a cored apple, telling Pierce to go down to the Thicket and arrest Phillips for assault or something. Some said he quit his delivery job the next day."

Leave it to Lane to come with a funny story to relieve the tension. It was the trademark of a local boy who used humor in the face of tragedy.

The visual image of Sheriff Pierce, belly overflowing his cowboy belt, approaching Ham Phillips's robotic enclave, thumbs in his belt loops, was the kind of stuff of which local legends were made. The story would be repeated around the stove at Whitehead's General, the feed store, and front porches on cool summer nights while the barbeque was smoking on the grill.

Tanner, however, kept his mind on the purpose of their visit, much as they tried to obscure it. He thought he knew why the two had come and said it. "So, bottom line is, you want me to go down there in the Thicket and talk to her. Is that what this is about? See what she has to say about what happened to Cole?"

They nodded in unison like two puppets on the same strings, relief evident on their faces. Johnson leaned elbows on his knees. "See, you're the only one who really knows her. And she likes you, I've heard the people say. Ever since you got that black man, what was his name? Moore out of prison."

Tanner gazed at the Thicket lining his cornfield feeling as if something were looking back through the dense tangle of growth. "True, we go back a-ways. We're both getting old. God only knows how old she is. They say when she takes off that gold hat—"

"Turban," Lane corrected. "It's a turban, Mildred says."

The young know everything. You know nothing of value. Acknowledge that.

"I doubt if she winds and unwinds it every day, but, okay then, turban. My point is her hair's pure white."

Johnson had only persistence in his favor and he applied that at every interval. "But Trey, he says she was singing there before—before the thing came, doing some hoo-doo worship."

"Tell him what he did to make her mad," Lane prompted with his soft voice.

"Cole poked her in the behind with a rifle butt and then, according to Trey, just disappeared screaming at the top of his lungs." Johnson cradled his empty glass in his hands, and raised tearful eyes to Tanner. "That's what he said, but he's not making much sense. We've got to take him over to Macon to get something to calm him down."

"These boys been smoking weed? Or meth? Sounds like a case of that rather than blaming something, you're not sure what, on that lady who was just there saying her morning prayers. Their religion believes in ancestor worship and they consider some places to be power spots where the earth's power is strong. Like the tree we call around here The Hanging Tree. But the hoo-doo followers think it's the mother of all trees so they call it The Mama Tree."

Tanner watched Johnson melt like butter on a hot stove in the presence of facts. They always did—these superstitious locals—so afraid of a tradition older than their pioneer culture. He relented, thinking of how his own family had reacted to anything other than the puritan values they'd inherited from their parents. Life was simple here, not subject to nuances, and certainly not open to variation in religion. He remembered when Catholics were suspect because it was said they worshipped statues. He thought they'd gotten beyond that kind of thinking, but then, the Springs was a backwater town in more ways than one. "Sorry," Tanner said, backing down from his role as self-appointed prosecutor. "Must've been an awful shock. Shows what happens when you don't go respecting other people's religion I guess. You sure it wasn't one of Ham Phillips' machines gone amuck?"

Johnson bristled slightly. "Wasn't no machine done ripped the boy apart like that. Trey says he saw eyes, big staring eyes come out of that whirlwind."

Lane traded looks with Reggie. It sounded like a bad drug trip to them. But Tanner felt Johnson's need for explanations, the community's need for closure, and above all, the need to save face. To give death some kind of dignity.

"Tell you what, I don't want Tinker Pierce to think I'm interfering in his job. He ought to be the first one to talk to her. After that, I'll go see her. I believe I know the way. Haven't been down there hunting in a while, ever since my leg got wonky, but I don't guarantee she'll tell me anything."

"Dad," Reggie put in. "I don't think it's safe for you to go down there at your age. I wouldn't even go down there in the Thicket. Last time I went down there to go hunting with you, I was eighteen."

Lane sensed Johnson's growing anger. "Get Lou Owl to

go with you. After all, he lives down there. He's a superstitious old coot, I know, but he always says the Chinaberry Man comes around when something bad's going to happen. Well, he's a bit late. He'd better come on, then, don't you think?"

Reggie's reference to his age was still setting on his nerves. "Then what're you asking me for? Get Lou to take Tinker down there. He knows the Thicket. Hell, it's his back-yard, he ought to." *Did he sound petulant, like a girl being the second choice as a prom date? Was his need to be needed as evident as that? Geezuz, he had developed into a crotchety old man since the war hero thing faded. He'd been sitting here sulking ever since.*

His nephew wasn't about to beg him. "Tell you what, Uncle Jordan, we'll just give Pierce a call right now and tell him that." He picked up his cell phone and dialed 911.

Instead of the emergency operator, Tinker Pierce himself answered the phone. When Lane asked him where to find Root Woman, Pierce readily admitted defeat. "Hell, she don't have a phone! She isn't even registered as a citizen, but everybody knows every move she makes, her complete history—or so they say—damn near everything, except where she lives. I wonder, does she even have a house or does she sleep in the damn trees? The whole town knows she's been here since God was a child. Why don't anybody know how to get to her house? Damn swampers, anyway. Why can't they live in civilization like the rest of us?"

"So if my Uncle Jordan and Lou Owl were to find her and ask what happened this morning to Cole Prescott, you wouldn't object?"

"I'll even loan them my phone to record anything she has to say. I don't do that for just anybody, you know. But this case is special. The Swamp isn't in my jurisdiction, see? Just the town of Julia Springs. That's the county sheriff's, but I'll bet you he can't find that damned woman either. Sure, sure, full speed ahead. Go for it! And tell Jordan I said thanks."

Lane grinned and tried to hand the phone to Tanner, but he waved it away. After Pierce had hung up, he said, "Finally, Uncle Jordan, you've got something to do."

Chapter 12

Tinker Pierce was clearly feeling the pressure of a man who had no answers. Seeking some clue as to what happened to Cole Prescott, he had slunk into Pop's Place, across the street from Saranji's where the white people hung out. While getting a burger and fries, he dropped broad hints like "Weather's looking bad. Could get another one of those skunk twisters like the one that tore up the Thicket this morning."

The people clustered around the tables knew exactly what he'd come to find out, but they had nodded and continued eating. Eating was a serious business around the Springs. A few people mentioned Delia Clark's death and asked how Des was taking it, but most just listened to Pierce go on and on about the grisly details.

Then someone asked, "When you going to find out what Root Woman had to do with that skunk twister, Tinker?"

And he was forced to confess, "I would, but I don't know where she lives."

"Did you try looking in the Yellow Pages under Hoo-Doo Magic?"

Everybody laughed at the jibe, yet there was an undercurrent of discomfort. Chief Price looked around at the weathered faces of the men he had known since childhood, reading them like the sports section of the Atlanta Journal. Skepticism was blatantly plain on some, discomfort on others, as if he had raised a taboo subject.

Lonnie Dorland took out a toothpick from the holder on the table and stuck it in the corner of his mouth. "Ain't nothing new for a twister to pick up somebody and throw 'em into a tree. You remember they found the Jennings' baby girl up in the crotch of a tree two days after a twister tore through Twin Pines. Right as rain, that baby was. Killed her poor mama and daddy, though, hiding in the bathtub like they was."

"He's right." Lonnie 's half-brother Walt always backed him up. "Hell, Root Woman is a big mama, but even she can't throw a grown man way up in a fifty-foot tree, now can she?"

"Maybe it was Chinaberry Man," said one of the other farmers at the counter. That brought a laugh from the assembled townsfolk.

Dorland laughed even harder. "Come on, that's plain crazy." Still, even he couldn't pull-off the confidence to put down the local legend.

The group quieted down, waiting. It wasn't a joke. It was something they all believed but never admitted to. The legend of Big Foot, some kind of man-animal that lived in the woods and no one saw by daylight. Hunters over the years, stretching back to Indian days, had reported strange incidents of someone or something tracking them as they hunted deer and wild boar in the deep woods. They told of hearing sounds of something huge moving through the woods, paralleling their path, its presence accompanied by the distinct odor of chinaberries.

A hush fell over the circle of work-stained, saddle-tanned farmers. Then they pelted Pierce with questions like buckshot at a tin can.

"What about chinaberries? Did they smell it?"

"Was there wind stirring in the trees, come up sudden-like?"

But Lonnie chucked the toothpick in an ashtray and said, "Most likely got a bad batch of white lightning. Both those boys drink whatever they get their hands on. I heard even anti-freeze."

"They just don't go uprooting trees." Pop Cooper, being a practical man, stated the obvious. In spite of the straggling trade, the restaurant's owner and his wife had attached themselves to the conversation. Ordinarily, Pop would rather injure a body part than lose a sale. Now, heads nodded as he pointed out the unthinkable. It was plain on their weathered faces that they were caught between myth and reason. Finally a voice said from the back of the group, "Hell, it ain't good, if he comes around again. You know what they say."

"Who you talking about, Lou? Chinaberry Man, you mean?'

"That's just a bunch of bullcrap superstitions." Pop Cooper was known to dislike Lou Owl because he had accused Owl and his brood of poaching on his land. He had even had Lou arrested several times, but Chief Pierce had always let him go for lack of evidence. One night, Lou had gotten even by nailing the hide of a missing calf on Cooper's barn door.

Now, at Cooper's challenge, all eyes turned on the speaker, an old man with Indian features and a graying braid leaning against the counter.

"Tell us, Lou."

"I'll give you a little history lesson, boys." Lou Owl gazed one by one at the apprehensive faces of the townsmen. "The elders say he showed up when Andrew Johnson was president and started his See the United States on Foot campaign for the Indians. And he showed up again right before WWI. And after that, the flu epidemic in 1937. Then he came around about the time the Atom bomb went off and again during the Cuban Missile Crisis. It's when something bad and big's going to happen to the people. He's kind of like a guardian of the people. A totem. An early warning system that's been around before even my people came here."

"Too bad he didn't warn us there was going to be a twister down in the Thicket this morning," Cooper said, looking around at the concerned faces.

"Oh, that Chinaberry stuff's just a whole bunch of hogcrap." Jake Fry shifted the wad of snuff to the corner of his mouth. "I'm going with Lonnie's idea of a freak twister. It was stormy yesterday for a little bit, and we're just a hair east of tornado alley. Happens all the time. The funnels jump the river from Alabama to Georgia and drop down but lose their momentum. The Weather Service don't record them 'cause they're under the radar, so to speak."

The consensus of the group was evident by a series of nods and grunts. Lou Owl continued staring over their heads and then, without a word, he paid for his coffee and left the restaurant.

"Crazy old coot," Cooper muttered, fumbling for a cigarette.

Walt Dorland leaned closer to his buddies, lowering his voice that the few women in the place wouldn't hear. "They say Root Woman's a witch—put the Evil Eye on more than one person around here. I even heard she does abortions then takes them dead babies out and makes some kind of potion with them."

Nods and grunts of approval rippled through the assembled group like an ominous wind. "Heard that, too."

"Time she was stopped from killing babies, that's what." Glances were shot Pierce's way, knowing he was married to a Catholic. He was aware of the implications and taking his Styrofoam container he got up and went to the door. "Says something against that in the scriptures, don't it? Killing babies before they're born and all?" Chief Pierce made those his parting words from the doorway, knowing what an impact they would have on simple minds.

"You go get that woman, Chief, or we will." Jake Fry lifted his coffee mug as if saluting a knight before a quest. "We know you can do it."

"Yeah, do it before we do something."

Cooper looked around at the customers for consensus. There were quite a few nods. Pierce only ignored them. It was knowing that his hands were tied that got Pierce seething with frustration. So, when Lane had called, he felt liberated. Now all he had to do was wait and do nothing. Tinker Pierce was good at doing that.

ဆၜ

Quade Walker had winced, just hearing the police chief's

querulous excuses. Pierce had gotten the job because Pierces had been the sheriff and the chief of police for as many elections as only Tanner and a few others could remember. Chief Pierce, the elder, for all the scandal of graft, wrong convictions, and racial profiling that had rocked his tenure, had all the other qualities the people of Julia Springs desired in a law enforcement office. The appearance of complete honesty and morality was a trade-off for accepting bribes from every two-buck bootlegger, pimp, and illegal gun trader in the eyes of the community.

Tinker III did all of that, including attending church every Sunday with his portly wife, Maria, and his excessively portly daughter, Tiffany. Many considered his choice of a Catholic Hispanic wife a detriment to his aspirations as state representative for the area. He could have chosen any number of local girls, instead of a Catholic and Hispanic at that, even though her father owned the gas station on the county highway.

Complaints were not voiced in so many words, but their community disapproval was reflected in their lack of support, the legend of Tinker the Elder notwithstanding. Tanner, however, owed a debt to the family he could never repay. As a young man, Tinker the Elder had saved his life and, consequently, Tanner continued his obligation through an entire generation. He was to the point now that, at times, he wasn't sure Tinker the Elder had done him any favors. Listening to Pierce's driveling on with excuses to cover his ineffectiveness as a city functionary on Lane's phone would have just sent his blood pressure skyward.

But Quade Walker just tuned his boss out, concentrating on the facts at hand. "What worries me is that people are starting to get up a hunting party and go down into the Thicket to look for her. Even though she technically isn't a citizen of Julia Springs, if something happens to Root—Miss Kahalia, you'd be responsible," he said, breaking into Pierce's rant. "I wouldn't be surprised if the NAACP doesn't get called in on it."

At the mention of that powerful organization, Pierce had to get himself another shot of Jim Beam and sit down abruptly.

"All because of Cole Prescott, a kid who wasn't the brightest bulb in the socket, was around when a rogue wind hit. And who are these people threatening her?" Playing Devil's Advocate, he sat back and put his feet up, the picture of nonchalant innocence. "Just a bunch of piss-ass farmers who love to hear themselves talk. And that's all it is, talk. You know people haven't got anything better to do."

But the chief was still stewing about the reception he had gotten down at Pop's Place, the downright smirks over his ignorance of what went on around there. "Tanner will go find her down there in the Thicket and tell her I want to talk to her, down here at the station, so everybody can see she's willing to cooperate with me."

In the end, Tanner had agreed because he remembered the night a long time ago, he had persuaded another man to go into town and a mob tried to lynch him, but he had also agreed to prove he was still useful.

Chief Pierce hung up, feeling like the incompetent idiot everyone thought he was, even his wife. It wasn't the first time the man who qualified as Julia Springs' only celebrity had put him in his place. On the other hand, Jordan Tanner was looked up to by the locals, primarily because he was a war hero and had punched out the governor of Georgia, for which he was thrown down the marble stairs of the state capitol building. He told Walker that story expecting the big detective to think as he did, that Tanner was just a has-been who needed something to do.

"Jordan Tanner came back here like a whipped dog with his tail between his legs. He was all washed up until the Winfields made him the administrator of the Winfield Foundation. I don't know why they did that, except their son Clay was a friend of his. Anyway, before Delia Clark took it over and cracked down on frills like parks, Tanner frittered away half the fortune on projects like a library and a town hall, and a dammed swimming pool for God's sake—desegregated!"

The bourbon was making him think aloud now, but Quade wasn't listening anyway, or he just looked like he wasn't. "Oh, yeah, I used to think that was the most awesome thing, to have a swimming pool everybody could go to. Was that Tanner's doing? I thought that was the most awesome thing. And the library, I used to spend hours in there waiting for my dad to get supplies. And punched out the governor? That makes him next to the Masked Marvel in my book."

The chief realized his complaints had the reverse effect on Walker and stooped to snipping over the city budget. "Damned waste of money if you ask me. We got to spend manpower, time, and gas policing those places. That's why you and I can't have a raise. Damned frills like that."

Walker got the drift. Nevertheless, if anyone could, Tanner would get Root Woman's statement and the whole mystery of Cole Prescott's death would be solved. Tinker leaned back in his creaky swivel chair, as his father before him had, and poured himself another two fingers of bourbon.

Chapter 13

Tanner wasn't particularly pleased he had let himself be sucked into another controversy. The tug-of-war over the administration of the Winfield Estate had reminded him how much he didn't like to be around disagreeing people, or for that matter, people in general. It got on his nerves—what was left of them.

"If Lou says something bad's going to happen, Root Woman'll know what it is. That is, besides throwing people up in trees. I'll get Lou Owl to take me down in the Swamp. If he's sober, that is. Last time we went hunting, I had to get a mule to bring him back home."

After the two men had left, Tanner sat back in his chair, staring out at the Thicket glowering beyond pastures dotted with Black Angus. It was gratifying to be needed by somebody other than Carolyn who, though dying, had him carrying out the garbage and chopping firewood, just "to give him something to do."

Lou Owl, however, was not a person who believed in illusions. Tanner always counted on him for the truth, and he certainly got it when he started to debate the wisdom of going down into the Thicket at night to find Root Woman.

Lou pulled up in his rattletrap truck just in time for lunch. Easing back in one of Carolyn's prized wicker chairs, he deliberately put his feet up on its neighbor. "You ain't getting old, J.T., you just getting bored to death, sitting up here on your porch all day. Look at you with that iced tea in your hand.

Bet you don't even have the good stuff in it, just plain old tea. That's when I know you're getting old, friend. I bet if you was hungry, you'd get up off your butt and get to tracking something to eat. Ain't that right?"

"I'm just asking, why at night? We don't have to go hunting down there at night. We can just as well look for Root Woman's place in the daytime, as not."

Lou's sarcasm bordered on derision. "You getting chicken? You know as well as I do you can't find no swampers' place in daylight—only at night, when they got lights on. I know now why you don't want to go. You been listening to Brice Johnson's stories about the Boogey Man what tore the arm off Cole Prescott and left him up in a tree. Maybe you are getting old, J.T. It just occurred to me, old is when you don't want to take chances anymore."

Tanner took the bait before he realized he was hooked. "Okay, then, Rambo, that does it. We'll go on down tonight and find Root Woman. I'll turn on the recorder on my cellphone and let her know this could be her deposition about what happened. Don't forget to bring your flashlight. No moon tonight."

"You ought to know I don't use flashlights. Let's everybody know where you're at and where you're going. If you're hunting, deer can see you a mile off. Meet you at the Hanging Tree," Lou Owl gave a hint of his fractured smile, "unless you believe all those stories about a bunch of Indian braves being hung up there for horse stealing a hundred years ago."

"Oh, quit trying to pull the 'injured native' on me. I don't believe in ghosts or the Tooth Fairy or even old Santa Claus. Stay for lunch. Maybelle's doing up crawfish and Reggie's here. He going to have a baby with that man he lives with."

Lou wore his usual bland expression. "Far as I know, two males can't do that yet. Got anything to drink around here?"

"You don't get it, Lou. They're going to get a woman pregnant and pay her money to carry it for them. Isn't that against nature or the law or something?"

"Damn, J.T., you were right. You are getting old—losing your sense of humor. What difference does it make how a child comes into the world as long it's loved and taken care of? Now, what have you got to drink in the kitchen?"

ఌఌఌ

The first thing Kenya saw was her tattered bloodstained dress draped over a willow chair near a stone fire fireplace. Then a large shadow loomed over her and she recoiled, squeezing her eyes tightly shut. She flinched as something cold, and yet warm, was applied to the side of her face and her seared eyelid.

"It's all right, daughter. Drink this and you will sleep." The voice was deep as a well and kindness itself. A hand lifted her head, carefully avoiding the wounds on her shoulders. Kenya drank something like warm soup and realized she was parched.

"Thank you," she tried to say, but the words didn't come out. Then the hand laid her down again, gently, on sweet-smelling hay.

"Sleep now."

And she did, wandering into a dreamscape more beautiful than anything she had seen in life, so beautiful she wanted to live there, to always have enough to eat, to have her body clean and untouched again, to wander along picking flowers and swimming in a silver stream. She remained there in the Beautiful Place until the next afternoon when she opened her eyes and found two large yellow ones looking into hers.

Kenya screamed and sat up, knocking the black cat away. It yowled in a fury of rejection. The wicker chair squeaked behind her and she turned in terror to see white teeth in a dark face.

"Shabaz, I told you not everybody likes cats, but you didn't listen and that's what happens. Hello, little one. How do you feel?"

Although the voice was deep and rich, it didn't belong to a man, so Kenya breathed more easily. As she tried to turn around to face the person, she screamed involuntarily. "Oh, oh, it hurts!"

"Yes, the cuts are deep in places, but healing up nicely. It's the burn, though. We may have to have a doctor look at that. Come, I'll help you sit up in a chair, and that will ease the pain some. You must be hungry by now."

"Yes, ma'am." As she tried to struggle to her feet, Kenya retched on the clay floor. Strong hands held her steady, applying wet clothes to clean her face.

"Poor baby. Come, take a step to the chair beside the fire."

"Sorry. So sorry. I'll clean it." The hands lifted her under the arms and swung her to the wicker chair and she realized she was only seeing out of one eye. The other was closed. Kenya moaned and wept. "I'll clean it up, Mama."

"No, you won't. Now, drink this."

The last thing she wanted to do was swallow something else, but the voice and hands were like those of the Lord, guiding her along the Valley of Death and therefore she did as she was told. After a few gulps, relief flooded her brain and seemed to permeate every nerve and vessel. She tried to smile, but it twisted oddly across her mouth. "Tankoo."

"You're very welcome. Tell me your name, daughter, and who did this terrible thing to you?"

"Shurkenyur." It didn't come out right.

"That doesn't sound right. Try again." The tall woman wearing a red shawl appeared within her vision range.

The girl shook her head. "Shurkenya. Joones."

"I thought so. Kenya Jones. I have treated your mother, Pearlene. You don't remember me? It was two years ago and she, your mama, lost her baby. I hear she got another one in a hurry, though."

"You're Root Woman? I member now. You do the root medicine. How I get here?"

"I just found you laying under the Mama Tree, all beat up. Who did this to you, baby? Can you tell me?"

Kenya was too drugged to lie, nor did she reflect any emotion as she said, "Mama did it. Mama." Unbidden, tears rolled loose, dripping from her chin unheeded. "She beat on me and whup me and burn my eye. Oh, Sweet Jesus, yes, she did." She tried to rock her body, but it hurt to move.

"But why would she do something like that? That's not love, is it? That's not the way a mama loves a child."

Root Woman knew the truth without hearing it, but Kenya had to say it first. To put it into the air, to have it blow away. It came out in wrenching sobs, the way a woman pushes a stillborn child out of the womb.

"It was him. Lewis Spencer. He done it to me every morning she sent me for firewood, and I swear she knew he done it. I swear she sent me out there, Miss Root Woman, right when he was out there. 'Cause I try to mix up the times, you know, so he'd be home already, and then I could go for wood or water and he'd be in the house—and when she'd even had firewood, but she sent me on anyway. And he come right after me and she knew it. Sure she did."

Root Woman did the rocking for both of them, rocked back and forth, making an um-um-um sound. Then she took a sage bundle from a basket beside the fire and held it until it caught the flames. Then she lifted it high while Kenya cringed, afraid she was going to be punished by fire. But Root Woman waved it through the air, creating a smoke trail and then dropped it back into the fire before it scorched her fingers. All the while, she chanted in some strange tongue Kenya had never heard.

"There," said Root Woman. "The air is clean of that ugly truth. Are you ready to eat, daughter?"

Suddenly, Kenya was ravenous. "Oh, yes, please, ma'am." Her open eye gleamed in the firelight as energy overcame fear. "Let me help." But when she tried to get up, she almost fell.

"Be still. You still weak. There'll be plenty of time to help me. But that comes later. Now, you must get your strength back."

It was the most to eat Kenya had ever had. There was roasted wild turkey, a shellfish stew with corn in it, and grits with honey. Over the sumptuous meal, she related what little of her life she remembered, how her real father, Willy Jones, had been killed by Lewis Spencer in a gambling fight, leaving her mother with an infant, and two small children. How the men had come and gone until Lewis Spencer came along and offered marriage. It didn't take long until it was clear what he really wanted, somebody clean and young. And all the time, her mama pretended she didn't know. Over and over, Kenya heard her tell Lewis he was her onliest man. If he left, she would kill her children and die. But Kenya knew he wasn't going anywhere. He had a warm fire, a woman to cook for him, and one for pleasure. Lewis thought he was the king.

While she purged her story, Root Woman listened, but her fingers never stopped moving. After she had eaten, Root Woman washed Kenya's gourd bowl in the hot water kettle and then brought piles of what looked like weeds and berries to the table. As Kenya talked, Root Woman's deft fingers sorted leaves and seeds into bowls and baskets. Then she dealt swiftly with a pile of gnarly roots that looked like twisted fingers, peeling off their skins and mashing them in a stone pestle.

Finally, Kenya had to ask. "What you doing there, Miss Root Lady?"

Root Woman's smile spread to her eyes that glowed like the coals in the hearth. "You'll learn soon enough, girl. Now, tell me this, do you want to go back to your mama or stay with me? You got a baby coming and you mighty young to be on your own. Fact is, I'm kin to you through your daddy, Willy Jones. Willy was my boy so you is my grandbaby."

Kenya was so stunned, that she put down her wooden spoon and stared at the tall woman across the table with her good eye. "You my Big Mama? How can that be? Nobody never told me. You sure?"

"You doubting my word?"

Kenya was so confused, she began to stammer, "O—oh, no, Mrs—I mean, no, ma'am. But why nobody tell me? My mama said we got no kin, least none to take us in."

"That's because your mama and me didn't get along, baby. And that fight your daddy got into wasn't because of gambling, it was because of her, Pearlene. Spencer called her a bad name and said bad things and your daddy had to fight him. I told him she wasn't worth risking his life for and he did anyhow because he truly thought the world of her. He loved you, too from the moment the Master of Breath breathed life into you, and Princess, your sister. You all was the apples of his eyes."

"He was big and tall like you, I remember." Kenya hugged herself with happiness, though her wounds still stretched across her back. "He would have killed Lewis Spencer, too, I bet."

Root Woman chuckled way down deep. "Now, you know that's the truth."

They shared a smile for the first time. "I love you, Grandma," Kenya said shyly. "That sounds so good to say— Grandma. I got one now, and I'll stay with you forever and forever. Grandma, I don't want this baby of his. Do I gots to have it?"

Root Woman looked long and hard at the ravished face of her granddaughter. "When you're strong enough, we'll go ask the Mama Tree. She'll know what to do."

❧❧❧

Holly and Gina staggered into Sara's Place, laughing so hard, they had to sit down before one of them fell down. They landed at a table where two church ladies were planning what to make for Sunday lunch. Seeing the disapproving looks on their faces just sent the two girls into more paroxysms of laughter until Saranji herself came out of the kitchen to see what all the noise was about. Seeing the look on her face sobered the two girls immediately.

"What you two doing here this hour anyway, let alone making all that racket?" Hands on hips, without waiting for an answer, Saranji started her investigation immediately, leaning on the counter in her apron, sharp eyes alert for any sign the girl was lying. "Where did you go after you left here last night, girl?"

Holly was still grinning at something Gina said, but seeing how serious Saranji was, her smile was replaced by a grimace of suspicion. "What d' you want to know for? You know where I usually always go."

Saranji zeroed in the word. "Usually Miss Delia's, but you didn't go there last night, did you? Now, you know you don't lie to me. No telling what you told your nana."

The girl struck a pose with folded arms and an expression that told her employer to mind her own business. "So what if I didn't? I called and left a message that I wasn't coming and asked if Ronda could just take my turn for once. Miss Wilkes don't do anything anyway but moan and groan about her feet hurting, and I didn't have her phone number. So I left the message on the machine. She's always there anyway and I just had other plans, is all."

Saranji pressed on. "I have to know, girl, and don't be using working overtime here to excuse yourself, either. I know what time you signed out and you better believe it."

Holly's defensive attitude began to crumble under Saranji's blowtorch interrogation. "I'm not, Miss Sara. You know Tony when he gets an idea he wants to do something."

"I don't know Tony, and I don't want to know Tony because he's causing you to get a bad reputation around here, Holly. I don't like the talk I'm hearing about him gambling and throwing his weight around like he's some kind of army dude just because he's been around. He's too old for you, girl, and you're going to end up in trouble if you keep hanging around with him. I don't suppose you know what's happened to Miss Delia? And don't be looking up at me with those great, big, puppy dog eyes now. I want the truth out of you."

"Holy smokes," a customer yelled from the porch, "Would you look who's coming now. Here come the Root Woman and her zoo parade!"

Gina spun off her counter stool and flew out onto the porch, but neither Holly nor Saranji took their eyes off of each other. She knew it was probably the only chance she would have to plead Megan's case in broad daylight. The two tens Megan had given her for a potion were still in her pocket and, as much as she feared Maureen's wrath if she ever found out, she couldn't get up the nerve to return empty handed to Megan. What if her sister did something to herself and died as a result? No, she couldn't let it happen, though she be damned forever for committing a mortal sin.

The men on the porch all got to their feet as the priestess, followed by her entourage, mounted the rutted sidewalk bordering Main Street. "And what in the hell else is that following her? Oh, my Lord, it's some kind of a little monkey! And she's got a parrot on her shoulder. It's a regular circus."

Inside the tiny restaurant, Saranji dried her hands on her apron and smoothed her hair down. "We'll continue this later," she said to Holly, who looked pale and had tears in her eyes. "As long as you weren't there in Miss Delia's house, you got nothing to worry about. Now, go out and ask Miss Kahalia if you can carry something for her. Lord, I got to tell you when to breathe air, too? Or can you do that much by yourself?"

Holly scurried out to join the small crowed gathering at the entrance to Sara's Place, but when she saw the strange caravan approaching, she shrank back, clinging to the screen door like the survivor of a shipwreck to a raft. "Sweet Jesus, that's a monkey! Don't let it in here, Miss Sara. I'm scared to death of those things."

"It's just a little brown monkey, Holly," Gina said, through the screen door. "It's so cute, like a little old man, kind of. Look at the big dog! And there's a pig with that little boy. They're bringing it for the barbeque, I guess." In a lower voice, she said, "Remember we're going to ask about Megan. You said you'd come with me to ask her."

"No, that monkey creeps me out. I'm not going out there. I don't care if Miss Sara cans me on the spot! Go out and help her carry what she's got. That'll be your chance. Go on then, if you ain't scared."

"I'll go!" Before she realized she was attracting curious glances from the onlookers, Gina was down the steps and dodging the gaps in the crooked sidewalk. At the front of the line was the tallest woman she had ever seen, even taller than her uncles, except Uncle Jordan. Adding to her impressive height was a gold cloth wrapped high around her head on which she carried a basket of colorful fruit. She was dressed in a long red and gold shawl, fringed in the same colors. Below that, a long skirt of similar weave bordered with gold threads peeped out with each measured step of her sandaled feet. Completing the outfit was a bird with gold and red tail feathers perched on her shoulder which looked around with questions in its round yellow eyes.

Behind her was a young light-skinned girl wearing a similar outfit, only much less elaborate. She was carrying a wide basket covered with leaves and river rushes. Trailing the young girl was a small boy alternately carrying and dragging a pig.

Bringing up the strange cavalcade was a small scruffy-looking monkey, which looked as bewildered as a child at school for the first time. It looked around with apprehension, chattering as if to calm itself. It took turns alternately holding onto the tail of a large shepherd mix and riding on its back.

Shielding her eyes against the molten morning sun, Gina took a deep breath. Approaching the regal priestess, she nodded and smiled at the young girl by her side. "Good morning, Miss Root Woman, can I help you with anything?"

The procession came to a halt. The little monkey was so startled, he jumped up on the dog's back, and the macaw shifted on the priestess's shoulder, flexing its brilliant wings. Opening its yellow beak wide, it looked as if it were about to answer for its mistress.

"Now, isn't that sweet of you? Have you met Kenya yet? This is Miss Gina Kelly, Kenya. Miss Gina, meet my granddaughter." Root Woman put her arm around the girl at her side. The girl's face had a raised burn running from her forehead to the cheekbone below her eye and another along the other cheek. When she smiled at Gina, it was easy to see that the older woman's love had put her at ease with her injuries.

"I know Kenya. Her family works for my Uncle Lane, right, Kenya? I haven't see you around lately, though. Where've you been hiding?" It was supposed to sound friendly, but came out as patronizing. Still, she kept her smile glued on as she lingered there under the glare of the crowd.

As the town's yellow dogs erupted into fits of barking from every vacant lot, the little monkey leaped from the dog onto the boy's back and then down on the pig which squealed in terror.

"That monkey'll be dog meat in three seconds." Standing on the porch, watching the interchange, Saranji had no tolerance for the exotic. "And Luther, put that pig down in the shed around back. Looks like he'll make some fine barbeque shortly."

Saranji caught a glimpse of Gina running to intercept Root Woman on the sidewalk skirting the edge of town and nodded at the desperation in every line of her young body. "You're a brave girl, but you don't need no love potion," she whispered to herself. "You not going to need it, baby, but I know somebody who is. Not many men going to love that freckled face but him who's coming."

Out in the glare of the hot sun, the saffron-robed woman put up her crimson umbrella with a red fringe to shield them. While Gina was included in its shadow, the small throng of locals had gathered outside Sara's Place stood hats in hand, eyes full of questions and petitions, but too reverent to ask out loud. They stood on the muddy sidewalk, the pride of the city council, costing each resident pennies they couldn't spare but did.

"Miss Gina, you are grown into quite a young lady now. And pretty, too. You look very much like your mama." Gina felt as if she were looking straight into the face of Minerva, the Goddess of Wisdom. It seemed all of her questions already had answers residing in those kind eyes looking down at her, as if they saw all the way through to her soul.

Nothing this woman could possibly say would be a lie. "I just wanted to ask you something if you promise not to tell Uncle Lane or even Saranji. I mean, Miss Sara."

"Now, Miss Gina, you know I cannot do that, especially if I think it is what you are going to ask me."

Stymied in mid-sentence, Gina tried to pose her request another way. "What I was going to ask you, it's not for me."

But Root Woman was way ahead of her. "If it's about Miss Megan, I can do nothing. I will do nothing to interfere with life. My powers are only for life, never death, though

some would say otherwise. As for love potions you are thinking about, you are far too pretty to need any and that Winfield
boy is not worth the shoe leather he walks on. None of the
Winfield blood is good. Don't waste your time. Someone else
is far more devoted to you than that scallywag will ever be. Is
there anything else you wish to ask me now, dear?" She turned
her gaze to the gathering crowd on the sidewalk. "I have many
more urgent requests to see to."

Gina looked over at the pleading women, children on
their hips, the poor, old and infirm nearly bent double from
hard work, children with sores and cuts attracting flies like fly
paper.

"No, ma'am. Thank you, though," she said, hot tears filling her eyes. "Megan just asked me to ask you. She gave me
ten dollars. Here," she said, knowing better than to offer it to
the tall proud woman. She gave it to the little boy peering
around the priestess' skirts. "Buy something nice for yourself,"
she said.

It sounded so condescending, Gina felt her face flush. As
the young girl standing beside Root Woman looked up at her,
Gina felt a thrill of revulsion and then sorrow. The heart
shaped face of Kenya, who had grown up at the McFarland
farm, and whom Gina had played with on summer nights,
stood there before her, keloid scars like zippers through her
golden skin. The morning breeze pushed the folds of her cloak
aside to reveal a thin cotton dress. There was a distinct bump
where none should be on that adolescent frame.

Root Woman smoothed the awkward moment. "Tell your
sister we appreciate the donation and we will pray for a
healthy child for her. Won't we, Kenya?"

The girl almost smiled and nodded in Gina's direction.
"Nice to see you again, Gina."

"Come over some time and we'll go swimming. Uncle
Lane's putting up an out-of-ground pool. We're having a
swimming party soon." She knew the invitation sounded desperate and that the girl would never come back to the farm.

As Root Woman moved forward at her regal pace, Gina
fell into step beside Kenya. The little group all walked under

the shade of the umbrella and moved as one through the crowd in front of Sara's Place.

As they passed slowly through the group, Gina slipped her freckled arm through Kenya's thin one. "Come on in. Sara's got the best lemonade tea in town."

The two girls wove their way through the crowd, requests falling on the crimson umbrella like raindrops. "Go along now, girls. Let me go to my people." It sounded like Moses leading his flock out of Egypt and, probably in the minds of the waiting followers, it was exactly that.

Pleading voices rose from the crowd gathered in front of Sara's Place. "Please, Your Excellency, I got the gout in both my toes real bad. I can't hardly walk."

"Your Reverence, please give my wife something for what's growing inside her. Big as an orange, it is. Doctor says it's a tumor and got to come out, but we ain't got the money for no operation."

They left her standing under the umbrella, the macaw lambasting the chattering people.

Inside, Saranji was back topping up customers' coffee and sweet tea. Holly was taking customer orders and didn't look up as Gina came in with Kenya. "Gina, sweetie, you better catch a ride home with your Uncle Lane. He knows you're here, so wait for him."

"How does he know that, Saranji?" Knowing what Lane would say about skipping school, Gina felt a thread of fear through her entire body.

"Because I called him to come get you. Now, Miss Holly, let's have a little meeting with Jesus."

Without waiting for an answer, she waved Holly outside the screen door. Gina was watching the crowd for her uncle's truck when she heard Holly's voice rise in angry protest.

"Yeah, I know I said I was going, but Tony showed up just as I was leaving work and said he'd give me a ride up there. Then he flat out kidnapped me off to some restaurant in Eufaula across the river. Said I could call on his cell phone and leave a message for Miss Rhonda to stay until Mr. Des got there. Honest that's the truth, Miss Saranji."

Saranji frowned, flicking at a lazy fly with her dish towel. "I guess I do. No, you too damned dumb to lie about something like that. But question is will the police know that?"

Speculation had just gravitated to the size of the latest rack of antlers brought in by deer hunters and all the hunters threw in their names. Killing something, even a buck, was the best escape for Julia Springs' hereditarily tough population. That was until Ernest Schultz brought Cole Prescott's arm into town. After that happened, things got ugly fast.

Gina sat on the rickety steps in the morning sun wishing it would burn her hair blonde and her skin tan like those Swedish girls who modeled weight-loss products on TV. She tried to rehearse what she would tell Megan when she got back that night. Megan would of course call her hopelessly stupid and want her ten bucks back. Then she would have to give up the ten she had gotten for having straight A's. Her dad said he would send fifty for such a good report card, and, as usual, forgot. So summer was looking bleak especially with Megan alternately screwing and cursing Art Gatewood because he wasn't worthy of her. She contented herself with thoughts of Vadim returning in a slick car and sweeping her off to go dancing in Macon at some fancy nightclub. She was so engrossed in daydreams she didn't see Uncle Lane glowering at her from across the street. Brice Johnson sat beside him, talking on his cell phone.

He shouted across the street so that those who lingered on the porch behind her heard and laughed softly. "I'm going out to Uncle Jordan's. You better get on back to school if you know what's good for you, young lady. Just tell them you're late because of a family emergency, but if they want to call me, they have my number. We'll talk later."

She watched the truck drive away and then started walking back to school. In her mind, Vadim walked with her, holding her hand, kissing her cheek. She began to smile, hearing the funny way he talked. She quickened her dragging feet, pulled up her bra strap, and headed back to the hundred year old building that held nothing that she needed to learn. She would put it all on her Facebook page when she got home, holding nothing back. *Dream lover, Dream lover, oh how I want a dream lover. I don't want to dream alone.*

Chapter 14

As daylight faded, they brought Tanner's truck as close to the edge of the Thicket as possible and parked it on the shoulder of the narrow lane that led across the soybean field to the tangled web of trees. It was known locally as The Jumping Off Place. Beyond it, the Swamp shimmered in a mirage of pearlescent mist, sent up by the vapors from the marsh, and the meandering creek.

As they reached the tree line, Lou Owl plunged ahead at a dogtrot that had Tanner gasping in the thick air. He sensed that peculiar claustrophobia when the sky was cut off by an interwoven canopy of vegetation.

Penetrating the Thicket, he felt as if he had plunged into an ocean of thick green water and that he was coming up for air only when the canopy briefly broke into open sky.

As Lou led the way, following a route only visible to a woodsman, the Thicket came alive with the sound of night creatures that was almost deafening, only to subside to a whisper at the first snap of a twig or human voice. Finally, it became so dark Tanner turned on the flashlight fastened to his belt so he wouldn't misstep.

"Put out that light," Owl's whiskey-rough whisper was the last human voice among the throbbing insect chorus as their muffled footsteps tread the tall grass in unison. Their eyes soon adjusted to the profound darkness, streaked with eerie yellow-green by swamp gas bubbling up from the vegetation.

In the darkness, he didn't see Lou move away, a crouching shadow slipping through the cypress and water oaks. Presently, he became aware of another sound, this one bold enough to pause the insect chorus. Only the bullfrogs were left to carry on the chorus, caught up in the rhythmic sound of their own voices. Tanner hesitated before taking another step, his finger sliding back to the safety lock on his rifle.

The sound stopped. "Hey, Lou," he called softly, "that you?"

There was no answer except the cacophony of bullfrogs and cicadas. Tanner felt his scalp start to ripple, stirring the roots of his hair with icy fingertips. Even the hair on his arms seemed to stand erect like the hackles on a hound on scent.

"Hey, Lou," he repeated, this time in a normal voice. The bullfrogs hesitated a few pulses and then picked up the cadence again. This time not even the crickets answered them. The night birds were still, as if frozen in their nests, listening.

He unsnapped his flashlight and turned the beam on, scanning over the moss hung trees which separated him from the path he thought Lou had taken. No deep voice cursed at him to ditch the light. Lou was gone in that stealthy, silent way he had learned as a child to fade into the cover of the water oaks and sweet gum trees as a child.

Then it came, on a soft breeze that stirred the Spanish moss in trees around him. The sickly, sweet smell of chinaberries reached his nostrils, sending a rush of adrenalin through his veins and his heart pounding. Parallel to him in the dark, a large shadow seemed to move in the depths of the velvet night and branches crunched under an unseen foot. It wasn't Lou Owl, whose tread was a mere whisper.

Keeping the light turned on, Tanner hurried more than was good for a white man to move through the Swamp, where alligators grunted under piles of leaves in the boggy places. Just as he was making progress through the gnarled trees, not ten yards away from him, something as large as a man paralleled his course, now crashing through the underbrush keeping pace with him. At that precise moment, his flashlight went out. Before he knew it, Jordan Tanner was running as he hadn't run since WWII France through German machine gun fire.

"Lou! Where the hell are you, man?"

The answer came not from the Thicket around him but from far away. "Tanner! Over here!"

Veering off to his left, he saw a sliver of light, which then disappeared as quickly as it had come, flicker through the curtain of leaves and Spanish moss.

"Lou! Shine your light over here!"

The light swung in his direction and he headed for it only to find, deep in the Thicket behind him, the footsteps crashed in rhythm to his own. As he ran toward the light, they faded in proximity. When he paused, out of breath, wheezing, he heard the splash of something heavier than a man, but striding on two legs, landing in the Hanahatchee Creek. He made the distance out to be at least a quarter of a mile away.

Having got his second wind, Tanner jogged toward the glowing light through thinning trees, determined not to betray his wholesale retreat to Lou. It didn't work with Lou, however.

"Tanner, what in hell was you running from out there? The Boogie Man?"

"Where'd you go? All of a sudden, I was alone out there."

Lou shouldered his rifle and the flashlight lit the amused twinkle in his dark eyes. "Didn't know you was scared of the dark, Tanner."

"Why didn't you answer me, then when I hollered for you? I heard you crashing around out there like a damn moose."

"'Cause you didn't holler loud enough, at least not loud enough for me to hear you."

"You didn't? You were about ten or twelve yards away, weren't you? You going deaf?" He made an effort not to sound irritated, but he was. He suspected Owl of playing with him, but there was concern in his friend's eyes above the light, not mischief.

"No, I was over talking to Root Woman. It was her you came to see, right? Hey, Jordan, you okay?"

"Fine."

He was lying and they both knew it, but this wasn't the time or place for discussing strange noises and stalkers in the dark. Later, over a bottle of good whiskey, the truth would come out. They had known each other that long, since they were kids growing up in two worlds and sharing only one, the wild one.

He hadn't seen her for quite a long time and yet, by the light of the fire, Root Woman didn't look any older. She was still straight as a loblolly pine, golden skinned with the eyes of a dark angel. Root Woman didn't acknowledge their presence for a while. The two men stood, rifles at ease, at the edge of her clearing while she addressed the sky with raised arms, asking for divine permission to invite them into her compound.

Tanner looked around the clean-swept yard with its piles of storage pots of all sizes and shapes. To keep her fingers limber for healing, Root Woman was a potter, composing all sorts of vessels from the red clay around the edge of the marsh. There was a strange female shape to many of the pottery creations, hinting at the shapes of the reproductive organs.

At a signal from Lou, they waited in silence as if they were seeking an audience with a dignitary. Dropping her arms and turning in their direction, the tall priestess beckoned to them.

"Welcome, gentlemen. Please come in." With a graceful gesture, she indicated the doorway of her little cabin which looked even cozier, now that the ghostly fog began to creep around them from the Swamp.

Inside it was even more welcoming, with a crackling fire in the stone fireplace and baskets of nuts and berries all around. Bundles of dried roots, smoked fish and meats were hung about the fireplace and along the rafters. A sweet oaky smell testified to the mixture of herbs, jerky strips, and dried flowers so thick it was like breathing pipe tobacco.

Settling in a large chair made out of a tree stump and padded with deer hide and raccoon fur cushions, Tanner started off, since no one else seemed inclined to speak. "I know this is an odd time to pay you a visit."

"Not at all. I've been expecting you," she said, gracious as the most practiced hostess. She was busy filling up gourd bowls with some kind of liquid. "Mr. Owl has told me you want to know about how Cole Prescott died." Coming over to him, she pinned him in his seat with her captivating stare. He was so fascinated by her face, he didn't notice she was handing him the gourd.

"Will you have some refreshment, Mr. Tanner?' As he was reaching out to take the gourd, something heavy landed on his shoulder. Still on edge from his experience in the Swamp, he swung up his arm, sending the bowl flying toward the fireplace. Its contents caused the fire to flare dangerously close to Lou who whooped with laughter.

"Rudiki, you bad boy! See now what you've done? Kenya, bring the mop and bucket over here."

The shadow moved away, making a clicking noise that caused the furry thing to follow it. Tanner was visibly shaking as a small, scruffy monkey leaped from his shoulder to the earthen floor to follow the shadowed figure into the next room.

He felt like a complete fool. "Sorry, I'm sort of on edge, I guess. Something seemed to be following me out there in the Swamp. Could have been a buck. Probably was."

"Not your fault at all. I should have warned you about Rudiki. He must have run away from a pet shop or someone's home, but he took up residence here long ago. He particularly likes male visitors as you can see."

He could have kicked Lou Owl who was still laughing. "Didn't mean to barge in like this, but Lou said—"

"You don't have to apologize, Mr. Tanner. A visit from old neighbors is always welcome any time. It's some of the new ones I don't care to deal with." With more class than Delia Clark in the Victorian mansion across the Thicket, she offered him a rustic-looking slice of bread.

Another movement in the shadows caused him to snatch his hand back to the gun at his side. He squinted through the shadows cast over the room to see the adolescent form of a girl. She kept her face averted, and head down as she crossed noiselessly to the hollowed out tree serving as a cupboard. Swiftly and silently as a ghost, she carried a mop to clean up the mess on the fireplace, and just as silently left them, all the while never lifting her head.

As the wraith passed, Root Woman said, "Thank you, Kenya baby, see that Frederick is in bed and bring back the dip in the blue jug, will you, honey?"

"Yes'um," replied the ghost in a barely audible whisper.

"Don't be shy. These gentlemen are friends. My grand-baby, Kenya," Root Woman explained, her great eyes glowing with pride. "She's gonna live with me now."

Lou kept erupting in chuckles, his eyes on the fire as if reading the future in the flames. Fed up, Tanner gave him an elbow in the arm and got back to business. "You were saying about the Prescott boy, Reverend Mother. How'd he get torn up like that? A rogue tornado, you think?"

The girl emerged from the shadows into the firelight, head down, proffering the sorghum jug. "Dipping sauce, sir?"

His stomach took a turn as she glanced up. Even though her face was swollen almost beyond recognition and a long slash raked across one eye, he had no trouble recognizing her. Her thin wrists bore raised welts suggesting the rest on her body could only look far worse.

"Say, young lady, your daddy works for my nephew, Lane, right? I've seen you minding some children in the yard."

"Yes, sir," she said, a slight sound with a tinge on grate-fulness to it, "but he ain't my daddy."

Tanner reached up and put his fingers under her chin. "Who did this to you, honey? What's your name again? Ken-ya, is it?"

By the firelight, her eyes shone wary and tense as a doe's in the Thicket. "Yes, sir. My mama did it, sir. That's who did."

He didn't bother to hide his revulsion. "Why in God's name would she whip you like that, honey?"

Without replying, the girl turned back to Root Woman whose own eyes blazed in the firelight, swimming in hot tears.

"It's all right, sweetie. You tell him."

"My step-daddy done got me in the family way is why. She said I—she said that I—" Kenya bent her head and pulled up her apron to cover her face, "—let him. But I didn't. Hon-est, I didn't. You won't tell Miss Milly or Mr. Lane, will you? 'Cause Lewis will kill me if you do."

Tanner got to his feet, towering above the child. "There, there, don't you cry, honey. We'll make him pay for what he's done. You can count on that." He put his hand on her shoulder and she flinched. "Don't you worry, baby. We're gonna make it all right."

When the girl left them, the three adults sat in silence, tangled in the web of their own thoughts. Root Woman stared into the fire while Tanner could be heard muttering, "Bastard!" to himself. In the distance, dogs began to bark furiously as if on the scent of their quarry. It brought Tanner back to the reason for his mission to this mysterious place where it seemed man was at the mercy of the natural world.

"Chief Pierce wanted me to interview you about the events of this morning. That is if, in fact, you saw or heard anything…unusual." At last he regained his composure and, clearing his throat, attended to the business of taking her statement.

Lou, however, dispensed with finesse. "He wants to know if you know how Scottie Prescott's kid ended up in a tree with his arm tore off."

Tanner turned on the recording application on his cell phone while Root Woman spoke in a voice deep and rich as the syrup in their bowls. "That's right, Mr. Owl. You see, there came up a sudden storm from the west with such a killer wind it uprooted trees near the creek and some distance inland, I believe. I heard shouting, but I was preparing to take cover just as the two young men approached me. I was saying morning prayers, you see. I was so worried about my grandchildren's safety, you know. I didn't know what happened to either of the young men until you told me just now. I'm very sad for their parents' loss, but these little downspouts have been getting very common in the area lately. They can be very destructive as you no doubt know, Mr. Owl."

"You bet I do. Oh, the other kid wasn't hurt, but he's had a bad shock. He said you told him to run. Probably saved his life, but folks around here don't think about things like that."

"Of course, I told Trey to run, but Cole didn't want to heed the warning. He kept insisting I leave instead. I even had to leave my offering bowls there and they disappeared into the air." The wily priestess leaned forward, as if talking into a microphone. "Is there anything else you'd like to ask me?"

Owl nodded. "We come down here to tell you the talk is in town is that you had something to do with it. I just wanted to let you know. They must think you whip up tornados in your spare time, then play dodge ball with them, and also kill babies and make potions out of them. Any truth to those rumors?"

She regarded him with glowing eyes. "You are always a friend to me, Mr. Owl. I appreciate you coming all the way out here to tell me. I'll come right on into town tomorrow and face my detractors. They need to understand that I had nothing to do with that Cole's death and I consider all life sacred."

"I'll tell them that. We'll tell them that, won't we, Tanner?"

"Of course," he said in spite of the growing suspicion she wasn't telling them everything that took place in that grove of tall trees. "I've got it right here for the record." He put his cell phone back in his pocket with a little flourish. "In the old days, I'd have to go home and write all this up. Now, I just pull out my phone and it's done." He handed her the gourd bowl. "Delicious," he said. "Just one thing, though. How did you know the young men's names?"

"I guess we'd better be getting on back, Miss Kahalia." Lou sopped up the last of the tangy dipping sauce with his bread. "Mighty fine supper, you fixed up. Mighty fine."

"Let me send some home with you, then. Kenya, fill up one of those jugs for Mr. Owl. How about you, Mr. Tanner?"

He was finding it difficult to switch the subject of a young man's violent death so easily, but he knew better than to not address humble hospitality. "I think we've already put you out enough, ma'am. Just thought you might have met these guys before. Apparently, they hunted here a lot."

They traded knowing looks. He could have left it at that and not pressed her. On the other hand, he had turned the phone off and put it back in his shirt pocket.

"I don't deny it, they've come around before. Quite a few

times, in truth. Riding their all-terrain vehicles down the creek and through the marshes, crushing life beneath their wheels to which they thought they were vastly superior. Each time we met, Cole Prescott informed me that the land my ancestors have lived on for hundreds of years now belongs to his father and that I should get out. In fact, last time he was here, before this morning, he threatened to set fire to my house so I would leave, said that I was a squatter and a poacher. I don't eat any meat, you know, so he must have meant I picked wild berries and fruit. Yes, indeed, I knew Cole and his friend and faithful disciple, Trey, but I would not wish them harm, no not at all. God takes care of me and mine."

He got to his feet with a slight lurch, grasping the tree chair to steady himself. "That stuff packs a wallop, Your Reverence. You should bottle it and sell it. Make a fortune and retire." Immediately, he regretted sounding so adolescent.

Apparently accustomed to the suggestion however, Root Woman smiled indulgently at him. "But I do, Jordan Tanner. I certainly do bottle it, though it isn't for sale. What the Lord gives us is not to be sold but passed along to others. Which is why I offered it to you. Have a good night and sleep well."

He thanked her, wishing the Lord had passed along wit as one of his gifts. At that moment, his phone went off in his pocket. It was a completely alien sound in the dense embrace of the Swamp. The silence hovered around them, suspended as if on tiptoe. He might have disturbed a high-level executive board meeting, so annoyed were the looks in his direction.

"Sorry," he said, without really knowing why he apologized. "Kids checking up on me. You'd think I was a teenager with a curfew the way they call around ten to see if I'm home. How about it, Lou? Ready to go back?"

"Think I'll stay here awhile longer and then get back to my place. You realize I only live about half a mile from here." Sometimes Lou could be a complete enigma, and this was one of those times. It was apparent to Tanner that some sort of contest was on between the two of them and he, Lou, was making all the rules. In some curious tribal custom known only to deceased warriors, this was Tanner's chance to prove himself

worthy of membership in the Dead Warrior's Society—a sort
of gauntlet he would have to run to be worth of the honor.

"In that case, guess you won't mind lending me your
flashlight since mine decided to die right out there in the
Swamp."

Grunting, Owl dug out his flashlight. "I need it back, J.T.
Got me a mind to gig some frogs later on, maybe even bag me
a gator."

"Then I just guess you'll have to come back with me to
get it." He kept on playing Owl's game, let him have his fun.
*He wouldn't be laughing if we ran into whatever was follow-
ing me out there.*

"Mr. Tanner, allow me to solve the problem." Root
Woman once again called the disfigured girl into the yard.
"Honey, bring me one of those roots I got drying above the
fireplace, hear? We'll fix up something that'll light your way
home, Mr. Tanner, and scare off any wild things you might
find on the way."

Ducking into the thatched hut, Kenya emerged with a
long twisted piece of wood, which Root Woman passed her
hands over and then dipped into a clay jar. From there, she
took it over to the fire which had settled down to a steady
glow. Touching it to the flame, she set the stick alight, at first
with a roar of blue fire and then settling down to a healthy yel-
low-gold.

"Here you are, much safer that a flashlight. You never
know when those batteries will go out," she said, handing
Tanner the torch. "Safe journey home, Mr. Tanner."

Glowering at Lou Owl, he thanked her and set out
through the trees around the clearing. Holding the torch high,
Tanner realized it was far better at illuminating the Thicket
than a flashlight would have been but more dangerous as he
passed under low-hanging branches dripping with moss.

He was heading for the creek which he planned to follow
since it led back to town where the trees thinned and marsh
grass rose to almost knee-height. He knew cotton-mouthed
moccasins and copperheads loved to nest there as well as alligators lying in wait for prey. Being nocturnal creatures, gators

very often hugged the banks waiting for deer to come for a drink. The flickering light would catch their ruby eyes and, being shy reptiles, they would move away. With his shotgun cocked under his arm, he threaded his way along the firmer ground.

As it had on the way to Root Woman's home, some ancient gland rendered useless in the electronic age, gave a telepathic alarm, sending his flesh crawling. Again, the hair on his scalp and arms rose like hackles on an alert dog. He stopped and listened to the Swamp over the thumping of his heart. It was holding its collective breath, waiting as an audience does for its star attraction and he was not it. The wild creatures, whose habitat he had invaded, were all too used to mankind. After all, the noise had almost been deafening a few minutes before.

Then, in the silence, it came again—a heavy step and then, at a length much longer than a tall man's stride, another footfall, not fifty feet away.

"Lou, come on. Quit playing now. I know it's you out there." Tanner was blustering and it caused his voice to waver as he lifted his torch. It flickered dangerously in a sudden breeze, as if someone were blowing on it. "Aw, crap, Lou," he continued talking to the shifting shadows as he went, "we're too old to be playing hide and seek. I don't want to belong to the Dead Warrior's Honor Society or whatever it is."

Reaching firm ground, he went at a dog-trot, rapidly winding him, until he had to stop. Still gripping the torch in sweaty palms, he bent down to catch his breath, which was coming in gasps. Since getting out of the marines forty years ago, he'd let himself go, and he vowed to get back in shape then and there.

Tanner straightened, and raised the torch in the direction of the footsteps deep in the Thicket. "Lou, I knew it was you."

"You knew who was me?" Owl asked, some yards directly behind him.

Tanner whirled around, nearly dousing the torch. Through the flickering shadows, Owl was coming at a trot, his flashlight in his snakeskin belt. Seeing Tanner, he slowed his pace and then abruptly stopped a few feet away, staring into the dark as if he had cat's eyes. Tanner had hunted with his friend too long not to know he had spotted something and he turned back in the direction Lou was staring. Like the two men, whatever was out there had stopped in its tracks, and Tanner had the distinct impression it was looking directly back at them through the tangled branches.

Then it came on the intermittent puffs of night winds rippling the leaves and moss—the odor of chinaberries, pungent to the point of being fetid.

So soft it was almost lost in the growing breeze, Lou began to chant in his native tongue, rhythmic as the bullfrog's croak yet barely rising above an insect whine. The moment was so intense with portent, Tanner felt hot sap from the root land on his hand and didn't flinch. His arm ached from clutching the rifle, but he wasn't about to lower the torch to shift it. Finally, across the Thicket, the crashing footfalls diminished as if the beast had been lulled into a retreat.

Owl came into the light. "Come on, let's go, J.T.," he said softly. "And you can carry your rifle on your shoulder. Let me have your torch. If you drop it, the whole place would go up like kindling. Fire always worries the wildlife. That's why they're so afraid of it."

"Was that why you were singing? To reassure that creature out there? What in the hell was out there, Lou? I've never felt like something was stalking me out here. Never once and I've lived here all my life. What the hell is that animal out there? I've heard a fire in the Okefenokee Swamps has run panthers and bobcats out of Florida, or maybe a buck deer. They can get nasty when you get in their rutting territory." He realized he was babbling and stopped.

Lou didn't answer. Instead, he grabbed the torch and led the way along the edge of the Swamp. "No place for a white man to be alone nowadays. Too many druggies and pot growers out here. Poachers, too. And don't blame me none for singing the calming down song. When I caught up with you, you was talking to yourself."

"You don't have to give me that white man junk anymore,

you know." Tanner tramped after him, making as much noise as he could. "This isn't Wounded Knee and, anyway, thought you were going home instead of playing hide-and-seek?"

"She told me to go after you, ungrateful skunk."

"Dammit, Lou, level with me. There was something in the woods out there and you know it. You've been dodging the subject like a hail of bullets. What the hell is it? You know and Root Woman knows and I don't like being treated like some damn hunter who just stumbled in off the road."

Lou turned to face him and the firelight appeared to send sparks into his eyes. The torch cast half his face in shadows and the other half was illumined, showing every knife scar and line etched into his swarthy skin. "Okay, I wanted you to get it firsthand. I wouldn't take the trouble to do that for anyone else, J.T. Only you. I hope you know that."

"Get what, Lou? Stop beating around the bush. What the hell is it that was following us?"

"You know, don't you?"

"The Chinaberry Man. That's what you think it is. That's why you let me go out there alone."

"If I told you, you wouldn't believe me. You're just like the rest of 'em, J.T. Got to have some damn printout to believe anything. There's things out there even I don't understand. Now, come on. It's even past *my* bedtime."

Tanner stumbled over roots and ruts to follow the torch-light. "Oh, I forgot. You know everything, Lou."

"Damn close. And what I don't know, I don't care about knowing nothing about."

ꙮꙮꙮ

Back on his front porch, Tanner sat in the old rocker, nursing straight scotch with a lone ice cube. Inside, the television flashed reassuringly and canned laughter kept him company, but he kept his eyes on the distant woods which hid its secrets well behind sentinel trees.

What the hell was shadowing my footsteps tonight? He'd have to go see tomorrow in the daylight, look for tracks, droppings—anything to reassure himself the thing he thought he saw was real and not some night-stalking figment of his imagination.

Suddenly, he saw a dark shape at the edge of the soybean field and was on his feet. "Come on, Rollo," he said to the pile of hair beside him. "Mosquitoes are getting bad out here. Let's go inside."

He took his shotgun up to bed, something Carolyn would have forbidden if she were alive. But, hell, she wasn't, and he had to have something to sleep with besides a dog whose digestive tract was as bad as his own.

He heard the phone through his pillow and, thinking it was his alarm set by some retroactive instinct, fumbled to turn it off. Knocking something metallic to the floor, he finally picked it up. It was his cellphone dancing around like one of Ham Phillips's infernal robots.

Probably Desmond Clark having a nervous breakdown. He answered with what he hoped was civility. It was Lane, his nephew.

"Sorry to wake you, Uncle Jordan, but Megan hasn't come home yet. I was wondering if you've seen her, by any chance?"

"At three o'clock?" These kids and the hours they kept. "What was she doing out at this hour, or should I ask?"

"Well, she was with Art Gatewood. They were going to some graduation party."

"In that case, I wouldn't expect her home before daybreak. You remember when you were a kid? Anyway, where was the party?"

Lane cleared his throat uncomfortably, "That's just it. I don't know. She skipped school today and said she'd call, but so far we haven't heard from her. Just wondered if you'd seen her, that's all. Milly and Joy are freaked-out, thinking she may have gone drinking across the river and you know how the Gatewood kid drives even when he's sober."

"Gina probably knows, but is too scared to tell, for fear Megan'll skin her alive. But if you're that worried, why don't you wake her up and ask her?" He didn't mention Root Woman. Lane would be on him to tell him where she lived. He wasn't about to do that.

But Lane was on it. "So did you see Root Woman down there?"

"Oh, yeah. We saw her picking some kind of herb by the creek. Asked her what the deal was with the Prescott kid and she said he got caught up in a land spout and got torn up. You need to tell Brice Johnson to stop believing in the Boogey man. Kahalia said she saw the sky turn black, lightning all around, and the funnel just dropped down like they do. I hear Johnson's making the natives restless with his talk about witchcraft."

"Thanks, Uncle Jordan. I'll tell him. Sorry if I woke you up, but you know how Milly gets. Joy's inherited the same hysterical gene, I'm afraid. Good night."

He could have kicked himself for lying to his nephew. On the other hand, what are you going to tell a weary farmer at three o'clock in the morning with a missing daughter and with two other women yelling in chorus behind him? That something large and dark was following him in the woods tonight? That he didn't believe Root Woman's story about the land spout tearing Cole Prescott apart?

With his mastiff, Rollo, beside him, Tanner went downstairs and got a piece of Maybelle's chicken out of the fridge and a cold beer. When he'd finished both, he locked the front door for the first time since Carolyn died. Leaving the light on in the living room, the way he used to for the kids when they stayed out late, he went up to bed. *Geezuz, I'm getting to be like an old lady, locking up tight and leaving lights on all over the place.*

જીજી

Sometime during the night, there was a strange thudding noise that set his windows rattling and the light in the living room went off. He didn't get up to investigate. Beside his bed, Rollo made strange growls in his sleep and his legs jerked as if he were chasing something in a dream. Tanner reached down, touched the shotgun beside his bed, and thought about firing a couple of shots out the window. Waiting, he realized he was holding his breath.

The first light of dawn was glowing outside by the time Tanner fell asleep.

Chapter 15

When Tinker Pierce described the circumstances of the missing arm's recovery to Mr. Prescott, the man dropped the phone and his wife had to take over. Neither of them wanted to examine the missing appendage and it was sent over to Tapley's mortuary where the staff wrestled with how to bury the parts with the whole. They debated whether to make a whole new ceremony or just sneak it in the coffin with due respects. The town of Julia Springs hadn't had that problem since WWII when local residents came home in pieces from places like Iwo Jima, Normandy, and the Ardennes to be reassembled in the process of internment.

Without waiting for the town weekly newspaper to carry the stories of Cole Prescott's mysterious death, Delia Clark's long-awaited demise, the missing arm, and what Lewis Spencer had done to his step-daughter, the entire population had passed the news via social media and by word of mouth in the barber shop and beauty parlor.

Trey Blake had to be given a sedative and two shots of whiskey to become coherent. He rattled on about eyes coming down, eyes above the trees, trees flying upward and Cole Prescott screaming as he shot into the air, catapulted skyward by unseen hands. Tinker Pierce kept nodding as if the boy were making complete sense, while across the room Quade Walker recorded the rant on his phone.

He made a few scribbled notes but mostly he was concerned with who else was there, what the sky was like, what time this all happened, and what the boys had been doing prior to that. He got none of that from the deranged Blake, which made him strongly suspect drugs were involved. He had seen soldiers in the military get hold of some weird-ass shit that either blew their minds or killed them.

By lunchtime the following day, word had circulated through the hamlet of Julia Springs that a monster was loose in the woods that tore people limb-from-limb and was under the command of Root Woman.

Christian women fled to their quilting circles, even if they couldn't sew a stitch, and choir practice where they didn't sing a note. Men hurried to Whitehead's Store or to Pop's Place until there was standing room only. The assembled farmers at Whitehead's chewed, dipped, and smoked almost all the to-bacco old Whitehead had in stock to his delight and his wife's fury. "I suppose you're going to let them sit in here all day, throwing their cigarette butts on the floor, and spitting wherev-er. Well, you clean up the mess then, dear. I'm going over to the church to get ready for Delia Clark's funeral reception."

The word was out that a three-legged calf had been born the night before and there had been meteor showers. Andy Dawson had lost six chickens to a raccoon. He found them with their heads torn off, still flopping around. Trey Blake kept talking about a monster in the woods and Delia's death smacked of foul play. Men and women together, or in their separate gatherings, all reached a quorum verdict. Root Wom-an was casting a spell on the town of Julia Springs with her heathen magic.

In contrast, Megan's pregnancy remained a guarded se-cret in spite of Gina Kelly's being seen talking earnestly with Root Woman and giving her money. The hint was dropped that perhaps Gina, who insisted on hanging around with that girl Holly, might even have a problem herself, but the idea was immediately put aside, buried under a wave of giggles. *Heav-ens no, she was so ugly with all that red hair and freckles, who in their right mind with sleep with her?*

The simultaneous discovery of Megan's pregnancy was not nearly as dramatic as the missing arm, but had just as much impact on the McFarland household. After Megan came home at ten o'clock the morning after the graduation party, she found her mother waiting for her, with a look that should have turned her to stone. Going about her usual chores, Mildred was emptying the bathroom wastebasket in the girls' bedroom and noticed several pregnancy test kits discarded with the trash. They not only confirmed her suspicions of Megan's behavior lately, not eating breakfast, hiding her slightly greenish color under too much makeup, and no discarded tampons when it should have been her period. She had been on the phone to Maureen immediately, telling her the news.

By the time Megan showed up from the party, "her situation" as it was referred to, was resolved around the kitchen table. Megan would marry Art up in Atlanta, and after a trip to Bermuda, the couple would live up there with Maureen where they would attend college. When they had the money, Arthur would receive when he turned twenty-one, they could decide their own lives. Period, end of discussion.

Though she was hollow-eyed and exhausted, when her mother laid down the plan for her life, which the family had devised, Megan's usually cool façade melted with rage.

"Oh, you've all decided what I'm going to do, have you? Well, get this! I don't want this baby, I don't want it at all. I want to give it away and come home and go to college. I don't want a brat trailing me around, whining for candy and milk and God knows what all. I want to get rid of it! If you help me get rid of it now, Mother, no one will ever know. I can go up to Atlanta and have an abortion this summer. Vacation starts tomorrow and then I can go. You can arrange it, Mommy. Oh, please, please, please."

But Maureen remained implacable. "You can't throw away a life, Megan. I'm surprised you'd even ask me to do such a thing. You know what the church teaches, dear. Now let me talk to the boy's parents. He's not a bad sort, Arthur isn't. A little aimless, is all."

"He doesn't want to marry me, either, Mother. He said so. Said he doesn't know if the baby is his, so you want me to marry someone like that? Besides, he's dumb as a board. Al-

ways going on about hunting and fishing. I don't want plain
stupid Arthur Gatewood when I could have my pick of boys!
No and I mean no. I won't!"

Maureen's arched brows nearly touched her hairline.
"What reason did you give him to think the baby isn't his, Megan? Tell me the truth! I want an answer now!" Her cobalt
eyes honed in on Megan's tearful ones. She grabbed her
daughter's thin shoulders and shook her roughly.

Gina said softly, "Mommy, don't. Leave her alone. She's
upset enough."

"Stay out of this, Gina! And let this be a lesson to you. I
don't work and slave up in Atlanta to send you all to college
and to the Atlanta just to have you whore around down here!"

As usual, Maureen wasn't allowing for the difference between her two daughters. What was punishment for one was
punishment for both. "I haven't done anything, Mama, and
don't intend to, so don't even say that."

But a thought occurred to Gina that put a guilty frightened
look on her face. *What if she sees my Facebook page? All that
stuff about Vadim and meeting him in the woods? Kissing and
coming to pick me up in his car? And all the comments? What
about all the comments?* They had been sweet ones before,
"You go, girl!" and "Shake that booty, Cutie!" from Holly and
her friends which were now Gina's friends, at least online.

"That's right, you're not going to either. You're going to
Miss Porter's up in Atlanta next year and that's that. Now, stay
out of this discussion. It doesn't concern you." Her mother
turned the line of fire back on Megan, who was shuddering
with sobs.

"I'm not—I'm not going to have this baby. It's not you.
It's not your body being torn to shreds. You've got no right
and some old man in Rome's got no right to tell me what to
do. It's my future, my life and I'm going to do the right thing.
Nobody wants to be a child that's not wanted. Look at us.
Look at Gina. She's even got a boyfriend none of you know
anything about. Daddy doesn't even want either of us or he'd
be here. He doesn't want you either, Mama, or he wouldn't
have left and stayed gone. I don't want to get married now or

even ever and I don't want kids. I just want to be normal."

Always one to deal with the problem at hand, Maureen put Megan's comment about Gina's boyfriend on the back burner, giving it far less priority than Megan's determination to have an abortion.

Dismissed, Gina headed for the safety of her room. Her thoughts turned to the boy in the woods that she had created a whole fantasy around. An imaginary lover. Thank God, her sister's pregnancy had taken over the entire household, giving her permission to romanticize again. Her dream had a name, Vadim something unpronounceable. He was so real that his blue-gray eyes haunted her, his lips curled in a smile. The touch of his hand as he reached to help her over a fallen log when they were blackberry picking. Was that love at first sight, when the idea of that person wouldn't go away, but drifted back at odd moments like this, unbidden, almost as if you wanted him to be there right beside you? Or was he, like Cole Prescott, just one of her visions? She hadn't told anyone but Holly about Vadim so how did Megan know about him? With icy terror, she realized somehow the word had gotten around to Megan about her sister's Facebook page. *Oh, God, please don't let her tell Maureen about it!*

But guilty pleasures are the hardest ones to give up. It made her feel wanted to have someone special whose attention was just for her and her alone—someone as handsome as a god with blond hair and gray-blue eyes. The kind of man Megan told her she would never get.

Finally, Maureen stormed off, talking to their father in New York on her cell phone, voice raised to scream level. "Well, how am I supposed to handle it, Mark? Sending money isn't going to fix anything. Well, of course, she can't stay here, you idiot! You have to take her with you for the summer—you and whatever-her-name is."

It was sort of ironic to hear her mother addressing her ex-husband's new wife as whatever-her-name-is. She knew very well it was Kim. Kim Yong Lee had married her father a year ago and they had twin daughters. Her father still didn't have a male heir and, like Henry VIII, kept going through wives until one of them produced a son. This was his third try and he had a raft of daughters to support and marry off. Gina had smiled to herself while she sat on Megan's four poster bed rubbing her sister's back.

"Why are you smiling?" Megan peeked through her fingers at Gina's preoccupied face. "What's there to smile about?"

Gina flopped down in the flowered chintz chair by the window. "Just Mama and Daddy. Does love ever last? Or are marriage and kids the kiss of death— correction—money, marriage and kids."

"No. I can tell you for one, it doesn't." Megan reached out and put her hand in Gina's. "Ginny, I just want to go back to my life like before this happened to me. Like I've just been sick or had an accident or something, you know? This...egg inside me—God, I sound like a chicken—it's not a person, is it? I mean, it's a fertilized egg at this point, that's all. People miscarry all the time about now. I mean, I remember Irene Johnson, old Brice's scaggy little niece, when she had to marry Ricky Whats-his-name, and three days afterward, she miscarried. They got the marriage annulled and Irene was free as a bird. Ginny, you've got to go to Root Woman and ask her for a potion. Beg her! Tell her I'll kill myself if she doesn't." Megan was up on her knees now, eyes streaming black with eyeliner. "I'll get her a thousand dollars. I'll give her Glory Road Church a thousand dollars for a new roof. They need one, Sara says."

Gina stared at her sister, hearing the desperation in her voice and seeing a strange look in her beautiful green eyes. *Almost crazy*, she thought. "Where are you getting a thousand dollars, rob a bank?"

Megan had that scheming Scarlett O'Hara look she got when she was devising a plan. "Who is the richest person you know?"

"Cousin Reggie. You're dreaming! He's not going to give you a thousand dollars without knowing the reason. Besides, he's supposed to be Catholic,"

"Who, besides him, are we related to? Uncle Jordan. No,

he'd just say have the baby and let Mildred and Joy raise it."

"Daddy? Well, then go to New York and stay with him and…"

"Kim."

"I had to think a minute. Almost said Chloe, but that was the one before Kim."

"He'll just tell Mother and all hell will break loose. Besides, I think they'll want me to stay and have the baby to see if it's a boy. Then Daddy will have one at last."

Gina wrinkled her nose at the thought. "Eeeew. Then they'll want to adopt it. That's really creepy but, knowing Daddy, doable."

"You're not getting the point, dope! I don't want to have a baby! I don't want to raise a brat and I don't want to even have one tearing up my body. I'm eighteen years old, understand? I don't care if I'm damned to hell. I don't want a baby. God knows! Look how we turned out—no mama around to speak of, and surely no daddy. Raised by aunts and uncles. No! No! No!"

Gina recoiled at the fierce way Megan grabbed her hand with both of hers. "Just be my angel and go and ask Root Woman if she'll do it for me—for a thousand dollars. I'll just tell Daddy I want—I know I'm saving up for my own car."

"He'd just buy you one. No problem. He said he'd buy you one when you graduate anyway. A convertible, too. No, that won't work."

"Yes, it will. He sends money all the time and I saw where he's listed as one of the new multi-millionaires in the United States this year. Did you know he's the founder of Hart Systems? That's what it said. Mark Kelly, founder and CEO of Hart Systems. Had a little article on him and everything."

"Great," Gina said without enthusiasm. "Wonder how they'd describe him as a father? Multi-Misogynist?"

Megan grappled with the joke. "What's that?" Though academically bright, Megan wasn't widely read.

"Never mind. Anyway, Root Woman doesn't do abortions so you're wasting your money. You need to go to the clinic in

Macon and maybe they'll do something there. I've heard they do."

"Oh and how will we get there? Fly? No, Ginny, you've got to be my friend and go back to her. Beg her on your knees. No, I'll go." Megan got her determined look on. She got up off the bed, her movements purposeful. "Art will take me down there. He hunts there all the time with his buddies. I spent all day making it three times with him, just so he'd make sure it was his."

"You did what?"

"Oh, don't look at me like that. You don't know men, Ginny. They only do something for you if you give them what they want."

"But you don't know where she lives, and she doesn't have a phone or anything. That's what they were saying when Cole Prescott was killed and they thought she did it. I heard Uncle Lane talking to Chief Pierce about it."

"Shit!" Megan suddenly seemed to realize the truth and was desperately seeking a solution. "I've got to find her before they do! Where's my shorts?" She pulled them out of the clothes hamper, holding her cellphone under her chin. "Artie, honey?"

Gina marveled at how her sister's voice changed from fierce to honeyed tones.

"Come pick me up, will you, baby? You want some more loving? Come on and get it while it's hot." Hanging up, she caught Gina's staggered expression. "Oh, don't look so stupid! You'll find out someday. I feel sorry for you when you do."

"Wait, Meggie. Just wait a second." Gina gave her confession with a sigh. "I saw Root Woman yesterday morning in town, okay? And I asked her...for, you know, something to get rid of the baby."

Her sister was aghast. "Oh, my god, you didn't! Why didn't you tell me?"

"Because Mama's here and I didn't want you to go telling her I was down at Sara's Place with Holly yesterday. She doesn't like me hanging out down there. What does she think Winfield High is, Miss Porter's?"

"Never mind that. So? What'd she say? Root Woman. Did you give her the ten dollars I gave you?" Her sister was on both knees now, like an alert rabbit frozen with tension. "Come on, what? Wasn't it enough? Did she want more?"

"She said she didn't do that stuff and she knew what I was asking for even before I asked her." Gina drew ten dollars out of her pajama pocket. "Here's ten. I gave her *your* ten dollars for the church."

Megan sat down like a cobra folding up inside its basket. "I knew you'd screw things up. And lost money to boot."

Gina hurried to redeem herself. "But guess who was with her?"

Megan was only half listening, her green eyes darting this way and that. "I don't care. The thing is, you asked her for the potion and she refused. Wait a second! Now she knows we're willing to pay big money, we've got to see if she'd do it for a thousand. She lives down there in the Swamp and I know she's got to be poor. And I *know* she does female stuff because she helped old Mrs. Winfield get rid of a cyst on her ovaries, or something like that before she died, and a couple of other girls I know with menstrual things. And Pamela Tate and Irene Johnson with their miscarriages. That's it!"

"What's it?" Gina was beginning to think Megan was getting deranged.

Megan leaned forward, gripping Gina's arm over the back of the chair until Gina felt her fingernails digging into the soft flesh. "We'll throw a scare into her. We'll tell her if she doesn't help me, we'll spread word around town that she had something to do with Cole Prescott getting killed, like turned her big ol' dog loose on him, and gave Pamela Tate and Irene something to make them miscarry. Let me do it! I'm better with words than you are. What do they call it? Veiled threats, that's it. Not in so many words. And I'll offer her the money, too. That's after she's turned down the thousand, which I bet she won't, though. But if she does, we just up the leverage on them, that's what Arthur says."

"You've been talking to him about it, haven't you? I can't believe you'd think of anything so terrible on your own. Besides, I honestly think she'd help you if she could, but not if you threatened her with lies that would get her in trouble. You remember Kenya, Pearlene Spencer's daughter, who ran away?"

Megan frowned and shrugged, annoyed at being distracted. "I guess. Why?"

"She was with Root Woman this morning at Sara's and she's pregnant."

"Go on. I heard her step-father Lewis Spencer raped her. So it's true."

"Her face was all torn up. Anyway, she did smile at me."

"Okay," Megan waved her hands with impatience, "so where are you going with this? How has that got anything to do with anything? I don't get it."

"Just I heard Root Woman ask Saranji if Kenya could work for her and Saranji said yes, any time after school. Root Woman then said, until she had the baby, she'd be home-schooled. And, Saranji said Holly would be glad to help her with her homework when things were slow in the afternoons."

But Megan wasn't listening. She was brushing her hair, a little smile playing across her curved lips.

"Megan, I didn't tell you Miss Delia Clark died yesterday, did I?"

Megan shrugged, wielding her curling iron at just the right angle to make a long, dark curl. "So? She was old. Oh, my lord! She did?" Suddenly, Gina had her sister's full attention. "She's Arthur's auntie! Maybe he'll get some money. She was so rich! She practically owned the whole town! Oh, that's wonderful!"

"They say she must have fallen down those huge stairs. That's why Uncle Jordan was in town. He's real good friends with Reverend Clark."

Megan had gone back to curling her long hair again. This time she was humming a little tune. "That's the best news I've had all day. Maybe Mother's plan isn't so bad, after all. I'll make it Plan B."

Chapter 16

When conducting an investigation involving morality, Mildred assumed a hawk-versus-snake position. "Then she isn't married."

"Holly said it was forced on her by her step-daddy, Lewis Spencer." Gina tried to avoid looking into her aunt's eyes, knowing there was condemnation there. "It wasn't her fault."

Joy and her mother looked at each other then back at Gina.

"That's rape," Gina said.

"Hush," Mildred cautioned her. "It's more than that. How could he do such a thing? Gina, go find Megan and tell her to wash up for dinner, will you?" She ended on a slightly skittering note. "What on earth will Lane say when he hears that?"

Gina looked from one to the other, unable to understand what the big secret was. "They're expecting about the same time."

"Go!" they said in unison. She went, but stopped outside the kitchen door.

She heard Aunt Mildred say, "You mean she was rrr…forced?"

"By her step-father Lewis, that no good piece of horse…"

She imagined Aunt Mildred, hand to chest, in a gesture of shock. Underneath her look of horror, she would be thinking what a juicy piece of news this would be to tell the Friendship Circle at church Wednesday night. "You don't mean it. He's a grown man. Oh, lord, wait until Lane finds out. I'll have to tell him and that will mean Lewis and Pearl will have to go and with all those babies, too."

When he heard the news at supper, without touching a bite, Lane went down and booted Lewis Spencer, his wife Pearl, and their children off his property. The last thing he heard Spencer shout as their loaded pickup pulled out on to the road was, "I'm going to kill that little bitch who told you, and you, too, Lane McFarland! Watch your back, hear?"

Lane's next phone call was to Tinker Pierce telling him to file rape charges against Spencer. Lane drank his supper that night for the first time since his oldest boy had gone to fight in the Middle East.

Getting away from all the ugliness about rape and unwanted pregnancies, Gina went upstairs to converse with her Facebook friends again on the secrets of romance. When she looked in the room she shared with her sister, it was empty. Megan had left without permission.

ෆ๑๑

The whole Blake family began having nightmares about being torn apart by a gigantic creature and the Catholic priest over from Macon, Father Carmichael, had to come and do one of those obscure blessings that keeps away specific evil spirits like the Baptists don't ever talk about in service. Even the black citizens got out significant crosses, but also gris-gris bags just in case this was an animal spirit haunting the town.

Then Brice Johnson volunteered the information that Gina had seen Cole Prescott standing in the side yard that morning, about the same time as his body was found hanging from the tree in the Swamp and an emergency ecumenical church service was called that evening.

Father Carmichael ate his dinner at Sara's Place, longing for a good shot of Jim Beam after listening for several hours to the wild-eyed Trey scare the living daylights out of everyone within ear-shot as he described his friend Cole being torn limb from limb.

Saranji herself brought the iced tea to his table along with a water glass of good Bourbon. "Half sweet and unsweet," she said discreetly.

"Just the way I like it," the priest said with a wink. "You must read minds."

"If I did, I'd make a lot more money than I do running this place," she replied. "But I'm not saying I don't know when a man has had a rough day."

The purpose of the church service was unilaterally agreed to by all participating clergy. Julia Springs was in the grip of evil and the cause was three-fold: the decadent lives young people were leading, lack of church support, and the whole community's preoccupation with materialism. Like guilty children, the assembled townspeople bowed their heads in shame, willing to shoulder the burden of communal guilt as Jesus had done.

On the other hand, Cole Prescott's father, Scottie John, had a much different agenda. Waving his baseball cap over their bowed heads like a magic wand, he singlehandedly lifted the burden of guilt from the shoulders of the townspeople and dropped it squarely on the Glory Road priestess.

"All that's well and good, preacher," he said, drawing a gasp from the ladies as he got to his feet, "but I got a boy up there in Macon General in the morgue and that Root Woman's to blame. She's been practicing some kind of hoodoo religion out there in the Thicket and set some kind of evil afoot. Someone's got to put a stop to it and, since I'm the injured party, it's going to be me. She and the rest of that scum who live in the Thicket are trespassing. I don't care if I do own part of a swamp that's got wildlife in it. I've wanted to get rid of the squatters down there for years. Now's the time! I'm going to smoke 'em all out and the EPA be damned."

By five, most people had gone home, more disturbed by the prayer service than comforted by it. Another hour had gone by before those who lingered on the steps of the Church of the Miraculous Waters, discussing the implications of the evening's events, noticed the peculiar light in the windows of Glory Road Church across the intersection. About the same time, customers at Sara's Place sitting outside under colorful umbrellas to eat their pulled-pork barbeques saw a black ribbon of smoke curl skyward above the cottonwoods. After a fraction of a second, the news came to everyone who had a phone. The Glory Road Church was on fire.

෨෧෨

Alone in her room, Gina waited for Megan to come home. It was nearly eight and she knew Maureen would be coming up to check on them soon. She played a game on her lap top. However, after a while, beating up monsters as they popped out of fake castles soon bored her and she turned on the music. Lying there looking up at the hairline cracks running across the old plaster, she shivered as the throbbing beats of soul rock rippled through her young body. The words spoke of pleasures she had only read about or imagined. Megan knew how it felt to let someone inside, but then Megan always went after what she wanted. Now she was pregnant and her breasts were getting bigger and Gina envied her older sister more than ever. Beautiful, talented, and now pregnant, Megan had it all, even boobs people could see.

But she, Gina Kelly, had Vadim, although she still didn't know if he was real or someone her horniness had just invented. Now, smiling to herself she replayed their accidental meeting at the quarry, wondering if, like Cole Prescott, she had conjured him up as well. *So I don't have to be alone...*

Megan's eighteenth birthday party had always marked the beginning of summer for young people in Julia Springs. They were sick of being under adult surveillance for drinking and necking. Always the main event of early summer, Megan Kelly's birthday party had lasted two days—the first for children and the second for adults which the kids attended anyway.

Even the Owl children were invited, all eleven, who usually brought some kind of wild animal as a gift, either dead or alive. Dead, if it were edible, alive if it weren't—except for the king snake which could have fallen into either category, depending on one's taste.

It was because of the snake, in fact, that Gina had met Vadim, and either God or Chinaberry Man. She never could quite decide which one was which.

The party had been a month earlier, in late May, and the earth was young again, stirring beneath the flowering ground just as mating instincts in adolescent bodies. After the presents were opened and food consumed, there was a heated debate: what to do with the king snake, a gift from the Owl children. Although some of the older boys suggested skinning it for its red and gold hide, most were in favor of letting it go. Gina went on the snake's defense, saying it killed rattlers and other poisonous snakes as well as mice. She said Saranji had told her snakes were good luck symbols and they guarded sacred places. After she convinced them they would all have rotten luck if they hurt it, someone suggested going down to the quarry and letting it loose to kill the water moccasins that hung around there.

"And he can kill Chinaberry Man," another soulless guest shouted, followed by a suspended silence while significant glances were exchanged.

"King snakes don't kill people, dummy. They kill rats and mice and stuff." Art Gatewood, Megan's boyfriend, was the one who knew everything about snakes and sex, or was convinced he did.

"Chinaberry Man ain't people. He's a spirit person." The girl's voice had such authority, everyone turned to look at Erin Owl, sixth among the Owl offspring. She was nearly Megan's age, a willowy golden-skinned girl. Everyone knew her dad had been a marine and was a real hero, even though he stayed drunk a lot now. He also a longtime friend of their uncle Jordan. "If you want to give our gift away, give it to Chinaberry Man. He will protect you because he is grateful."

Art responded with the conviction of a soul that had been saved in the muddy waters of the Hanahatchee creek. "I don't believe that old Injun hoodoo. It ain't even Christian, either. My mom says its heathen nonsense. C'mon, let's go swimming."

"You better watch out where you swim, Arthur Gatewood. The tie snakes will snatch you and pull you down and you won't breathe air again."

At the mention of the old native legend, even the master of all information looked uncomfortable for a brief moment, shifting from one bare foot to the other as if he had stepped on fire ants. "Aw, fuck you, Erin. Go play with your snake. Anybody who would bring somebody a snake for a birthday present is a damn fool." Taking the snake by its tail, Arthur swung it twice around his head like a whip and flung it high into the tree canopy, sending the party guests running for cover.

Activity was suspended for a breathless moment while the guests looked from the slender girl standing on a boulder above the pool to Gatewood, his spiked hair standing up like a water sprite, glistening droplets flying out like sparks in the sunlight.

"C'mon, last one in has to kiss a snake." Megan shattered the moment by tearing off her skimpy dress and running to the dark water in her expensive but barely visible underwear. Gatewood could hardly resist the invitation, and the rest of the partygoers knew better than to resist Gatewood's example.

Erin turned on her heel and bounded into the woods with only a few siblings following her.

Gina was outraged by Megan's behavior when she was around Gatewood and also the discourteous way she treated Erin. "I'm not going. You're all crazy if you go after a fool like him!" she yelled at their backs. "There's quicksand in that quarry. It eats your skin off! Everybody knows that."

"We're not going to swim in that part, stupid. Ditch little sister," Art yelled back and the rest took up the cry. "Ditch little sister! Ditch little sister!"

Gina followed Erin deep into the Thicket until she was exhausted by the sweltering heat. She sat down on a tumbled boulder and looked around, searching for any sign of her friend's movement—a startled bird or moving branch. It seemed the older girl had melted into the scrubby trees, avoiding the blackberry brambles and Creeping Jenny which had scratched her own legs until they bled. It was as if she had turned into a tree herself, the way the gods had changed a maiden. No snapped twigs, no rustling branches, Erin had simply vanished as if the forest had absorbed her.

No one knew exactly where the Owls lived in the Thicket or the Swamp-side, but they had lived there for over a hundred years, wherever it was. Uncle Lane said it was true. They were the remnants of a native people who fled when the whites ran all the natives out of Georgia and Alabama so they could take over their land.

"Good afternoon, Miss."

The man's voice came out of the trees behind her so suddenly Gina felt as if she had turned to into the granite rock she was sitting on.

"Don't be scared, miss. I don't mean to frighten you, believe me."

Stories of young girls disappearing, later to turn up dead, in just such remote places as this terrified her to the point her teeth were locked and chattering. She nodded. "Uh-huh."

He rose up and stepped from the pile of boulders behind her, tall and fair as a god in the afternoon sun. The young man was ragged and filthy, but he bowed slightly as if he were at a formal dance and was asking her to sign him up for the next one. "How do you do? My name is Vadim. Please excuse me if I frightened you, miss."

"Gina. My name's Gina. That's short for Regina. It's a stupid name, but I'm named after some aunt or something." For some reason, she knew instantly he wasn't from around Julia Springs. Maybe because of his courteous formal speech? Whatever the reason, she relaxed a little to the point of being able to speak coherently.

"Regina. It means queen. Is Italian name, no?" He looked around, as if trying to formulate small talk before killing her, which she was certain he intended to do. Or even worse. "Very hot day, yes?"

Too terrified to scream for help, she kept up her end of the conversation. "Going to be a hot summer, yes, sir."

From the start of their conversation, she had noticed something strange about his stilted sentences. Maybe he was an escaped lunatic from the state asylum at Milledgeville. Or he could be retarded, hiding away in the basement of some well-meaning farmer's house, educated on the Bible by an over-protective mother. In was common in their small community to adopt these people into their midst without a ripple.

"Did you fall down here or something?" She nodded towards his ragged clothes.

"Fall?" He seemed puzzled for a moment, looking up at the trees as if trying to connect the word "fall" with the seasons. "No, working here. Not looking where I was going, I took a tumble down. Oh, I see. You mean I fell down. Like Jack. As in 'Jack fell down and broke his crown,' no?"

Even worse than she thought. A mentally retarded convict wanted for rape and murder who had been working in the quarry and managed to escape. She wished she had watched more news on TV like America's Most Wanted, but she hated the squiggly black-and-white screen with all the gritty faces leering from their mug shots. Now they had invaded her world of birdsong and green-gold sunlight.

"But you aren't hurt? Other than that, I mean."

He seemed to be about to bolt into the woods like a deer at any second, looking over his shoulder toward the sound of the laughing party guests. "Oh, I am very good, thank you for asking. Only mosquitoes are terrible. And I have only a little clean water left. So I must go back and finish work now. I am pleased to make your acquaintance however, Miss Gina. Have nice day."

"To prison?" It was out and he was going to kill her. "I mean, back where?"

The man who called himself Vadim began to laugh and hushed up fast, glancing around again. But she had seen a row of perfect white teeth in his dirty face, and a glimpse of something else, pride. "Oh, you think I am convicted person," he said. "Oh, no, miss. I am not convicted person. Only little bit lost and very dirty."

She looked at him dubiously. "Lost?" He might really be crazy, but she didn't want to rile him by calling him a liar. "Are you from America?"

"I come from Ukraine five years now. Work as surveyor

for chemical company. See, down there by little stream?" He pointed toward the sluggish creek running through the Thicket. "Company want to buy up all this land," he said with a sweep of his arm. "So I am coming back from creek and not looking. Then falling—no rolling down—down until big rock stop me. I am becoming little bit unconscious, I think." He pronounced it "sink."

In spite of meeting him in a quarry, she was beginning to believe him. A warning bell had gone off somewhere. The first step in the killer's mind was getting close to the victim, she remembered reading somewhere. "So you did get hurt. How long ago was this?" It was on the tip of her tongue to ask him if he had seen Chinaberry Man, but on the other hand, she just might be talking to him.

To her surprise, he pulled a cell phone out of his pocket and consulted it. "About 9 o'clock this a.m. What is this place? A pool for swimming?"

She was now thoroughly disarmed. "No, that's just my sister and her friends playing in the rainwater that's built up on the island side. They used to quarry limestone here. On the rocky side there's quicksand and water'll eat your skin off. So stay away from there. There's a path that winds back up this side here. It's about half mile from the creek from there. They used to float the limestone down to the river on barges, my uncle told me."

"Ah, yes. My boss says to check the railroad bridge on the creek. I am going to do that after I finish survey. This quarry hole is not on my map so I don't know it is there. Imagine my surprise when I fall down, down, down like Alice through the hole." Again, the laugh and smile.

At least, he was well versed in children's literature. She wondered if she could believe him, this golden man besmirched by mud and burrs. Gina got to her feet slowly. "I have to be going, too. I'll walk with you to the path that leads up to the creek so you can find your back from there. Like I said, we had a big birthday party today. That's all that shouting and carrying on you hear down by the water. *Warn them there are other people nearby, never hurts in case he tries some-*

thing. Joy's instructions on date rape sprang to mind.

"Is party for you? May I ask how many years you have?"

"I'm sixteen years old, soon to be seventeen," she said, formally correcting his English. "And no, the party's for my sister, Megan. She's eighteen. How old are you?"

"I am twenty-one. My day of birth is November."

"Mine's August. Then I'll be seventeen." Why did she say that? Was it too much information about herself?

"I have sister of that age back in the Ukraine. Her name is Lara. And one older brother who is here in States. Chicago, Illinois."

"You must miss your family back home," she said, stopping to pick blackberries from the brambles that blocked their way, "your sister and all."

"Oh, yes, very much, but I like States, too. Many opportunities here."

She gave the first handful to Vadim who received them with pleasure. He ate them as if he were starving. Soon, they were raiding the brambles for every last berry they could find, until their mouths and teeth were purple.

"Do you want to go back there, to Russia?"

"Ukraine. Oh, no, no, Miss Gina. I like America and I want to stay. My mother and father are old and my sister will stay in Ukraine. I don't want to go back there. No, freedom is best for me." He bent his golden head for a moment then took out his cell phone. "Yes, I am almost through. I will text you my report when I finish." Closing the phone, he said, "I must go, Miss Gina. You have made this day most pleasant, but boss is chewing me up. I must finish job and get report in."

It was only then she noticed the quarry no longer rang with laughter and shouts. The swimmers must be getting ready to go back, and she hoped by now Megan and Art had rejoined them, making her re-entrance easier.

Finally, they found the path leading through the quarry and up the forested side of the quarry winding around tumbled boulders. They shook hands solemnly and then she watched him vanish into the new foliage, climbing upward with strong steps. Turning the opposite way, she headed down toward the pool in the deepest part of the quarry, but the path was hard to see in the lengthening shadows. Then it abruptly ended at the dense undergrowth growing along the steep rock face of the pit. She turned around and walked back the way she had come, but the path again petered out in the scrubby Thicket where volunteer pines and oaks had sprouted up.

It wasn't there. Somehow, she had walked around to a completely different part of the quarry than the place where she had come in.

The sun was sinking, sliding like melted butter across the spring sky when she found the pool at the bottom of the quarry. By then, it was cast in shadow, a black mirror reflecting the jagged wall above it. Behind her, the Thicket was in deep shadow, coming alive with insects and strange rustling and cracking noises as night creatures stirred from their sleep. Instinctively, she chose the only direction light would lead her—straight up the rock wall of the quarry.

She thought briefly about yelling for help. And then realizing no one could possibly hear her, she measured the distance across the water to the wall with her eyes. Either someone had placed a log or a tree had fallen down in a storm across the narrowest part of the pool. Countless scores of swimmers had used it for a diving board until it was nearly submerged. Nevertheless, using it as a tightrope walker uses his wire, Gina carefully placed one foot in front of the other until she was at the end. There remained nearly three feet of water until she could be on firm ground and, giving a huge leap, she cleared the gap, coming hard up against the rock face. She had long ago taken off her party shoes, a pair of one inch heels Maureen had brought down from Atlanta. They were to become casualties of her predicament if she were to climb the wall to the top.

A slight sound that echoed across the dark water made Gina look behind her, sensing another presence. A deer driven by the heat came out of the Thicket to drink the brackish water.

The climb up the quarry wall, easy at first because the stone cutters hadn't completely finished chiseling away large boulders at the bottom, became a grueling ordeal as the razor sharp rocks cut her bare feet until they bled.

In the middle third, the granite shafts became smoother, leaving larger spaces between footholds. Her hands worked in tandem with her feet in perfect coordination in order to pull her body up through the gaps. She dared not look down, remembering the warnings about climbers who did and died, paying the price.

By the time she had reached the upper third, the sun was a narrow strip of light along the lip of the quarry. Its slender rays stretched toward her—probing fingers of light touching the jutting edges of the rocky face as if the sun itself were pointing out the best grips for her desperate fingers. Near the top, yet not near enough to grasp the grassy edge, she found herself with nothing to hold on to—no crevice in which to pry a hold, no foothold for her bleeding feet and her arms were getting weak. It wouldn't take any great effort just to let go and fall to certain death on the jagged boulders below.

She clung to the granite chest of the earth, envisioning her funeral. Her mother would be crying, blotting her mascaraed eyes, which always looked like a circus clown's when she cried. There would be lots of prayers and food, with people loading up their plates to take home what they would eat in their parlors and watch TV. Gina never thought death would be something not to dread, as simple an act as just ceasing to struggle—just letting go.

"Help," she whispered, too exhausted to shout. "Somebody, help! Vadim!"

Her body, however, had different ideas. It had come out of her mother fighting for life and wasn't about to give up, never. Born a month early, running the gamut of childhood illnesses, nearly dying of pneumonia—oh, no, it wasn't giving in to some harebrained whim of the mind. No, it clung to the granite wall like a frightened child to its mother, fixed barnacle-like.

Then she smelled chinaberries, sweet and primal and something ordered her to look up straight into the retreating sun. *Reach up your hand, child,* said the sun, and she did, pry-ing loose the fingers of her right hand and stretching, stretching toward the light. That was the last thing Gina had remembered.

Her mother came from somewhere, overwhelming her with expensive perfume, smothering her with kisses. "Oh, baby, we were so scared. We searched and searched everywhere and didn't even think of the quarry until that tramp told us where you were. And oh, I don't even want to think about what he might have done to you."

"Then don't," Aunt Mildred said. "Have some lemonade, Gina. Your hands look like raw pork chops and your poor feet, I can't even describe them. Like you got caught in a food grinder. What on earth have you been doing? And how did that young foreigner know where you were? I'll bet that's a story not even you could make up."

She never told them the real truth about the man called Vadim or Megan and Art skinny-dipping and coming up all stuck together like a couple of yard dogs mating. The fact that Megan and Art hadn't admitted they had left her behind in the quarry seemed irrelevant now that she was safe. Her excuse was simply falling asleep and waking up as it was getting dark.

At the time, a lie seemed safer than saying she had met a good-looking young stranger with a foreign accent and picked blackberries with him. The very fact that he had dropped by the house to make sure she was safe must mean something— that he could care about a sixteen-year-old girl with wild, red hair, freckled arms, and a big butt.

No, she wanted Vadim all to herself, not shared with suspicious, nosey relatives in whose minds all foreigners were linked to acts of violence and terrorism. Her relatives were simple people with simple values: fear the unknown, accept the known for what it is, and ask no questions for fear of confusion. The beautiful young man in the woods became the stuff of dreams and would come back out of love for her, in spite of all dangers and distances. She would eventually choose to go with him and everyone would say, "I never thought Gina Kelly was so much like her sister, Megan. I guess that goes to show you, still waters run deep."

Chapter 17

Nearly two hundred miles north, in an Atlanta industrial park, Vadim Ivanovsky studied the computer screen intently. Behind him the office door opened and his boss, Alex Foster, passed his cubicle with a casual, "What's up, man?"

In the stuffy air of the small office, the odor of whiskey floated down to him like feathers from a sick bird. "I'm wondering if you approved that order for shipment of liquid chemicals from North Georgia Chemical."

Foster sounded slightly annoyed, the way he usually did before getting his afternoon nap. "Yeah, why? What's wrong with that? It's a sizeable deal for us, making that connection with Florida for five carloads of benzoyl chloride gas."

"The reason I ask is because...did you read my report on the bridge at Julia Springs?"

Impatient for his post-lunch nap, yawning openly, Alex Foster smiled automatically, showing his perfect American teeth. He always smiled when he lied. It was expected of a Foster whose firm had been in chemicals since the 1940s.

His family had lived, talked, and represented the chemical industry all his life. His grandfather had started Foster Chemical Co. during World War II and sold out to a major corporation for millions. Like many entrepreneurs, he saw the real opportunity was in transport and, by extension, in tanker cars and rail lines. Staying alive just long enough to see his ideas pay off handsomely, his demise left his son, Alexander Foster

II, as the nominal head of the firm. Even in his declining years, the old man could easily see a board of directors would have to keep their collective thumb on his globe-trotting, sport-fishing, ski-bum son.

Foster, who had been raised on the golf links of the Atlanta Gold Club, had joined the firm when his father decided to take up yacht racing fulltime with his third, very expensive wife. The board of directors of Foster Chemical Transport was ready for him. He was smart enough, had a degree in chemical engineering, and an MBA. Moreover, he had chemicals in the brain, and knew the industry inside and out.

The board, on the other hand, knew enough to play to his weaknesses—in order to keep power in their hands and their salaries high. Give him just enough money to indulge his pleasures, which were many, and drained him. Let his wife go to Paris twice a year to see the collections with newly-rich friends, and they, the board, could run the company.

His six figure salary allowed him to stay on the links and in the bar, but not quite enough to manage his two families and a very greedy mistress. He always needed more, which kept him in the office until at least Happy Hour. He was, granted, always in touch electronically, even in bed with his honey.

"Yes, I think very wrong," Vadim said. "Problem is the bridge there across Hanahatchee Creek is not safe. Army Corp of Engineers say bridge is only 40% sound."

"The Army Corp of Engineers is only about 40% right half the time. Besides when was that study done? Back in 1960, I'll bet."

"Correct. 1965. Over forty years ago. Then only forty per cent sound. But when I do inspection last month, not even forty. Perhaps twenty—perhaps zero. One support footing exposed completely." Vadim looked up at Alex Foster, his regular features lit by the glow from the computer screen. "It is unsound, Mr. Foster, sir. Unsound for train to pass over, certainly."

"Hey, look, kid—" The situation was becoming tense, judging from the way Foster suddenly invaded his cubicle and fell into the chair. He was a big, handsome man with a casual,

slow grin which had earned him the name Slick in his fraterni-
ty. "I've got the green signal from the DOT commissioner for
the shipment, don't I? That's all we need to clear the way to
the plant in Florida."

"But—"

Foster waved away his protests. "You know what, you're
a good kid, Vadim, but you worry too much. Get it? That's my
job, to worry, okay? Just forget it and do your work."

As Foster got up, swaying slightly as he eased through the
doorway, Vadim rose to his feet nearly matching his height.
"But please, Mr. Foster, I saw the bridge. No repairs have been
done to it. The track—"

Foster yawned and used the cubicle wall to steady himself. The entire section swayed under the impact of his weight.
Vadim reached out to hold it steady.

"Yeah, I read it. You said."

"In the file I am looking now. There is no confirmation
number in record. No DOT confirmation number for your request to move freight. No HAZMAT inspection number, okay?
Got to have both to move chemical."

Foster was becoming visibly annoyed. "Okay, look, Von.
You do your job and I'll do mine, okay? I spoke to the commissioner personally on the phone. He knows my dad and he
gave the permission to move the shipment, okay? Said he'd fix
it with the HAZMAT people, so no sweat, okay? I appreciate
your concern and all but mind your P's and Q's. That's why
you're only a temporary employee here so I can see how we
get along together, get my drift?"

"Sir, I got to take absence this afternoon." Vadim stood
resolute, waiting to get fired on the spot.

Foster turned around and glared at him. "What? Why the
hell is that?"

By now, Vadim realized his job was in jeopardy and visualized his life in the Ukraine as if it were still an open wound.
Always hungry, waiting tables in some sidewalk café, and
watched by secret police because of his role as an activist in
the uprisings against an oppressive government. Over the tops
of cubicles, he saw one of the draftsmen pop his head up and

nod his head. Marv was a black engineer who had befriended him his very first day at work.

Marvelous Marvin, as he called himself on his weekend gigs as a DJ, had taken the young immigrant under his tutelage. "You got to learn good English, man, if you want to meet girls around here. Right now, you talking like one of those robots in some bad sci-fi flick. You know, the 'Take me to your leader' thing."

Now Marv came around the gray cubicle wall as if he were on urgent business. "Hey, Vadim, how's the grannie doing? You take her to the ER yet?"

"ER? What is this?"

"Emergency Room. Hospital, you know the drill. No point waiting for the doctor to see her. Afternoon, Mr. F. Lunch at the Sports Bar again? Got any scores? Baseball, I'm talking about." Whatever Marvelous Marv said, it deflected Foster's anger away from Vadim and on to the Braves pitcher.

"Hell, we started off the season the hottest we've been in years, but the left-handed line up's hurting us, man. If we switch the heavy hitters to the right, we still got a chance at the playoffs. Whaddaya think, Marv?"

"When Ellis comes up to the mound, you can see the opposition dugout getting on their walking shoes, man. They need Diego up there with his curve ball killer."

"My grandma she is sick. Needs to see doctor," Vadim blurted out loud enough for Foster to flick a glance his way. "It is emergency."

Foster pretended to have forgotten Vadim was still standing there. "Oh, yeah, go on, kid. But make up the hours before payday, you know the drill." As Vadim hurried to the office door, he added, "And say hello to Granny for me. I hope she's pretty." Dropping his voice he said, "Kid's got to learn better English. Like talking to a damned robot."

In the parking garage, Vadim studied the schedule he had downloaded to his phone. The shipment of hazardous chemicals would have left North Georgia by now and would be nearing Atlanta at two. Traveling at fifty-five mph with two fifteen-minute stops, it would reach Julia Springs by around seven. He had plenty of time to get there before the train pulled out of Carrollton and warn the authorities there to delay the shipment while they checked the bridge supports.

He almost couldn't bear the thought of what would happen if the train wrecked, spilling benzoyl chloride so near that little town. People near the spill would die or be so sick that they wouldn't get to the hospital in time. And the land, the beautiful woodlands where he'd met the girl, would all be ruined. He'd never forgive himself and she wouldn't either.

Melding cautiously in the fierce afternoon traffic, he steered his two-year-old sedan through the bowels of Atlanta's narrow South side and on to the Interstate. That girl in her pretty blue dress, that incredible hair the color of fire cascading down her tan shoulders crept into his mind where she lingered like the notes of a love song. "My name is Gina. That's short for Gina," she said, with her lips curved in a smile. "I'll be seventeen in August."

"I'll be twenty-one in November," he said to the direction finder.

"Recalculating," it replied.

℮℧℮℧

The sleek silver sports convertible was parked with the top down because the couple inside needed more room to make love. They had parked there quite often in the months leading up to graduation as their lust for each other grew into a mating frenzy.

Finally, Megan sat up and started pulling up her bra. Arthur tried to pull her down on the back seat again, but she resisted, shrugging his hands off.

"Come on, Meggie. It's early yet. Your folks know you don't come home when you're s'posed to, anyway. Once more, honey please. You got me so horny now, I'll have to jerk off down by the creek."

"Go on, then. You act like I'm your whore or something." She pulled up her blouse but he began kissing her neck.

"Well, you are my little whore when it comes to lovemaking. I've never had anything like it, even when I paid good money."

Swinging her whole fist around, Megan socked him squarely in the face and lunged forward to open the passenger door. But Gatewood's arms went around her waist, holding her back on the seat. "That hurt, girl! I'll teach you to hit me!" Pinning her down under his superior weight, he forced open her legs. She kept hitting him with her fists until he finally stopped.

Meanwhile, the creature witnessed the struggle from his hiding place near the train tracks. There the undergrowth was untouched by the hairless ones who came to the creek fishing, leaving their garbage on its banks. He had grown to have a taste for their food and the guts of their fish which they often left behind. It was an easy meal.

Now, he watched with a different kind of hunger as the couple wrestled in the back seat of the shiny vehicle. Lifting his nose to the air, he smelled a strange new odor, that of mating. Feelings he had never had before stirred in his loins. He stood up on his hind legs to see better, curious, beginning to ache with pleasure in an organ he had never used that way before.

Abruptly, the couple parted and the girl leaped out of the vehicle half-dressed. "Rapist!" she shouted through angry tears. Hair flying wildly, pulling on her short skirt up around her waist, she ran to the railroad tracks and over the trestle to the far side of the creek. He crouched again as the boy tried to cut her off at the bridge, but she was too fast for him. His shorts had slipped below his buttocks and he had to stop to fasten them, all the time muttering to himself.

Then the young hairless male leaped up on the trestle and started shouting angrily at the forest on the other side. He even ran part of the way into the Thicket just as lightning forked across the darkening sky. Mystified and curious, the creature hunkered down and waited. When the hairless male left, he could follow the scent of the female easily. In the distance, thunder rumbled, but what he could identify, the creature didn't fear.

Not the lightning coming ever closer, even setting alight a tall old pine deep in the forest. Or the crash of thunder like a thousand kettle drums at close range. It was something else, a new sound that kept him from pursuing the female, a sound that superseded lust. The hairless boy apparently didn't hear it yet, it being imperceptible to human ears. It was the vibration of the rails up on the track as if a huge beast were on its way, each footstep jarring everything for miles.

The creature crouched in the thick undergrowth and waited.

৩৩৩

"Come on, girl, time's a-wasting. Soon it's going to be getting dark and I have to start my cooking fires." Root Woman pulled the clean cloth over the reed basket, brushing away the small monkey who tried to pull it off again.

"Where're we going, Nana?" Kenya rose from the hay mattress where she'd been napping and buttoned her shift. "Town again?"

"No, ma'am. We paying a visit to the Mama Tree."

Kenya got a pear to eat on the way. "What for? And why do you call it the Mama Tree? I think it should be called the Grandma Tree 'cause it's so old."

Root Woman laughed in her quiet way. "Maybe so. We're going 'cause it's a holy place, for one thing. We got to leave our offerings for the ancestor spirits, for another. And then we got to ask it something."

"I thought ghosts couldn't eat nothing. What you want to waste good food on them for? Besides, trees can't talk. So what you expect it to say?"

With Kenya still rattling off questions, they made their way along a path that Root Woman's feet had worn over the years. The girl soon quieted down, caught up in studying the flowers and fruit trees that lined the route to the towering oak tree. There were peaches ripening on several, persimmons on another. Bright quince blossomed on the bushes and blueberries.

"Did you plant all these or did they just grow by themselves?" Kenya asked the tall, old woman who led the way.

But Root Woman didn't answer. Her lips were moving in a mantra and Kenya quickened her pace, knowing better than to talk when her grandmother was praying. Presently, they came to the ancient tree and Root Woman laid down her gourds, each with a prayer. When she had finished she said, "Come here, child."

Kenya went to stand beside her. Root Woman put her shawl around the girl and began chanting again. Then she put one hand on Kenya's belly and the other on her shoulder, swaying with the chant. The girl swayed with her grandmother, lulled by the foreign but somehow familiar words. Then she gasped as a twisting pain tore through her body. Root Woman held her closer and chanted even harder.

"Oh," Kenya said loudly. "I feel like something bad's wrong. It hurts! My stomach hurts! Like it's breaking apart!"

Root Woman stopped singing and swaying. "Then She has answered. Let's go home, baby. I smell smoke. Something's burning. I hope I didn't leave my cooking pot too close to the trees."

෧෨෧

Gina Kelly lay on her bed looking up at the cracks in the eighty-year old plaster molding around the ceiling. The music on her headphones was sexy and soft. Behind closed eyes, she offered her entire body stretched out for this invisible lover to take. *Vadim, Vadim, come back to me. I think I love you, Vadim. Come save me again. Let's get naked together and swim in the dark night.*

Getting up slowly, she got back on her laptop and opened up her Facebook page. She couldn't believe the number of comments had mushroomed to twenty-two from three that were posted that afternoon. Some of them were just a few words and some, paragraphs. And there were pictures as well: of her face touched up to resemble Satan's, of witches plunging knives into babies, of Megan with a huge distorted abdomen and the word Slut in bloody letters written across her face. Horrible things! She read the comments with whispering lips, unable to believe what she saw but magnetized to the screen in horror.

"Ugly Bitch Witch." "Red-headed Satan Lover" "Why don't you die and break the curse?" And there was a picture of her hanging from a tree.

She didn't hear the phone ring in Lane's office and her uncle leaving in his pickup truck, red emergency lights flashing on the dashboard.

Following the beat of the Facebook streaming music, she danced away to a dream space where the erotic turned to terror. Gina woke up ten minutes later with a scream, her blouse soaked in perspiration. She had seen Megan running from something huge. Her mouth agape with terror, forming the words "Help me."

The creature behind her was closing the distance between them with giant steps, huge red eyes glowing in the dark. He had almost caught her when she woke up. She looked at the clock. Eight-thirty. She knew immediately that Megan had gone into the Thicket to find Root Woman, but something else had found *her*.

Gina sat straight up with a gasp as the waking vision of Megan screaming for help, running through the Thicket with something huge following behind her played out before her open eyes.

At the same moment, she heard Joy calling, "Ginny, come down now! We have to go to town! Something's happening and I want to see if Dad's okay!"

Chapter 18

Tanner had just dozed off on his porch when he heard Rollo growl. He awoke to find Lou Owl sitting on the steps, sipping straight from the whiskey bottle he was sharing with Reggie at lunch.

"Hell, you getting old, Tanner. Asleep in your rocking chair like an old geezer."

"In case you hadn't noticed, Lou, I am in geezerhood. So are you, you damned bastard."

"Let's go, then."

"Go? Where? It's gonna be dark soon and a storm's coming. See those thunderheads building up in the west? I can smell it and I saw lightning flashes over there over the Thicket."

"That's why we got to go. Get on your waders and your jacket. We got to go down to the Swamp again."

"Hell no! I'm not going down there at night. There's something roaming around down there that doesn't like humans. Some damn big animal that smells like Freon or something. What for, anyway? What's so damned urgent it can't wait until daylight?"

Owl lit a quick cigarette. In the dark, it glowed like a firefly as he dragged on it and exhaled with a juicy cough. "There's a lot of talk going on in town about how Root Woman done this and done that. Scott Prescott's threatening to set fire to the whole damn place and I wouldn't be surprised if he don't try tonight while everybody's tied up fussing around old

Delia Clark's dried-up, old, dead body. Come on, get your boots on and let's get going. Creek's already flooding and it's raining down by me." Tossing his cigarette aside, Owl stood up and picked up his rifle. For the first time, Tanner noticed he was carrying a backpack.

"Hot damn, the things I do for you, Owl. I've had the day from hell and I was catching a few winks when, no, you have to come and wake me up."

"You sound like an old woman bitching away about losing a night's sleep. Hurry up. Sooner we start, sooner we'll get there. Hell, what's that now?"

The sound of emergency sirens reached them across the open fields. Looking in the direction of the sound, the two men noticed a peculiar glow lighting the sky over Julia Springs.

"Looks like something big's on fire."

"Get your old ass in gear, man. Old Precott's on the warpath." Lou trotted off in the direction of the Thicket.

Simply because he'd never known his friend to be in a hurry about anything, Tanner dragged on his waders and grabbed his rifle and what was left of the whiskey.

"Wait for me, dammit," he called. But Owl had been absorbed into the sunset, as if he were a part of it.

ເ∽ຈເ∽ຈ

Plunging into the deepest part of the Thicket, Megan ran blindly along the creek, mosquitoes clinging like fleas on a dog to the bloody scratches left on her arms and legs by vines and branches. A light glimmered through the dense forest and then was gone as the trees began moving with a sudden wind. Falling into marsh ooze, she felt something skitter away from her arm. She screamed as a snake, terrified by her flummoxing, slithered over her leg in flight. Keeping up the staccato screeches, she stumbled to her feet, only to fall again into the slippery ooze. Tasting mud in her mouth, she spat and retched.

"Somebody help me!" No one answered, but the light came back again. She was getting closer and sheer panic gave her the momentum to get to her feet. "Help me, please!"

Behind her, she heard something large and heavy crashing through the undergrowth. Looking back, she expected to see Arthur Gatewood lumbering along in his best offensive tackle mode, preparing to bring her down on the forest floor to rape her again. Freezing like a stalked deer, she heard him splashing through the pool she had just floundered in. Silently now, she crouched down, weaving through the water oaks and kudzu screens, until the light flashed again. Her heart, which seemed to have stopped beating, launched itself wildly in her chest. The light was steady now, a beacon reaching fingers of light through the thick tangle of vines and stumpy water oaks. She aimed toward it and saw a large figure emerge in front of it, the light framing her like a halo. It was Root Woman carrying a lantern.

"Who's out there? Come this way, so I can see you. Kenya, go look and see if you can find the person who is hiding out there."

A wispy figure darted into the trees. "Who's out there," Kenya called, her voice shaking slightly. She took a few hesitant steps into the darkened woods. "Don't you know the woods is on fire?"

Erin Owl pushed the younger girl aside striding into the woods as if she owned them. "All right, who's there? Show yourself now."

"It's me," Megan barely had enough strength to speak and then she fainted, falling on the gnarled toes of a water oak.

"Miss Kahalia, look who's here!" Erin Owl called to the tall woman in the clearing. "Megan Kelly, come to pay you a visit. Gee, I wonder why?"

With a secretive smile, Erin slapped the pale cheeks of the girl who had barely acknowledged her presence through four years of school. If she slapped them a little too hard, she told herself it was justified since she had restrained herself from doing it so often over the years. "You better came to, Miss Peach Crop Princess, or we'll leave you here for the Boogey Man to get you, and I don't mean Arthur Gatewood either."

Kenya intervened, lifting the girl's mud-soaked head gently to administer spirits of ammonia. "There, there, Miss Megan. It'll all be all right. You'll see," she said stroking the pale cheeks as if reassuring herself.

Root Woman couldn't suppress a smile. Erin's vindictive behavior contrasted sharply with Kenya's lack of spite. "Bring her along, girls. We need to be getting to town. I think I feel something bad happening there." She and Kenya loaded their bundles on their backs and waited for Megan to get to her feet and come stumbling into the clearing, covered with mud and scratches. "Can you walk, girl?"

Through tears of humiliation and relief, Megan nodded, too grateful for human company to speak.

Erin picked up a basket of pots and herbs and shoved it at the shivering girl as it began to rain. "Then make yourself useful and tote this," she said. "Carry your weight, Miss Peach Crap Princess."

Through the dense forest behind them, they heard someone running, calling Megan's name. She turned, terror taking control of her entire body, and she clung to Erin's arm.

"Don't let him get me," she said. "Please don't."

Erin thrust her hand away. "It's only dumb ass Arthur. You better be nice to him, seeing the situation you're in."

Gatewood plunged out of the woods like a rutting stag, and stopped. "Megan, honey. What'd you run away for? I've been looking everywhere for you."

"Go away," she screamed, shrinking against Kenya' supporting arm. "Go away! I never want to see you again, you rapist!"

He looked sheepish under the accusing stares of the women. "Okay, okay. You don't have to freak out about it. I just wanted to tell you I'll bring the car around so if you want a ride—"

"Go to hell! I'll never get in your car again! Never!"

Kenya suddenly doubled over with pain. Dropping her basket, she fell to her knees holding her stomach. "Ohhhhh, help me! There it is again! It hurts like I'm gonna die!"

The women lifted the stricken girl to her feet and were making their way toward the entrance to the Thicket with an uncomfortable Gatewood lagging behind when someone else came stumbling out of the lengthening shadows behind them. It was Holly, looking pale and winded. Her usual cool attitude was gone, replaced by uncharacteristic urgency. Her hair, usually straightened and tidy, stood out like a dark halo all around her head. "Oh, thank you, Jesus! Thank you. I thought I was lost down here and with that fire coming. You all got to hurry up and get out, hear? The whole woods is on fire." She stopped to get her breath. "What's wrong, Kenya, honey, you hurt?"

"Holly, what in hell are you doing here?" Erin Owl demanded an explanation even if the others didn't care. Holly belonged in more sophisticated environments, not in Erin's world of outhouses and squatters shacks.

Holly took offense at Erin's demanding tone. "Like, who are you, the FBI? For your information, Miss Nosey, Grandma sent me to warn Root Woman that old Mr. Prescott was setting the woods on fire. They're old friends, you know. Not Prescott who runs the Klan around here. She and Root—Miss Kahalia."

"That's so kind of her to think of me—breathe deep, honey lamb—" Root Woman put a protective arm around her granddaughter's shoulder, "seeing as how she goes saying she doesn't like that "Demon Worshipping" church as she calls my mission. Shows how we misjudge people, doesn't it?"

Kenya shrieked again, and doubled over. This time she screamed at the sight of blood gushing down her legs. "Help me, Grandma! Am I going to die?"

Root Woman said in a soothing voice. "No, baby, it's a perfectly natural thing that's going on. The Mama Tree sent you a blessing, is all, but we got to get to Miss Lois's in a hurry. She'll take care of it. Her house is right up the way here. Lean on me, now." With Holly helping her and Erin and Megan following behind, dodging the trail of blood as they went, they made their way to the walls of Lesbos.

"Who goes there?" shouted a voice from a round turret made from adobe brick. "Oh, it's you, Miss Kahalia. Let me radio the gate to let you in."

"And please call Miss Lois to come immediately. My granddaughter's got a female problem. She's in quite a bit of pain."

"Female problem. I've near heard it called that before."
Erin looked around to see if Megan appreciated the joke. "I
would have called it a male problem. A horny male problem.
My mother has had eleven kids and about that many problems."

"I don't get it." Megan caught up with the other girl.
"What's going on?"

"She's miscarrying. Getting rid of the baby, stupid. Miss
Kahalia's just too polite to put it that way. A female problem,
she calls it. I say it's a male problem, get it?"

"Or she's just too guilty, you mean." Megan fixed blazing
eyes on Root Woman. "That's not fair! I offered you money
and you wouldn't take it. But you would get rid of your own
granddaughter's baby to make potions with, I'll bet."

"Megan, you know that a lie." Erin tried to defend Root
Woman against Megan's outrage, but Root Woman was more
than capable of defending herself.

"What's all this fuss about? Can't you see Kenya is in
pain?" Root Woman turned her sympathetic eyes on Megan.
"Do you want this to happen to you, Megan Kelly when you
have a chance of delivering a perfectly healthy child? It's just
nature's way of getting rid of something that's not perfect,
that's all."

"Oh, but you're Mother Nature, right? You know all the
secrets to getting rid of a child that's not wanted, I know you
do. What about Phyllis Overby and Susan Braithwaite? They
lost their babies because they bought your poison to kill them.
That's how the Glory Road Church got built, with the profits
from killing babies. But you wouldn't help me get rid of mine,
oh no! Let Megan Kelly suffer hell and damnation. She deserves it. Well, I'm gonna see you get what you deserve and
we'll see who suffers then. I'm going to report you to the
law!"

℘℘℘

Beside the train tracks, the creature waited for the silver
vehicle's owner to return. His heart sang out in pain, but the

only sound he made was his breath through flared nostrils. Then he lifted his nose to inhale another scent—one that brought a warning of danger, superseding passion. Smoke drifted on the growing wind, creeping along the canopy, forced to the ground by humidity. Lightning began to rocket across the leaden sky and the smell from the west was acrid, fueled by manmade substances that reeked of the four wheeled beasts. The odor put fear into his being, unknown except around the hairless ones. Eons of defense mechanisms stimulated his pineal gland, causing his scalp hairs to rise up forming an arch from his collarbone to his forehead.

It seemed a long time before the hairless boy got back to the car and, with a spatter of dirt, drove off on the logging road that cut through the forest at an oblique angle. By then the first few raindrops were falling and he put the top up, cursing all the while.

But the creature still waited. The vibrations in the steel rails meant the beast was coming closer. His hiding place afforded him safety and the beast would probably pass him by unseen. Still his whole being ached for a mate and he wanted to follow the hairless female with the long black mane. A distant whistle—what was that? It was a sound not unlike the one he made through his teeth when danger was near. Could the oncoming beast have spotted him from this distance? Now confusion overtook the creature and he squatted in place afraid to move.

A flight path through the jungle-like swamp formed a visual map in his mind. A vibration of the steel tracks resonated throughout his body, signaling a new danger. This time, he could not identify the warning sensation that sang through his veins to his muscles and from there, throughout his entire being. He crouched by the steel lines, dreading the giant beast that pressed ever nearer, rattling the ground under his feet as it advanced.

Some mile and a half up stream, the last retaining wall of Arnold Wheeler's catfish pond gave way as the force of the flooded creek spilled over the crude dam. It released a torrent of water, boulders, and timbers into the path of the flood.

Chapter 19

They trotted single file through the dense forest until Tanner had to call a halt to the pace. He bent over gasping for air, not caring what Lou Owl would say.

When he could manage speech again, he managed a fractured complaint. "Where the hell are you going? To a damn fire?"

"Funny you should say that." Owl put his rifle down against a tree and rested in the crook of a branch. "Have you looked over to the east?"

"I haven't been able to take my eyes off you since we started out, afraid you'd start playing hide-and-seek again." Tanner straightened up, finally able to inhale again. "Oh, good lord, what in hell's that over there?" Through a gap in the canopy of interwoven oaks overhead, he saw a red halo above the horizon. "Hell, it's another fire!"

"You ready, now?"

"Tell me where we're going before I take another step, just in case you decide to take a shortcut."

"First stop, Ham Phillips, then Andy's place, then Root Woman. She's probably already started for town by now since that was her Glory Road Church on fire."

"How the hell do you know this stuff? You don't even have a cell phone."

They hadn't moved twenty yards into the jungle when a clear voice called, "Papa?"

Tanner was grateful for any opportunity to stop, but to see

a slender form walking out of the green plant wall was a particularly welcome sight. Lou Owl's daughter, Erin, looked as though she were walking along a city sidewalk window shopping as she came through the woods.

"Your mom and the kids in the truck yet?"

"They were packing up when Mama sent me to Miss Kahalia's to tell her. Papa, the Thicket to the east of us is on fire. Old Mr. Prescott's gone crazy, saying he'll burn us all out." There were tears on the girl's cheeks, but her large brown eyes were as alert as a hunted deer's. "He's already set a bunch of fires at the east end of the Thicket."

Her father seemed unimpressed. "Prescott never had any brains to go crazy with. Erin, girl, I got a job for you. Go to Miss Kahalia's place and make sure she's gone. If she's left that monkey critter or the dog or any other animal behind, bring it back with you, okay? Go now."

"I've already been there, Papa. Mr. Tanner, I am to tell you Megan has gone with Miss Kahalia and they're all on their way into town except Holly and Kenya who had to stay with Miss Lois and Isis because I think Kenya's miscarrying. That dirtball Arthur Gatewood and Megan had a big fight, I guess, Mr. Tanner, and he was trying to make up to her. You know, the rumor is she's pregnant. Art's been smoking weed again. I could smell it on him."

"No. I didn't know that, Erin," Tanner said, "but I'm not surprised. Megan's a little wild. I'll call her uncle to come get her at the Jumping Off Place."

"Don't stand around here gossiping, Erin, then. Go on and help your mother with the kids or something." Lou sounded so irritated, she immediately shrank back into the shadows.

"Yes, Papa." And she was gone.

"Now you sound like a grumpy old coot, Lou. You're sending that girl on a wild goose chase with a brush fire in the neighborhood."

Lou turned on his heel. "Ham Phillips next," was all he said.

As if to emphasize the urgency of their mission, lightning forked overhead and thunder rolled across the Thicket in the path of the fire. As they lapsed into the dog trot again, Tanner found he had passed the first stage of the long distance runner, and was finding his breathing space. He remembered that from boot camp after running many miles with a full backpack every morning. Somehow Lou Owl was finding a path through the Thicket as if following a city street, curving around fallen trees or marshy pools.

Following the glimmer of Owl's rifle barrel in the shadows, Tanner realized his eyes had adjusted to night vision. All at once, Owl stopped abruptly, causing Tanner to nearly collide with him.

"Just when I was going good," Tanner said. "What's the mat—"

Owl's finger in the air silenced him. The signal for danger. He knew enough to listen as his friend had taught him, with his entire body—and smell. Listen to the sound of the forest, the wind, the odor of fetid moisture on the wind. Then it came, a crunching in the underbrush. Tanner's neck hairs rustled and his scalp tingled.

Owl took the safety off his rifle and Tanner followed suit.

"Who goes there?" a voice boomed out, startling swamp birds and sending deer out of their thickets plunging wildly through the underbrush.

They peered into the shadows where a red light gradually approached them, swinging from one side to the other as if were suspended from a metronome in midair. The light was accompanied by crashing and crunching noises made by bulldozers in a clear-cut operation.

Tanner whispered, "Whoever they are, they're riding an ATV or a backhoe—only thing that will cut through those woods. Either way, get ready for trouble. It's got to be Prescott and his boys." He hoped his nonchalant tone didn't betray his overwhelming relief that whatever was approaching wasn't Chinaberry Man. Not unless that mysterious creature had developed speech along with an unsteady gait.

"Aw, hell. It's just one of Ham's robot guards." Lou snapped the safety back on and saluted the lumbering machine that came lurching out of the brambles on to the path. "All hail, Lancelot IV. Take us to your master. Better yet, can you take a message to him?"

"Prithee, who goes there?"

"Lou Owl and Jordan Tanner."

"Follow me." The machine made a drunken circle and lunged back off the path into the forest.

"Never try to reason with a machine," Lou muttered, following the robot.

The mechanical voice sailed back at them through the muggy night air. "I heard that disparaging remark, sir. I have my orders, varlet."

Tanner fell in behind his friend. "Put you in your place there, Sarge."

Even before the scraggly dogs, deer, and pigs came out to greet them, the odor made it to their nostrils, even through all the smoke. As they followed the trampled undergrowth Lancelot IV left in his wake, Lou said in a low voice, "Don't stand around gabbing with Ham. We got to make tracks down to the bridge."

Crunching woody roots under his truck wheels, Lancelot IV turned around, recording their features as his single, red eye passed over their faces. "You are not to worry. My next mission is to escort Her Reverence, Miss Kahalia, personally. I trust you can find the rest of the way to my master."

"Right," Lou said, elbowing Tanner in the side. "We'll just follow our noses."

"He didn't get it," Tanner said as the machine went crashing away through the forest. "I think Ham won't program in a sense of humor because he's afraid they'll tell better jokes than he does."

"Ha, ha, ha," echoed back to them through the thick twilight air.

Chapter 20

Quade Walker was not so preoccupied with the fires Prescott and his sons and neighbors were setting that he didn't forget to buy livestock feed after he got off work at five. He went to Whitehead's, glad to take his mind off the day's events at least for the moment. But even that brief respite was clouded with rumors, questions, and speculation by the group of crusty, old men leaning on the counter or sitting on the porch so they could spit into the dirt.

"I hear Lewis Spencer escaped the law by running into the Thicket. That so, Captain?" Captain was what the locals called Walker, referring to his rank in the service as they always had in the South since the Revolutionary War.

Quade nodded curtly and continued shopping, but one old wag said, "Yeah, he's probably at Deacon Slade's place thinking what child they can snatch next. No telling what two perverts'll think up when they get together. Two perverts together, ain't that nice, though?"

"Probably Chief Pierce can't find them either."

Loud laughter followed that gibe at Pierce.

"Anything else, Captain Walker? Pigs ears for the dogs? We got them specially priced this week, and we got a special on pumpkin and squash seeds." At the counter, Buck tried to drown out the gossips on the porch. Lowering his voice, Whitehead leaned closer. "Don't pay any attention to those old men. They don't know nothing about nothing."

"Maybe old Prescott's got the right idea. Flush 'em out

with fire. That includes that old witch and her familiars: monkeys, parrots, pigs, and I don't know what all." The stranger looked directly at Walker standing at the counter. "Since what passes for law enforcement in this town is too sissified to do it themselves."

He said it loud enough so that Walker couldn't ignore him. All the conversation stopped while Quade Walker slowly turned around. The man whom he didn't recognize faced him squarely with an attitude of arrogance about his stance, but his eyes were fearful and didn't remain on Walker's for long, sliding slightly to the side.

"No offense, Officer," he said with an attempt at bravado.

"None taken," Walker said. He shouldered the fifty pounds of chicken feed and grabbed a feed bucket while somebody opened the door for him.

The stranger stood back as Walker passed, his eyes straight ahead.

As he walked out of Whitehead's, someone said, "Now there goes a gentleman and an officer."

In his truck, Walker got out his cell phone. "Why didn't you tell me Lewis Spencer got away from the sheriff's deputies when they went out to arrest him?"

Pierce's whiny drawl was like a worm in his ear. "Because I didn't know until late this afternoon. I been on the phone with half the county since then, wondering what's on fire. That's the least of our worries. Scottie John Prescott has lost his marbles and he and his kids and their friends are setting everything on fire. With a lightning storm coming, the damn fool! You're not leaving just yet, are you? You can't, Walker. It's an emergency!"

Like Tanner said, everything with Pierce was an emergency. "I'm going out to the farm to feed my animals, but I'll come back in if you need me."

"Don't leave me with that fool, Martin, long, okay? He don't know his ass from grass."

He would, if you ever told him what to do, Walker thought, but didn't say it. "Okay," he said and rang off. *It's a good thing that wars happen when they do*, he thought, putting the truck in gear. *If Tinker Pierce were ever drafted, he would have a command under him because he'd gone to college, and one of his own men would have to shoot him in the butt before he did something to kill them all.*

જ્જ

Vadim drove the speed limit even though cars passed him on the interstate as if he were standing still. At one point, he pulled over at a rest stop and dialed the Julia Springs City Hall and police station.

The message machine came on, droning that they were out of the office and would return the call.

"This message is for police chief. He must to call DOT central in order to stop chemical shipment coming to Julia Springs on way to Soledad, Florida chemical plant. Is shipment of hazardous chemicals on board and bridge is not able to support weight of train. Please give message to mayor or somebody in authority. Goodbye."

It was getting dark by the time he turned off the county highway to Julia Springs. The old asphalt was rutted from spring rains and the sky looked as if another downpour was imminent. He had made only one quick stop to get a barbeque sandwich from a roadside stand which he ate back on the road. He needed to pee, but the first thing he wanted to do was find the police station to see if they had received his warning. Then he would find Gina and stay by her side until the danger had abated or—he was unwilling even to form the thought—a disaster occurred.

Keeping his eyes on the two lane road, he was weaving around the potholes to avoid damaging his tires when a flashing blue light in his rearview mirror snagged his attention from the road. His blood seemed to freeze as a booming voice told him to pull over and step out of the car. It happened frequently in the Ukraine where the police were always watchful. Now, it had happened here, in this remote place with its wandering dogs and chickens and children playing basketball in desolate front yards.

He pulled to the shoulder, nearly overwhelmed with relief. Opening the door, he stepped out of the car and turned around to find himself facing three men with automatic weapons. The driver of the police car stayed behind the wheel, as if he were ready to chase him in case he started to run. A black SUV pulled up beside his car and four more men jumped out wearing yellow protective vests.

The leader, with a face like death itself, pointed an automatic weapon at him. "Freeze! Put your hands up against the car now, buddy! Pat him down, boys! Spread 'em, mister."

"Maybe he don't speak English, sir," a reasonable voice said. "Sprechen Sie Deutsch?"

"Well, he'd better learn. Damn foreign terrorist."

"You make mistake, I am not terrorist." Understanding the chatter, Vadim tried to comply with the confusing directions while forming an explanation, but as they cautiously approached him with automatic weapons at the ready, he began to reach into his pocket for his wallet. "Look, I show you.ID."

A bullet dropped him in the dusty road.

One of the SWAT team acting as the paramedic raced up to the lifeless body and touched his white throat with delicate fingers. He looked up at the leader with a slight shake of his head.

"Geez, did you have to ice him?"

"Why not? They've killed enough of us," the captain replied, with a shrug. "See if he's got explosives strapped to him then send some men to check that railroad bridge he was talking about on the machine. Hell, it could just be a decoy, too. These bastards are so twisted, it could even be a church or a school. They want to play hard ball. Paybacks are a bitch."

Chapter 21

As they struggled to enter Ham Phillip's compound, Walker and Tanner found the inventor already packing what appeared to be a truck, but after closer examination turned out to be a tractor with a chicken coup on a platform. Various robotic machines lurched about the cluttered yard, trying to follow Phillip's orders, but colliding with each other in the process.

Phillips was affable as usual, hailing them merrily as he set another struggling bird inside the coup. "Thought you'd be along so I sent Lance IV out to ease the way for you. What do you think of my Cooperator? She's a multi-purpose vehicle run on chicken and pig shit. Comes in handy for such events like this. I'm dying to see how she works. First opportunity and all that, you know."

"Which event is that?" Lou Owl asked, putting down his rifle to hand Phillips a piglet.

"No, no, I have a special place in back for piggies." With surprising agility, Phillips climbed down from the tractor, jumping to the ground, shoulder-length, gray hair flying in all directions. "Don't you fellows know? Haven't you heard? Scottie John Prescott has started fires at the west end of the Thicket. Traveling at about fifteen miles an hour," Phillips glanced at his watch, "no, twenty the way the wind is picking up. It should be here in less than an hour."

Tanner thought aloud. "Just in time for the train, if there is a train."

Phillips nodded rapidly, obviously distracted by the malfunctioning machines running into each other, dropping whatever they were carrying, bumping into each other again as they tried to retrieve things with mechanical claws. "You've heard about that, then. Shipment of benzoyl chloride, I believe."

Tanner caught Lou's eyes sliding sideways, his silent signal to get back on the path. He had to ask one more question of the physics genius, however. "But do you think the bridge will hold, Ham?"

"Would I be packing up if I did? No, no, Scrap. Turn around and bring something else. Let Porkie clean up the mess, that's a good boy," he said to a pair of colliding machines. "Children never do what you tell them the first time, do they?"

Lou had always considered Hamilton Phillips a lunatic—but a smart lunatic, he was fond of adding. With a touch of sarcasm, he asked, "How do you know all this stuff, Ham? I mean, Doctor Ham. You been down there getting some scrap metal off those old pylons, maybe? Great stuff for making robots—s'cuse me—your kids with."

The former Ivy League professor stopped trying to load squealing piglets into the back of the Cooperator and regarded Owl with a condescending look. "My dear Owl, it's really quite simple, just by listening in on all the land lines in town. I can do wireless phones only when the humidity rises and the signal is clear, which is now since rain is on the way. I picked up the DOT dispatcher verifying the train's existence as it passed through the Carrollton switch. Also the warning of a young employee of the chemical company which owns the train and leases the tracks. He left a message on the machine in Pierce's office and that simpleton has obviously not taken it seriously."

As a bolt of lightning forked across the night sky, immediately followed by an enormous thunder clap, Tanner said, "In that case, we'd better get going and warn the neighbors. Deacon Slade and his brood. All his wives and kids."

"Oh, I wouldn't bother, J.T. I've already sent Lance IV over to Kahalia's and Rambler VII to Deacon Slade's place. I daresay he's all alone at the compound now since all his wives took their offspring and formed a commune of their own. They call it "Lesbos" after the ancient Greek poetess Sappho's retreat. I thought that was very clever of them and sent one of the kids over with two chickens and a small coop to get the enterprise started. They're planning to sell eggs and their Ezekiel bread in town. I hear them singing and playing the guitar into the early evening hours. Much like muses in archaic times, I imagine." Phillips went back to loading animals until the Co-operator resembled the Ark on three wheels.

"You keep up with everything that goes on around here," Tanner said, trying to adopt a cordial tone. "We didn't even hear about that one in town. Old Deacon's started that one-man tribe twenty years ago. Some of those girls must be going on forty by now."

"It really wasn't for public knowledge," Phillips said, a confidential note in his voice. "Just one of the kids picked up the row they had when Slade tried to keep his harem from leaving and they, in turn, beat him up pretty bad. Boy, from the yelling on the mike, I couldn't even tell if he was still alive when they got through pounding on him or not."

"You mean you had a recorder on one of your robots?"

The icy stare Ham Phillips turned on Tanner told him clearly he had blundered. "They're not robots, sir. They are my creations, my offspring. In short, my children. Would yours were so smart and so obedient, and as moral, from what I hear."

Tanner bristled at the obvious reference to Reggie's liaison with his lover Brandon, which, no doubt, Phillips had picked up while listening in on their conversations on the wireless band.

Seeing Tanner's growing fury over the remark, Owl intervened. "Hey, Ham, we'd better get moving. Glad you told us about old Slade. Hope he makes it out in one piece—or several."

"That's what he deserves associating with humankind. On to Pater's place, children. We'll have to make our home in Magnolia Alley until it's safe to come back." Phillips took one last look at his thatched compound, and then whistled for the two little machines who lined up behind him like ducklings following their mother. As Tanner and Owl turned to leave, the smaller of the two called Porkie stopped and wheeled to face them, blocking their path.

With a lurch, the tractor started up, and towing a flatbed trailer with a load of machine parts, the professor set his caravan in motion. The smaller machines, goats, dogs, and deer followed the roaring, cackling, whining machine down the Swamp path to the road and on to Julia Springs.

Still bristling and forming some kind of retort at the pointed reference to Reggie's liaison with Brandon, Tanner stood looking after the procession until the last animal and machine faded into the Thicket.

Lou punched him hard in the arm. "Hey, that guy gets to be more of a lunatic every year. He's acting more and more like one of those scrap metal skateboards he calls kids. Imagine them running around that barn of a place he calls Magnolia Alley." Breaking off, Owl lifted his nose to the wind. "There's smoke on the downwind. Even if the rain stops it, the wind'll still drive parts of that fire pretty far into the Swamp. Damn it! I bet the wife didn't carry my cows with her to town. Come to that, she probably hasn't even left yet. Always forgetting stuff at the last minute."

"As long as she doesn't forget one of the kids. Anyway, Erin just told you they were on their way, so relax."

"Robots have feelings, too, you know," said the small robot Porkie, turning to follow the truck. "And don't go by way of the creek. There's a train coming and the bridge isn't safe." They recognized Ham Phillips's voice coming from the machine. "Goodnight, gentlemen."

Lou tried to outrun the little machine. "Hey, wait up! When's the train coming? What time?"

But Porkie picked up speed, disappearing into the Thicket.

Lou shook his head and trotted back to Tanner. "Kind of a shame what one bad trip will do to a mind like that. Let's go, J.T. Smoke's changing direction, which means the fire's found a new path. It ain't raining hard enough to stop it, either."

They were trotting down the trail through the Thicket as clearly marked to the swamper as any highway to the motorist. Terrified deer bolted in all directions as long as it was away from the tongues of fire.

"Lancelot IV, come in, please." Hamilton Phillips's voice sailed above the clatter of the Cooperator's engine, sending fleeing animals running in circles. "What is your location?"

In the murky water of the creek overflow, Lancelot IV did a systems check. Although all his command receptors were switched into high gear, his two-horsepower engine only whined, sending showers of mud all over his aluminum exterior. With every rev of his engine, his wheels only sank deeper into the sinkhole. Lancelot IV did another systems check. The report was bleak. His wheels were now two inches deep in water and he was running out of gas.

"Lance, can you hear me? Come in, Lance."

"Oh, woe is me," were the last words Phillips heard over the roar of the tractor engine.

დადდ

The creature set his internal compass for the South and the safety of the Great Swamp. The course sent him across the path of the crouching black beast that by now was no more than yards away. As it rounded the curved track and he saw its single eye roving back and forth, he realized it was simply another of the two-leg's machines, but without teeth or claws to tear at him. He simply had to remove himself from its path and proceed.

It did not appear to be able to follow him and he was confident he could elude it if it did leave its rails. He had seen many of these running along the rivers at night, their single eye staring straight ahead into the night, unaware of him hiding in the rushes and reeds on the banks or floating along in the swift currents.

He felt such relief that he paused and faced it for a few seconds in defiance of its power, before the night and the forest swallowed his trail.

ℰↃℰↃ

The Florida bound shipment of benzoyl chloride had pulled out of its second to last stop at Carrollton right on time and rolled right down the line toward Julia Springs. The engineer and his assistant passed the time playing chess on their phones and then ate their boxed lunches ordered beforehand from the catering service.

"Who'd want to live down here in this god forsaken place?" the engineer asked over the phone to his wife back in Rome. "Looks like nothing but tree, trees, and more trees." Turning his eyes back to the winding tracks, he continued on a subject that made him feel less lonely. "Kids had fun swimming today, I'll bet. Swimming in Grandma's pool." He interrupted the desultory conversation to call to his assistant. "Hey, buddy, looks like there's some kind of fire off to the left, Zack."

His assistant barely took his eyes off the game in front of him. "Probably slash and burn. That's all they've got down here are trees, like you said."

Clutching his cellphone between ear and shoulder, the engineer took a sip of his coffee. "No, it's nothing, honey. Julia Springs is coming up. Probably something on fire down there. Looks like a couple of fires in fact. There's one in town and one a few miles east." Peering out of the window, the engineer said, "Hell, I don't like hauling chemicals, but we get hazard pay. Don't even want to think about fire."

His assistant grunted agreement, never taking his eyes off his game. "Four more hours and we're home free," he said. "We're coming to the crossing over Hanahatchee Creek. Quarter mile ahead. Geezuz, what kind of name is that? They've got the hardest names to say around here. Ossahatchee, Chattahoochee. I come from Ohio and everything around there has four or five letters. Mostly four like Damn River or Shit Creek." He laughed at his own joke. "Haven't been down this way before. Check the stats on this crossover, will you?"

The engineer checked the bridge's statistics on the computer. "Sixty per cent solid. 1961. COE. DOT clearance. 1990.

Man, typical BS. Wish they were the ones driving this buggy and not us peons crossing this bridge."

Zack looked up briefly. "Don't forget there are two of us in here."

Ernie, the engineer was on the cab phone this time. "Check DOT clearance on bridge at Julia Springs. Crossing Four. COE clearance. Aw, hell. Over and out." Staring straight ahead into the darkness, he slowed the train to twenty then fifteen. "The hell with their deadline. I'm taking my time. There are two railroad bridges, each with sixty to sixty-five reliability. That means a forty percent chance we may fall into the river with a load of flammable chemicals, man. Somebody had to be on crack or booze or both to declare that a safety margin."

"Faster you go over, faster you get to the other side," the assistant said, glancing over at the speedometer. "I say make a run for it."

"I'm driving it, buddy. Guy at the last stop in Carrollton, he said there was heavy flooding. Could have loosened the footing." The engineer put down his cellphone and studied the bank of cameras overhead presenting different views of the track.

"We're losing time. Already behind schedule due to delays." Switching on the two-way to headquarters, Zack said, "Approaching the bridge at Julia Springs. Please advise."

"Proceed with caution," came the sleepy voice at the other end. The orders over the two-way were clear. They were on their way down to Florida.

"Bastards," Ernie said, flipping the speaker switch.

Chapter 22

Root Woman stared at the ruins of Glory Road Church, her arms limp at her side. With her orange robes and turban of bright gold lamé, she might have been the bronze queen of a scattered people, destined to reunite them under a new aegis.

"We'll rebuild, no doubt about that. It is God's will and we cannot deny it," she whispered to the subsiding flames.

"If you set up a fund at the Farmer's Bank, I'll get the word out on social media."

She turned her amber gaze on Chief Pierce. "That won't be necessary. The funds to rebuild will come."

Shifting his weight nervously, Pierce winced. He never knew how to say the right thing. "Holly and Kenya are still unaccounted for."

From the crowd that had gathered around the fire, other voices rang out. "Gatewood says Art hasn't come back yet. Says he's got Megan Kelly with him." There was a little ripple of gossip through the spectators and nodding of knowing heads.

One of the firefighters came forward out of the smoke and debris. It was Lane McFarland, barely recognizable in his firefighting gear, his face blacked with soot. "Pierce, my niece's gone to this dance and party with the Gatewood kid and we haven't see her since morning."

Root Woman turned her head away from the ruins of the church her followers had built with their own hands and their own money. "Arthur Gatewood took us up to the main road in his car. Then he and Megan went their own way," she said nodding at the little boy beside her, clinging to her robes. "Then me and Frederick here got a ride into town with friends."

She placed emphasis on the word "friends," implying that Gatewood would hardly meet the qualifications for the term, leaving McFarland and Pierce to only imagine what indignities she had suffered during the ride out of the Thicket.

Root Woman left them to their imagination without explaining how Gatewood, reluctant even to give them a ride in his new car, finally let her and Frederick get in the back seat. He had said the paved road was as far as he was taking a black woman who had killed his friend, Cole Prescott. In addition, he hoped she and every other swamper got burned out of their land forever. He told her how old man Prescott was going to drain it and develop it as a discount shopping mall, the first in this part of the state, and how she wasn't a Christian since she refused to help Megan in her present state, but she would kill her own granddaughter's fetus probably to make more potions.

Finally, after enduring his vituperative harangue for two miles, which was mostly for Megan's benefit, in spite of the rain and ground-seeking lightning, she got out of the car. But Arthur had the parting shot. "Yeah, get out, Witch Woman! I hope lightning strikes you dead! That'll save the State the expense of Death Row!"

Root Woman had given Megan one more glance before she and Frederick got out in the rain that had settled over the land like a benediction. But the girl sat looking straight ahead, her long dark hair snaking over her bare shoulders. Gatewood's letter jacket lay in her lap as if she couldn't decide to wear it or not.

Lane shook his head and put his helmet on again. "At least, we know she's safe. Thanks, Miss Kahalia. Now, let me go back and see what needs doing."

Chief Pierce was now in the driver's seat in a real emergency and he relished the role, even if he wasn't sure what to do. "I'll find out who done this, Miss Kahalia, honest I will, when I got time. Right now I got a dead terrorist out there I got to deal with." The chief put his hands on his belt with his customary swagger, avoiding the incredulous look she turned on him.

"You think a terrorist did this, Chief Pierce? No, wasn't a terrorist at all. It was somebody we see every day and goes to church right across the street." She nodded at Sacred Waters Church, standing gleaming white in the glow of the flames and floodlights. "But you don't have to worry about an investigation. In fact, I prefer it if you don't even start one, because that person is forgiven by each and every one of us. It is only in being like our Lord that we succeed as worthy of him."

"You don't get it, Miss Roo—Your Reverence. We got a dead terrorist out on the road who warned us already he was going to do something to the railroad bridge over the creek. You know all those terrorists are atheists. They hate Christianity and have sworn to wipe it off the face of the earth—that includes burning and looting churches."

Gina, who had been holding Frederick's free hand and trying to tell him pigs are smarter than humans, smart enough to run away from a brush fire, could hear Pierce's voice above the crashing timbers of the disintegrating church.

"Excuse me for interrupting—"

Mildred reached out to grab her arm, but Gina slipped away from her and moved to Pierce's side.

"This is an adult conversation, Gina. Excuse her, Chief. Miss Kahalia. I'm sorry for all this." With a helpless wave of her plump white hands, Mildred apologized for the town, for the cruelty of inequality, for racist bigots, and specifically the incivility of her niece who didn't recognize a tragedy when it was before her very eyes.

However, Root Woman took Gina's hand and drew her closer, drawn by her sudden agitation. "What is it, Miss Gina? You look worried about something child."

Gina struggled to put her fears into words. "You said something about the railroad bridge. What exactly did the man who called say?"

"Something about a shipment of something coming down

here on the way to Florida. Said the bridge was no good. Look, honey, love to chat with you but I'm on duty. Got to check out the bridge myself. Already sent some of those SWAT team types down there to see what's going on, but have to check it out myself." Pierce sighed wearily as if his workload was overwhelming. "The buck stops here, you know."

"But—"

"Listen to the girl, and stop talking for once." Root Woman's stern command brought a hush to the chattering spectators and froze Pierce where he stood. "Go on, Gina. Why are you asking?"

"Well, I never! Taking orders from her. Next she'll be paying his salary," came the voice of one from the crowd of onlookers.

"You're kidding, right? She don't pay taxes what pays his salary," said another.

But Gina only heard Vadim's voice asking her what her name was. "What did he look like and did he talk funny? Like a foreigner?"

Pierce, still chafing from Root Woman's rebuke, pulled out his cellphone from its holder on his belt. Flipping it open, he thrust it Gina's face. "There he is. You ever seen him before? I suppose you been over to wherever it is he come from. Russia or some commie country like that."

Gina stared at the photographs flipping across the small screen. Vadim his head and torso covered with blood sprawled on the red clay shoulder among the weeds. A close-up of Vadim's bloody face, mouth agape, blood in his golden hair. eyes rolled up in his head. Vadim, in what had been a white shirt and tie, his collar open, blood everywhere. She slowly slipped to her knees and then sprawled on the muddy, red ground.

೧৩೧

She awoke in the Fellowship Room of the church, stretched out on the bed in the nursery. In front of her was a picture of Jesus, blond hair, blue-eyed native of Nazareth.

Dimly, she heard Mildred's voice in the hall, sputtering

like a hen who has just laid an egg. "A—and when he showed her the pictures, she just passed out, p—poor little thing. Imagine seeing that stuff just shoved in your face. No, she doesn't know anything. Gina just has some strange spells sometimes. You know she kept telling us she saw Cole Prescott after he died. She used to tell us things were going to happen and then they would. A clairvoyant, yeah, I guess you could call it that. When she was little, I don't know, about four or five, she dreamed about an airplane crash, described the plane and all. Sure enough, do you know about a week later some CEO and his girlfriend or wife and a couple of other people were killed in a rainstorm about three miles from here when they tried to land the plane on one of Lane's fields."

"How're you feeling, honey?" Joy's small, cool hand pressed her forehead. "Don't listen to anything Mama says. She's just worried about you is all. Can you sit up? Want a sip of water?"

Gina sat up on the sagging cot and swallowed a mouthful of water. "He's dead. Vadim's dead. He wasn't a terrorist. A student. He was only a student."

"Now, honey, you didn't even know the man. How could you? He was from Atlanta, they said. Just one of your bad dreams, is all. We should go on home. It's almost—my goodness, nine-fifteen." Joy looked at her phone as though it had just spoken. "It's been quite a day! Come on, we'll go home and make some popcorn with lots of butter and watch a movie on TV."

Jumping off the cot, Gina swayed dangerously for a moment, steadying herself on the back of her cousin's chair. "I have to go. I have to see—"

Joy got to her feet, putting an arm around her shoulders. "Oh, no you don't have to go anywhere. You're going to get in the truck and we're going home. Mama, get off the durn phone! Ginny's having one of her spells."

Drooling uncontrollably, Gina grabbed her arm. "But you've got to tell Pierce. He said the bridge wouldn't support a train. He works for the company that sends the train." Her fingers bit into Joy's plump white arm.

"Who does, honey? Chief Pierce said he's sent some guys down there to check on the bridge, okay, sweetie? Oh, Mother, get off the phone. Look, I'll phone Chris. He knows a lot of people. Maybe he can think of somebody"

But Gina was enveloped in the approaching tornado that came down out of the high ceiling, sending her helplessly spiraling out of control. She flailed her arms up and down, turning this way and that as if she had been blinded and lost her way. "You've got to stop it. It's coming. Now!" Her body began to jerk convulsively and her eyes rolled up until the whites showed. Foaming spittle oozed from the corners of her mouth, and she fell to the pine-board floor, writhing and gagging.

Joy screamed, putting her hands out to stop the convulsive girl. Then having to dodge what might have been a hard blow from Gina's wildly swinging arm, she stepped back and shouted, "Mama! Come help me with Ginny. She's gone out of her mind! She's having a fit! A convulsion, that's what it is! Hurry!"

In the end, Dr. Morrissey, who had come to help an injured firefighter, came over to the church and, seeing Gina stretched out on the floor, now relaxed and seemed to have fallen asleep, shook his head. "What you're describing sounds like a seizure, but a pretty serious one," he said, smiling at Joy whose face was as white as an egg, her blue eyes in stark contrast in the colorless oval. "What's her relationship to you? Your sister?"

The color returned to Joy's pale cheeks and her dark blue eyes widened. "My cousin," she said. "My name's Joy. Hers is Ginny. Gina. I mean, Gina Kelly."

"Do I get to choose which one I like best? Anyway, I'm glad there's some kind of Joy around this town," he said, smiling at her again. He got to his feet and lifted Gina on to the cot. "She'll be okay if you just let her sleep. Has she been diagnosed with seizure disorder?'

"Of course not! I'd have known what to do if she had." Joy regretted her tone immediately. "Look, I'm sorry, but she scared the bejesus out of me. She suddenly fell out and started to jerk and swing her arms all around. I'd have known what to do if I just had some warning." She tried to hide the tears of relief that filled her eyes. "Do you think she'll have another one? She just had a real bad shock. Chief Pierce showed her pictures he'd taken of that man they shot who was going to blow up the bridge and Gina is so sensitive. I guess she got upset."

The young doctor smiled sympathetically. "Yes, I took a look at him and he was all shot up. That would be enough to upset anybody not used to seeing that kind of thing. I did my residency at Grady Hospital in Atlanta and I can't tell you what all I saw. If you'll just call my office and make an appointment, I'll run some tests. Has she had a spell like this before?"

She walked with him to the front door of the church. "Just mild ones. Not this bad, ever."

Opening the door, they saw the burning skeleton of the Glory Road Church, and in the distance, fire lit the horizon. "Enough to make anybody sick," the doctor said, more to himself than to her. "There seems to be a lot of hatred here."

"No more than any other place," Joy said. "But lately, everybody seems to be on edge. You know, like they're expecting the worst to happen, and blaming each other for making it happen. They aren't always like this."

Morrissey looked down at her and smiled. "I hope not because I was thinking about opening an office here."

After telling the doctor she'd make an appointment with him for Gina, she returned to the nursery where her mother was straightening up the cot, patting the pillows in place. "Doctor Morrissey's a good-looking young man," Mildred said, without looking up. "Saw his picture on the front page of the *Journal*. Must be a good doctor, too. Whatever he did, fixed Ginny right up. Put her right to sleep. He coming to see her again?"

When she straightened up, hands to her back with a groan, her daughter was gone. All she heard above the shouts in the street was Joy's high heels clicking on the wooden hall floor. Mildred followed, going to the front door of the church to see what the commotion in the street was about.

Across the street, a group had gathered around Root Woman, either making her the target of their angry comments and taunts or defending her from them, she couldn't tell. What she could tell was her husband was weighing in, driving the crowd back with shouts of "Get back! Get back! This building's gonna fall any minute now and somebody's going to get hurt! Y'all go on home, hear? Nothing to see now but ashes and ruins. We got to clean up and maybe go home sometime tonight."

"Shame you brave firefighters got to risk your lives for somebody like her," was heard from the retreating crowd. "Her Reverence or whatever name she calls herself probably started the fire so she could collect on the insurance."

"Yeah, I wouldn't waste any more of our water on the voodoo church. Good riddance to bad rubbish, I say."

A few grumbles followed in their wake but none loud enough to be heard above the shouts of the firemen as they pulled their lines back to the ladder truck. Breathing a sigh of relief and reminding herself to warn her daughter about the dangers of getting mixed up in matters of race, Mildred returned inside to prepare Gina to get ready to leave.

But when she returned to the nursery where she had left her niece sound asleep, she got the shock of her life. Gina was gone.

Joy threaded her way through the mob to Root Woman's side. "C'mon, Miss Kahalia. Our truck is over there," she nodded at the parking lot across the street. "You and Frederick can stay out at the farm with us tonight. Come, Freddie, my man. And the dog, too." She glanced at the angry faces around them. "Bet you all are first in line when the Glory Road Church, along with the other churches in town, hand out the Thanksgiving turkeys this year, and they hold their chili cook-off free to all and sundry. Or maybe you think they put a voo-doo curse on the food, too. Didn't stop you chowing down in years past, though, now did it? Come on, Miss Kahalia. Don't mind them. Must've got their cable cut off and got to watch something even if it's a church burning." Joy's stinging wit was well-known around town and no one wanted to cross words with her, knowing they'd hear about it for years afterward.

Root Woman was still staring at the charred timbers instead as if they were the prophecy bones in which she saw the future. "But I can't leave Holly and Kenya," she said. "I have to stay here and keep watch over this holy place."

Saranji stepped forward and took Root Woman's arm in hers. "I'll go get them if you tell me where they are, dear Miss Kahalia."

In the glow of the flames, the stately priestess looked confused and both the younger women felt a twinge of sorrow that such an icon of female strength should be the target of so much hate. "Why, they both should be at work by now. Holly should be at Saranji's since Miss Delia's passed on. And Kenya should be there, too." She turned to meet the sympathy in their eyes, "No, no, wait now! I left them both at Lesbos with Miss Lois because Kenya wasn't feeling good and Holly wanted to stay with her."

Just then the crowd parted as Mildred came running up, looking frantically around for Joy. When she saw her daughter, she burst into tears. "You've got to call the police, the National Guard, somebody! Gina's gone. I came out to see what the commotion was and when I came back, she was gone."

Joy spoke calmly, knowing Mildred's tendency to become hysterical over the unexpected. "I'm sure she hasn't gone far, Mama. She was probably looking for me and I was just telling Miss Kahalia we'd take her and Freddie to our place for the night."

"Let me go see if she's at Saranji's. I'll go down there and in case she shows up. Saranji will give you a call. I'm sure she's all right," Root Woman added, patting Mildred's plump arm, knowing it was what the distraught woman wanted to hear. What she didn't tell Mildred was what she had seen in the embers of the Glory Road Church.

"I'll catch up with you later, but you're right as always, I'd better run Mama back home," Joy said. "I'm sorry about all this, Miss Kahalia. I really am. You better believe we'll help you rebuild your church," she added with a forked glance at the few grumblers who remained.

The flames caught up in Root Woman's glowing eyes. She enveloped Joy in her flowing robes like an epiphany. "Bless you, Joy McFarland. I believe you will." She just couldn't bring herself to say *But the foundation will be built on the blood of those two young people, the way churches often are.*

As always, great happiness was tempered by great loss. Knowing this, tears filled Root Woman's eyes and she turned away. Freddie took her hand and led her through the thinning crowd and down the main street.

Chapter 23

Y ou know more than you're saying." Tanner raised his voice above the rising wind.

Lou resembled an old bullfrog, crouching on the bank of the rushing stream, studying the water. "What about?"

"Oh, shit, Lou, come on now. Something's going on around here and I want to know."

"That's the trouble with the white side of you, J.T., you always want to know. You want to know everything, like you're entitled to know everything like you was God's chosen or something. Well, get the message, you ain't."

"Oh, I suppose you are."

"I'm what?"

"Chosen. Special. Like you hear something and I don't. Like I can't and ain't meant to." He was plain irritated and he didn't care if his old friend knew it. "I thought we trusted each other and there I am, thinking you're right there in the woods alongside me and you take off and get to Root Woman's place just to show me up."

"What in the hell are you talking about?"

"I want you to explain what's going on around here, how plain is that? Okay, first this kid gets thrown up in a tree, and I get stalked by some big old critter the size of a box car while I'm supposed to be with you on the way to her house. Don't tell me you're so innocent, it's like what're you talking about, man. Come on, Lou. It's just the two of us. You can trust me with a secret. You know you can."

The narrow path had become visible as they made better time away from the Thicket. Here and there backwater flooded across the path so that they had to wade through it, but otherwise their first instinct was to get away from the advancing flames. After that, warning the residents of Julia Springs and the Thicket took priority.

Finally, Tanner slowed to a weary walk. "I haven't run this much since I sold my treadmill to Reggie for five bucks." He had been trotting after Lou, feeling twice his friend's age because of the old wounds which hampered his every move. His bad leg was killing him every step and he began to limp.

In the misting rain, the Thicket sweltered like a field hand's armpit, the smell of burning vegetation overriding the fecund odor of overheated plant life.

Sluggish gators and moccasins fixed beady eyes on them from the tall grass where they had taken refuge from the rising, muddy water. To his right, nearly obscured by the Thicket, an earthen mound rose on Tanner's right. It was a remnant of what Owl was content to call the Old People, prehistoric civilizations presumed to be Mississippian spin-offs. Long since looted for artifacts, gaping holes like eyes dotted the sides of the structure. Tanner always wondered why early settlers even placed a value on the artifacts of the civilization they had so ruthlessly dismissed as savages.

"Hell, I thought you said slow down, Lou."

The answer came from ten yards ahead. "Come on, Pappy. It's right up here."

"Damn well better be worth it," Tanner said. He arrived beside Lou gasping for his next breath, embarrassed because he was so out of shape and quite bitter about it. "Okay, what did you have to show me while giving me a heart attack? This smoke's getting thicker and it's gonna be nightfall soon."

"No kidding," said Lou. "Look up, J.T. The reason he's come around's right in front of you."

"This is one helluva time to play the inscrutable savage. What in hell are you talking about?" Then he looked up at trestle above them. "Okay, it's the old railroad trestle up there. Remember we used to walk across it as kids. The creek was higher then and sometimes, we'd lose somebody diving off the trestle, breaking their neck in the creek, remember?"

"Yeah." Owl stared into the swirling water. "My oldest brother. He got drunk at graduation and dove off. Broke his back and lived in a wheelchair 'til he got hold of a gun and shot himself."

"You've got the cheeriest family stories, Lou. It's a wonder you survived."

"Either one of us, you dumb bastard. You know what I brought you down here to this old trestle for?" Lou hadn't slowed his pace before now. But arriving at the base of the old railroad bridge, he stopped so abruptly Tanner, who was close behind, almost ran into him.

"Shine your flashlight up there." Lou was indicating the trestle itself with a wave of his arm.

Tanner who was out of breath, fumbled for his flashlight in the creeping shadows, aware that the usually sluggish creek sound as if it was boiling over its banks. "Why? You want to hold hands and jump off together or something? Owl and Tanner together for eternity in the happy hunting ground?"

"Cut the jokes, dumbass. This is a time to be serious." Lou climbed down the shallow banks and lowered himself into the rushing creek. "C'mon, fearless."

Tanner was aghast at his friend's daring. "Hell, I've been baptized, Lou, and I haven't got night vision anymore. Without my glasses I can't see two feet ahead of me. And it might surprise you to know, I haven't got a death wish yet."

"Quit bitchin'. Just follow me." Lou Owl slipped on the mossy boulders strewn along the creek bed, regained his footing, and moved against the current, all the while keeping his rifle over his head.

"Famous last words. Sure as hell glad you weren't my commanding officer in Nam. He got more people killed than the Kong knocked off."

Though he was a tall man, considerably over six feet and well-padded, Tanner found the current of the waist-high water much swifter than he remembered it from fishing last fall. Silently thanking Lou for telling him to wear his wading boots, he found himself half floating, half wading up to the first pylon which had sprawled across the creek since 1941, threading the tracks like a needle through the Swamp and Thicket into the town.

The original trestle was built just after the turn of the century, replacing an even older wooden bridge crossing the muddy creek. Its trestle bed was made of steel as were the pylons which were stuck down into footing of concrete blocks. Tanner saw the problem before Lou had even pointed it out with the barrel of his rifle. The water level had risen almost to the top of the concrete footing of the second pylon. Still, it was easy to see erosion had eaten away the bank of the creek to the point the entire concrete base of the footing was exposed.

Lou was bobbing up and down, his rifle barrel point straight up like the needle of a compass pointing due north. "That's what he's been trying to warn us about. Chinaberry Man. Right there."

Tanner looked up, saw boards missing in the rail bed and others just missing and whistled. "Sonofabitch," he said. Then pointing his flashlight over at the bridge footing, he muttered an astonished curse. The concrete block resembled a giant piece of Swiss cheese with a bite out of it. The pylon wouldn't support the weight of a car, much less anything larger. The lapping waves sprung up over the top of the crumbling footing as if they were hungry to eat the rest of it.

"I suppose this Chinaberry guy went to Georgia Tech," Tanner said, shouting over the wind and water. Then dirt cascaded down on his head as something rattled the loose rails overhead. He looked around in alarm, half-expecting to see the creature himself looking down from the embankment.

Instead, Lou hissed, his signal to be quiet. "Listen!"

✧⋄✧

The creature lingered beside the train tracks, its instincts battled for supremacy over whether to hide from the behemoth who approached with an ever-increasing roar, or take flight like the other forest dwellers. The hairless two-legs, however, always reacted differently to every situation, he noticed. They often ran toward the tongues of flame, rather than away and shouted when they ought to have been silent, causing their quarry to flee in the other direction.

He longed for the sanctuary of the Great Swamp where there were few of the unpredictable hairless two-legs and even fewer of their mechanical beasts. The smoke was a well-known peril to him and his ancestors and had felled many of them in the North woods. Even though places could be found to avoid the tongues of fire that ate the trees and bushes that provided food, while the smoke crept into their hiding places. It had killed his parents and sent him fleeing South through swamps and down rivers at night, only to hunt him even here.

If the burning tongues came, even if he managed to avoid confronting the huge adversary who was lessening the distance between them at frightening speed and with a terrible roar, he would have nowhere to conceal himself afterward. The bright flames would have destroyed all sanctuary. On the other hand, the forest would provide him the most cover from the eyes of the two-legs and they were, by far, the greatest threat of all.

Taking the path of least resistance, he emerged from the safety of the Thicket and with great strides, crossed the tracks. Before he plunged into the woods, however, he turned to face his enemy. The vibrations coming up through his feet told him an adversary the like of which he had never encountered was approaching at a speed he could not measure, and his keen hearing detected a mechanical clicking sound that matched the vibrations. Clickety-clack. Clickety-clack. The approaching animal's paws covered ground like nothing he had ever known, its claws clicking against the earth with a warning they were killer sharp and protruded from the feet of this giant animal like scythes.

There was no doubt in the creature's mind that this was a new challenger for the territory he had counted on being his own. As he was very young and had been, up until now, unchallenged for supremacy anywhere he went, the creature felt fear and something else—loss. Let this oncoming victor reign supreme over all wildlife for miles around, even the two-legged hairless female with the fine black tuft of hair. He didn't care. All he wanted was the safety of his leafy home, free to eat the chinaberries, when the fragrant blossoms turned to fruit, walnuts, figs, pears, and, best of all, pecans.

But something else, another emotion made him linger there as the beast came around the corner and he faced his nemesis, standing up on his hind legs as if ready to do battle. It had a single eye that searched this way and that. The creature was mesmerized by terror, wondering why the immense beast didn't stop and prepare for territorial battle.

Then came the sound like a thousand eagles screaming.

ᘓᘓᘓ

The *Warrior's* engineer switched off. "Bastards," he said as if they could still hear him. Then, "Holy crap, what the hell is that?" The engineer put on the brakes by hand and then dialed down the speed on the console. Then he blew the train's horn twice in warning. The wheels dug into the track, screeching like bats escaping from hell.

"What the hell?" Zach lurched forward in his seat, dropping his electronic tablet on the floor. "What's the matter? What is it?"

"There was some guy on the track. No, more like a bear or a gorilla or something just huge!" The engineer peered into the darkness. "About fifty yards down the track. There, there, on the right side. See it! See the bushes waving where he just went into the woods?"

His assistant engineer stared ahead for a moment, then seeing nothing, turned to the older man. "You want me to take over, Ernest? You been working back-to-back shifts. You know, everybody starts seeing things after you've been looking at the track for that long."

The engineer rubbed his eyes. "Naw, it was there. It walked right up to the track and just stood there looking at us. I even saw its eyes flash red like wild animals do. Whatever that was, it was standing upright like a man."

The train engine screeched to a halt, followed by a lurch

as the successive tanker cars piled into their couplings behind them.

Zach was fully alert now, looking ahead and then at the cameras covering the rear of the train. "I don't like the sound of that. Maybe just a cow, huh?"

"Not unless Babe the Blue Ox has been practicing hand-stands." The engineer was still craning forward, studying the track. "Hell, now what's that?"

Zack was equally nervous now, straining to see through the darkness. "What? Did it come back? Maybe it was a bear. They walk on their hind legs when they're scared-like. But they ain't got no bears down here—a few up north, not down this far. You seeing the animal again? Where at?"

"No, I mean the track. Something's not right," Ernie said in a shaky voice. "Gimmee my flashlight and the gun out of the holster. I'm going to take a look. You check the couplings, okay?"

"No, I'll come with you. We'll stick together in case there's really something out there."

They followed the rotted rail bed along the tracks towards the bridge. The engineer straightened, stopping squarely on the tracks. "Listen," he said. "That's water. Lots of water, moving fast."

ↄ⌒ↄ

Although Owl's keen ears had heard it first, even with his punctured eardrum, Tanner picked up the diesel engine sound-ing its whistle. Dirt began to rain down on them as the old rail bed above their heads began to shake with anticipation of a load it couldn't possibly bear.

"Let's get out of here!" He didn't have to be told twice. The current carried them swiftly downstream until both men could get their feet under them and climb out of the frigid wa-ter. They both flopped like fresh caught catfish in the marshy grass, sending sluggish water snakes sliding away.

Getting awkwardly to their feet again, both men began shouting and waving their flashlights but their efforts to stop the train were drowned out by the sudden screech of metal on rusty metal as the engineer applied his brakes and the *Warrior* came to a halt just short of the bridge. Presently, two lights came slowly dancing through the fog coming toward the place where the trestle crossed the rising creek.

"Look up there! Somebody's coming over the tracks." Lou Owl looked almost happy, happier than Tanner had ever seen him, as if a long held conviction had suddenly been proven. "Damn it, Jordan, he stopped the damn train. Ain't that something else now?" The lantern lights of the two trainmen now appeared at the entrance to the bridge. "Hey, they're coming over the bridge! Hold your light up high so they can see us."

Like two lunatics, they shouted and waved their flashlights and guns around. "Hey, up there! The bridge won't hold you. Bridge is damaged. Stay where you are!"

Over the rush of water and rumbling thunder came the reply. "About time somebody noticed," someone said in a Midwestern voice.

"Smartass." Lou lowered his voice only slightly. "I don't suppose you noticed a fire heading your way, too?" he shouted to the trainman standing on the bank above the rushing stream. "What's your cargo?"

Again, the laconic voice said through the smoke and fog like some Delphic oracle, "Chemicals."

"What kind?" Tanner shouted back.

"You know something I don't know or something, Tanner?" Lou asked him.

"Just pretending I do. When in doubt stall for time."

The trainman's voice came back, bristling with suspicion. "Who wants to know? You the DOT inspector or something?"

"'Cause I live here, that's why. What kind? I'm asking you nicely." Tanner noticed the increasing edge in the man's voice. "Or maybe you want to talk to the HAZMAT guys?"

"Benzoyl chloride, if you wanna know," came the reply from above them.

"Now, that just about makes it a perfect evening, right?" To Lou he muttered, "What the hell is that?"

"For you and me both, buddy." At the edge of the bridge, the young assistant engineer squatted and shone his flashlight at Lou, scrambling for the bank, now waist-high in the gathering current.

"What made you stop?" Gaining solid footing on the path, Lou walked even with the two trainmen. "The train. Why didn't you go on over?"

For a long moment, the trainman didn't answer. Then he said, "You guys got bears down here?"

They answered in unison, "No bears."

The younger man spoke up. "Thing is, engineer says he saw some kind of animal crossing the tracks. It was upright on two legs. Only animal I know walks that way are monkeys and bears. Far as I know, you got neither one down here." Zack held his lantern higher but the light just bounced off the curtain of smoke mixed with fog.

Lou called, "What's he been smoking?"

They shared a laugh. Ernie remained silent, and vigilant.

"Whatever he was seeing stopped the train from going over the bridge, right? Next time you guys are back this way, bring me some."

Tanner's leg was beginning to ache and he was sick of the rainwater running down his back and into his shorts, but he moved closer to Lou when the talk turned to mysterious animals. *Besides, it's hard to hear over the rushing water and thunder,* he told himself.

When it seemed the casual banter would end, he called, "No one uses that bridge anymore. Last freight came through fifteen or so years ago. What made you guys think it was safe to cross?" He got out his flask and had a shot of bourbon before he passed the flask to Lou. The two trainmen could probably use a drink by the sound of them, but nobody volunteered to cross the sagging trestle to get it.

Through the fog, the voice of the engineer came back. "We radioed the central office and they gave us the okay to cross. The company who ordered this shipment is supposed to check the bridges with DOT ahead of any shipments. It's just our job to get the load there and keep the old *Warrior* on schedule. Now, we can't back up without jumping the track so we'll just have to wait here until they send a relief engine from the switch yard outside Carrollton."

"Well, whatever they're sending, make it fast," Tanner shouted "No telling where this brush fire's going to go and if it jumps the creek or lightning strikes on that side, I hope you guys are out of here by then."

"You and me both."

The four men faced the rushing creek, each aware of the implications.

"I think I should warn you this chemical we're hauling," Ernie said finally, "it's got a reputation for being unstable around water and heat over a certain temperature."

"I'm not going to ask what'll happen if that brush fire jumps the creek," Lou said. "I'll just use my imagination. Whoever okay'd this bridge had his head up his ass, if you ask me."

"My thought exactly," said the engineer. "I know one thing, though. I'm too old to go swimming in freezing water up to my ass."

Lou grunted, which passed for laughter among his people unless they were drunk. "Your dumb ass, you mean," but he lowered his voice so it couldn't be heard over the rushing water. "Hey, Tanner, you and I have fished here since we were kids. You ever know this water to be cold in summer? This creek is being flooded by something else upstream. And I'm beginning to wonder if, with all this rain we've had lately, old man Arnie's makeshift dam has broken down entirely."

"I'm not even going to ask how you know all that. Arnie doesn't have a permit to dam up the creek because it runs through inland marshland."

"Take my word for it, he does, and he has some big old bass and catfish in it. I've got a whole freezer full to prove it."

The voices of the trainmen came back across the torrential creek. "We're heading back to the train now. Thanks, fellas, for the heads-up. We won't be bothering you again after I file my report on the state of this bridge."

The younger man said, "If we'd fallen into that flooded

creek, you better believe whoever was responsible for this shit would make headlines."

"Glad we could help," shouted Tanner.

"Yeah, let's hope that'll be the last we see of each other," said Lou.

But the two trainmen were going back up the track by then, switching their lights from side to side as if they expected trouble. The engineer kept his pistol at the ready, in case anything should come charging out of the woods at them.

When they reached the train, Ernie put the gun in its holster, and got out his cellphone. "I'm calling Headquarters Emergency again, telling them to get down here on the double. We have a potential disaster on our hands and, if that fire jumps the creek, those two yokels are right, we'll all be blown to hell and that little town with us."

⁊∾⌀∾

In the opulent Atlanta industrial park, behind his massive desk, Alex Foster had passed out from a combination of sexual exertion, Scotch whiskey, and general ennui with life. He drank his dinner, picked at his carryout Chinese, and felt like a dog for letting his kids know what a dirt bag he really was. The call from the emergency dispatcher woke him up.

Answering in monosyllables, Foster listened, feeling sick at his stomach, more from drinking than from the news. He touched his computer screen and there it was the whole picture from his engineer's phone. Adrenaline snapped him to attention, and even while he listened, grunting into the phone to the dispatcher's report, he opened the file Vadim had referred to earlier. With his forefinger pressing hard on the Delete key, he erased the entire file except where the DOT representative had given him the okay to ship. Vadim's entries, describing the bridge as "damaged and not sound enough to support even the weight of a handcart, much less a diesel engine," vanished.

Snapping a few terse orders at the dispatcher, he hung up and rushed to the bathroom. There he retched for close to half an hour, rinsing his face in cold water when he was through.

Then Alex Foster closed the office, turned off his cell phone, and went home to his upscale bachelor pad with pool and sauna. There he slept in his clothes, sprawled out on the king-sized bed.

Chapter 24

The Julia Springs firefighting crew battled the wind-driven blaze which pressed them ever nearer to the old quarry. Taking refuge on the far side of the pit, they battled it with hoses from the pump truck until the line of flames ate up the vegetation between them and safety. One unit, their retreat temporarily blocked by flames, climbed down into the quarry for safety in the murky water if necessary.

As they stood watching the flames shoot past them, blowing up tall pines, setting them alight like mobile fireworks, one volunteer decided to take a leak in the fetid water. With a yell that caught the attention of his crew, he came running back from the water's edge.

"There's a body down there," he said, pointing back toward the black pool where the flames above them were reflected as on a giant onyx. "Looks like he fell in."

They waded out as far as they could go without getting sucked into quickmud. "Some black guy. Been there a couple of days at least, judging from the smell. We'll get the EMTs to go down and get him tomorrow. Whoever he is, he ain't going nowhere."

Following the swollen creek, dodging the deeper places where it had overflowed, Lou kept a northward course along the flooding Hanahatchee Creek.

They had agreed Lou would check on his pigs while Tanner would turn inland to check on Deacon Slade at Deacon's

Heavenly Hollow and then to the last isolated community and the newest, Lesbos.

Tanner pressed forward in the driving rain until Deacon Slade's cerulean blue compound walls loomed above him, like remnants of some ancient city through the drizzle. Made of adobe mud brick and painted with murals of undecipherable symbols, the adobe brick walls were rumored to represent Slade's prophecies for the future of mankind. He claimed it was written by unseen hands in the heavenly skies and he had spent years reproducing it deep in the woods, using his wives and children as forced labor.

Pushing aside the arched gates over which was printed *All Who Enter Are Blessed*, Tanner stood and looked around the compound yard.

Animals of all sorts milled around the grassless yard. Overturned feed troughs and bins lay everywhere, a testimony to hunger. Goats, sheep, chickens, dogs, mules, and several ribby horses all surged forward as one and he was forced to wave his arms and shout to drive them back. Finally, he fired his rifle into the air and, as one, they dove backward, huddling together in the night.

"Slade!" he shouted. "Slade, come out and show yourself, damn you! You've got to feed these starving animals!"

There was no reply so he began to search the small apartments around the yard. Except for shards of broken pots and a child's doll, they had been emptied of all furniture and evidence of human habitation.

Tanner sat down on what was left of a dirty cushion near the apartment door, aware a goat and a mule that had stuck their heads into the room in silent supplication. As he surveyed the ransacked room, he found them watching him with near desperation.

"Let me rest up out of the rain a minute and then I'll go looking around for the feed. Surely they wouldn't leave you all to starve, would they?"

"No, they would not be as cruel as he," a lilting voice behind him said. "Away with you, Jarvis and Sam. I will come with food shortly." The goat and mule withdrew their heads in obedience, stepping aside to let a slender young woman enter the room.

"The grain store is through this doorway, Mr. Tanner. I wonder if you would mind helping me pull the doorway open?"

"You know my name, but I'm at a disadvantage, not knowing yours," he said, getting unsteadily to his feet. Unfolded to his full height, he towered above the girl feeling as awkward as a teenager on his first date.

"I am Isis," she said with a regal incline of her head. "My mother, Sappho, is mistress of Lesbos. She sent me to fetch you and, knowing you would rest here, and feed the animals as well. She knew Deacon Slade would not and she, as always, is right. Pig shit, that's what she calls him and so he will remain."

He followed Isis to an adjoining room, warm and dry although the rain kept a steady drumbeat on the tiled roof. Watching as she opened the door, it occurred to Tanner he had never seen the girl in town, although he certainly would have remembered if he had.

She was dressed in a long gown, off one shoulder in the style of classical Greece. Her waist length blonde hair was loosely held in a loop of braid, the rest cascading down her golden back, nearly reaching her chain-link girdle. She stooped gracefully down to scoop grain into pottery bowls to feed the waiting animals huddled together outside in the rain. He couldn't help but notice she had no underwear other that the chain link girdle.

Tanner helped carry the grain-filled bowls out to the livestock, noticing they edged back and waited until he set them carefully down in front of them. The larger ones were fed last and then Isis shut and locked the door, stuck the large metal key in her belt, and touched his arm.

"Now, we must leave. There are many dangers abroad—fire and flood to name the most pressing. It is the beginning of the remaking of the earth, Mr. Tanner. My mother is particularly fond of protecting you, although she will let other men die."

Without a backward glance, the girl set off into the storm, as if she were walking in the summer sun. After making sure the door to Slade's hut was securely closed, Tanner followed her, sinking into water ankle deep with the first step out the compound door. Taking out his cellphone, he dialed 911, hoping to get the dispatcher. His phone was wet and had gone dead.

Following Isis through the downpour, he reflected on the commune dwellers purpose in remaining isolated from the rest of Julia Springs. Like everyone else in town, he had heard about Deacon Slade's commune, a harem, the locals called it, saying he wasn't a deacon of any church except where he was the divine being. Tanner had even run into the Deacon himself a few times while hunting. Slade had the appearance of a 70s hippie combined with a biblical prophet, although his prophecies were anything but biblical. Like his closest neighbor, Ham Phillips, he had become impatient or disillusioned with modern society and withdrawn to recreate the universe according to his own specifications.

According to Slade, his was the seed that would repopulate the earth after Armageddon, not idol-worshipping Abraham's. His flock was taught to be self-sustaining, making everything they used, ate, or wore. They were educated in the classics, Roman and Greek literature, and they were all excellent mathematicians although they did not have the concept of zero, since it was introduced by the Arabs in the Middle Ages.

The entire brood was self-perpetuating, with the progeny of his first wife intermarrying with the offspring of his second wife and third and fourth. This was frowned upon by the locals who reported Slade to the Department of Family and Children Services. They investigated, and promptly removed the children, which by that time numbered twenty with four more on the way. Slade was charged with everything from child abuse to bigamy and sent away to a mental hospital. Finding him perfectly sane, just decidedly weird, they sent him back to Julia Springs.

His wives promptly beat him to a pulp and, with their remaining children from other marriages, left Slade's World to form a matriarchal society where Tanner found himself on that stormy night.

Resembling Slade's World in architecture and construction, Lesbos, too, was surrounded by a high wall made of adobe brick. There the similarities ended. As he and Isis approached over an arched wooden bridge spanning the marsh, Tanner felt as if he had stepped back in time to the Middle-Ages. Slender white towers with Gothic arched windows rose behind the compound wall. Guard shacks stood at each corner of the whitewashed battlements and, even through the rain and mist, he made out a light in each one.

Each ivy-covered tower with its fluted red-tiled roof sported several colorful flags which, even as he watched, changed order as if signaling some urgent message. His guide, Isis, came to a halt and held up her hand.

"There will be a short wait, Mr. Tanner, while I announce your presence to the queen. Wait here in the shelter until I come back for you. I promise I won't be long." Pulling her hood down, Isis let the droplets from the trees sparkle in her hair, decorating it as if they were diamonds. Tanner found her beauty almost other-worldly, reflecting the uniqueness of her surroundings. She smiled gently as if she knew what he was thinking. "Come, I will show you to the gatehouse."

By this time, he was weary enough to curl up under a tree and sleep, but he followed the girl a short way into the forest to a smaller version of the guard towers. He couldn't help but notice the resemblance to the home of the Seven Dwarves, complete with antique brass latches, flower boxes, and shutters.

Stooping to avoid hitting his head on the lintel, he followed Isis into the small structure, wondering if this was where the Lesbos children played house. There was a table covered with a checkered red-and-white table cloth, a jug of beer, a round loaf of bread, and a hunk of cheese. He had been catapulted back to medieval times and actually contemplated tugging on his forelock as was the custom.

"Just help yourself and I'll be right back," Isis said with that archaic smile. "I know you are very tired and you have come all this way to warn us of impending danger. Queen Sappho will be very pleased to see you."

But Queen Sappho, who turned out to be Deacon Slade's oldest wife, Lois, was not pleased at all. Instead of inviting him into the compound, she came out wearing a red velvet cloak and some kind of headdress which resembled the Statue of Liberty's crown of lights. In fact, in her long dress in classical Greek style, Lois, Queen of Lesbos, might have been the model of the New York Harbor monument.

"Mr. Tanner," she said, sailing into the small guardhouse.

She was a large woman, with meaty arms and ample bosom. She had a deep voice and a take-charge manner that dismissed resistance as futile. In fact, he was reminded, by her stature and demeanor, of Root Woman, but the resemblance ended there. Where Lois was commanding, Root Woman had the power of wisdom. People did her favors because, when they needed help, she was there to heal and comfort them. Still, Lois was a strong leader and, like Root Woman, she was the object of right-wing scorn and had suffered many hardships before gathering disciples to her cause.

"It was very gallant of you to come and warn us of fire and flood," Lois said. "But we are not without the modern convenience of a computer. What on earth made you bring him here, Isis? He will only bring us trouble and we've had enough of that lately." To Tanner, she said, "This is a female community, Mr. Tanner. We do not allow men, do you understand?"

Meanwhile, Tanner had gotten to his feet only to bang his head on a crossbeam. Cursing beneath his breath and rubbing the knob on his scalp, he replied, "Sorry, ma'am. Just wanted to see if you needed any help packing up, in case that was necessary."

"I'm sure he meant well, Mama. Mr. Tanner helped me feed Pig-shit's animals. They were starving and very afraid of the storm. I brought him here because he needs to rest before trying to get home in this storm and with the fire so nearby—"

"I see. You're right, as always, Isis," the regal Lois said, relenting a little. "Very well, you may rest here, Mr. Tanner. Then I will send an escort with you to the edge of the Thicket.

There are many dangers present tonight, the fire and creek flooding not the least of them."

"You heard about the old railroad trestle giving out, then." He wondered how the evening news picked up the story so fast. "About the train stalled there just ready to cross?" That hit the mark. Both women stared at Tanner, obviously hearing about the danger for the first time. "I thought Ham Phillips would have sent word by now."

"Professor Phillips," Queen Sappho said, "means well, but he is a misogynist nonetheless. Please go on about the train. What is it carrying?"

"Benzoyl chloride. They've sent for a relief engine, but chances are this brush fire will jump the creek before then. I won't impose on your hospitality, ma'am. I better be getting on home, and I know the way. Been hunting out here since I was a kid."

Lois' reaction was immediate. "Isis, go look up that chemical and report back to me. And sound the alarm to take cover, just in case we need to." Turning back to Tanner, Sappho said, "Please drink up, eat something, and have a rest before you go. You were always a hero in my eyes and so you will continue to be, Mr. Tanner. Now, I must attend to Kenya, Kahalia's granddaughter. She is having a prudential miscarriage. You see what indecencies the male sex can wreak upon our bodies? We are here to prevent that."

"I understand, Miss Sappho."

She smiled at him for the first time. "Still Lois to you, Jordan."

Alone in the king-sized dollhouse, Tanner sat down on a stool made for midgets and filled a mug with ale.

෴

After getting as close as he dared to the body floating in the acidic water of the quarry identifying it as belonging to the fugitive Lewis Spencer, Quade Walker left the firefighters battling the fire line and climbed up the wooded side that led to the creek. Volunteers from the town were chopping down brush and trees to clear a fire break which made the small footprints easier to see. He had been hard at work for several hours, clearing brush and sapling tress, but when the fire had chased the whole group down into the quarry, he had seen the footprints in the muddy earth even before the man's body was discovered.

They had been particularly noteworthy because the person who made them was alone. There was no evidence anyone else had been around. They were at least a couple of days old, and they had been made by someone wearing soft leather shoes, the kind without commercial soles. Intrigued, he followed in the direction the footprints were leading and encountered a detachment of fire crew from nearby a station who were creating an escape route consisting of a rope bridge across the swollen creek which was secured to the remaining bridge pylon.

ℰↄℰↄ

On the other side of the creek, the two trainmen watched the overhanging branches parched from the winter drought, catch fire and drop into the creek-turned-river below. The engineer calculated the damage a load of benzoyl chloride exploding and spilling into this waterway would do to the little town that lay in its path.

His assistant, meanwhile, was thinking how fast and how far they would have to run to get away from the deadly fumes if the fire reached them.

Besides millions of dollars in property loss, the chemical carried health risks as well as environmental destruction. They both saw their jobs going the way of the rushing water which swept everything along with it.

ℰↄℰↄ

Ignoring the warnings that the fire could skirt the fire line at any moment, the detective loped along the muddy path around the edge of the pit, eyes on the wet ground. So intent were the fire crew, they didn't even notice he was gone until someone turned to ask what they ought to do about the body of Lewis Spencer.

"He don't say much," someone remarked. "Kind of a lone wolf, if you ask me."

"Don't knock him," responded his sooty companion. "He's all that stands between us and that ding-dong Pierce."

"You ever see him take out a drunk? Dropped with one punch. Man is tough. I wouldn't want to mess with him."

"Make sure you don't. I'd hate to be your dentist if you do."

Skirting the flooded edges of the creek, Walker picked up the small footprints on the other side, noticing the inland direction they were taking. Girl, not very old, slim from the shallowness of the footprint, wearing some kind of soft leather shoe, maybe a sandal. Went to the quarry and back within the previous couple of days, which accounted for the tracks being washed out by the rain.

The footprints led into the Thicket, following a route he had forgotten existed, but had discovered as a boy. Walker slowed down, suddenly overwhelmed with tears for the childhood that might have been his. He felt an emptiness of memories that had been wiped clean from his mind by war and the explosion that had blown him from his Humvee, by the relentless concentration on how to stay alive that made yesterday and tomorrow lose all significance. His step-father didn't even recognize him anymore, a victim of Alzheimer's and heavy drinking, which was all right with Quade Walker. His real father took off when he was just a baby. Ryan Walker had made a poor substitute, beating him with the buckle-end of his belt for every minor offense until the boy became a man. Then one night after a football game in which Quade had made three touchdowns by running the length of the field on stolen passes, the showdown came.

After that night, his mother threw him out—ostensibly for his own safety. He lived with one of his uncles, Gabe, until he joined the army. So tough inside, he visualized his own feelings as something like an onion, layer-upon-layer, but each as tough as boot leather. Now tears hydrated the outermost layer of the onion as he followed the path he had discovered as a boy, running away from or running to what might have been.

From his uncle Gabe, he had learned his mother, as a single woman with a child to raise, was always dependent on a man. Instead of doing better for herself, she had taken up with a drunken bastard, Ryan Walker, who hadn't even graduated from high school, but sported a Georgia Bulldogs shirt and license plate like he was an alum. Walker had sworn to kill him if the bastard ever hit his mother during one of his drunks. Since they both knew he was capable of killing, his mother had made it clear, after he had returned from the Middle East campaign, Quade was welcome to visit when there were witnesses around, preferably with some weight on them.

Now in the middle of a storm, following a trail that disappeared into the marshy ground, Walker had never felt so alone, even guarding a mountain pass in Afghanistan. At least there, he had buddies who would understand how he suffered. He was suddenly shamed by his blubbering and, slowed to blow his nose between his fingers in the rain.

"Hey, what's up?"

The man was trotting toward the fire instead of away from it. That was the first thing Walker thought was odd about the lithe figure coming through the rain. The next thing he saw was that the man was carrying a shotgun chest-high like a soldier which made Walker automatically put his hand on his service revolver.

The man trotted a few more steps, and then stopped. "Hey," he said, still holding the rifle to his chest, "You're Quade Walker, right?"

"Right. Where're you headed?" He recognized Lou Owl, an old native whose family dotted the small hamlets around here like so many bee hives. "There's all kinds of trouble if you're headed along the creek. Stalled train, bridge out, brush fire's getting worse. Better turn back."

"Son, I've been heading for trouble all my life. Can't go dodging it now. Besides, I live down here. Got to check on my wife and the pigs. Make sure they okay. I already been down at the bridge. Where you headed, back to town?" Though he moved like a man half his age, Lou was old close up. Two long gray braids dripped with rain and two fingers of his right hand that were supposed to grip the rifle were missing. Two dark eyes looked into his with sudden recognition. "You're Marlene Sumter's boy, aren't you?"

At the mention of his mother's maiden name, Walker shivered. "That's right, how did you know?" He had an eerie feeling that the man was headed for certain death, that he had to make an effort to stop him. "Look, come on back to town and we can talk. I'll buy you a beer, how's that?"

"Something about you reminds me of her, that's all. How is she, good?"

Something struck Walker as strange—standing in swirling mist and rain, talking about his mother. "Yeah, good, good. Look. I wouldn't go back down there tonight. I'll call and make sure the residents are all cleared out west of here, okay? Livestock, too." He got out his phone but Lou Owl shook his head, moving past him slowly as if he hated to leave.

"Give my regards to your mother. We knew each other once, long time ago." Lou Owl picked up the dog-trot, only looking back once. "Bye, Quade."

Walker turned to watch the man disappear into the mist. "Wait!" he called. "Come back, it's not safe." But his voice became weak and he suddenly began to cough as though his lungs were coming out. "Wait!"

He fell to the ground, trying to get his breath through the deep racking coughs. He felt dizzy and faint. Lying there in the rain, he saw a light coming toward him.

Walker finally got to his knees and saw a girl standing in front of him. She was holding a lantern which illumined her beautiful face within the hood of her cloak.

It was a good thing she spoke first because he couldn't make a sound. "Hello, I am Isis," she said. "Are you lost? Sick?"

"No, um, no, ma'am. I mean, miss. I'm sorry, what was your name, again?" He sounded like a complete idiot, but the girl didn't seem to mind. Maybe she was used to idiots stumbling around in rainstorms in the dark.

"My name is Isis, sir, and may I know yours?"

She was so calm and gracious, they might have been getting acquainted at a neighborhood party instead of in the dead of night with a storm raging. He was acutely aware of his running nose and dried it on his sleeve before saying, "Walker. Quade Walker, Julia Springs Police. I'm—I'm just trying to warn people of the brush fire and creek coming out of its banks. I expect you've heard about it by now. Helicopters and all been making enough noise."

He was actually apologizing for the calamity that they were facing. He couldn't believe his ears, but she put him at his ease.

"That's very kind of you, Mr. Walker, sir. But we're quite aware of the dangers and have taken precautions to be safe. "

"We?" He might have known this one was taken, although he wondered what man in his right mind would allow such a beautiful girl to intercept strangers in the dark, especially one blowing his snotty nose in the rain in the middle of a forest.

"We are residents of Lesbos, my mother, siblings, and myself. My mother is Sappho, Queen of Lesbos. I think you know my father as Deacon Slade. Now, come with me, sir. You need to get out of the rain. You look like you have a bad cold. Follow me."

He could do nothing else, but follow her like a hungry dog. All perception of danger seemed to vanish, washed away by the rain cleansing the darkness from his soul. Isis, Lesbos, her mother was a Queen of Something, her father the reprobate Slade, drunkard and jailbird. Her profile, turning to check to see if he were behind her, was exquisite, so perfect that he hated to come at last into the light where his scarred face would be revealed to this vision.

But when they came to the lighted walls of Lesbos with its guards in their towers, trading flags furiously, he forgot how he must appear. Instead, he stood in the rain wondering how this castle could even be in the same countryside as Julia Springs with its stagnant main-street from the last century or even before that.

With its scruffy yellow dogs and boarded buildings, caved roofs, and houses taken over by kudzu and sticky vine.

"You live in here? I didn't know there was an apartment complex in Julia Springs." As he said it he realized it came out like something Tinker Pierce would have said.

Isis turned her face up to him, laughing with delight. She was even more beautiful when she smiled. Her hood fell away when she looked up revealing her golden hair, plaited in a braid that disappeared into her cloak. "It isn't an apartment, sir, it's a castle with many rooms. I will tell Mama you are here. She's expecting you, so she asked me to put you in the gate house. Mr. Tanner is already there waiting out the storm, and I will bring you refreshment. He has probably drunk all the ale by now."

Ale? The gatehouse? Was this a dream?

Beckoning him to follow, she led him to the gatehouse and knocked before entering. Then she put a finger to her lips and motioned him inside. Bending to avoid hitting his head, he stepped into the small room where Jordan Tanner lay stretched out and snoring on a bed about a foot too short for him.

"See what I mean? It looks like someone refilled the ale pitcher and there is a clean mug besides. Help yourself to bread and cheese and I'll be right back with the queen. Eat all you like, Mr. Quade Walker. It's organic and very good for you." She backed out the door smiling, leaving him alone with Jordan Tanner.

Chapter 25

"Tanner, wake up! It's Quade Walker. Where the hell are we, the Magic Kingdom?"

"Huh?" Jordan Tanner squinted at the large, dark form bending over him. "Walker? That you?"

"Yeah, it's me. Here's your specs." Quade handed Tanner the glasses that had fallen to the floor as he slept. "Now tell me how you came to be here in this…this place and who the hell is Queen Sappho?"

It took Tanner a couple more cups of beer and about half an hour to catch Quade up on all that taken place: Ham Philips loading the Cooperator and telling them about the impending train, about signaling the trainmen, and about meeting Isis. Walker was a good listener helping himself to a couple of mugs of ale but, at the mention of Isis, he slammed down his mug so hard, the table jumped.

"That's who I want to know about, Isis. Isn't that the name of some sort of Greek goddess or something?"

"Egyptian. The goddess of a lot things. It changed with the dynasties. She's a beauty, though. I'm sure you noticed." Recognizing the bewildered look of a man uncertain whether to fall in love or not, Tanner chuckled and shook his head. "I thought so."

Walker looked self-conscious and changed the subject. "This place must have been built by the seven dwarves." He looked around the small room. "Or it was a kid's playhouse?"

"I heard Isis call it the gatehouse, but then I was in a time-warp when you came in and set me right straight again." Tanner finished the last of the ale and set his mug on the table. "Now that I've told you how I got here, how about telling me how come you're here? The Swamp isn't your usual beat, is it? Hell, I believe Pierce wouldn't dare venture past The Jumping Off Place if he knew a bunch of Amazons were roaming around down here."

Walker flashed a rare smile at the thought. "You're right about that. I was at the quarry when they found Lewis Spencer's body. Followed a set of tracks that would get washed away by tomorrow. Passed some guy who said he was going to check on his pigs and his wife. That's when I met that girl, Isis. It's like she was waiting for me or something."

"I know. They must have radar back at the castle. You need it down here with all the meth labs these days." Tanner leaned back and then they were quiet for a few minutes, listening to the storm. "That was Lou Owl you passed. Damn fool was going to check on his pigs and his wife in that order?"

But Walker seemed distracted and restless, looking around for some hidden assailant. "Right. He said his name was Owl. I invited him for a beer but he said he was going to check on some pigs. Tried to talk him out of going back by the creek. That bridge is getting ready to fall down by the looks of it, groaning and swaying back and forth. Good thing that train stopped before it went across."

"Yeah," Tanner said, trying to focus Walker's attention away from the shadows in the doorway. "You said you were following tracks? As in footprints or animal?"

"Footprints. A women's. A girl about five-foot-three, five-foot-five, 110-115 lbs. About like that girl Isis, in fact. Where'd she go, anyway? I'd like to talk to her."

"You honestly don't think she had anything—"

"I didn't say that. I only said they led me—"

"—right to here. Have you seen what they've done here? I mean right here in the Swamp? They're practically self-sustaining. Selling electricity back to the grid. Raising their own food, building a place that looks like a palace out of totally biodegradable materials."

"Whoa, wait a second! I'm not working for EPA, Tanner, just Julia Springs Police. And I have a dead body on my hands on top of a storm, a brush fire, a bridge collapse, and a stalled train full of flammable chloride."

Tanner was silent for a minute, thinking of the implications for the little community which lay nearby. Walker shivered suddenly with uncontrollable movements that reminded Tanner of soldiers he had seen in Vietnam suffering from malaria.

"Damn!" Walker said. "Damn this rain!" He was seized with such violent fits of shaking that the mugs danced on the table. Lapsing into a coughing fit, he fought for a clear breath.

Tanner got to his feet in concern. "You've got a fever, Quade. Here, let me cover you with a blanket and get Isis back here. Surely they've got something—"

"No. I'm okay, just leave me—" But Walker was *not* okay. He was shivering so hard his teeth were chattering and sweat was mixed with the moisture on his face.

"Alone? Isn't that just like a man?" The door swung open and Queen Sappho swept in followed by a bunch of tough-looking female guards. She leaned over the detective, lifted each eyelid, felt his forehead, took his pulse, and straightened up. "Pneumonia," she pronounced. "Hoist him up, girls. That's the way, easy does it. He's got some heft to him. Mr. Tanner, follow us. And watch your head. Don't want another causality tonight, do we?"

"Could I ask where we're going?" Crouching to clear the doorway, Tanner felt like a supplicant asking his monarch for a favor.

"Why, into the castle compound, of course. The fire could change direction any minute and the creek's flooding, not to mention the threat of a chemical spill. There's not a minute to lose." Clapping twice, at which signal the handmaidens marched out with Walker on their stout shoulders, she sailed into the stormy night.

"But I thought no men allowed." He followed her into the rain across the drawbridge and through the gate to a long, empty hallway. There the procession carrying Walker headed one way and Queen Sappho the other. She paused, seeing his confusion.

"Mr. Tanner, I have sons by that odious human piece of shit who claimed to be a man, but that isn't my children's fault. In danger and when we are born, we are all equal. It is law and culture that changes that. Now this way, please."

Chapter 26

Gina ran through the graveyard and out the gate over which there were printed, in rusting iron letters, Julia Springs Cemetery. She headed blindly in the direction of the Swamp and the brush fire without concern for her safety. She only knew she had to find Vadim, to make certain their dream was safe, and to be with him if he was in danger. She'd find him working by the creek to save the town with the other men, she was certain.

When she reached the western edge of the Thicket, Gina stopped, confused by what she saw—a blackened tree line denuded of its foliage still lit by patches of the fire that had devoured the habitats of thousands forest dwellers.

How could Vadim have possibly escaped from that inferno? Dismayed, she stopped and burst into tears. She was standing there, weeping, when a loaded pickup truck stopped on its way into town.

"Need a ride?"

When Gina didn't answer, the driver hopped down and put a comforting arm around her shoulders. "There, there. It can't be all that bad, pretty little thing like you. Come on, now. Let's get you out of the rain for starters, then you can tell me what a little red-haired girl has to cry about. My name is Slade. They call me the Deacon around here."

Once seated in the truck, Gina made an effort to thank the man behind the wheel. "I thank you for giving me a lift, Deacon, but I really have to find Vadim. See, he was coming to see me tonight, but I went to watch my uncle fight the fire and the police chief showed me some pictures of a man they shot outside of town and I know it wasn't him, but I just have to find him to make sure he's okay."

She was surprised by the vehemence of the driver's reply. "Stupid police! That's just how stupid they are, showing pictures like that to a young girl like you. What's your name, honey? I've already told you mine." He stared hungrily at her through the dim light from the dashboard.

"It's Gina, but my nickname is Ginny." She didn't want him to think she was too young to be out at night by herself. The way he stared at her made her increasingly uncomfortable, so she edged to the far side of the truck.

"Gina! I like that name. It sounds like church bells chiming. Re-gin-ah! Re-gin-ah!" He sang it out like a hymn until she laughed and touched her hair self-consciously. "A beautiful name for a beautiful girl. He leaned closer so that she smelled liquor on his breath. "How old are you, Ginny, honey?"

"Old enough to know the difference between love and infatuation, if that's what you're asking." She looked at him around the edges of her hair which had curled tightly in the rain.

"Really?" said Slade, taking her reply for flirtation. "How old's that?"

"Seventeen. Vadim is twenty-two. That's only five years difference."

"Seventeen, huh?"

Eighteen was an adult, close enough for consensual sex and this girl wanted it, he could tell. She kept hinting at it all the time, bringing it up while acting so coy. Slade looked out the dirty window of the pickup truck. The fire was past his compound now, and down to the creek. He weighed the consequences of taking the red-haired girl by force versus luring her to his compound and obtaining her consent by drugs mixed with alcohol.

It had become lonely at the compound since that bitch, Lois, left, taking even his youngest wife with her. He'd never forget the scornful look she gave him as they left, carrying their belongings on their backs. Pigshit is what she called him. Pigshit is what she called the father of her four children. And she added to that "You old goat!" Just because he made advances to one of his own daughters. Isis, her name was. Beautiful name for a beautiful girl whom he hadn't recognized as one of his own, because she'd been gone so long when they took her away and put him in the funny farm—just for playing house with young girls—just showing them what marriage expected of them.

Slade turned toward the girl beside him as if he had a sudden thought. At the same time, he slammed on the brakes, sending Gina into the dashboard. "Sorry, baby. I forgot something back at the house. Won't take a minute to run back and get it."

"But the fire. Hadn't it burned your way yet?" Rubbing her elbow she banged up against the peeling dash, she looked around at the piles of trash piled in every available space: boxes, stones, firewood, scraps of food. Maybe he lived in this truck.

He was busy turning the truck around in the road. "Matter of fact, I think I've seen a young stranger hanging around down by the creek lately. Kind of brownish hair."

"Blond." She corrected herself. "Well, maybe a little brown mixed in."

"Right, blue-eyed and kind of tallish." He checked with her, gratified when she nodded.

"I'll be darned, that's him then, Mr...What's his name again?"

"Vadim. It's Russian."

"Talks funny, like...like those spies in the movies? God be praised! He's alive and well and staying at my house, waiting for the storm to slack up. He took refuge with us when it got too bad. You want to see him, I reckon, to make sure he's okay and everything." Slade looked at the girl, hopefully, like a hunter watches his traps.

"I knew he wasn't dead! I don't know who that man was they shot, but it wasn't Vadim. That Captain Pierce is such a dope. Probably shot some perfectly innocent man that came to help fight the fire!"

"You're right about that, baby doll." Slade was elated. She had fallen for it, hook, line, and sinker. Now, he had to figure out how to get her into bed. He looked over at the redhead beside him, savoring the moment when he'd be alone with her, going over everything he'd do to her young body. "Shoot first, ask questions later, that's the police around here. Why, they came to my house one night and accused me of running a meth lab and took all my children away. All because of a dirty rumor, no evidence whatsoever."

"How many children do you have?" It was a perfectly simple question and she wondered why he looked so funny, like he had something to hide.

Careful now. This could be a trap. Don't want to seem like a dirty old man. A family man, that's the ticket. A family man. Rock solid, hard-working, trustworthy family man.

"Just three: little Michael, he's three, Charlene, she's six and a half, and David, my oldest twelve. I pray every night to Jesus to get my children back, safe and sound."

"Poor things. I know they miss their daddy, too. Where are they now, in foster care?"

"With their mothers, darling girl, with their mothers." Then, under his breath but loud enough for her to hear, "Those harlots. Hussies, every one of them."

He realized he had revealed more about himself than he should have when she asked, "How many times have you been married?"

"One too many. Glory be, praise the Lord! Would you look at that?"

"Look at what?' Gina looked out the window at the unfathomable darkness. "I don't see anything."

"That's just it. The fire's burned past it. My place is saved. Hallelujah! The good Lord is my fortress and my shield! Praised be the Lord! Let's go see if your boyfriend is still there, and if he's not, where he went. Those firefighters got cellphones and all. They'll track him down."

In the face of such overwhelming joy, Gina was helpless

to demand she be taken back to town first—before this weird old man went back to wherever he lived in the Swamp. She allowed him to drive through the curtains of rain that were sweeping the land like wraiths dancing manically through the night.

Finally, he drove about a quarter mile up a dirt road and, when the road ended abruptly in weeds, Slade brought the truck to a stop. "We'll have to run the rest of the way, little lady. It's not far. 'Bout a quarter mile. If you hurry, you might even catch the fire crew and find out if your boyfriend is with them."

Something about Slade made Gina uneasy. Maybe it was his wives desertions. Maybe it was the way he kept looking at her and touching her shoulder. On the other hand, he had seen Vadim and could take her to him.

But Slade was well experienced with reluctance in fe-males. "I dunno. There are some bad characters around these parts. Drug dealers and sex perverts. Why, just last month, a twelve-year-old girl was snatched right from her front yard. Hasn't been seen since. You're a lot safer with me."

Finally, Gina went with Deacon, partly because she want-ed to make sure Vadim was alive, and partly because she be-lieved his protestations of being a godly sort of man like John the Baptist, living in the wildness eating locusts. Shivering at the thought he'd offer to share some with her, she left the shel-ter of the truck and followed him down a muddy path into the Swamp. He must surely have a phone, wilderness prophet notwithstanding.

Chapter 27

In the Lesbos castle, the rooms allowed for male visitors by giving them more headroom and urinals made from old toilets without seats. The room Tanner was given was comfortable enough, although it reminded him of a cell. Something about its starkness and the fact it was windowless reminded him of a minimum security prison.

Queen Sappho had apologized for the sparseness of the decoration by saying, "We don't have male visitors as you can see, but you'll be safe here and I hope comfortable. Now I must see to Mr. Walker. Anything you need just ring the bell for the night staff." She indicated a long elaborate bell pull dangling from the ceiling. "Good night, Mr. Tanner. Sleep well."

The door shut firmly behind Lois Slade, alias Queen Sappho.

Down the hall in a similar room Walker slept fitfully under a pile of blankets. From time to time he'd thrash and moan and cry out, "They coming. Hit the dirt. Take cover! Incoming! Incoming!"

Isis would dab his forehead and murmur softly, "They're gone. Rest easy, they're not coming back. Shush. You're safe with me."

Sometime during the night he opened his eyes briefly. The first thing he saw was Isis asleep in a chair beside him. She looked so much like an angel that at first he thought he was dead, and up in heaven, where the powers of the Divine would decide whether or not to throw him out when he got better.

"Please let me stay, Lord. Please. And let me do some good for all the bad things I've done," he said or thought he said.

Isis stirred in her sleep, resting her cheek on her other hand and sighed, "Hush, now. They're not coming back. You're safe. I won't let them hurt you anymore."

He fell asleep wishing he were that hand, the one resting against her cheek.

ဢ

Tanner checked his cell phone messages. There was one from Reggie asking him where he was and did he want him to come get him. *Fat chance.* Tanner chuckled. Reg wouldn't know where to find this place. Very few people would and, if they did, they wouldn't gain entrance to Lesbos. If it hadn't been for Walker falling ill, neither one of them would have been allowed in.

The other three were from Melissa asking where the hell he was and was he playing hard to get, because if he was, she going to drive out to the farm and get him to stay with her 'til the storm was over. There was one wildly worried message from Mildred, Lane's wife asking if Megan and Gina were with him and, if so, call her immediately. No, call her any way. And the last one was Melissa, sounding frantic, near hysteria. Some firefighters had come upon his truck parked at the entrance to the Swamp. Had he gone hunting in this weather? The fire was now out of control, there was a stalled train full of chemicals on the tracks, the old bridge had been swept away, and she was going out of her mind.

He tried to call to reassure her that he was all right, but there was no signal. Thinking there might be reception outside in the hall, he went to the door, and found it was locked from the outside. "Do you need something Mr. Tanner?" said a pleasant voice from somewhere in the room.

"I was trying to make a telephone call but I can't get a dial tone. I wanted to step into the hall a minute to see if I can get a signal there."

"Sorry," said the voice. "We don't allow visitors to make phone calls. Strictly against rules. Good night, Mr. Tanner. Sleep well."

☙☙☙

Following the path along the creek, Lou Owl watched the rising water with conflicting feelings. If the fire leaped the creek, its embers being driven by the wind to the forest on the other side, then the crippled train was directly in its path. On the other hand, the ever-widening creek provided a natural barrier against the wall of flames being driven westward by the storm winds. There wasn't enough precipitation to put out a raging brush fire fed by a glut of spring drought.

But, if luck held, and he prayed to the Great Whoever, then the flames would be stifled by the flood. He was so intent upon concentrating all his energy on this outcome, he didn't see Death coming. Lou Owl had faced Death all his life, thought he knew its face and its form. He didn't expect it would come through the things he loved most—the rivers and the trees. He had worshiped them all his life and he would have been the first one to reflect on the irony of the situation. On the other hand, he had always wanted to die outdoors by the hand of the natural world itself. So the Great Whoever granted his last requests through its own—a tree.

The means of his death was a respectable water oak, nearly Lou's age to the year, seventy-six years old, still full of life, and even capable of planting offspring every year. It was a venerable tree with roots the size of a man's thigh, but life had always been tenuous for it, planted as it was on an ebbing and flowing water route. The Hanahatchee was a venerable waterway itself and so the pair had lived side by side, the means of life and death for the tree. It had, in turn, spread its branches over the water, providing shade for spawning catfish and freshwater bass.

He had always wanted to die here. On its banks, as a kid

of seven, he had found shark's teeth fossils and even made a necklace of them. Because the ancient oceans had once covered this area, he would find the fossilized skeletons of seagoing creatures he couldn't even envision: giant lizards and fish with teeth capable of tearing flesh. Along its banks, Lou, his father, and brothers had dug up the Magic Root that the Chinaman paid well for, sat on the knees of the giant cypress, and killed gators to sell their hides. He had his Vision Quest here, in the manner of his western cousins. A tree with all the animals sitting on its branches and him sitting at the very top appeared to him in a dream, asleep in a deer stand one night. Then he had killed a sixteen-point buck with one clean shot and his whole family, in their multitudes, came out of the forest to the feast.

What seemed so ironic to him, he who was always alert, who rarely slept an entire night, didn't see it coming. The tree, swept down by the broken dam, rode the tide sideways, its branches cutting down saplings of ten years like a scythe blade.

It was a Cossack saber, carried on the crest of the rising creek, riding the flood plain of the Hanahatchee like a half-sunken ship wreck. Lou looked up from his fierce address to the Great Whoever to find the ship-tree before him, indeed overhead. It was too late to dodge death, too late to roll as he had always avoided man-made gunfire. He met his termination as a physical being, the way he had met all the challenges in his life—head-on. The Great Whoever welcomed him home.

ᥱᥬᥱᥬ

The entire western half of the Thicket was now ablaze and the firefighters had to escape across the creek, the prevailing winds driving the flames toward them. They regrouped around the captain who was yelling at the two engineers to move the damned train.

He got the same reply he received half an hour ago—the relief crew and engine were on their way. Meanwhile there was nothing else they could do but sit tight. If they tried moving the train with that bad coupling and the splintered track, it would derail and that would be the worst possible scenario.

The slicker-clad fire captain moved closer to hear the engineer above the noise of the storm. "What the hell is benzoyl chloride anyway? Is it flammable? And what's your company doing moving a shipment over this old track anyway? That bridge hasn't been used for over thirty years."

They made a strange contrast, the bespectacled engineer and the exhausted fire chief both trying to cope with circumstances beyond their control—beyond anyone's control.

At that moment, the sky lit up with brilliant lightning and, in seconds, was followed by a tremendous clap of thunder.

"God, that was close." Returning to his crew, the captain gave a warning they all dreaded. "Be on the lookout for fresh flare-ups on this side of the creek, boys. That last strike was close to home. If it gets too near the tracks, we'll have to evacuate pronto."

Before he finished speaking, the sky seem to open up overhead and engulfed the men in a deluge of water, as if someone was emptying a giant bucket over their heads. As the rain intensified, a loud cheer went up from the men. The tongues of flame eating up the distance between them suddenly vanished under the blanket of miraculous water.

They dispersed to put out hot spots and do damage control in a few places that the fire had spread along the creek. They worked with white grins on their blackened faces and traded jokes, comparing the rain to a cow peeing on flat rock or the chief after three beers. A relief crew came all the way down from Macon and the tired firefighters gladly went home to their families where they were welcomed as conquering heroes.

℮⌀℮⌀

The train track and jammed coupling were repaired and a switch engine towed the crippled *Warrior* back to Atlanta for repair. It became known as the Night of the Triple Threat in local lore and, like legends, it had its heroes and its villains.

The terrorist played a large role in villainy along with the Atlanta company arranging the shipment of hazardous chemicals across a unstable bridge.

The relief crew from Macon found Lou Owl's body some fifty feet from where the tree hit the bridge. The trainmen tentatively identified him as one of two men who warned them the bridge was out. That's when the hunt began for the missing Jordan Tanner whose truck had been found parked at the Jumping Off Place, a local entrance to the Swamp.

Gina and her sister Megan were among the missing, although Arthur Gatewood had called home to say they were going to another party, across the river in Alabama, and wouldn't be back until God only knew when. It was hoped that somehow Gina had joined them until Lane talked to Megan and told her to come home.

"And bring Gina with you. Tell her for me she's grounded indefinitely for running from Joy with all that's going on. Worrying her Aunt Mildred like that. What's got into her, I don't know. Something's upset her."

"We're across the river at Bobby Turner's house. And, Uncle Lane, Gina isn't with us. Do we still have to come home? Party's just getting going good. Puhleeze don't make us come home yet! Gina's probably with Holly somewhere."

"Glad somebody can have a good time tonight." His voice was heavy with fatigue. "Then where is she? She ran out of the church after having one of her spells and nobody's seen her."

Megan was getting impatient, he could tell by the whining note in her voice. "I honestly don't know. Did you call her?"

"She left her purse at the church. Her cellphone is in it. That's why I'm calling you. Okay, you can stay 'til one, not a minute longer, you hear?" Lane cut off his cellphone and ran his hand over his grimy face. "Girls. Teenage girls. They're like sticks of dynamite ready to explode."

Joy put a comforting hand on her father's shoulder. "I was a teenage stick of dynamite once. Still am. Look, you get some rest, Pop, and I'll look for her. I'll bet anything she's with one of her girlfriends. Holly, most likely."

Mildred got off the house phone and came into the kitchen looking worried. "That was Holly's grandmother. She hasn't come home either. She was wondering if we heard from them."

Lane banged his hand on the pine table so hard the coffee cups jumped and the women started nervously. "See that's just what I mean. Going off on some tangent down to see God-knows-who on a night like this. Doesn't think of the danger involved. Doesn't think about her family. Doesn't think period!"

"I'm sure she didn't mean to worry us. Ginny's got a good head on her shoulders although she was acting kind of strange tonight."

"What do you mean strange?"

Aware both her parents were staring at her waiting for a reply, Joy chose her words carefully. They were too expert at reading her facial expressions to soft-pedal the truth. "Well, you know how she gets when she has one of her spells. Sort of spacey, you know?" Joy looked from one of her parents to the other and was gratified when they nodded in unison.

"You think she had one of those episodes at the fire where Glory Hall burned down? That'd do it," he said.

Mildred looked at her exhausted husband who was fighting to stay awake.

"Dr. Jim said you never know what's going set them off. A car crash, a fire, any kind shock. She seemed awfully upset about something when Chief Pierce showed her pictures of the terrorist, or who they think was a terrorist, anyway. She fainted clean away. Doctor Morrissey said he'd like to run some tests on her. Thought she might have a seizure disorder," Joy added.

"Look on her phone, Joy. I read somewhere if you want to know about a teenager's life, look on their phone. See when she made her last phone call and who she called." Mildred sat down at the table and watched as Joy scrolled through the calls.

"Just one early this morning 8:35 am to Holly. That's all." Putting the phone down, Joy kept looking at it as though she expected it to ring. "Uncle Jordan can't be reached either. There must be some dead spots out of service because of the storm. Could they be together do you think?"

"Not if Jordan's gone hunting. He goes with Lou Owl and they get so bombed they couldn't hit the side of a barn three feet away from it. I'll give him a call though and leave a message on his voicemail. Won't hurt this time of night. If he's with Lou, he'll be asleep by now anyway." Lane left a brief message and hung up. "Just as I thought, probably got the thing turned off. Don't know what use a cell phone is when you turn it off all the time."

Chapter 28

Following Deacon Slade through the Thicket bordering the Swamp was like following some giant primordial bird to its nest through a tangled mass of vegetation. He dodged, ducked, and weaved through the underbrush, his coat tails flapping like wings behind him.

"Just a little bit farther now. Got to catch those firemen before they move on. Just a few more steps now and we'll be home and dry. Ah, what do I see ahead, but home? We'll be cozy in a jiffy. There we are, my sweet Ginny, home be it ever so humble." Slade disappeared through an opening in the wall of a fortress and then stuck his head out again to make sure she was coming.

The rain was coming down hard so that all Gina wanted was shelter. Still, she hesitated when she saw the peculiarly shaped doorway just beyond the gate. It was in the shape of a minaret or, she couldn't help noticing, a phallus like the dirty drawings boys in her class made and stuck in her book when she wasn't looking.

"Come right in and I'll soon have us a warm fire going." Noticing her hesitance to enter the compound, Slade flapped around the room that was round, busying himself with making a fire, chattering about wet firewood making smoke and how they must avoid smoke because the fire crew would see it and turn their hoses on it.

"I thought you said they'd be here, anyway." She stood just inside the doorway, a puddle forming at her feet. A feeling of uneasiness was nibbling at the edges of her consciousness, which had become clearer after running through the rain, as if the rain itself had washed away the fuzziness that had taken control of her for the past two hours.

"I'm sure they're on their way, dear. Now just make yourself all comfy while I get us some hot milk. Chocolate milk, all righty?"

The only light in the room was a lantern which cast an eerie light over the scene. In it Slade's sharp features took on a predatory look as if he were a vulture disguised as a man. He seemed to hop around the room lighting on things the way vultures pounced on carrion in the road.

"Of course, you're anxious to know if your boyfriend is safe and I'll call just as soon as I get this fire going."

"I think I must've left my cell phone in your truck. It's in my purse. I'll just go get it."

But Slade rushed to block the doorway. "You didn't have a purse with you or I'd have seen it, but I'll go look, to make double sure just in case, as soon as I get this fire going and our milk warmed up. First-things-first, I always say. Don't want to catch cold, now do we?" He took her by the arm with a surprisingly firm grip and steered her to the fire. "Sit here, my darling, while I go get the milk. I'll be right back, I promise. Milk is in the fridge in the kitchen."

He slipped out an arched doorway which led to the interior, still babbling something about summer pneumonia being the worst kind and one of his parents dying of it. His absence gave her time to think about what she was doing in the Thicket in this strange room with the even more peculiar Deacon Slade late at night. The rain was still pounding on the roof, but she was already wet, anyway, and Slade's predictions of pneumonia weren't nearly as frightening as some other outcomes that her imagination came up with. She was at the outer door when Slade ducked back in the room holding a clay jug.

"You're not thinking about leaving in this storm, are you, Miss Ginny?"

"I was just going to look in your truck for my cell phone."

"Oh, I'm glad I took the precaution of locking the door. I

wouldn't want to be responsible for your getting lost, now would I? Now let me just put this milk on to heat it up and then I'll show you where you can sleep."

"But my family'll will be worried about me. They'll have a search party going, I'm sure of it." She struggled to unlock the door, locked from the outside. Gina made a dash for the arched doorway, but Slade seemed to anticipate her next move and was there before her blocking her way. She evaded his grasp as he reached for her arm and grabbed the pottery milk jug. "Come a step closer and I'll break this over your head!"

"That'd be a waste of good milk. I milked that goat only this morning. Now come on, Ginny, be sensible. Nobody's going to be hunting for you in this pouring rain. I'll take you home first thing tomorrow. Now be a good girl and put that jug down."

She circled the room holding the jug over her head until she was at the door again. "Unlock this door now or I'll throw it."

"Suit yourself. Sleep in here then. Good night and sweet dreams." Picking up the lantern, he disappeared around the doorway. Though he took the light from the room, she could see his shadow as he lingered in the next room to see if she'd follow him.

After a half hour or so, he apparently nodded off at his post. She waited until Slade began snoring and tiptoed over to the doorway. Deacon Slade was slumped against the wall, asleep, the lantern beside him.

Just beyond Slade was another room and she could see another beyond that one. *Slade's World was laid out like a series of mole hills, each adjoining the other through a curtained doorway and like a mole's tunnel,* she thought. *It must have two entrances or possibly, a third.*

Gina picked up the lantern and quickly crossed through two rooms. In the second, she found a bed. And as quietly as she could, dragged it to block the doorway. She added a couple of chairs and cushions to the pile in case Slade should awaken and come looking for her and then picked up the lantern and hurried on. The next two rooms were littered with goat and chicken droppings which she tiptoed over. High above the noise of the storm, and the neighing noises of frightened animals, she heard another voice. She stopped, listening with every fiber of her nervous system.

Turning toward the sound, she noticed a small door. Pulling on it with one hand didn't budge it. Putting the lantern down, she put her whole weight against it and succeeded in getting it open. It led to cellar stairs, and at the bottom sat a teary-eyed girl of about twelve.

At first the child was terrified, cringing like an animal at the bottom of the stairs. "Where's that old man? Who are you? Please let me out of this dark place. I want to go home."

Gina heard a sound behind her, too late to react. The next thing she knew she went flying down the stairs, colliding with the girl at the bottom. The girl shrieked, clawing at her, beating her as they rolled backward under Gina's weight.

"That'll teach you to threaten your Deacon, Miss Ginny. Think about repentance in there awhile, and then we'll see what we can pray about together." The cellar door slammed and they were plunged into darkness.

For a few minutes, they lay there together and then Gina sat up. She had fallen on the lantern but it hadn't broken. Slade hadn't noticed it because his flashlight had been so much brighter and it had tumbled under her as she had fallen. She set it upright on the cellar floor and looked around. The place was filled with rubbish, boxes, and littered with mice droppings and cobwebs as far into the dark as she could see. Then she turned and looked at her companion who was sitting up staring back.

"How long have you been in here?"

"I don't know. I've lost track. He, that old man up there, he only lets me out to go to the bathroom. I tried running away, and now he won't let me out but once a day. My mama must be looking for me. I know she is. I can hear her calling in my head, and, when I'm asleep, I sometimes see her standing right over there." She pointed to the darkness behind them.

"I am sure she is. My name's Ginny. What's yours?"

The girl replied, "Caroline. But they call me Carrie for

short. I'm sorry if I scratched your face. I was just so scared. Sorry, Ginny."

"That's okay. Now, we've got to get out of here somehow." Getting to her feet she explored back as far as the dirt floor went, pushing the cobwebs aside until she ran into an earth wall. She was about to turn around when she felt a drop of moisture. Raising the lantern higher, she tried to find the source of the water, but the glow of the lantern cast the ceiling in half light. Gina stood on her tiptoes to touch the place where the ceiling sloped downward.

There was a line of moisture running along the top of the wall. "Carrie, will you come hold the lantern for me?"

Carefully the younger girl picked her way through the trash on the floor. "I'm scared of rats. I seen some. Their eyes were glowing red in the dark."

"Here, hold it as high as you can. That's it, like that." She steadied the lantern and scraped a little dirt away from the dark line where the wall nearly met the ceiling. It grew wider as she scraped. She took off her sandal and scraped with the hard sole of the shoe.

"Better, but it'll take forever, and we haven't got that long."

Hunting among the rubbish, Gina found a shard of glass and dug at the wall with it. After succeeding to tunnel through a small hole, she stood on a box to see where the moisture was coming from. On the other side of the cellar wall, rain was falling somewhere far overhead and pooling up just below her line of sight. Gina held her breath. Through the night, sounds of the Swamp came the reverberating echo of raindrops hitting metal.

"Hand me a box. No, two."

Caroline brought two of the cartons over and stacked them against the dirt wall of the cellar. "What do you see? Is there a way out of here?"

"We need to make this hole a little wider and it's already starting to get light out. Hurry and see if we can widen it just a bit more so you can get through."

It was close to dawn when the tunnel was wide enough for their slender bodies to slide through though they would land waist high in the rain barrel at the bottom of the cistern. Bracing her back against the wall, she saw the grate a good four feet above her head and above that, blue sky. The storm was over and most of the brush fire had been extinguished by the rain.

Looking behind her through the tunnel, she saw the faint light reflected in Caroline's eyes staring back at her and, in them, fear and confusion.

Trying to keep the urgency out of her voice, she called, "Come on, Caroline, pretend you're at the swimming pool and going to sit on the side of the pool."

The faint whine reached her through the faint light. "I ain't never been swimmin', Ginny. My mama never had the dollar to get in."

"Well, I'll take you to the pool every day this summer if you'll hoist yourself up on this barrel like I am."

"Okay, here I come. Catch me 'cause I don't want to fall into no water and drown." She came headfirst, her dirty face emerging first.

After several attempts at jumping, Caroline landed on the rim of the barrel, squealing with delight as she succeeded. "Just like getting out of the creek at home when it's flowing good!"

"Hush, now! You've got to be quiet 'cause that old Slade's got ears like a donkey. Now climb on to my knees and see if you can lift that grate and move it over. If you can, I'm going to count to three, and then climb on my shoulders, okay? Just like acrobats in the circus."

"I never been to no circus either, Ginny. But I seen pictures of 'em in my little sister's coloring book she got for Christmas from Santy Claus. Okay, like this?" She stood on Gina's knees, and with surprising strength pushed the grate aside.

"Now up and out you go." Counting to three, slowly Gina straightened her back and stood up with Caroline standing on her shoulders. With a final wiggle, Caroline was crawling on her belly legs waving in the air. Moving the heavy metal grate a little way back over the hole, Caroline bore Gina's weight with two hands long enough for her to grasp the solid iron grate with both hands. Gina swung both legs out of the hole and Caroline grabbed one arm. In the next second, Gina struggled free.

They realized with dismay they were still inside the compound and the animals in their pens were making noise as if they were hungry. Slade would be awake any minute and out to feed them before he checked on the cellar. They would have to hide some place near the wall but away from the cistern area. Caroline spotted a clump of banana plants, on the other side of the sheep pen, and they were moving through the sheep when Slade came out and yawned while peeing in the front yard. They froze crouching down behind one particularly fat ewe who didn't seem too overjoyed to have two humans clinging to her mud encrusted wool.

"I'm coming, girls, I'm coming," Slade yawned again, and putting down his robe, went inside. The girls took the opportunity to bolt across the yard to the safety of the banana trees and in doing so, neglected to close the gate to the sheep pen. The hungry sheep wandered out into the yard, pulling at anything green including the clump of banana plants.

"Hey! Get away from them bananas! Shoo, now, shoo. I got to get a new latch on that gate when I go back into town. The Deacon takes good care of his girls, he does. Got to go feed those two bitches after they repent and say they're sorry. Shoo in, that's right. Go on, now." Slade cooed like a grandmother rocks a baby to sleep, dreaming of bygone days when the baby was her own as he herded the loose sheep back in their pen.

Through the broad banana leaves the girls watched, not daring to breathe. When he had feed the sheep a bucket of smelly slops, Slade went inside calmly, whistling through his teeth. They rose slowly, preparing to run to the gate when he rushed back out carrying an axe.

"Thought you could get away that easy from the Deacon, did you little bitches?" He ran straight toward them and before Gina could stop her, Caroline bolted from the cover of the palms, screaming at the top of her lungs. Gina looked for a weapon and found a shovel lying on the ground a few feet away. As Slade chased Caroline, axe raised above his head, Gina followed him, shovel gripped with both hands in case he turned on her.

As they passed the front gate, the wooden door came crashing down and Quade Walker bolted inside, pistol drawn. Slade stopped, axe over his head, and turned back to swing at Walker, but the detective shot it out of his hands. Slade looked popeyed for a full three seconds, apparently convinced that he was immortal.

Aghast at the blood spurting from his palms, he cried, "You've shot Jesus, you fool!"

"Get your hands in the air, Slade," Walker ordered, but Slade did a little dance of pain and then suddenly dashed through the destroyed doorway into the Thicket where he disappeared like a fox going to ground.

Jordan Tanner and Isis, who were each armed with a rifle in case Walker missed, took aim as one, firing shots through the doorway, but by then Slade had disappeared into the bushes.

"Let him go and let's see to the girls. I'll radio for a search party. Jesus, my ass." Walker grinned at the astonished girls who were frozen where they stood—Ginny with shovel still raised over her head, Caroline ready to run for her life. "Miss Ginny, you've given us all quite a scare. And who's this other young lady?"

Caroline burst into tears, sobbing in hysterical gulps. Isis rushed to her, enveloping the sobbing girl in here arms.

"Her name's Caroline. She's only twelve and no telling how long she's been a prisoner here. She's lost count of the days."

Isis looked over the girl's head at Walker. "I can tell you she's been missing a month and three days. Now you know why I was out in the storm last night. I saw Slade's truck go out and was trying to search for her in the compound."

"I'm sure glad you were," he said, his eyes gentling on her. "But I wish you'd told me you suspected he was the one who kidnapped her in the first place."

Isis looked away. Walker was surprised to see tears forming in her eyes. "He is pigshit, but I guess I come from pigshit."

"Your—he was your father?" Walker looked stunned. "I'm sorry, but I had to shoot. He could have killed one of the girls with that axe."

"Oh, I knew it would end this way. That's all right." She brushed a hand across her eyelids. "I guess I weep for what might have been, that's all."

Tanner put his arm around Gina. "I swear if you didn't look like you were ready to do battle. A real warrior-girl."

Gina let the shovel fall to the ground, her knees sagging suddenly as if her bones had dissolved.

"Can I go home now, Uncle Jordan? I haven't had a wink of sleep all night."

"I should say so. Your mama's down from Atlanta and Uncle Lane's got the entire town out looking for you." Walker nodded his agreement and Tanner put his cellphone to his lips. "I've got her," he said in a low voice. "Meet me at the Nest."

"I'll be talking to you, Miss Gina, when you've had some rest, that is." Walker met Isis's gaze over the top of Caroline's head. "After we all have had some rest and a good think."

He was calling for back up and the county sheriff's helicopter when they left the compound. Outside the gate, Gina hesitated. "Wait, Uncle Jordan. Hey, Carrie, you still want to go swimming some time?"

The girl raised her head from Isis's shoulder and looked at Gina with a tear-streaked, red face. "Sure. I mean, sometime."

"I'll call you. I mean, like send you a message or something. Give me a hug. We're sisters, remember that."

The younger girl had the beginnings of an uncertain smile on her face as she hugged Gina. "I remember, forever. Sisters in distress."

"Pinkie promise." Their grimy pinky fingers curled around each other like earthworms, hooked tight, then each let go.

"See ya," Gina said and went back to Jordan Tanner. "Let's go home, Uncle Jordan."

They emerged from the Swamp just as the sun crested the flooded fields, its rays refracted by countless droplets and puddles until it seemed they were walking on a path of light.

Chapter 29

Deacon Slade watched the helicopter circling over the Swamp from his hiding place in the thick underbrush, being careful to stay in the patches untouched by last night's fire. He would wait until dark to move on, wading across the creek, where it ran over boulders to the far side, and from there to the main road. His wounded hand was wrapped in rags made from his nightshirt, but it throbbed mightily so that he began to feel lightheaded with pain.

He slumped against a tree and slept fitfully until darkness fell then awoke with a start. Something was moving in the woods nearby, something that walked in measured, ponderous steps.

Slade whimpered from terror and pain, suspecting another policeman with pistol drawn was hunting him like a wounded animal. *Oh, Jesus, deliver me from mine enemies.*

But no, whatever it was just beyond the curtain of branches and leaves was, at once, too silent and too loud—footsteps as if they were made by something too big and heavy for a man. A buck maybe, pray God, driven this way by the fire. Too silent for a human—silent breath, occasionally pausing as if sniffing the air. Or him!

He tried peering through the branches, but could make out nothing. Nothing but an odor...what was it? Like something that ate chinaberries passing gas. A sweet fetid smell. Slade stood up, thinking that would scare it away. That was a mistake, his last one as it turned out. The last thing he saw was a pair of eyes looking down at him from a great height, hating what they saw.

The creature had always hated this he-human, hated him because he had watched Slade beating his animals and his she-humans. He had heard their piteous cries and felt the blows echoing on his own powerful body so that he had flinched with their pain.

Now was his chance to inflict pain and he did it, bringing pleasure to his loins with every screech the he-thing made. The creature, blinded by rage, let out an unearthly sound, a high whistle that could be heard for miles, and a deep growl that sent animals within earshot scurrying for their hiding places. A boiling rage suffused his brain, rendering it incapable of caution. He hated all humans then, saw them as an implacable enemy. He had seen them pouring kerosene on his beloved earth, setting the chinaberry trees and blackberry brambles alight and turning the Swamp into a roaring inferno so that he was driven to eating grubs to keep from starving.

When the he-thing was finally hanging from the limb of a half-charred pine, the creature looked under the bloody, torn nightshirt just to make certain he hadn't been playing with a she-human as it had shrieked and cowered without putting up a resistance. Growling, satisfied deep within, the creature strode away.

ლოელა

They found Slade, or what was left of him, about a mile from town, hanging from a tall tree by his nightshirt or what was left of it, his skinny legs dangling as if he were a broken marionette.

Little did they guess he had borne the brunt of retaliation for the sins of them all.

"Whatever happened to him, he deserved it and it'll save the Georgia taxpayers a heap of money," said one volunteer deputy, looking up at the dangling body.

"Danged if he don't look like Jesus hanging on that tree limb, don't he, though?" His companion stood, hands on hips, surveying the devastated area. "Must have climbed that tree to hide from the bloodhounds."

"What'd he do, pole-vault up there?" came the reply. "There's no branches on the lower half of that pine. Whatever he done, that's the end of a nasty little man and I say good riddance. The only problem he's gonna give us now is how to get him down."

ezezo

Reg was in the kitchen with Maybelle when Jordan Tanner finally drove into the flooded yard, causing all the dogs to come running to greet him and then inspect his pungent clothes to see where he'd been all night. He said hello, took a piece of sausage up to bed with him, sprawled across his bed on a bunch of papers, and went to sleep.

Waking at near noon, Tanner shaved and when he looked in the mirror, he started asking himself what the hell went on last night. He remembered the bridge collapsing and the train full of chemical gas stopping just short of going down in the creek. And then he remembered Lou Owl going upstream for some reason and him heading back to his truck. From there, it got a bit hazy. He decided what he needed was a drink and was heading downstairs to get a shot of bourbon before lunch, when Melissa popped up out of his leather arm chair.

"My word, Jordan, let me just say you had us ready to get the bloodhounds out and our waders on and go after you into the Swamp. Do you put your cellphone in your tackle box when you go in there or what?" She planted a kiss on his chin just as the kitchen door swung open and Reg came out with two drinks in his hands.

"Here, Dad. Drink your breakfast." He was not smiling, unusual for Reg because he always seemed to be apologizing for being alive. "You'll need it."

"Why all the long faces? I mean, what the hell is this, a wake? I'm alive, damn it! We've survived fire and flood, a near chemical spill, and a kidnapping!! We ought to be celebrating!"

Reg and Melissa traded meaningful looks, indicating there was something he didn't know and they weren't going to spring it on him until he'd had a round of drinks.

"We are, Dad, albeit quietly. A lot of people around town are hurting." Reg handed the other glass to Melissa who shook her head.

"Never before four in the afternoon or it causes facial muscles to sag."

Reg finally lightened up. "You remind me of my mother. She used to say that same thing." It was easy to see he liked Melissa and she saw in him the son she never had. She needed somebody to love and mother. That was the Southerner in her. In the South, the South Melissa grew up in, that was what women were good for—mothering sons and, badly, daughters.

Reg saw in her, Tanner realized, as though someone was standing by his shoulder telling him what was going on, the mother Frenchy wasn't—dedicated, perfect, comfortable in that role. He looked from one to the other, reading their faces until they realized he was standing there.

"Dad," exclaimed Reggie as if seeing him for the first time, "how about some real food? You must not have eaten any supper, right?"

"I feel my face muscles sagging because of what's in this drink. Bring me a bourbon on the rocks. This stuff isn't fit to brush your teeth with."

She patted his cheek and gave his glass to Reg. "Bring that stuff he keeps under the sink for medicinal purposes, or so he says."

The defeated look crept over Reggie's face again. "I thought you liked Bloody Marys—just vodka, bitters, and tomato juice. I'll be glad to change it to bourbon though. I've got something I need to talk to you about, Dad, but it'll keep."

He surprised both of them by his lack of patience. Last night and all its implications, to say nothing of lack of sleep, all made their way into his voice. "Not about Brandon again, is it? Because if it is, Reg, I've got more pressing issues to find out about right now."

"It is and it isn't about him. And by the way, I'm paying

for everything so you don't have to worry. It's all taken care of—the birth, everything." Again, that hurt expression weakened Reg's fine profile as he turned away and Tanner regretted his sharp reply immediately.

"Then what's the problem?" Tanner cursed himself for the petulant note in his voice. It had been a long night and he still hadn't heard what happened at the bridge. Did the train go through or did the bridge fall? And he hadn't heard from Lou Owl. That weighed heaviest on his mind. He had said he was going back to check on his animals or some such dingbat thing.

Meanwhile, Reg was doing a little dance the way he indicated he had to use the bathroom as a child, as if using the actual word caused him anxiety. *That was probably the damned duke's fault, the prick Frenchy left him to marry because she needed stability. If she had found it, it certainly hadn't trickled down to Reg.*

"No problem. No problem at all, Dad. Just that Brandon doesn't want to be saddled with a kid and I do, that all. So we officially split up. Here, I'll fix you that bourbon and branch if you don't like the Bloody Mary." He seemed eager to get away now that the news was in the open.

"Stop. I'll do it. Let me. I'll be back in two shakes of a lamb's tail." Melissa grabbed the glass from Tanner's hand, recognizing the men had talking to do and, muttering something about dying for Maybelle's pizza ball recipe, went through the kitchen door like melted butter.

"Actually, I was going to find out if anyone has seen Lou Owl because he never misses a drink after an adventure."

"Probably got washed out and followed his wife and kids to stay with relatives." Reg obviously wanted to talk about things other than his father's VFW friends. He needed approbation for what he was doing, electing to raise a child on his own. He fervently wished his step-mother, Caroline, were here. She would have reasoned with his father like she always did, making sense of situations he didn't want to deal with and didn't see why he had to. "There's a million Owls scattered from here to the Florida line. Lou could be with any one of them. I'm glad you found Ginny though, Dad. How'd you do it?"

"The real heroes were Quade Walker and Isis. I was just along for the ride because I still had my rifle."

"So who is this young femme fatale? Isis, is it?" Melissa asked, coming in from the kitchen with his drink in her hand. "Someone is into Egyptian mythology around here. I knew there was another woman involved. Cherchez la femme, as the French say."

"She's Deacon Slade's daughter and her mother is Queen Sappho, although you probably remember her as Lois Thompson."

"Good lord, you don't mean it! Isn't she the child who accused him of—you know the story—keeping her as a sex slave?"

"Yes, she's one of them, but she's turned out to be a perfectly lovely girl." Tanner rose to her defense even though he shared Walker's suspicions that Isis might have been complicit in her father's luring the two girls to his compound. But he wanted to give her the benefit of the doubt because she had led the way back to Slade's when Quade Walker had asked her whether she had seen Caroline at her father's place. She hadn't really seen the girl that Slade abducted, but she suspected him of being up to no good because he was being secretive about going into town for supplies.

"I never knew him to be anything but secretive, keeping his harem and all those kids out there in the Swamp. My daddy put him away for ten years, but he got out in five 'cause the rest of the inmates were threatening to lynch him. Just knowing he's locked up again, I'll sleep better at night." Melissa gave a little shiver and slipped an arm through Tanner's.

"Go on, Dad," Reggie prompted. "What happened after you and Walker got there?"

"They were okay, aside from needing a bath." Tanner deliberately downplayed the suspense, the suspicion that they would find them dead or tied up and abused in some god-awful way. He could tell what they were thinking, both girls had been ruined, beyond disgrace, and the town would have to find it in their Christian hearts to feel sorry for them instead of blaming them.

"Poor kids. It must have been a scary situation. They'll have to have a lot of therapy to get over being locked in a cellar with some old creep prowling around."

Tanner looked at his son as if seeing him for the first time in a long time. Reg always could see other people's side of things. He always put himself in their place, as if he was suffering with them, as if he knew what it was like to be a victim.

"Fear is a good thing, son. You know, those two babies had tunneled right through the cellar wall into a cistern where Slade had set up a rain barrel to catch drinking water, I guess. They were headed for the gate when that old bastard spotted them. He was chasing them with an axe when we got there. Quade shot the bat out of his hand, but he got out the gate and into the Swamp. They're looking for him now."

"Holy shit! That was close! You guys are heroes."

"Correction. Walker's the hero, and that girl, Isis. We wouldn't have known where they were except she took us there."

"But if she knew beforehand, why didn't she alert the police? He could have done anything to them by then. Did Walker question her about it?"

Suddenly, a wave of weariness rushed over him. "I guess he's going to when the dust settles. First, he had to take the other little girl to her mother. Tell Maybelle I'm going to catch a little nap before lunch. You and Melissa go on and eat, hear?"

"You all right, Jordan?" Maybelle stuck her head out of the kitchen door, her brow furrowed as she looked at him with concern. It didn't take a degree in logic to figure she had been listening the whole time.

"It's probably the whiskey and no sleep. I used to stay up all night and drink my breakfast," he said.

"You used to be a whole lot younger, too." She handed him a plate of food. "Tell you what. You eat some of this barbeque and then stretch out in the den on the couch."

After he had left them standing outside the kitchen, looking after him as he retreated to the sanctity of his den, Melissa turned to Reg. "He never answered your question, honey. Why that girl never told the police."

"Maybe Dad doesn't want to speculate on motives. He'll have to testify at Slade's trial and he knows he could sway a jury just by angling his testimony one way or another. After all, one of those girls was a member of his own family."

In his den, Tanner turned on the TV and, without tasting it, wolfed down the barbeque and cornbread. The den was cool and shadowed the way he liked it in the early summer afternoons. He stretched out on the leather sofa as much as he could. It had seen better days and smelled of dogs, several generations of children and babies spitting back sour milk. In short, life in the Tanner family had left its mark in its tufted body. It had been the longest Carolyn could get at the time, seven feet to contain his six-feet, four-inch frame. But in order to do that, it had to be curved at either end which was awkward for a big man like him to manage.

"I'm not shaped like a question mark," he had told his wife when Kirby's Department Store had delivered the thing all the way from Macon. The irony of that remark hit him and he chuckled, snuggling down into its smooth odorous depths. He was shaped like that now since age had curved his once wide shoulders and sent his neck down between them like an old buzzard.

Tanner was just drifting off when he was aware of another presence in the room. In fact, someone was watching him, probably Maybelle back to pick up the dishes or Melissa tracking him down to see if he needed anything. No, no, it was a male presence, no doubt about that odor. It wasn't Reggie who smelled like expensive after shave and horses, or Lane who had the distinct smell of fertilizer about him.

He opened his eyes to find Lou Owl gazing at him from the doorway to the garage. "I thought it was you. Nobody smells that bad. Did you get something to eat yet? Maybelle's got barbeque in the kitchen."

Owl looked like he had something on his mind or he had forgotten something important, and was trying to think what it was. Accustomed to his friend's frequent silences, Tanner closed his eyes again. "Whenever you're ready. Meanwhile, I'll go back to sleep. Got about two hours last night. Damn women kept waking me up."

But Owl was back again in his dream or dreaming awake, whatever it was. He was standing on the other side of a river. Waving. "See you on the other side, Jordan," he said. "Whenever you're ready. Got to go home now."

Before Tanner could ask him where he was going, Lou Owl walked through the closed door and into the Thicket where he had live all his life.

"Aw, Lou, come back." Tanner sat up and looked around. The den was empty. "Just kidding. We'll get a drink and—"

"Who you talking to, Jordan?" Maybelle was standing in the doorway, looking around suspiciously. "Ain't nobody here and ain't nobody gonna be, if I have anything to do with it. I said leave that man alone and I mean leave him alone, end of story. That includes that Bulloch bulldog, too."

Tanner yawned and rubbed his eyes which were red and scratchy from smoke and fatigue. "It was just Lou Owl. Comes and goes through the garage as if he owns the place."

Chapter 30

Maybelle stopped collecting the dishes and silverware and looked up at him. "Lou Owl, you say? That's who you as talking to?"

"Yeah, why?"

Tanner risked a lecture from Maybelle and lit up a cigar. After a long, satisfied puff, he exhaled a cloud of smoke into the still air. Maybelle was still looking at him. He expected her to tell him Lou Owl was a poacher and stole chickens and occasionally pigs and was no good to hang around with because he could get tarred with the same brush.

Instead, she said, "I guess you ain't heard, then."

"Heard what? About Lou? Heard what about him, Maybelle?" He tensed, sitting forward to see her earnest face in the slanting light coming through the half-closed blinds. "Is he hurt or something? Family all right? He looked okay, but he could do with a bath as usual. Personal hygiene never was his strong suit. What?"

"He's dead, Jordan. Lou Owl's body is at Tapley's waiting for the family to tell them what to do with it when they get back in town, whether they want a Christian service or to do an Indian one. You know how they is." Maybelle stood there, tears welling up in her eyes. "You just seen the ghost of ol' Lou. He come to tell you good-bye." She wept silently into her apron.

It didn't sink in, couldn't be aligned with what he had just seen. "What? No, wait a minute, now. He was standing here a minute ago, big as life, same smell, everything. They got the wrong stiff down at Tapley's, if they think that's Lou. Some poor chump but it's not Lou Owl."

Drying her face and gathering up the dishes, Maybelle hid the soft glance of pity behind her usual façade of hopeless inefficiency. It was all too familiar in the Quarter where she had grown up a skinny, cross-eyed kid who needed glasses. She knew denial when she saw it. Then reality, then grieving, then finally acceptance—the Lord's will or whatever they chose to do with death.

"Okay, I may be wrong and it wouldn't be the first time. Best thing to do is get it straight from the horses' mouth. Quade Walker is out there waiting for you. I got to get back to work anyway. You want me to send him in here so you two can talk in private?"

"Send him on in, I guess. I'll set him straight."

It couldn't be Lou. They could put that thought right out of their storm-addled heads. Japanese bullets couldn't destroy Lou Owl. Years of drinking everything from corn liquor to bathtub gin hadn't made a dent in his liver where it had killed mere mortals. No, they had the wrong corpse, and if they gave it a pow-wow funeral, Lou would be there to dance with the best of them.

"Tanner?" Walker came in the study, looking dark as death in the half light. He looked for a place to sit, a little like a hawk circling before it lands. "Okay?" he said indicating a chair.

"Let me get some light on."

"No! No, this is fine. Okay the way it is. Mind if I smoke...inside?" It was clear the young detective thought he had bad news and Tanner knew what that felt like. As a much younger man, he'd had to tell the woman he worshiped that her lover was dead and watch her dissolve before his eyes, never to fully recover.

That had been Reggie's mother, Francesca or Frenchy, the beloved that still haunted his dreams. That had started Frenchy on a downward spiral she never pulled out of.

Pouring them each two fingers of bourbon, Jordan Tanner

decided on a preemptive strike. "Walker, Maybelle just told me you think you've got Lou Owl down at Tapley's but you're mistaken. It's not him because he was just here. Came right through that door over there big as life." He could tell Walker was indulging his senior-ness, sitting there through layers of smoke like Buddha, letting him get on with grieving.

Finally Walker said, "I'm afraid it is him, Jordan. He must've, I don't know, got wiped out by a tree or something. All tore up and that. But it was him, right enough. Daughter ID'd the clothes he was wearing. Ring, everything. Poor kid, but she was brave, I'll say that for her. Erin's her name."

Tanner had to somehow acknowledge the truth and it was the ring that did it. It was their high school class ring. Lou had made a concession to only native jewelry by wearing it. His only acknowledgement of mainstream society and he wore it at his wedding, too. It almost did Tanner in. But neither Lou nor Walker would have approved of him grieving any other way than hanging one on.

"I'm sorry." Walker seemed to be working through something of his own. "I know you two were buddies and all. If it's okay, I'd like to share something with you that I've been having to work out by myself. See, I had the same experience you did when my brother died, killed in Afghanistan, and I didn't—I couldn't wrap my mind around it—the fact he was dead. I saw him just as I see you sitting here, I mean."

Through the shadows, Walker seemed more anguished than he was, and Tanner leaned back on the sofa, trying to make a connection between the pain of the living and the serenity of the dead. "I didn't know you had family, Quade."

Walker made a sound that could have been an ironic laugh or a grunt of pain. "He was it. My brother. Four years younger, football player, two years of college and he joins the army. He wanted to be like me, he said. Girlfriend would have to wait 'til he got back, he said. She got married to some dude two months after—after his unit got pinned down outside some little village. Rockie bought it after a house-to-house search for—never mind how. Anyway, I was back in the States undergoing treatment for shrapnel wounds when they told me.

But the funny thing was—I had just been talking to him in my hospital room."

Walker went on, saying how there wasn't a scratch on him. All dressed up in his uniform. He thought his brother was just visiting him on leave. "After they gave the news, I just couldn't take it in, you know? I thought they had the wrong guy. Talk about denial. Hell, I really fell apart after that. Drinking myself to death. Nothing to live for. We didn't have the same fathers, but we were brothers just the same."

Tanner's mind had been hijacked, however. He wandered, stranded on some barren island of the mind's making, in search of an escape route, a ship home to sanity. He found it in a Scotch blended whiskey bottle he had been saving for the birth of his grandson, or barring that, some momentous occasion. This was it and the baby wouldn't know the difference.

He poured two fingers neat for Walker and one for himself. "To your brother and to Lou. Both heroes. Both gone home."

Walker joined him and they finished the bottle in the twilight, talking and drinking until nothing they said made sense any more. People came and went as if to pay their respects or to ask questions of Walker, then realizing they had intruded on anguish, left quietly.

Walker spent the night on the porch in the old wooden swing, chintz cushions with ruffled flounces protruding beneath him as if he were some kind of scary Valentine. Tanner slept in the big leather recliner chair, Rollo beside him on the floor. All three of them snored at different intervals, making a noise "like my grandpa's old John Deere tractor," Maybelle said to Melissa who finally gave up and left, leaving her cell phone number in case Tanner had forgotten it.

"Best thing for them." Maybelle paused, listening at the kitchen door to the sound of whistling and sonorous inhaling. "Tomorrow'll bring its own set of troubles and a hangover that'll make them wish they'd died, too."

Chapter 31

There were several memorials in Julia in succeeding days. Meanwhile, ovens were heating up in spite of the June temperature and humidity to the chagrin of most of the male population. As casseroles, cakes, and roasts sent the thermostats into orbit, one-by-one the men lost the battle with economy versus the unhealthy Southern tradition of wakes, food for the grieving families, funerals, and memorial services.

On the issues of funerals and memorial services, The Blessed Water Baptist Church of Julia Springs was under siege.

As Dowager Queen of the Springs, Delia Clark's funeral was expected to rival that of Europe's crowned heads. The Clark's monuments already took up more than their share of the small cemetery just outside of town to the point that locals referred to it as Clarksville.

Not to be outdone, the Prescott family wanted Cole's re-assembled body to be interred on the same day as Delia's and threatened to withdraw their memberships, which numbered at least thirty people, from the small church if their demands were not met.

Finally, a peace agreement was worked-out that Delia's would be in the morning and Cole's would be in the afternoon.

Delia Clark's was attended by the dutiful Desmond and his kids and their families and a few ladies who were afraid she would come back to haunt them if they didn't. Members of the Winfield Foundation showed up in navy blazers and ivy league ties, but left right after the service.

"All of his life, Lou Owl had one foot in two cultures. Try as he might, and that wasn't hard, he didn't quite fit in with either of them." That was what Tanner said at his memorial service.

There was one to satisfy the white daughters-in-law at the Evangelical Word of God Church outside the city limits, at which members handled rattlers and moccasins to prove that God loved them, and that they were saved. The Methodists and Baptists who had turned up to watch the show, and eat the feast, did so furtively, as if they were afraid any minute a rattle snake would escape its cage and come after them, causing their faith to be put to the test.

Tanner gave a eulogy, praising the hero that had saved lives in raising the alarm about the washed out bridge. Behind him, the rattlesnakes shook their rattles in the cage rear of the blue velvet curtain as they warmed up to strike at anything that moved.

"I'm sure Lou would love being so close to danger," he told the mourners, "but I don't, and he knew that better than anybody. I can hear him laughing now as I get the hell—or heaven—out of here."

"Best words I ever heard at a funeral," said one good old boy. "I got to wishing I had brought in my shotgun in from the truck."

The native side of Lou was celebrated long into the night, in fact all night, until the orange sun came up and then for two days after that. Walker showed up for that one, and to Tanner's surprise, joined the dancers circling the huge bonfire. As he took his place among the swaying dancers, Walker looked more at peace than he had since Tanner had known him, as if he had made up his mind about something important.

Lewis Spencer had been reviled even before word was out about what he had done to Kenya. The quarry was where the entire population of the Springs thought Spencer was going to meet a fitting end, and a sense of fitting justice greeted the news as it spread around town.

The disposal of his body was another story. No one came forward to claim it, not even Spencer's wife. Pearlene Spencer wouldn't even put out a few dollars to bury him. "Throw him back in the damned quarry, good-for-nothin' that he was. Serve him right for putting my daughter in the family way. Regular damned goat, he was."

e⁄ɔe⁄ɔ

Out of habit, the sheriff scratched his bald patch, with an expression of surprise to find no hair. "I'll ask Mary Ann if we got discretionary funds for a situation like this. Usually, somebody'll claim the body. A relative or something."

"It's kind of hard to tell what he died of, seeing as he's such a damned mess." Newsome Tapley tried to keep the examination on track so he could get back home. "Between the buzzards and the quick lime, old Mother Nature done a number on him, I'm telling you. Skull's got a big hole in it, but that could have happened when he fell."

"In the back, ain't it?" His face screwed up against the odor, Sheriff Pierce leaned a little closer to the remains and pointed his ballpoint pen in the direction of the gap in the skull. "People generally fall forward, not backward."

"Unless he was standing with his back to the quarry and somebody shoved him backward or he lost his balance." Tapley was trying to stifle the impulse to laugh out loud at Pierce, who finally resorted to putting a hanky over his nose. "Anyway, he's been dead awhile. Happened about midnight two days ago, I'd say. I'm going to send for the forensic team to examine the skull for debris, just in case."

Dr. Morrison looked up from the corpse. "One funny thing about it, Mr. Tapley."

"Funny?" Tapley considered the young physician an upstart, not knowing anything but what he graduated with from medical school.

"I meant strange. Thing is, he and Delia Clark died the same way. Wound is just about in the same place. Back of the head. And there's no water in his lungs so he didn't drown. His neck is snapped like a matchstick. Only forensics can tell if that happened before he fell or when he landed thirty feet later. Plenty of boulders in that old quarry."

Walker shifted his weight from one scuffed boot to the other. "Somebody could've hit him from behind so he would fall, and Miss Clark, too. From what I hear, there are plenty around who had motives."

Anxious to get on the road, Richards stirred restlessly in the airless mortuary. "Hell, I'm just going to let forensics take over. Every death I've seen since I took office, they got run over by their own tractor or shot clean through with a bullet. I'm just going to put it down as death from a fall and wrap this buzzard bait up until forensics get here. Tapley, stick him back in your cooler 'til they come."

Newton Tapley III covered the body with a sheet. "I hate to get stuck with him. From what I heard, he fathered a kid with his step-daughter. Maybe she did him in."

"Hardly say I'd blame her," Tapley agreed.

"If nobody don't come forward, I say put him in Potter's Field and say a few words."

"Potter's Field?" Walker looked around at the others. "Where's that?"

"Wherever we got room." Chief Pierce put his hanky down and took control of the situation which surprised everyone, especially himself. "I'll get Root Woman to come over. She passes for a minister among the colored folk around here. She'll do her hoo-doo thing, throw in a few dried chicken's feet and we'll be done with his stinking corpse."

After the other men had left the morgue, Tapley pulled the body bag up over the corpse and slid it back into the bank of steel cabinets.

ε∽ε∽

Back in their office, Walker met Sheriff Pierce's pale blue gaze across the desk. "I didn't want to say this around Newsome because he'll just go down to the feed store and stir up a whole hornet's nest of wild talk. But ol' Spencer didn't fall down in no quarry and he didn't get pushed neither. His body was too far away from the quarry wall."

"What'd he do then? Fly down?"

"Damn near. There was so much stress and strain on his leg joints it damned near separated his feet from the upper part of his legs."

Pierce looked plain stupid for a moment. "Say what?"

"I mean, it looks like something picked him up by the ankles and slung him around like a cat by the tail then sent him a-flying into the quarry like a damn Frisbee."

"Ain't nobody that strong. Hell, Spencer was a big man, over six feet and close to 250 pounds."

"I know one thing, it wasn't that little step-daughter of his. She barely weighs a hundred pounds, poor little thing. Must be the same person that put Cole Prescott up in the pine tree." Walker's smile was ironic, but Pierce took him seriously.

"That's messed up, Q. You don't believe in that Chinaberry Man stuff, I know you don't."

Walker slipped his phone back in his shirt pocket and tuned to leave. "All I know is we would've kicked ass in Afghanistan if he'd been on our side."

❧❧❧

Nobody showed for Lewis Spencer's bleak service except his mother and sisters. They stood dry-eyed as his wooden coffin was lowered into the grave and turned away in a huddled group before the minister had finished reading the service. They said they were late for a graduation ceremony and Lewis was going to hell, anyway.

Chapter 32

Sometime that night or in the early hours of dawn, Tanner got a call. It was Sheriff Tinker Pierce, Jr. He asked Tanner to come over to the hospital in Macon. It seemed Quade Walker had tried to commit suicide—again.

"Is he dead?" Tanner had a flashback to Walker dancing the night before, that resolute look on his face.

"Almost, and I don't know why not. Missed his heart by a hair. Damn kid. I tried to tell him he had everything to live for once, in a friendly way, you know what I mean? But he has this monkey on his back, I guess from over there in the Middle East, something that he can't shake. I don't know what to do. Can you come? He thinks the world of you, Jordan. Like a father or something."

"I'll get dressed and be right over, and I'm bringing someone with me— someone *he* really thinks the world of."

❧❧❧

The Swamp was still soggy as Tanner made his way towards Lesbos, the orange light of dawn warned of raid lighting coming his way. He was stopped by the ever-vigilant guards in the towers as he rang the bell for entry.

"Who goes there?"

"It's me, Tanner. I'd like to see Miss Isis, please. It's an urgent—"

The door opened in the wall and Isis hurried out. She

looked fresh as day, clean, and, instead of robes, she was dressed in jeans and a tank top that matched her enormous blue eyes. "Yes, I know. It's Mr. Walker, isn't it?"

"I'm afraid so. He's in a bad way. Up in Macon at Memorial Hospital."

"Let's take my motor bike out of the Swamp. We can go faster that way. You left your truck at the end of the road? Hop on, I'll take you there."

"No thanks. My legs are too long for that little thing, but you go ahead. The keys are in the truck and he'd much rather see you than me. I think he loves you, Isis."

She bent her head as she slid her red helmet over her long hair. It fell loosely over her shoulders like tangible streamlets of sunrise. "I'm not worthy of his love, but if it heals him, he can have it."

With a smile, which made going without his morning coffee worth every moment, she zipped off, hardly making a dent in the damp earth.

He started back, but had only gone a few steps when he heard a familiar voice call his name.

"Mr. Tanner."

He turned to see Queen Sappho standing at the door. It was hard to tell if she was still in her nightclothes since she always wore long flowing robes.

"Hope I didn't wake you," he said, looking guilty. It was obvious he had. Like Isis, her hair wasn't braided yet. *Her handmaidens were probably still sleeping,* he thought.

"Would you like some coffee before you go? I believe the kitchen has some fresh eggs, too." He was dumbfounded. He, a male, was actually being invited into the inner sanctum for breakfast. His amazement must have been evident because Sappho smiled. "It's all right," she said. "All our shots are up-to-date."

"I thought you'd be angry with me for barging in like that, for getting Isis to go to Macon to see that boy in the hospital."

"Oh, we knew about it right after it happened," she said all-knowingly. In the enormous kitchen of the labyrinthine castle, Sappho personally poured coffee into a huge mug and helped them both to a plate of eggs, sausage, and grits.

"How is that?"

She placed the plate in front of him and poured herself a smaller cup. "That young man had something dark in his mind, a kind of cloud covering his thoughts. Suddenly, simultaneously, although we were in different rooms, we—Isis and I—sat straight up in bed last night. I dreamt he called Isis's name, and called and called. I thought he was outside and went to look, but at the same time, so was Isis. We met in the hall, looked directly into each other's eyes, and then it dawned on us—we both had the same dream! Except she had heard him very clearly say her name. She has a cell phone that she turns off at night, but it registers calls. He called exactly at one o'clock."

"Did he leave a message?"

Sappho shook her head. "No, but he didn't have to. She was afraid he would do something like that. She has the gift—she's a special girl, that one." She stirred her coffee. "You know Slade raped her when she was fourteen and she has a child, don't you?" Sappho waited for him to swallow his food and grab a sip of coffee to wash it down.

"No, I didn't. That's what she meant by she wasn't worthy of Walker's love, I guess."

"That and other things he did to her and the other girls." The laugh wasn't really a laugh, more like a sound people make when they're wounded. "Why is it the victim gets all the blame and, on top of that, self-loathing? Will you tell me that, Jordan Tanner?"

"I'm afraid I can't, Miss Sappho. I've never figured it out myself, but I do know it's the way things are—but pity can be just as bad. Isis doesn't want that, I know. And I don't think that boy Quade cares. He's in so much pain himself. Where's the child now?"

"Here. But he has problems we can't deal with, so I've made arrangements for him to get treated at an institution up by Atlanta. He has a congenital heart malfunction, among other things."

"I see. I'm sure that's the best thing for him." He didn't

know what else to say and she didn't expect him to. Tanner pushed his plate back and sipped his coffee. "That was a mighty fine breakfast. I appreciate it."

"You'll want to be getting up to Macon yourself shortly." Sappho took his plate to the sink and scraped it in a pail. "Take it to the pigs," she instructed a girl who was washing cloth napkins in the sink, "after the children have all eaten, of course."

"I'll be going then. It's a long walk back to the house." Tanner felt reluctant to leave the great kitchen with its red clay walls and wood-burning stove. Sunlight streamed down from the skylight overhead and a brown thrasher could be heard singing on a tree branch somewhere inside the compound. Beside him, Sappho smelled like a woman in the morning, of vanilla and musk and faintly of sandalwood.

The moment came to him like an unexpected gift. He was savoring it when she said, "You'll come again and be welcome. And Jordan, I heard your friend, Lou Owl, died during the storm, but I dreamt he passed by here on the way to your house yesterday. It wasn't unusual. He used to bring us fish he'd caught down at the creek, and sometimes fresh venison. Then I learned only his spirit was visiting. A breeze came up that shook some peaches off our trees. Then it went away as quickly as it had come." Sappho opened the great door to let him outside. "I think you were very close, almost like brothers."

A sudden wave of emotion gripped Tanner and he wasn't able to speak for a few minutes. Tears welled up in his eyes and he turned away.

"I know," she said, "I know," and closed the door.

Chapter 33

He walked back out of the Swamp, still enjoying being alive, breathing in the morning freshness filled with the faint odor of charred wood. When he reached the Jumping Off Place, his truck was where he had left it earlier, parked where the road ended. Isis had ridden the motorbike all the way into Macon.

He found her there beside Walker in ICU. His eyes were closed, but she was whispering to him earnestly some lovers' secret only meant for two to share. He didn't disturb them, but managed to snag a passing nurse who directed Tanner to inquire up at the nurse station for updates on patients' conditions.

There he encountered the surgeon who had operated on Walker. "Are you related to him?" the doctor asked.

"Cousin. How's he doing? Will he pull through?"

"This isn't the first time he's tried this, I take it. He's a vet and we're transferring him to the VA Hospital as soon as he's stable. Judging from the other scars he's got, he's been wounded by shrapnel and gun shots. I'll tell you...what was your name again?" Tanner told him. "I'll tell you straight. He's got to want to live, that's what it boils down to—something to live for. I've seen 'em with the best chances, just give up, and some, with nothing going for them but love, hang on and pull through. Shot up as he is—only he knows the answer to that question."

Tanner looked back at Walker's room where Isis had laid

her bright head beside his dark one. Her lips moved against his ear in earnest litany. Whatever she said got through the sedatives and, without opening his eye, Walker moved his hand in her direction. She covered it with hers, still whispering in his ear.

"I think he's going to pull through, doctor. In fact, I'm positive." Tanner was just about to leave when a familiar twang stopped him.

"Tanner, what's she doing here?"

He turned to see Tinker Pierce coming toward him, a scowl on his biscuit-colored face. No matter what time of day or night it was, Tinker always seemed to have a mouthful of something, or maybe it just looked like he did because his cheeks were so pudgy.

"Who do you mean?" Tanner faked complete innocence, knowing Pierce was easy to fool. All the local felons knew it, too, unfortunately. The district attorney's office would think they were going to throw the book at some three-time loser only to have Pierce let him slip from their grasp for lack of evidence.

"Her," the police chief said, jerking his head toward the room where Isis still lay beside Walker stroking his hand. "That's Slade's daughter in case you hadn't heard the story. The one he ra—molested, and he's got a child by her. Kid's nutty as his old man so they say."

"Looks like she's doing Walker some good. At least, he's responding to somebody. Doc said it's touch and go. Better touching than going, I'd say. And no family's showed up so far, not that he's got a whole lot around here."

"Listen, buddy, I think she's a slick little number. Walker told me yesterday she knew where those girls were all along. You ever think she could be just setting them up for her daddy?" Tinker dropped his voice when he talked about sex as if there was something lewd about the subject to be shared only among good old boys like himself. Tanner felt sorry for his wife who had a look of desperation all the time.

He couldn't resist teasing Pierce just to watch him squirm. "Setting them up? What are you getting at, Tinker?"

"You know, he had a harem and a gillion children. They say he liked young girls, the younger the better."

"All I know is we wouldn't have found them without her. And you know what she called her father? Pigshit. I don't think she had anything but contempt for him. When Walker came along, she was trying to figure out a way to get them out of there. She would have led us right to them except Walker had a bout of malaria or whatever it was. And half the Swamp was on fire, if you remember."

"Well, why not tell me? I'm the law. Haven't they got phones out there?"

"'Fraid not. Computers. No phone."

Pierce sidled closer and dropped his voice to a confidential level. "Is it true they've got a regular castle out there the women built themselves? No telling what goes on in there. I wouldn't be surprised if they were all lesbians."

"In that case, Isis wouldn't be interested in procuring young girls for her father, would she?"

The chief looked at Tanner, confusion crossing and re-crossing his face as he tried to rationalize the two conflicting statements and failed.

"Guess not," he said finally. Pierce straightened up and adjusted his belt to rest below his paunch. "Well, guess I'll go have a chat with the doc as to when it's okay to question Quade. He said something about footprints around the quarry in his report last night. Said they might have belonged to a woman. Oh, and by the way, Jordan, if anybody asks you, just say Walker was wounded by a prowler. Don't want word getting around about...you know what I mean." Pierce put the word suicide in the same taboo category as sex. "You heard we found old Slade, hanging way up in a tree, just like that poor ol' Prescott kid. 'Cept he was pretty much together, Slade was. Can't figure out how he got that far up the tree, but it don't matter much. All we have to do is bury the sucker. Saved the State a pile of money."

Tanner watched Tinker Pierce, Jr. walk away with a slight swagger the way his father used to walk. But instead of looking big and bad the way his father had, on a little man like Junior, the same sway of the shoulders actually looked comical.

Tanner stepped out into a ripening summer morning. Life had never seemed more kind to him. He felt as though he had lived at least nine lives, each as distinct from the other as if they belonged to other people. In his youth, he had taken risks, as if there were no tomorrows, but there were tomorrows and this was his. He longed to tell that young man lying in the ICU that there were reasons for surviving. Then he remembered when he didn't care either, and decided to let Walker find out for himself. He was inhaling the odor of flowering Bradford pear trees that marched around the ground in well-measured paces when his phone rang. It was Melissa Bullock sounding artificially sweet, but the underlying tone was anxious.

"I finally caught you sober! Good! 'Cause I'm inviting you to dinner at six tonight. Be there or be square. And don't say you're busy. I checked with Reggie and you're not."

"I'm not and I haven't heard anyone say square in forty years. Did your significant other cancel? And since when is Reggie privy to my social calendar?"

The comeback was light as the white pear blossoms pooling up below the trees. "I don't have a significant other—yet. Dress is casual."

"What else have I got?"

"See you at six. And don't think of any more excuses not to be alone with me. I've got a suite for two at the Caracas Hilton booked for a week from tomorrow—for two whole weeks, in case we want to stay that long."

She hung up and he was suddenly back in the world, as it existed for other people. People like Melissa who had a social calendar and made entries like "Thompsons for cocktails and possibly dinner." Frenchy's world who demanded a man by her side, clever conversation, keeping in touch, presents at Christmas, cards at birthdays, and just for fun, and closeness. Above all, closeness. Closeness as Frenchy defined it was not the kind he and Lou had known, a male thing.

No, with Melissa it was an arm around her narrow waist, a lingering look, an occasional kiss on the lips for all her single friends, and reliability. After a lifetime of being unreliable,

Tanner decided to give it a try. *What the hell, reliability couldn't be that bad.*

☙☙☙

That evening, he was as prompt as he had ever been, which was forty-five minutes late. "Sorry, I didn't realize Rollo was out of kibble and I got buttonholed by Chief Pierce as I was leaving Whitehead's General, and you know how that is…"

Tanner had trotted out his old, white, linen blazer for the occasion only to find one of two buttons missing, and the bottom one was snug, but wore it anyway with his shirt open at the neck and black loafers that even Caroline had a hard time with.

"For one thing, they could use a good polishing and for another, one has a tassel and the other one doesn't," she would say, whereupon he had pulled off the remaining tassel and torn the leather off with it.

Melissa, however, knew enough not to be picky about small stuff. She would straighten it out by simply buying him a complete wardrobe, shoes and all. A maid showed him into the grand drawing room of Bulloch Hall where light and music and the sound of dozens of people making scintillating conversation nearly drove him back out through the front door.

But Melissa, in a plunging turquoise halter dress that dared anyone to guess her age, pinned him in the spotlight, seizing his arm and pulling him down to whisper in his ear, "Can't wait 'til we're alone and can actually hear."

Rich and beautiful women like Melissa didn't believe the word "no" was meant for them. She reminded him so much of his first wife, Francesca, who, like Melissa, was raised by an indulgent parent and took it for granted that she would get her way.

He drank too much, ending up in Melissa's enormous four-poster bed snoring away with his hostess nestled beside him as if she had always belonged there. He was glad to be part of the world again.

Chapter 34

S he has seizure disorder. It could disappear or if the episodes get close together and more severe, it could get
worse. We'll put her on a trial of medication and see
how she responds." Dr. Morrissey gave the EEGs a final
glance before facing the McFarland women, especially Joy, the
patient's cousin, whose onyx eyes met his, asking for honesty.
"That accounts for her recent episodes of blacking out, seeing
things, and so on. She's not going crazy by any means. Probably brought on by situational stress."

There was a collective sigh of relief among the ladies
seated in front of his desk.

The patient's mother, Maureen Kelly, an angular, attrac-
tive woman with red hair and critical green eyes said, "I hope
you don't object, Doctor, if we get copies to take up to special-
ists in Atlanta. Second opinion and all that?"

"Aunt Maureen, don't make a big deal out of it. He said
Ginny's okay. I would think that's enough. We don't want to
upset her anymore. She's upset enough over the storm."

"And I suppose you mean over her imaginary boyfriend
getting killed, don't you? That's what I mean by not being
normal. It's her flights of fancy that worry me, Doctor. She
thought this terrorist fellow was coming to see her—her personally. Never mind that he was some Russian spy who threatened to blow the railroad bridge up. Good thing they killed
him before he got loose around town. No telling what he
would have done."

"Police Chief Pierce said later he thought they had made a mistake by killing him. Said he listened to the message again and he thought the man said the bridge was going to collapse. Chief said the SWAT team took the tape as evidence they'd killed the right man and told him not to tell anyone." Joy looked from her aunt to her mother and, finding no comfort in either one, at Morrissey.

"I notice he didn't mind that order," Maureen said wryly.

Mildred wiped a tear away and made an attempt to join the meeting. "Said they went off half-cocked because he was a foreigner."

But Morrissey and Joy were still looking at each other, each thinking something different.

They had both witnessed the state Ginny had been in at the fire and Joy had remembered she was babbling about some man who worked for a company in Atlanta whose shipment was going over the old bridge. Some man she had called Vadim.

"I think there's a possibility she's right, poor little thing." Joy said it with such conviction, even Maureen didn't contradict her.

"Have the police interviewed her?" Morrissey felt an attraction to this young woman who believed in the validity of her own opinions. It didn't hurt that she was very pretty with her black eyes and wavy black hair falling to her shoulders. But he was semi-engaged to a nurse, shared a bed on weekends at her place in Atlanta when he could get away. Still, it didn't hurt to admire her looks and the direct way she spoke up. No Southern beating around the bush, just out there.

"No, and they're not going to." Maureen answered again—slim as an explanation point and just as emphatic. "I won't have my daughter dragged into this mess. Especially with the oldest one causing a scandal. This is a small community, doctor. Word travels like wildfire— forgive the pun. I won't lay this on my sister's family. They have to live here."

At that, Mildred who had remained quiet and tearful all throughout the appointment burst out angrily. "What happened to Megan is not our fault! She's always been a willful child and if she's pregnant, she knew what she was doing. That's all there is to it."

Megan's pregnancy was a subject that had lain just below the surface of small talk ever since Maureen had learned of their elopement across the river to Alabama the night of the storm. Stung by the allegation that her daughter was somehow morally defective, she countered the attack. "Well, if you had been stricter with her, it never would have happened in the first place."

"Oh, well, that's good coming from you! Why did you leave them with us then, instead of taking them to Atlanta with you? Because it would cramp your style, Maureen. That's why!" Mildred's resentment toward her sister boiled to the surface in spite of her determination not to let it come between them. She had married a farmer and not only raised two children of her own, but after Maureen and her husband had split up, her two nieces as well.

Maureen had taken a glamorous job up in Atlanta with an advertising firm and, citing as her reason "...so as not to disturb Megan's promising music career with the Mercer School of Music," left the girls with the McFarlands. But Mildred knew mother and daughter were alike in their headstrong approach to life. Megan, even from the beginning, was hard to manage—always teasing her younger sister, running with the privileged crowd at school, called into the principal's office for breaking rules.

All this the McFarlands had borne with grace—after all, she *had* been deprived of her father and mother. But sex before marriage and causing a scandal they would have to face every time they went to church or sewing club or even the post office! That was cause for sharp words.

The doctor was accustomed to family scenes in his general practice and sat back in his chair, glancing at the clock. Joy, on the other hand, was mortified. "This is about Ginny, not Megan, for once. If we could just finish up here and let the doctor get on to his next appointment."

Maureen jumped up abruptly. "If you'll just send the X-rays, or whatever they are, up to Emory, I'll make an appointment with a specialist up there. Thank you for your time, Doctor." She pivoted on one high heel and left the office.

Mildred dabbed at her eyes with a tissue, and then put it back in her handbag. "Guess you're privy to a lot a family secrets, Doctor Morrissey. I apologize for intruding on your time with our troubles."

"How far along is your niece's pregnancy, Mrs. McFarland? The reason I ask is, she must have told her sister before it was revealed to her mother, and this might have some bearing on her condition—Gina's, I mean."

"I never thought of it that way." Mildred's round face crumpled again. "Poor little Gina. Megan must have forced her not to tell. I wouldn't put it past her. Oh, she's a schemer, that one."

Joy who had been thinking of Ginny's odd behavior lately—wearing that T-shirt about premarital sex, concerns about her behind and dressing up for school—remained thoughtful. She got to her feet, and held out her hand. "We've taken enough of your time, Doctor Morrissey."

He stood up and took her hand. "Not at all, Miss McFarland. I'd like to see Gina in a couple of months, that is if she doesn't have any more episodes. Here, I've written her a prescription for seizure prevention. I hope it does the trick."

"I'm sure it will, if we can just stop this bickering and see that she has a good time this summer, she'll be back to normal in no time." They were still clasping hands and she slowly withdrew hers. "Come for dinner next time you're down our way, won't you?"

It was just something country people say, but he jumped at the chance. "Do you mean that? Because I have to come down there tomorrow. I'm opening an office in Julia Springs with two other associates. We went to Emory together, sort of buddies, if you know what I mean."

Before Joy could say anything, Mildred interrupted. "Bring them along, too. The only place in town to get something decent is Sara's Place, and that's just barbeque. Guaranteed to give you heartburn that won't quit."

"Can I call you? About whether we can make it or not?"

It was meant for Joy and he hoped it didn't come across as too obvious.

But Mildred didn't have a clue about subtly. "Sure, you can. Joy will give you our number. The more that merrier, I always say." She went out into the lobby, blowing her nose, where Maureen was ordering the EEGs sent up to Atlanta.

"You know that dinner means lunch and supper means dinner down here." Joy handed him her business card. "It has my cell phone. Give me a call if y'all can come out. Anytime is fine."

"'Joyful Noise.' What's this? You're an entrepreneur?"

"Doctor, your next patient is here," came over the intercom.

"Just something I do on the side. See ya." She hurried out to join the others in the lobby, passing the nurse who gave her the onceover as she passed.

"She's very pretty," said the nurse, putting the patient's chart on his desk, "in a country kind of way, of course. That why you want to open an office way out in Julia Springs?"

"Might be, and the fact that I have a growing practice out there. Who've we got now?"

The nurse droned on about the patient's vital signs while Morrissey watched Joy McFarland in the waiting room. She was talking to her mother, rather listening and nodding her dark head, then, as though she was sharing his thoughts, she turned and looked back at him. They exchanged a smile and a lingering look until the nurse closed the door with unusual force.

Chapter 35

Walker mended quickly. He was accustomed to pain and bore it without any other comment than a strained look on his face. For three days, Isis slept in his room or one of the break rooms at the packed VA Hospital. Occasionally, one of the residents of Lesbos brought her a change of clothes and asked when she was returning home.

"When he gets well," she said, looking at Walker who stirred restlessly in his morphine-induced sleep.

But Walker was in for the long haul. He told the doctors the gun went off by accident when he was drunk and asleep—grabbing it in a PTSD nightmare about the Taliban overrunning their position.

They didn't believe him and put him on suicide watch until the unit got too full. Then they assigned outpatient therapy and discharged him, giving Isis a list of symptoms to watch for. There was no question that he wouldn't go home without Isis. He didn't even have to ask. Walker saw it in her eyes.

She settled into his snug apartment, the upstairs of Mrs. Booth's place, as if she'd always been there. The downstairs remained empty since the old lady was in a nursing home. To Isis, it was the grandest place she had ever been, with flush toilets and central heating. For the man who had brought her there, making all this possible, she had a kind of reverent worship, a devotion that was like a religion with its own liturgy and its own practice. They would lie in each other's arms at the end of each beautiful day, each longing for more intimacy but fearing to test the shimmering bubble that captured them.

When he asked her to marry him, she said, "We don't have to. I think it's better if we don't."

"I'm afraid I'll lose you, so it's a selfish reason, see—and I don't think I can make it without your love." He brushed back the glistening curtain of hair that half veiled her face.

"Is it so hard to say you love me?" She leaned over him, her long, pale hair like a waterfall of light fibers all around her shoulders. "Is it?"

"More that life itself," he answered. "That's what you are to me. Life." He told her about meeting Lou Owl in the woods just before she had found him so ill that night. "There was something familiar about him, like I knew him from some-where. I went to his funeral and I don't even know why. I was surprised to see my Uncle Gabe there. Seems they had known each other because they had worked at the same place. That's when Gabe told me the truth. Lou Owl was my father."

Isis traced the wounds on his face. "I knew Mr. Owl. He would have been so proud of you. He was a soldier, and brave, too, my mother said. He once beat up my father when he beat one of my brothers so bad they had to take him to the hospital. He was one tough old man."

"But I knew he was going to die that night. I felt it, like…I don't know what you call it."

"Premonition?" Isis smiled her archaic smile. "I have those, too. In fact, I knew you were coming because I saw you in a dream."

"You did?" He looked at the girl in his arms, as if she were a vision liable to vanish any minute.

"Well, continue," she said, seeing the adoration in his eyes.

"I tried to talk him out of going on, but he wouldn't listen. Oh, God, there was so much I would like to have asked him. Like why he never claimed me. Why my mother had to marry that bastard just to give me a name. But I remember when he said goodbye. He said my first name. "Bye, Quade," he said."

"Maybe she didn't tell him. Maybe she kept it a secret. Women do, you know. Keep secrets from their children."

"That's what my Uncle Gabe said. Because he wasn't white like her, she was ashamed of sleeping with him. And he was much older than she was. I called her up and she told me she had always wanted to forget about the whole thing. That she just needed some loving that night and he was drinking with my uncle. So I was the result of a one-night stand. I told her his funeral was tomorrow and she said, "Good." Then she hung up on me."

Isis laid her bright head on his chest. "You have me now."

"I don't need anyone else, if that's really true," he said, stroking her hair. "I just need you. You are my world now."

ເ⁄ຈເ⁄ຈ

Meanwhile, one of the part-time deputies, Petey Martin, had to fill in. His ineptitude—although he was legally correct—drove everyone crazy, including Chief Pierce who had to undo all the messes he made. Martin gave a parking ticket to one of the Winfields who had double-parked his Cadillac outside the hair salon. He was inside getting his hair cut when he looked out and there was Martin writing a slew of tickets. Martin then had the Health Department inspect Sara's Place, scoring a whopping fifteen violations, closing the place for a week. Pierce got them to rescind the most negligible so people could get something to eat without having to drive halfway to Macon.

Finally, he called Walker. "I can't stand anymore. Get your tail back here so I can get rid of this moron. He's driving me to drink. And oh, by the way, I passed the word around town that Slade shot you when you rescued those girls. Just to cover any gossip about you and that girl, Ice or whatever her name is."

The next day while Walker was at work, Isis left for Lesbos.

She left a note. It said, *I can't live in your world where people judge you by what you are instead of who you are. I am not my father's daughter. I am Isis becoming a person. I can't give you all the love you need. I have my mother, my sisters,*

and my brothers to protect. I love you and always will. Good-
bye, Isis.

His day turned to night. He was a man groping in the
dark, trying to find his way through each and every hour. He
read rejection in every line she had written. How could he believe she could love a loser like him? His mind turned to darker thoughts. She was just making sure she wouldn't be charged
with obstructing justice or being an accomplice to kidnapping.

Walker buried himself in his work. There was nothing
else to live for. He became rough and bitter, drinking himself
to a coma every night.

The case of Reverend Slade made the news as the GBI
and FBI took over excavating his weird compound searching
for the bodies of missing girls. They came by the McFarland
Farm to interview Gina and Caroline, who held hands and
would not be separated.

Gina did most of the talking. "No, he didn't do anything
to us, but he was going to. We barricaded the cellar door to
give us time to tunnel out. I think he had kept somebody else
down there because we found food and stuff. I knew we had to
make a break for it and so we tunneled out."

The third day of their investigation, the agents discovered
Lesbos. "What in the hell is this, a motel in the middle of the
jungle?" They looked at Walker who looked as though he
wanted to be anyplace but outside Isis' front door.

He covered up his apprehension with a shrug. "There's all
kinds of places out in these woods. Some are nice and some
are just ramshackle huts strung together. Depends on who lives
there," he said, trying to appear nonchalant.

"Who lives in here?" asked a female agent. She was a
bottle blonde who wore a weapon on her hip and was sweating
slightly in the June heat. It made her dark roots even darker.
"Snow White and the Seven Dwarves?"

"Just women and children, that's all. No men, far as I
know."

Her attitude told him he was just a dumb local cop, who
might even have a connection to one of these ladies, probably
as a customer from the looks of the place. "That's informative.

These ladies have a name and means of support, or do they do guided tours for a living?"

At that moment, one of the guards, still pulling on her Kevlar vest, called out from the tower to their left, "Halt! Who goes there?"

All three agents reached for their guns and badges simultaneously, until Walker, fearing a shootout, called, "It's just Deputy Walker and some friends. We just wanted to speak to Miss Sappho, if it's convenient. That's all. If you would please tell her we're out here?" He dropped his voice to a rough whisper. "Put your guns away, damn it. That's all we need."

As one, the agents took their hands off their hips, but got their ID's ready. They glanced at their leader, the blonde, who nodded approval, but rolled her eyes at Walker.

"Looks like the dwarves are packing heat these days."

Walker ignored her, walking to the tower so the agents strained to hear what he was saying to the guards above. "Look, they just want to ask a few questions, okay? Ask Sappho if she would come on out here, please. I promise they only want to ask a few questions, is all."

But that wasn't all the Feds wanted. When Sappho came to the door, smiling graciously, the agents demanded to be admitted.

With a show of badges and a search warrant, they launched a search of the premises, rounding up the occupants out of bed where they shuffled out into the bright sunlight. Isis stepped out of the kitchen where she was preparing lunch to see what the commotion was about.

When she saw Walker, she gave him such a look of pain, he felt wounded all over again.

"Is this your doing? Your revenge? I thought you, of all people would understand!" Without waiting for a reply, she turned around and slammed the kitchen door.

"That girl is hiding something," the blonde leader said to the other two agents who were standing nearby trying to make conversation with the children. "Find out what it is." One of them ran up to the closed door and hammered on it.

"Open up, please!" Before he could repeat the knock, the

door opened. This time it was Holly who opened it. Kenya stood beside Isis, who had her arm around the girl's thin shoulders.

"I expect you want to see us." Holly turned and indicated the younger girl. "About Lewis Spencer and how he ended up in the quarry."

Chapter 36

"T ell me about your boyfriend. Was he sweet to you?" Caroline asked Gina.

They were sitting beside the pool, drinking sodas and pretending they enjoyed burning up in the late June sun. Both girls looked milk white compared to the other brown ones frolicking in the pool. Caroline was uncomfortable at first without her clothes, but she held a towel in front of her skimpy swimsuit that Megan had outgrown.

"Very. He brought me flowers. Candy. Once he even picked blackberries and fed them to me one by one. He was so funny. He said that made a blackberry smile that wouldn't go away even if I was sad."

Caroline looked up in Gina's face from her deck chair. "And did he ever make you sad?"

Gina glanced over at the girl she had come to regard as her little sister. Around town, they were the girls who had escaped from Slade's captivity, which had a tinge of notoriety to it. In spite of an outward show of thanksgiving at the churches around Julia Springs, there were always questions in the back pews. *Wonder what he did to those girls? You know he didn't leave them alone, especially that twelve-year-old. Now, the McFarland girl, she's a feisty one and would've put up a fight, but that Caroline's just a child, and you know what perverts like him do to children.*

"The reason I'm asking is 'cause I've never really had a boyfriend. My mama just runs them off." Caroline looked at

Gina under her lashes, shielding her eyes from the July sun. "I hope you don't think I'm being nosey or anything."

Gina shook her head and continued staring at the swimming pool shimmering in the sun like a mirage. "That's okay. Only when he left. Only when he left."

Caroline thought that over, and then asked, "Will he ever come back, do you think?"

"Only in my dreams. See, he's dead, Caroline. Someone—they killed him."

Caroline stared at the puddle of water splashed up on the poolside by some boys doing cannonballs off the diving board. "My brother died that way, too. Somebody shot him dead outside the liquor store up on the highway. He was only twenty at the time, stacking boxes in the dumpster to earn some money. They robbed the till and then, as they were leaving, they ran into Ronnie. He must've tried to run away because they shot him in the back, right through the heart. My mother ain't been right since it happened."

Gina took her eyes away from the bright glare on the water refracting into tiny diamonds of light, over and over, as the boys dove from the high board. For a moment, she looked at the girl beside her, drawing hearts with finger in the puddle beside her chair. She opened her mouth then closed it and broke into a sob. She turned over on her belly so people wouldn't see and adjusted her big sunhat so it shaded her face. She looked so ugly when she cried, she didn't even want Caroline to see her, but Caroline got up and sat beside her, stroking her freckled shoulders as they shuddered with sobs.

"There, look what I done," she said, her thin voice barely rising above the boys' raucous shouts of laughter. "I didn't mean to make you sad. That's how Mama does when we start talking about how 'Ronnie used to do this' and 'he used to say that,' just cries and cries. But I say, just remember the good times and not the bad. Don't do no good, anyway. Won't bring him back. Just makes the heart ache, that's all. You got to do something about it. A good thing to wipe out the bad one."

Gina raised her head. Her nose was streaming and she wiped her face on her beach towel. She didn't care who saw what a mess she was. Let them gawk and talk, that's all they did, anyway. She was almost glad Maureen was putting her in some Catholic girl's school up in Atlanta.

"It's so unfair that he died trying to save the town. He was doing something good and got killed for it."

The painfully thin Caroline, with her wispy blonde hair and pale eyes, presented a sharp contrast to red-haired, red-faced Gina with her softly rounded curves. Yet there was a bond growing between them that began with their harrowing adventure, but had matured beyond that to shared losses and a feeling of trust.

"Then he's got a crown in heaven and he'll take his place at the Lord's Table with all the heroes, gone before him, who died doing something good."

Sitting up, Gina looked out at the pool again. It was calm again and the afternoon sun looked like butter melting across its flat surface. The lifeguard was talking to the boys, telling them they were disturbing the other swimmers and, if they cannonballed one more time, they could get dressed and go home.

She turned to the girl beside her, who like her, was mesmerized by the pool of light. "Then we'll have to try, too. Do something good, wipe out the bad. Pinkie promise."

Caroline crooked her little finger and held it up for Gina to see. "Pinkie promise."

"I lied about Vadim. I said he brought flowers and candy. That was a big lie and I'm sorry for it. He wasn't even my boyfriend yet, but I just knew he would be."

"That's all right. He would have brought flowers and presents if he lived. You got to remember that. Oh, lord, that lifeguard looks like he's coming this way. Wipe your nose again and smile pretty."

"You sound like my mother."

They were laughing when the lifeguard stopped at the foot of their lounge chairs. "Hey, Gina. Glad to see you're okay and all. A lot of people got hurt in the storm and brush fire around town." He was a tall, muscular boy who had graduated last year, but she couldn't remember his name.

"Yeah, we're okay, thanks. And thanks for stopping those boys from acting up. They were soaking everybody and scaring the little kids."

"Yeah, I told them not to come back without an adult to supervise them. So what are you doing this summer?"

She smiled and sat up, pulling on her cover-up because she was getting pink across the shoulders. "Just hanging out. This is my friend, Caroline. I'm sorry, I know your face, but I can't remember your name. I'm really rotten with names."

She squinted up at him shading her eyes. His blond hair glistened in the sun. For a moment, it seemed Vadim had come back to life like Jesus rising from the dead.

"I am, too. It's Victor. Just call me Vic, though. Victor Albright. My mom graduated in the same class as your uncle. They go way back, those two. Well, I got to back to work or I'll get canned. Can't be seen talking to girls, especially cute red-heads. The guy who runs the pool complains about every little thing. I'd love to talk to you some more, though."

"Sure. Any time." In her own ears, her voice sounded flat, surreal like an echo down a tunnel. It matched the whole situation, like Cole Prescott standing in the azalea bushes after he was dead.

"I'll take that as a 'yes.' Nice to meet you, Caroline. I knew your brother. Nice guy. Well, see you." They watched him walk around the pool and climb up in the guard's chair. Neither girl spoke for a long time, each thrown back into the sad past.

"Let's go. I could use something to drink." With a rush of energy, Gina slid on her flip-flops and gathered up her sunscreen and towel.

Caroline scrambled to follow her. Victor Albright saluted them from his post, but neither one saw him. Gina tried breathing deeply once she got to the truck, but the heat had sucked all the available oxygen out of the air. The truck was like an oven even though they had put up the sunshade. She opened the door, started the motor, turned the air conditioning full blast. Orange balls of light were going off in front of her eyes, her breath left her body, and then everything went black.

Chapter 37

Jordan Tanner went to Melissa's party the first night she invited him, and to subsequent ones at Bulloch Hall—which turned out to be part of her plan for *his* life. The other was to be part of *her* life—which she had stated from the day they had bumped into each other earlier in the summer.

It was melon season now and the air was just as sweet and juicy as the ripening fruits lying under the vines in the fields.

He was feeling a return of simple lust, at first brought on by Melissa's plunging cocktail gowns—which left nothing to the imagination—and then by her intimate little touches, placing her hand on his buttocks while they were dancing, playing footsies, and caressing his inner thighs under the table. That is, until he got over the shock and started to rather enjoy himself.

Then he realized where she was steering him, right into a political career and over a virtual cliff as far as he was concerned.

To his amazement, one night a former senator asked him if he were available to be appointed to an interim spot left vacant by the death of the incumbent. He was so drunk he would have agreed to anything, even serving in a government that had once seen him thrown down three flights of marble stairs in the state capitol building for punching the governor.

The reality sank in once he was sober. He could have been shot where he stood, except the governor—a weasel from a succession of weasels, put in office by a well-oiled political machine—knew Tanner knew too much and probably had all the information stored away somewhere in cyber-space to be released like so many guided missiles. So, instead, he was discredited by a secret power cable which passed the word everywhere Tanner sought employment: universities, news organizations, even high schools. Jordan Tanner, war hero and crusader for the underdog, was a commie and a gay one at that.

His father-in-law, Bancroft Murphy, had died so he couldn't go back to work for the local newspaper, making peanuts. So he went back down to Julia Springs to run the Winfield Foundation and live off his wife's substantial inheritance. Carolyn was always uncomplaining and practical.

"You know, you've been avoiding the obvious, Jordan, dear," she said, bustling around the kitchen putting everything in order, including his life. She was always doing three things at once. He found that annoying since he could do only one, and then only if no one interrupted him.

"What, that I'm washed up? Seems that's been thrown in my face so many times even I got it."

"Oh, stop feeling sorry for yourself and listen to me." When she got that tone, he knew she meant business especially since she stopped straightening things and came over to him. "Has it ever occurred to you that your family needs you? This farm needs you and this community, too. Bloom where you're planted and stop trying to relive the past. Move on, darling."

He had taken her advice and settled for life on the front porch. Until now, when he'd been offered a chance to get back in the game by the very people who had thrown him out fifteen years ago. In his role as an elder statesman, maybe he could do some good.

Melissa had a different take on the position. "Look, honey, you got your sweet skinny ass kicked a long time ago. This is your chance to kick theirs. Don't tell me you've lost all that fire down under because I, for one, know better. I'm behind you and beside you 100%, if you want me. Daddy always said you'd make a name for yourself, so don't make him a liar."

"I did make a name for myself and it was mud, remember? After he said my first wife was nothing but a whore. Anybody would have done the same."

"No, not anybody," she said, moving so close to him that he could feel every curve in her slim body, "Only a true champion of justice like you. Besides, that old man needed punching out if anyone ever did. He was a nasty old thing—tried to feel me up at a campaign party, not once but twice. Oh, please tell Senator Trip you'll take him up on the offer. Pretty please?"

The face she offered up to be kissed was so appealing, he could see why Melissa always got her way—she offered herself with it. She was like Frenchy that way, all or nothing. That's how Southern girls of that class were taught to bend the rules of society. He wasn't equipped to resist that kind of pressure. Few men were.

"Okay, what can it hurt to take this interim appointment? I'll just sit there in session, looking dumb as a board anyway."

She kissed him long and hard. "No, you won't. You'll vote the party line, be a team player, and when the position comes up in the next election, you'll be a shoo-in."

That was the catch he knew was hidden in all this talk of a new start and kicking ass. There was always a catch. He should have known.

Chapter 38

Walker, Holly, and Kenya were parked in Walker's SUV outside the Frosty Freeze on the main highway.

"I think you ought to let Miss Kenya speak for herself," he said.

Walker had driven the two girls all the way up to the highway to get them hot fudge sundaes and himself a coffee. He knew that would put the two at ease, so he could get them to talk.

Kenya looked like she didn't know what to do with it, but Holly dug in as if she had been deprived of sweets. Then she looked up, spoon midway to her mouth, when he added, "Then you can tell me about your boyfriend, Tony, that right?"

Holly put the plastic spoon back down, stilled heaped with a bite of chocolate ooze. "Yeah, that's right. What do you want to know?"

Either she was playing dumb or she didn't know the guy had a rap sheet full of misdemeanors and the army had finally kicked him out without pay. Walker was taking a gamble that she didn't know. After all, guys in fatigues and desert boots were all over the place.

Hunters got desert camouflage outfits from supply stores, until South Georgia resembled a state under martial law. Add a smooth storyline, a little plastic flashed around, possibly even a flashy car, and presents…

What was a small-town girl like Holly, living with her

grandmother, supposed to think? He was a change from the hicks around Julia Springs.

"Be thinking about what you want to tell me. Right now, Miss Kenya, you're supposed to eat that stuff before it melts all over you." In spite of the fact his job brought all kinds of heartbreaking situations with it, Walker couldn't help a surge of pity for this girl-child who sat with a hot fudge sundae looking like it was some kind of bomb about to go off in her lap.

She took a tentative bite of ice cream and pleasure lit up her pensive face. "That's good," she said and took three successive spoonfuls. Then she put down her spoon and refastened the plastic covers. "I'm going to save the rest for Frederick. He loves ice cream."

"Silly, it doesn't save. You go on and finish it and we'll bring Frederick here when I get my driver's license." Holly looked at Walker like a fellow conspirator. "What are you going to do with somebody like this child? She's barely used an inside toilet, much less had a hot fudge sundae before."

Walker started up the SUV. "She's lucky she has you to look out for her."

"Where're you taking us now? Jail?" Holly reached for Kenya's free hand. "Don't we get a lawyer first?"

Walker almost smiled behind his sunglasses. She was edgy about something. "Why? Have you done anything to go to jail for? You'd better tell me if you have. Makes my job a lot easier."

"Okay, I admit I told Tony a lot about the house—Miss Delia's house. I said it got creepy at night because the carport door didn't lock good, and that she kept a lot of money in there. I wouldn't even go downstairs if I heard a noise, not even to get something to eat. He asked me a lot of questions about stuff. I can't remember exactly what. When he asked me to go out to dinner and dancing, well, how could I say no? Nobody's ever asked me in all the years I've been dating. He said he'd buy me a dress and shoes, you know, the works. How was I supposed to know Mrs. Wilkes couldn't stay? She always fills in for me, or Reverend Clark, or even Mrs. Clark, although she didn't get along with Grannie Clark. That's what I called her, Grannie Clark. She loved it, but wouldn't admit it."

"Did you know this guy, Tony, had a record for a bunch of stuff, including breaking and entering?"

Holly's eyes widened with sudden realization. "He was with me all night. It couldn't have been him."

"He had a buddy who was a real burglar do it. We even found some of the jewelry he tried to fence over in Macon. The police are questioning Tony and, from what I hear, these guys make a routine out of learning where the goodies are kept in big houses like the Clark's and fancy hotels by chatting up the maids that work there."

Holly's eyes filled with tears and she covered her face. "I can't believe that I am that stupid. Here I was giving all the answers he needed and he wasn't giving me anything but a line."

"Don't be too hard on yourself. It happens. You aren't the first person to want to believe somebody really cared for them or that it would last."

He looked so sad for a moment that Holly stopped being afraid of him. "You're talking about Isis, aren't you?"

"Among others, yeah." Walker pulled out of the parking lot and on to the highway which led to the Thicket. "Better finish that," he said. "It's starting to melt all over the place."

Kenya, who had been licking her spoon and scraping up the last vestiges of ice cream, put her bowl down on her knees. "I didn't kill my step-daddy. I meant to, 'cause he tried to get me to go with him. I was fighting him and he fell down and I got away. I heard him yelling like he was hurt, but I didn't look back. I just kept running 'til I reached Mrs. Queen Sappho's place. I hoped he died though, after what he done to me. I hope he's in hell."

"I figured. The quarry was pretty messed up what with firefighters having to shelter there and all. But there was a girl's footprints there, and I followed them and met Isis. Was she waiting for you?" The memory flooded back, bringing her presence with it. He pictured Isis standing in the woods with a lantern the night of the fire—it was carved into his memory like the scars on his body.

"No, that was way before, like two or three days. My grandmother, Kahalia, she sent me out to pick blackberries by the quarry and me and Frederick was filling up buckets to make jam. All of a sudden, Lewis Spencer, he popped up out of the bushes and grabbed me. He was like high or something 'cause he was saying all his troubles was owed to me, that I told on him and he was going to kill me before I could testify. Then he started dragging me to the quarry, saying all the time he was gonna throw me down there. Poor little Frederick tried to fight him off, but he sent him flying and Freddy ran away. I have a stick to beat off wild dogs and hogs with and I grabbed that and hit Lewis hard and he fell down. That's when I ran." The scar over Kenya's forehead was thickening, pulling her eyebrow into a cynical quirk. "I'm glad he's dead, but I'm glad I didn't kill him. At least, that ain't on my conscience."

Walker could visualize the scene: the struggling panicked girl, the terrified little boy, and the desperate Spencer. "I'm just going to put it down as accidental death. The coroner's willing to swear to it and so am I. No witnesses. No weapon. No case. One thing, though, Lewis' body was found quite far from the quarry wall. Nobody could've even jumped out that far and landed where we found him. It's almost like he was thrown or dropped from a helicopter or something. You said you heard him yelling like he was hurt. Did you see anyone or hear anything else besides him?"

"Maybe he landed in a blackberry bush," Holly said, bursting into relieved giggles. She didn't even know he had escaped from the county jail.

But Kenya didn't laugh. She looked down at the dish in her hand, playing with the chocolate ooze at the bottom. "Grandma says, 'The Great Ones are our guardians.' They, like, protect us because we protect them. Looking out for us, warning us when there's danger."

"Where'd you hit him?" asked Walker, remembering what Tapley, the coroner, had told him. That the blow that probably killed Spencer was to the back of his head, not the front as it would have been if he were struggling to drag Kenya to the quarry.

"Right up the side of his ugly, old head."

Like a karate chop to the jugular, Walker guessed, *enough to knock the wind out of a grown man.*

"So what you're saying is you think this guardian saw you fighting for your life and when you got away, he saw Spencer get up and come after you again and stopped him. That about it?"

Holly said in a defensive tone, "You can think whatever you like. She didn't kill Lewis Spencer. Now, can we get home? My grandma is gonna have my hide anyway for ending up with swampers. 'Course Miss Kahalia doesn't really fit the usual description of a swamper, does she? What I'm saying is, can we go home now?"

"Sure," Walker said. "By the way, Miss Holly, what were you doing at Miss Kahalia's place the night of the fire?"

Holly stopped checking her appearance in her compact mirror and shot Walker a wary look. "I was trying to chase Gina McFarland, if you must know. I knew she was going to ask Miss Kahalia something and I figured that's where she was going."

"She picked a strange time with the fire and storm and all," he said mildly. "You sure there wasn't another reason?"

She was on the defensive again. "Like?"

"Like hiding something or somebody." He kept his eyes on the road, deliberately slowing down to the irritation of the eighteen-wheeler behind him. Kenya gave it away by staring at Holly fixedly, as if she knew the truth.

"See, I chased your friend, Tony, all the way from Macon. He got wind I was on his tail and booked straight down here. What was the attraction that made him brave a storm like that and a brush fire? Was it you, Miss Holly, or was it that he stashed the money and jewelry down there in the swamp?"

She sighed and wiped silent tears as they rolled down her cheeks.

Kenya patted her knee. "Tell him. Tell him the truth."

"Okay, the truth is, I knew what he was planning. I didn't know his friend would do the actual stealing, though. Honest, the plan was just to get money and stuff from the safe. That's all. I told him not to go upstairs and wake up the old lady. His friend must've done that."

"But you were there, right, Miss Holly?"

It took her a moment to get the truth out. Holly took a deep breath and let it go. "Okay, but not during the robbery. I waited in the car outside." She cut her eyes at Walker. "Okay, I let myself in the front door and called out to the old lady. Mrs Wilkes was on the phone, gabbing at her husband as usual. I just went to the carport door and unlocked it, that's all. Then I just sat in the car until it was over."

Walker sighed. "After they couldn't get the safe open, my instinct tells me they must've asked Mrs. Clark for the combination and she told them she'd open it. That's why her fingerprints are on it and not theirs." He pictured poor, old Miss Delia dealing with these two hoods in her dignified manner, bewildered about why they wanted antique jewelry and the money to run the household Desmond gave her every month. "Go on."

"See, I don't know what all they took. Tony asked me where he could hide some stuff, where it would be safe, and I thought of this old fishing cabin down in the Swamp. It used to be my grandpa's when he was alive, so I took him down there. He said we'd go on a cruise to the Bahamas when he cashed his share in. We'd hop off the boat and go live where nobody could find us."

"So you thought you'd meet him there at the fishing shack and run away with him to the islands?" He never ceased to be amazed that women would fall for the oldest con artist line, beside the one where the guy promised to marry the girl.

"Yeah, but it didn't turn out that way." Holly covered her face with her hands. "When I got there, Tony was leaving the shack. He wouldn't take me along—said I'd only get in his way. He just laughed, got the box, and left. Left me there in the woods with the fire coming and the storm and everything. That's when I caught up with Miss Kahalia and Kenya. I decided to stay at Lesbos, thinking it would all just go away. But it doesn't just go away, does it?" The girl beside him uncovered her face and sat up, staring vacantly ahead at the road to town, her cheeks still glistening with tears. "What're you going to do with me? Whatever it is, I deserve it. I know."

"It ain't nothing compared to what I'm going to throw at Tony Baloney. Starting with having sex with a minor and breaking and entering. You'll probably do some time in the Youth Detention Center, and maybe the judge will sentence you to probation and a year of community service. We'll see if this has taught you something. By the way, we picked up your friend the next day in Macon and he turned state's witness on his buddy. Said he just stayed downstairs but his buddy went up to Miss Delia's room and got the old lady to open the safe. He said they told her you were with your grandmother at the hospital and they wouldn't let her be admitted unless you got the money. According to Tony, she said, 'Oh, if it's for Holly, then take all you need.' She must've been climbing back up to get Mr. Desmond when she fell."

"There, don't you feel better now that you spoke the truth?" asked Kenya, her face brightening to a smile. "My grandma says—"

"Oh, I don't care what your grandma says. I'm just afraid what mine is gonna say after she hears. I'm in big trouble in more ways than one."

"Oh, are you going to have a baby, too?" Kenya clamped her hand over her own mouth.

But Holly silenced her with a scathing look. "Kenya, you know, sometimes you can be downright tacky! Shut the fuck up!"

They rode in silence after that. When they pulled up in front of the police station at Julia Springs, Kenya said, "I just want to tell you something, Mr. Quade, if you don't mind my butting in your business."

"Fire away, Miss Kenya. I'm pretty well the town's business now." His rough face wore a gentle expression when he looked at the scarred girl. "Take your time," he added, thinking she wanted to tell him something about Holly.

"It's about Miss Isis, see?" Seeing his expression harden, she quickly blurted out, "See, she loves you so much it's tearing her to pieces." Now he was staring open-mouthed. She took it as a sign to go on. "She's hiding down there. She's hiding because it's been her home ever since she come back from foster care. You know they took all those kids away from Miss Lois and Deacon Slade."

At that point, Holly picked up the thread. "Yes, the State did them like they did me, except my grandma stepped in and got custody. All kinds of shit goes down in foster care especially when you've got looks like Isis does. They had those kids in all kinds of placements and finally had to split them up."

"Okay, I was talking first, Holly. Let me finish. He hasn't got all day, you know." Kenya ignored Holly's furious look and continued. "Mr. Quade, see she's just scared of the world, that's all. My grandmother—"

Holly rolled her eyes. "Oh, Lord, here we go again!"

"My grandmother has worked with her, giving her all sorts of gri-gri bags to fend off evil and such, but I told her you were the best one for that. After all, you've been a soldier and you didn't die when they blew you up so you must have guardian spirits. So if she married you, they'd protect her, too. Then she said she was afraid it was because of what your mama done—you don't trust women. That's what I got to say." She opened the passenger door.

"Wait!" His voice was so commanding, that both girls started nervously. "What did she say when you told her that? About me being better than a gris-gris bag?"

A soft smile briefly made Kenya pretty again. "She said, 'That's right, isn't it?' like she had never thought of it that way before. When it was only you two, she says she felt safer than she ever had in her life. But when you started leaving to go to work, she couldn't take it no more, and I know what it's like, 'cause when my mama would leave me alone and men would come in...well, let's just say I know what it's like having your protection up and leave you. I think you should go to her, yes sir, I do, Mr. Quade. Listen to me, telling a policeman what to do, now." She bowed her head as if apologizing for the greatest flood of words she had ever spoken at one sitting.

Walker studied the steering wheel as though driving for

the first time. "Thanks, Miss Kenya, for telling me that." Then
he was all policeman again. "Ready to go, Miss Holly?" But
this time there was hope in his voice as if everything was going to be all right.

"Yeah, but my first call is going to be to my granny,
okay?" Holly gripped Kenya's hand for a minute. Then she
said, "Let's get this show on the road!"

❧❧❧

Later that night, the tower guards at Lesbos called out,
"Halt! Who goes there?" to the large figure of a man carrying a
flashlight as he emerged from the Thicket. It was Quade
Walker.

"Would you tell Miss Isis I want to talk to her, please?"

She was there at the gatehouse within minutes. He tried to
speak, but the words he had prepared died on his tongue as
though they had turned to ashes. He stood and looked at her
with his soul in his eyes.

"You don't need to explain," she said, moving so close he
could smell the hyacinth scent of her hair. "You came back
after I treated you so cruelly, that's enough."

"I love you, Isis," he said in a strangled voice. "Please
marry me." It was the best he could do, but apparently it was
enough.

She melted into his arms as if she belonged there. "Oh,
yes, Quade Walker. Yes, I will."

❧❧❧

Reverend Desmond Clark was so glad he didn't kill his
mother, he didn't stop to think maybe when he heard her up
out of bed and talking to someone, he should have checked on
her instead of going back to sleep. That is, until his wife Marilyn accused him of hiding in bed long after the robbers had
finished doing what they came to do—then coming out of his
room to find his mother lying sprawled on the harlequin marble floor of the entrance hall.

They were in Delia's huge house, doing their best to sort out ninety-three years of living by a woman who had too much money and didn't want to share it. Marilyn seemed to have another agenda, though.

As she paced along the landing overlooking the marble entrance way, she stopped abruptly, looking furiously at her much smaller husband. "I mean, I don't understand why, Desmond, if you could hear your mother's scratchy little voice, you could have certainly heard a man's deep voice, too?" She looked at him accusingly with scorn in her dark eyes he had once thought were her best feature. Now, they were stones cast at the sinner, ready to condemn without mercy. "According to that girl, Holly's, story, there were two of them, in fact. I don't believe for a minute her boyfriend didn't go upstairs, so you'd be hearing two grown men and a little old lady screeching, 'Who are you?' Didn't you hear that, Desmond? My god, I know you did! Admit it!"

"You're jumping to conclusions without any proof as usual, Marilyn dear." But his voice gave him away, quavering when he needed to sound indignant. "I tell you now, as I have said a hundred times or more, I was asleep and I thought Mrs. Wilkes had stayed, and Mother was talking to her. There was a door between us and a long hall, don't forget. I don't know why all of a sudden you're attacking me when you should be—"

His wife cut him off as cold and sharp as a knife blade. "Supporting you? Because I fail to understand cowardice, that's why. I just fail to understand it. The men in my family would have grabbed a gun and gone after those hoodlums and turned them over to the police after they got through beating the tar out of them. That's what a real man would have done, if his own mother was there in the house being robbed."

"You forget I don't carry a gun like the Neanderthals in your family who enjoy killing things." He got a little surge of satisfaction over the little jab at her red-neck relatives, but she quickly squelched it.

On the way out the door, she half-turned. "Well, you could've called the police at least. But no, you were afraid they'd hear you, that's why. Really, Desmond, you're disgusting."

"Wait, where are you going? We have to get these rooms sorted out by next month so we can move in. I can't do it all, you know. Someone has to help me." His quavering voice reflected his fear of being left to fend for himself, first by his mother and now by his wife.

"Oh, you can keep it all in this museum to the Clarks. I'm going home to stay with my Neanderthal relatives. At least I can count on them to protect me."

When the front door slammed behind her, even the hundred-something etched glass panes rattled accusingly.

Chapter 39

"Miss Gina?"

Behind her eyes, she saw him again. This time whole, healed without a trace of blood in his shining hair. Her lips moved to say his name, Vadim, but no sound came out. It was only a thought that said it, *Vadim*.

"Look, she's opening her eyes, Mama! Come here quick!" Joy's excited voice pierced the white fog. "Hi, Ginny, sweetheart. How do you feel? Doctors said the surgery was a success. Tumor's all gone." Joy's usually confident voice wavered slightly. "Well, most of it—that is. Lucky for you they found it at Emory. Look, Mama, Ginny's looking at us."

"Don't be talking her arm off, Joy Faith. Give her some space. She don't want to hear all that stuff about tumors. Hi, sweetieheart. How you feeling?" From somewhere in the marshmallow-thick fog, Aunt Milly was speaking in Georgian country tones.

But Vadim was talking, too, telling her he had found a place where blackberries grew without thorns, and his boss didn't care how long he stayed, and he wanted to take her there. She rose to join him, but not before telling her relatives goodbye, though they only saw her lips move. She was going to walk hand-in-hand with Vadim where blackberry brambles and wild roses grew.

When her eyes fixed and the heart monitor went flat with a screech, the room erupted in chaos, but she only looked back once. Then she took Vadim's hand and walked away, leaving the crash cart team to work on her lifeless body. It was two days before her seventeenth birthday.

ぴぴぴ

Two weeks later, Megan Gatewood had a baby boy, born one month prematurely but already weighing eight pounds, three ounces. "One more month inside Mama and he would have walked out on his own," the doctor said, drying his hands. "How do these little girls have such whopping babies?"

"'Cause they eat everything in sight," replied the nurse, putting the instruments away. "I've got a teenager and I might as well have a horse."

ぴぴぴ

Two weeks following that, Quade Walker and Isis Slade were married by Desmond Clark in the Church of the Blessed Springs and, as night fell, by Miss Kahalia and Queen Sappho in a combined ceremony in the forest that, among other things, incorporated the four elements—earth, wind, water, and fire— and jumping over brooms to the beat of African drums. Just witnessing the rituals sent Chief Pierce to confessing before the congregation that he had witnessed "pagan worship" for three consecutive Sundays. But old timers like Jordan Tanner and Jake Fry said Lou Owl would have loved it, jumping right in to dance to the drums.

From his hiding place in the part of the Thicket left un- touched by the brush fire, the creature peered at the he-human and his mate standing in the middle of the candlelit circle. Studying them intently, seeing them nuzzling each other, he felt an odd twinge of loneliness rising in his throat. Root Woman still talked to him, fed him dried fruits and nuts, but she and her animals now lived in town among humans while her church was being rebuilt.

The winds of late September nights were blowing colder when the last candle was extinguished and the jubilant guests trooped back through the dark woods to Sara's Place for a barbeque prepared especially for the occasion. A whole calf was turning on a spit over an open fire outside after being buried in a fire pit for two days. The very sight sent Chief Pierce back to his office to consult the Fire Safety Code manual, the County Health Code, and the OSHA website.

The creature was left alone in the dark Thicket as the laughter of humans faded, leaving behind only the moaning night breeze. He sniffed the air, picking up faint traces of roasting flesh. Then he stood up on both feet and gave a high-pitched, mournful whistle like the sound of a midnight freight. There was no answer, only the night wind. Deeper in the forest, a doe and two fawns scampered away. The creature was alone, without his she-humans to watch and protect. He whistled again, plaintively like a whimper.

Then the creature went to the still rapidly-flowing creek and slipped into the water, making barely a ripple. He knew the way south, the way the water flowed to the Great Thicket many miles away. There, he would find a mate as his parents had found each other in the Great Forest to the north.

But when he reached the new bridge, the creature tugged himself out of the stream and under the shelter of the overpass, looked behind him at the place that had been his home for many years. There was a curious sensation somewhere in his broad chest and he put his paw there to find it, but it eluded him as if he had indigestion from eating too many berries. It pained him, clawed at him like the disagreeable winds of coming winter. The creature wanted to roar in his pain, but he was too close to humans to make noise. So he sighed, his great chest heaving, tapering off to a whimper, and then slid back into the creek, flowing south to a new life.

↩↪↩

In Atlanta, some two hundred miles away, Jordan Tanner felt the pain of separation from his home as he listened to some representative from Buford drone on about the merits of legislation he was sponsoring about better regulation of the chicken processing industry. His detractors kept interrupting with shouts of, "Hell, we can't even afford fried chicken anymore, much less eggs!" Mumbling something about a bathroom break, Tanner got to his feet and wandered up the aisles of the Senate, saying to the smiling page as he passed "Call me if they decide to vote on something. Will you?"

In the House lounge, he stared out the huge window at the city turning on all its lights like a woman putting on her jewelry. The city had so changed since he worked here fifty years ago—was it that long? Now, he shared a swank apartment with Melissa who had settled right in as part of Atlanta's glitzy social circuit. Every night he would come home to find strangers sipping cocktails in the living room, or go to strangers' living rooms to sip their cocktails, and try to figure out what was their relationship to him. Melissa, however, told him these were just people he ought to meet and he should be his amusing, rustic self.

"You know, down home country but smart, darling."

On top of that, he didn't know what she took, but she rode him like a witch on a broom at least three times a week after insisting he take injections for erectile dysfunction. Tanner sighed, thinking this was going to be one of those nights. *You know, sex keeps you young they say.* "Now I know what killed my grandfather," he said to one in particular.

As if it were listening, his cell phone vibrated in his pocket. It was Hamilton Phillips calling from home. His voice was surprisingly clear.

"I managed to get the Chief's WiFi passcode," he said. "They've got the strongest signal in South Georgia. I won't waste time, Tanner. I'll get right to the reason I called you."

Tanner was so glad to hear a voice from home that he didn't care if the conversation went viral over the airwaves. "Ham! I haven't seen you since the brushfire. Still holed up at Woodbury Hall?" He had driven by once, imagining the look of horror on the elder Phillips's face if he could see the lawn of their country estate cluttered with rusting robots, parts of mechanical bodies, along with various machines in various states of disintegration, including whole cars.

"Yes, and I'm kind of liking it, getting back to civilization as it were—flush toilets and running water, that sort of thing. One doesn't have to spend what's left of their gray cells on mundane projects like that. Instead, I'm focusing on larger projects, and that brings me to what I called about."

"You said larger projects." *Here goes the plug for local perks*, he thought. Appreciating politicians more every time he got asked to do somebody a favor or promote a pet project in the House. Probably with Ham it would be funding for a putting a robot programmed to say, "The South will rise again" on the moon.

"Well, you remember Lancelot IV? I believe you ran into him the night of the storm?"

Tanner said he did, thinking with a twinge of sadness that he had been with Lou Owl that night.

"You see, I traced his signal to where he was stuck fast in a tangle of roots that night and yanked him out of there with tow chains tied to my truck. I had a lot of cleaning to do, so basically, I just let him sit until I got around to dismantling him. When I got to his camera and recorder, I tell you it nearly knocked my socks off."

Thinking Phillips had come near to electrocuting himself, he said, "Oh, no! You okay now, Ham?"

The scientist got that edge to his voice when he thought the person he was talking to had the IQ of a frog. "No, I meant shock of the other sort. Surprise, to say the least, because when I ran the frames back, there were what sounds like Arthur talking to somebody. And then suddenly, this face appears for two frames and then the light goes out. Remarkable! Stunning!"

Tanner was unimpressed and his impatience crept into his voice. "I don't get it, Ham. Whose face?" He immediately hoped it would be Lou's, hoping for one last glimpse of the old scout, but Ham's reply put all logic on hold.

"Would you believe me if I said I think it's the legendary Chinaberry Man?"

There was an awkward silence in which Tanner tried to think of the right way to suggest Phillips had finally gone completely around the bend. "But no one's ever seen him, Ham."

"That's the whole point, isn't it, Jordan? I think this is the first photograph of him. Before that, the critics were saying he didn't exist! That he was a hoax! I can prove to the world there is a Chinaberry Man! It's right there, in living color. Thank God I loaded Lance IV with color film that very morning because I ran out of black and white!"

"But why would you want to do that, Ham? I mean, expose his habitat to the world. It's been a secret up to now. Let him live in peace, wherever he is. Remember, you wanted to get away from the world once."

"You're right, Jordan, and I don't want to get called a fool again. I don't need that. Scientists can be such sanctimonious assholes, and then there's the cretin public. Good advice and I'll take it. Stop by the Pater's old place when you're back in town. I'll show you the film. Oh, don't worry, I won't destroy it. In fact, I've made several copies and archived it in the Cloud. But I'll leave it to the National Academy of Science after I'm gone, along with my robotic systems."

"Take it easy, Ham. Don't touch any live wires." Tanner ended the call, reminding himself to see what funding was available for robotic research in the State coffers. Somewhere in the echoing halls of the state capitol building he thought he heard Lou Owl laughing. Glad there were still a few mysteries left in the world, Tanner poured himself a drink and toasted everything that made him happy.

છબછ

At Sara's Place, as she worked cleaning the tables and stacking dirty dishes, Kenya began to sing in a voice as thick and rich as sorghum syrup. The customers smiled and nodded, leaving her big tips. Sometimes she added a few dance steps and they clapped out a rhythm, glad to be participating in her emerging joy.

"Kenya ain't darkened the door of the church yet, but she sure has got the spirit in her," they said.

છબછ

Hearing the voices in her head, Root Woman paused on her way to gather wood and looked up at the Mama Tree. The tree answered with leaves falling like tears. *When the spirit moves her, she'll come.*

About the Author

Even as a child, Trisha O'Keefe was impressed by the inherent power of alternative medicines. Indigenous healing practices are an ongoing theme in her novels. As a native Southerner, O'Keefe claims to have "a lot of red dirt" flowing in her veins. Growing up, she spent summers on her uncle's farm in South Georgia, "mainly getting into trouble." That trend has continued throughout her life. After traveling abroad for fourteen years, running into revolutions or governmental coups nearly everywhere she went—even Britain was in the midst of a labor strike when she moved there—she returned to the States. She is the daughter of Jimmy Jones, a well-known journalist for the *Atlanta Constitution* under Editor Ralph Magill. One of her earliest memories was the sound of a typewriter rattling away in the middle of the night. You would think that would have cured her from ever putting two words together, let alone a book. Still, at age 6, she co-wrote *Spot, The Dog* with her sister, followed a long time later by *Hanahatchee, Poseidon's Eye*, and *Love Song of the Chinaberry Man*. Two more novels, *The Magi's Well,* and *The Mama Tree* will be published in 2016. "I guess some things you can't cure," O'Keefe says. "You just have to go where they take you."